GRACIE'S SIN

GRACIE'S SIN

Freda Lightfoot

Hodder & Stoughton

Copyright © 2002 by Freda Lightfoot

First published in Great Britain in 2002
by Hodder and Stoughton
A division of Hodder Headline

The right of Freda Lightfoot to be identified as the Author of
the Work has been asserted by her in accordance with the
Copyright, Designs and Patents Act 1988.

2 4 6 8 10 9 7 5 3 1

A CIP catalogue record for this title
is available from the British Library

ISBN 0 340 82000 4

Typeset in Centaur by Hewer Text Ltd, Edinburgh
Printed and bound in Great Britain by
Mackays of Chatham plc, Chatham, Kent

Hodder and Stoughton
A division of Hodder Headline
338 Euston Road
London NW1 3BH

To David, for being there

ACKNOWLEDGEMENTS

I am indebted to Elsie Taylor and to Betty Kirkland for the information they made available to me on the Timber Corps and the nature of the work they did. They kindly checked my manuscript and pointed out my mistakes which I hope I've accurately corrected, though I have still allowed my own timber girls to use tents on one brief project. I hope I will be forgiven for this. My thanks also go to Ulverston Library for the information on Grizedale Hall. For the sake of the story, I have taken a few liberties with the facts here too. Grizedale Hall was a grade one security prison for high ranking German Luftwaffe and U-Boat officers and it is doubtful that it would ever have accommodated NCOs. I chose to ignore this fact because it would have been against the Geneva Convention for a higher ranking officer to do manual work on the land, or to be allowed the kind of freedom that I give my fictional POWs. In every other respect, I have made the setting and situation as accurate as possible.

Chapter One

1942

The train shuddered to a halt at Bodmin Road Station on a gasp of steam. Although there was no indication on this anonymous country platform set in thick woodland that this was the correct destination, all signs having being painted out because of the war, passengers scrambled to their feet and began to lift down bags from the overhead luggage racks.

'Is this it? Have we arrived already?' Lou felt an unexpected stinging at the backs of her eyes, and a small sob escaped her as she squeezed closer to Gordon's side in the overcrowded carriage. He grasped her hand, held on to it tightly and she was pleased to see that even his normally cheeky grin was a bit lop sided.

She'd meant to be so brave, so matter-of-fact when the moment came for them to part and here she was on the point of blubbing. But then they'd only been married five minutes. Two whole weeks in actual fact though it felt like five minutes. A month ago she hadn't even known Gordon Mason existed, now he was her husband. The very thought made her insides turn to water with excitement.

It all started when Lou and her friend Sybil had decided to

spend a week in the West Country on a much needed holiday. They'd found cheap digs in Brixham and were having the time of their lives, paddling in the sea, sitting on beaches, exploring quaint harbours and pretending there wasn't a war on at all. Then up had strolled a couple of sailors and that was that. Within seconds her whole life had changed. Sybil had given Gordon the glad eye, of course, as she usually did with fellows, but it was clear from the start it was Lou he fancied. He'd proposed to her that very first day.

The following morning, having smuggled him in through her landlady's back pantry window and up to their room where he'd slept like a lamb on the floor, after a few satisfying clinches of course, Lou had sent a telegram to her mam, telling her not to expect her home. At the end of the week poor Sybil had returned alone to the factory in Rochdale, where they both wove silk for parachutes, in something of a huff, while Lou set about making other plans for her life.

The landlady of their digs had been sporting enough to stand for her at the short wedding ceremony, choosing to wear a pink-flowered hat and leopard-skin coat for the occasion and quite taking it in her stride that these two young people, who had only just met, should rush into lifelong matrimony. 'Happens every day, dear,' she told them. 'What with the war, and all these poor lonely sailor boys. I'd wed one meself, given half a chance.'

'She'd be better off adopting one,' Gordon had remarked with one of his wry grins.

Since then they'd only managed to spend two entire nights together, though Gordon had somehow managed to wangle enough free passes for it to seem like more. He'd even got quite nifty at sneaking off the Plymouth base without a pass at all, and there'd been no further need to smuggle him into her digs now they were legally married. He could walk in quite openly. Lou felt, in fact, as if the last two weeks had been one long honeymoon.

She lifted her hand, twisting it about so she could admire the shining gold band on the third finger of her left hand. Her new name still sounded strange. Oh, but didn't she just love being Mrs Lou Mason instead of boring Louise Brown. What would Mam say if she could see her now?

Someone jabbed an elbow into her shoulder and she came out of her day dream with a jolt. Doors were being flung open; weary passengers stretched aching limbs, rubbed grit from their sleepy eyes as they clambered stiffly down from the carriages. The honeymoon was over and real life was about to begin.

'This is it, love. Keep your chin up. Think of it as an adventure, and I won't be far away.'

It had been the day after the wedding that she'd seen the poster asking for women to join the Timber Corps, a section of the Women's Land Army, offering work on estates in Cornwall. It had seemed the perfect solution for it meant she could stay near Gordon. Lou had signed up without a second's thought.

Now Plymouth seemed a million miles away. And, as Gordon frequently pointed out, he could get his sailing orders at any moment and be sent heaven knows where, right into the thick of it. Lou kept her mind deliberately vague and unfocused on this point because it made her go all sick inside at the thought. She wished suddenly that she was back home with her mam and three sisters, for all they spent the whole time worrying and waiting for news of their various husbands and boy friends as well as Ronnie, their brother, who was in the army somewhere in Singapore. At least she wouldn't feel quite so alone.

She tried to smile but it turned a bit wobbly. Even her legs felt like jelly as she stepped on to the platform. Gordon handed down her kitbag then pulled the carriage door closed with the leather strap and leaned out through the open window.

He looked so handsome standing there in his sailor's

uniform, neatly pressed collar flapping gently in the breeze, round, tanned face beaming at her with stoic brightness and love for her shining out of his dark brown eyes.

'It's all the wrong way round, isn't it? I should be seeing you off,' Lou told him.

'We're seeing each other off, each to do our bit. Equal partners, eh, love?'

'I love you,' she said.

His face went oddly still and serious, then, reaching down, he grasped her by the arms and half lifted her off her feet so he could kiss her. That was the wonderful thing about Gordon. He never seemed to notice that she was five foot seven and what might politely be termed voluptuous. He called her a pleasing armful and handled her as if she were light as a feather, kissed her deep and long, as though they hadn't kissed anywhere near enough these last weeks, and left her as breathless and limp as a fourteen-year-old schoolgirl, rather than a practical young woman of twenty-three.

When he put her down again, Lou's cheeks were all flushed and her hat had fallen off and was rolling between the feet of a group of soldiers and airmen who were milling around, some, like Gordon, holding adoring sweethearts close. Others hoisted laughing children into their arms before marching off for an eagerly awaited leave, grinning from ear to ear. She felt a shaft of envy for their good fortune. If only she could turn back the clock. How could she even get through one day without seeing her husband?

Snatching up the hat, Lou rammed it back on to her head, quite ruining her chestnut curls carefully arranged into bangs, and ran back to grasp Gordon's hand as if she meant never to let him go.

An aged porter hurried forward to collect a dowager's smart brown leather suitcase, sensing the opportunity for a tip; squabbling children were being admonished by harassed

mothers; there was the sound of quiet weeping and family
members clutched each other in relief or fear as the train
breathed noisily beside them like an impatient animal eager to
be off. Then came shouts from the station master, the banging
of doors and blowing of whistles, and finally the clunk and
rhythmic turning of wheels, the contented hiss of steam as the
train began to inch forward, anxious to continue on its journey.
Still holding Gordon's hand, Lou walked along with it.

'Don't fret, love. I'll nip over to see you as soon as I can.
This isn't forever, not by a long chalk.'

'I'll write when I find out what free time I'm to have.'

Their hold finally broken, they stared helplessly back at
each other, nothing left to say yet so much unspoken reflected
in their eyes. Gordon leaned out of the carriage window, waving
till the last possible moment, till the train had rounded the bend
and he'd been swallowed up by a swathe of greenery and a belch
of steam. Lou felt as if he were being sucked away, out of her
life forever – which was nonsense. Hadn't he just said he'd see
her again soon? Eyes smarting, she went back for her luggage.

Within moments the mêlée of people had vanished, the
porter and station master had returned to their respective
hideaways for a welcome cup of tea, and only two people
were left standing forlornly on the deserted platform, Lou and
one other, a girl of about the same age.

They gazed at each other in open curiosity, aware that they
couldn't have looked more different. One was tall and statu-
esque, the other petite with long straight blonde hair. Where
Lou's gaze was frank and open, lit by the warm friendliness of a
wide smile, the other girl had an oval childish face, pale-
skinned, her huge grey eyes giving every appearance of terror, as
if she couldn't imagine how she came to be there on that
deserted platform in the middle of nowhere, but would really
like to turn tail and run after the departing train, were there any
hope of catching it.

But in one respect, at least, they were entirely alike. They wore identical smart brown overcoats, woollen stockings and highly polished brown shoes, neat brimmed hats and, most telling of all, the same shiny new badge in the form of crossed brass axes which marked them as comrades. Lou thrust out a hand.

'Louise Mason, Lou for short. I take it you're heading for the same place as me? Timber Corps training camp?'

'Yes, I suppose so. Gracie Freeman.' Hands were shaken, grins exchanged, and with an air of awkward embarrassment at being pitched together in this way, two strangers in an unfamiliar situation, they busied themselves collecting bags, various brown paper parcels and gas masks. Lou swung her kit bag up on to her shoulder with ease, as she had seen Gordon do many times with his. The smaller girl made no attempt to follow suit but seemed happy to drag the long kit bag by its neck cord.

'Dratted thing took up more space than me on the train,' she said with a wry smile.

'Aye, it would, seeing as how it's nearly as tall as you are. You could do with a dog collar and lead, then happen it'd come by itself if you whistled.'

That voice, Gracie decided, was North Country, rather than her own Hereford accent with its distinctive Welsh border twang, but it was warm and somehow reassuring. She visibly relaxed, beginning to feel better already. Laughing, they walked together off the platform into the station yard, which seemed to be equally deserted, the only sound in the still September day coming from some unidentified bird high in the trees that lined the track.

'By heck, is that a song thrush? You don't get many of them to the pound in Rochdale.'

'A blackbird actually. Is that where you come from? Lancashire?'

Lou beamed proudly. 'For my sins, as they say. What about you? Come far?'

Sin! Gracie's attention was caught by the word, one she had come to hate. There was rarely a Sunday morning in chapel she hadn't heard it on the lips of some lay preacher or other, her own father in particular. It had always seemed to the young Gracie that if anything at all might bring happiness or pleasure in life it must be a sin. How fiercely she had resisted all those stern rules; the limericks she'd hidden in the pages of her New Testament when supposedly learning scriptures; the scarlet and azure ribbons she'd kept in her handkerchief box to brighten up the sober colours of her homely skirts and blouses; the secret dance lessons with her more frolicsome mother. She felt a pang of guilt, remembering. Her mother would miss her badly, though she too had played a part in Gracie's decision to leave.

She could see her now, standing at the door, delivering doom-laden warnings about 'this ridiculous notion to be a *Lumber Jack*'. Disappointment had soured her voice and she showed not the slightest sign of amusement when Gracie corrected her, saying that they were called Lumber *Jills*, not Jacks; an attitude coloured by her lost dreams of the solidly respectable career in teaching she'd so carefully mapped out for her only daughter.

Gracie's father's reaction had been to gaze mournfully at her with an air of wounded reproach, guaranteed to fill her with guilt, saying how he'd hoped she'd join him in the shop, how he'd worked hard all his life to ensure that his precious daughter would have a good business to inherit, and here she was throwing his generosity back in his face. He'd sent her to her room to 'examine her conscience', as if she were still a naughty child needing to be punished for missing Sunday School. She'd stayed there for a week on a diet of bread and water but it had made not the slightest difference. Her mind was made up.

Though it hurt Gracie deeply that her parents were more concerned with their own opposing ambitions for their only daughter rather than with her wishes on the matter, she'd held fast to her resolve. 'I mean to go. I need to lead my own life,' she insisted.

'But how will I manage without you?' her mother had mourned. 'You know what he's like,' nodding darkly in the direction of the shop.

Howell Freeman claimed to be Welsh, though he was born in Chester, and hated the English, including his own wife who hailed from Liverpool. Brenda Freeman, on the other hand, maintained that she'd spent her formative years in the best part of Cheshire and had married beneath her. The animosity between husband and wife had been the blight of Gracie's young life as each called upon her constantly to take their side and act as referee in their frequent arguments. She had never fully understood the cause of their marital failure. There was perhaps too much of the ascetic in her father, while her mother pined for more money in her purse, pretty gew-gaws and a measure of independence she claimed never to have enjoyed, going straight from the strictures of her father's repressive household to that of her husband. But whatever the reason, Gracie was heartily cheesed off with being the sticking plaster which held the pair together.

It was seeing a poster of a girl in a smart uniform which had finally made her recognise that it was time to break free; that her parents and their conflicting ambitions were no longer her responsibility. Such decisions are easily made, of course. Carrying them out quite another matter. Yet Gracie had held to her resolve; had no intention of looking back, of apologising for her decision, or showing one iota of regret.

Now she considered this stranger whom she instinctively liked, laughing as Lou vociferously complained about the vicious grip of her new hat as she wiped the sweat from her brow, making her chestnut brown hair tumble down all anyhow about her flushed face. It was no doubt against the rules to remove the offending article while in uniform but Gracie sensed in this new acquaintance a healthy disregard for authority. Her own hat felt stuck fast to her head, as if she would never have the courage to take it off without permission. Yet this would be an inaccurate assessment of her personality, for wasn't she a rebel too, at heart, despite her prim and proper veneer?

'I feel I've been travelling for days. God knows how I've managed to get here at all, the number of changes I've had to make. I'm worn out before I even begin.'

Lou didn't like to say that she was worn out, too, because it was for an entirely different reason.

'So what now?' Both girls looked about them at the empty countryside, the gently rolling green hills and what appeared to be acre upon acre of thick woodland. 'If this is Bodmin I don't reckon much to the town, do you? They don't even have a Woolworth's. I suppose we have got off at the right place?'

'I think the town is some distance off. Perhaps we could ask the station master, though, just to check.'

Barely lifting his nose from his pint mug of tea he bluntly told them that they could catch a train to Bodmin Central if they'd a mind to go into town, otherwise they could walk to the camp, assuming they knew where it was. Having delivered this unhelpful information, he buried his nose once more in the mug and slurped loud and long.

The two girls returned to the empty yard. Here they settled themselves to wait, with what patience they could muster, on a low stone wall. The wait was long and dull and boring. One hour passed by, then another. Halfway through the third thick grey cloud blotted out the sun and a thin rain started, cloaking the woods in pale mist. They huddled together for warmth.

'D'you reckon we should set out to look for this camp?' Lou enquired.

9

'And risk getting lost?'

'You're right. Better to stay put.'

Their discomfort increased as the rain grew more persistent but they kept on talking, keeping their spirits up, using the time to glean a good deal of information about each other. They discovered that though they had little, if anything, in common, there was an immediate bond between them.

At eighteen, Gracie was, in fact, almost five years younger than Lou, and single, though she loved the tale of Lou's register office wedding and the reception afterwards with three drunken sailors at the fish bar on the Barbican. Lou had been brought up in a mill town, one of a large, noisy family, while Gracie, as an only child, had lived behind her parents' village shop deep in the countryside. Lou claimed to be untidy, bossy and cackhanded to the point of being all fingers and thumbs. Gracie admitted to liking things to be tidy and organised, with a fondness for any sort of craft, even needlework.

'You could happen darn my stockings then. They're allus full of bobbie's winders. That means holes, if you need the translation.'

'Only if you'll help carry my kit bag.'

'It's a deal.'

They beamed at each other, well suited.

They were at least alike in two things: eagerness to do their bit for the war effort, and equally to have fun and enjoy life while they could. Dusk had begun to fall and it wasn't so easy now to pick out the thread of road, or the shape of the woods and hills beyond.

'Looks like we might be spending our first night camped out in the station yard,' Lou dryly remarked, and was instantly interrupted by the roar and cough of a lorry's engine, the grinding of gears and a loud tooting of its horn. It lurched to a stop in a huge puddle, spraying them both with muddy water. A freckled, oil-streaked face appeared through the driver's window, looking decidedly harassed. 'Lost the use of your legs then, you two?'

'We didn't know where to go, and were afraid of causing trouble by getting lost,' Gracie said, surprising Lou by her spunk at being prepared to speak up. From the look of her, she didn't appear to be the sort to say boo to a goose.

The girl frowned. 'Weren't you given a map?'

They looked at each other in dismay. Were they? Neither could remember. Arrangements had been made so quickly, and so much had happened to each in such a short space of time, they couldn't be entirely sure. This time it was Lou who frantically attempted to disguise their confusion. 'The station master told us somebody would fetch us, if we'd the patience to wait.' A slight stretching of the truth and the oil-streaked driver snorted her disbelief, clearly doubting its veracity.

'Bert knows only too well that hell could freeze over before we namby-pamby any new girls here. Well, don't stand there gawking, we haven't got all night. Hop aboard.'

The flat back of the lorry being six foot from the ground, hop was not the word which sprang to mind as the pair struggled to clamber aboard without losing either their belongings or their balance. They were laughingly assisted from above by half a dozen other girls who commiserated with Lou and Gracie's rain-soaked state. They themselves were well protected in capes and sou'westers. The bedraggled pair landed unceremoniously, flat on their stomachs, completely winded and all dignity long gone. With nothing to hold on to but the sides of the wagon, and the road being full of pot holes, it proved to be a hazardous trip. For the whole of that terrifying, lurching journey, they clung on to each other for dear life, quite certain that at any moment they would roll off the back and be left for dead on the open road, while each of them privately wondered what on earth they had let themself in for.

✤   ✤   ✤

The lorry drove along a series of roads and tracks that led through the dense woodland filling the valley of the River Fowey, passing over a humpbacked bridge before finally turning left through a pair of ornate gates by a small square stone lodge with a single smoking chimney. Inside, unseen from the road, a young girl stood at the kitchen window, hands resting in hot, soapy water. She tucked a stray lock of hair behind her ear, leaving a soap bubble caught in a shining black curl as she watched in silent envy. The lorry trundled past, as it did every day, to and fro, backwards and forwards, morning and night, full of happy, laughing girls. She had grown accustomed to the sound, yet marvelled that they could still find the energy to sing after a long day working in the woods.

Rose had once been fond of singing herself. She'd always believed in starting each day with a light heart, but that had been before certain individuals had devoted the rest of it to draining that exuberance from her.

Almost on cue, the sound of squeals and a different sort of laughter came from the living room behind her, followed by the voice of her brother, slurred with drink.

'Come here, Gertie, me sweet maid, let me warm ye up. Rose, when you've finished, fetch in another load of logs, there's a good girl.'

Rose let out a heavy sigh but made no response. She hadn't sat down for more than a minute since she'd left her bed at six, or was it five, this morning. There always seemed something needing to be done, some task to perform, even now, at the end of a day, when she'd thought herself free at last.

She leaned forward to get a better view of the road but it was quite empty now of the lumbering vehicle. Despite the mud and the rain, the long tiring days felling, the sparse food and probably harsh discipline at times, Rose wished she could be one of them, one of the laughing girls in the truck, so that one day it might carry her away from this existence she called a life.

She longed for this impossible dream with all her young heart. She envied their freedom, their energy, their ability to laugh at nothing. Most of all, she envied them the warmth of loving companionship.

Rose couldn't remember the last time she'd had a friend of her own. She had a vague memory of playing with some children long ago on a beach, so she must have had friends once, mustn't she? But then, perhaps not. The only one she could truly recall ever having was her darling mother. Sometimes Rose's heart ached with the pain of losing her.

When Eddie had got this job at Clovellan House, she'd thought they'd landed in heaven. It had been the first good thing that had happened to them in over two years, ever since poor Papa's death which had followed on so quickly after Ma's that Rose had thought the pain would go on forever. Everything would be better now, she'd thought. Eddie would feel he had a purpose at last, that he was valued, and his temper would improve. Now she knew different. His inexplicable resentment of her had continued to fester, quite beyond her comprehension.

No matter how hard she tried to please him, however much she assured him of her deep respect and love for him, her darling brother, he seemed determined to hold her responsible for what he perceived to be his parents' rejection of him. Rose knew it was only because of the deep grief he suffered, but her own helplessness in the face of such obdurate misery filled her with sadness And, beautiful as it was, here the empty rooms, the formal gardens, even the woods around them, seemed to echo with her loneliness.

'Rose, d'you hear me? We're bloody freezing in here.'

'Coming.'

Chapter Two

The rain had finally stopped as the lorry continued along a private drive through open parkland, allowing the girls to catch enticing glimpses of a rambling stone house set at the end of an avenue of elms. Granite walls, ghostly pale, stood out against the deepening blue of dusk, interrupted at regular intervals by rows of windows that seemed to blink sleepily beneath eyebrows of typically Cornish hood-moulds. Built around a large forecourt, the house sported battlemented walls, formal gardens, neatly clipped topiary and stone balustrades along its elegant terraces.

Gracie thought for one delicious moment that they were about to be billeted in a stately home but the lorry turned away from the house and drove on, labouring up a gentle slope with much crashing of gears. By the time it finally drew to a halt it was almost dark and she could see very little but a row of huts, what might have been a large marquee and a queue of girls making their way into it. The whole site appeared to be surrounded by a belt of beech woods. They climbed stiffly down from the lorry, nursing their many bruises, and were soon inches deep in mud.

'Oh, great! This is all we need. Don't attempt to drag your kitbag over this, little Titch, I'll carry both,' Lou announced, and did so, one on each shoulder.

Following a supper of Spam, lettuce and tomatoes, they found themselves billeted in corrugated iron huts, each one accommodating twenty girls in bunk beds. Gracie and Lou chose to share one near the door.

'Might be useful,' Lou pointed out with a sly wink, opting for the bottom one since she claimed to be less agile than her smaller friend. Gracie guessed that she meant it would be convenient for allowing its occupant to slip easily in and out of the hut, should the need occur.

They quickly stowed away their gear in the adjoining lockers, then made up their beds with the sheets and blankets provided but, instead of a mattress, found they were expected to sleep on 'biscuits'. These were so thin and hard, it was necessary to have two, or even three, on top of each other. That first night Gracie hardly slept a wink as the 'biscuits' slipped about, entirely defeating her attempts to rest. Then it seemed she'd no sooner managed to get off to sleep when they were woken by the loud clanging of a bell. It was barely six-thirty. Lou leaped out of bed shouting 'Fire!' which made the other girls laugh. But the new recruits soon learned that snatching a few extra minutes' sleep was unwise as that bell meant action.

'Stand by your beds!' a stentorian voice rang out, followed by the wheezing figure of Matron. A substantial woman, whose uniform was as severe as her unforgiving face, she rolled, rather than walked, into the room. She was so huge, Lou half expected her feet to make imprints in the planked floor.

Inspection had begun.

It was made clear that for their first morning only a somewhat lenient attitude would be taken. Hereafter it would be very different. In future by the time inspection was called, they needed to be up, washed, and dressed in their shorts and PT shirts with beds neatly made and lockers tidy, ready to march outside for physical training the moment it was over.

'Good lord,' Lou complained. 'Have we joined the army?'

'Indeed you have,' came the strident voice once more. 'The Women's Land Army, and *don't you forget it!*' Despite the promise of leniency, a few unfortunates were unceremoniously stripped of their coverings and tipped from bed, a rude awakening to the day.

Sleepy girls stumbled over each other in their efforts to line up at the wash basins, find the right clothes and make their beds, all apparently at the same time. Once everyone was finally dressed they were given punctilious lessons on folding and stowing away gear, polishing badges and shoes, and how to make proper hospital corners. Lou foolishly asked what these were as she'd never had to do one before and received a brisk lecture in return for her honesty. She was made to strip her bed and remake it, not once but four times, until she had done it to Matron's complete satisfaction.

'Got it now?'

Arms and back aching with the effort of her labours, Lou hastily assured her that she had.

'Excuse me, Matron. Could I just have a word?' Gracie approached the enormous woman, looking rather like a kitten addressing an elephant for all her manner was friendly, chatty, almost as if they were two old friends who'd stopped for a gossip over the garden wall. Lou held her breath. What on earth was coming now? 'Could I just say that these "biscuits", as you call them, are most dreadfully uncomfortable?'

'Are they indeed?' Matron's tone was so freezingly pleasant, Lou could almost see the icicles forming on her breath. 'I dare say you have a feather bed at home?'

'As a matter of fact, I do,' said Gracie, in pleased surprise that Matron should know such a thing. 'Feather beds are so comfortable, aren't they?'

'Well, you won't get a feather bed here.'

'Oh, no, I didn't expect to.' Gracie seemed to treat the growling response as some sort of joke and smiled sweetly at

Matron, who gazed impassively back. Lou briefly closed her eyes and issued a silent prayer to the Almighty to strike her friend dumb within the next half second. Unfortunately, He must not have heard for Gracie blithely continued, 'But I do think we should have proper mattresses else how will we get any rest?'

There was a collective indrawing of breath. Matron was clearly not a woman to mess with. Lou took a step closer to her friend's side, as if to offer protection from the retaliation which would surely come, or at least alert Gracie to the dangerous path she trod. Apparently oblivious of the warning, her friend was off again.

'Oh, and then there's the matter of the lorry . . .'

'Lorry?'

Lou felt her insides shrivel to nothing, knowing it would not be pleasant to see murder done before her very eyes. The silence in the hut was profound.

'Probably the state of the lorries isn't your responsibility.' Gracie gave a polite little smile by way of apology if this were indeed the case. 'But perhaps you could tell me to whom I should speak on the matter because I really do think that they should be covered.'

'You do?'

'Oh, yes, to keep the rain out.'

'I take it that you don't like getting wet?'

'Not really, no.'

'How unfortunate for you.'

'Even the other girls, who were wearing sou'westers and capes, were almost as cold and wet as we were. And there was absolutely nowhere to sit, or to hold on to. We were falling about like skittles all over the place. There could easily have been an accident.'

Lou would have liked to have had something to hold on to right then. This slip of a girl, who had seemed so quiet and inoffensive at first sight, possessed the heart of a lion, no doubt about it.

Matron's flabby jowls quivered as she shook her head in disbelief at such temerity, dark eyes narrowing to pin points and burying themselves within the folds of her fleshy face. 'Dear, dear, dear. Now I wonder what we should do about that?'

Apparently oblivious to the caustic edge to her tone, Gracie calmly suggested that a tarpaulin might be useful. The colour of the woman's face turned slowly from pink to red and through to dark purple but Gracie seemed not to notice that either. She gave every impression of accepting the thin-lipped smile as entirely genuine. 'And maybe seats of some sort?'

'Indeed!' The woman seemed to swell in size, like a bristling cat confronting its enemy. 'Perhaps you would care to visit my office later, so that we may discuss these complaints in more detail.' The sweet tone of voice dripped acid.

'Before breakfast?' asked Gracie brightly.

Matron's voice dropped by several octaves. 'This evening will do very well. After supper. You might even have thought of a few more problems by then.'

'How very kind.' Gracie remained seemingly impervious to the undercurrent of danger.

As the older woman half turned away, her expression like carved stone, Lou sprang to life and slapped a hand over her friend's mouth before, as she later explained, Gracie could put her foot in it again.

'I thought she was jolly understanding,' Gracie protested as Lou continued to hiss furious warnings at her underneath her breath as they made their way outside.

'Of course she sounded bloody understanding! She's the sort to smile even as she issues the ten lashes.'

Lou grumbled that PT was a form of merciless drill better suited to the Marines as she bent and stretched, jumped and pounded, marched and ran – but then hastily retracted these

remarks, fearful Gracie might add them to her list of complaints. 'It's just that I'm not built for leaping about. Too much
wobble. I shall have to buy a more serviceable brassière. In this
one, I'm very likely to knock myself out if I jump too high.'
"Which remark left Gracie so helpless with laughter that she
tripped over her own feet and fell flat, which did not endear her
to the PT mistress.

Following an hour of this torture, there was just time to change
quickly and again stand in a shivering line at the basins before
breakfast at eight-thirty. This was followed by a medical; an
embarrassing and humiliating procedure in which Gracie was
bluntly told that she was really rather small, and was she
absolutely certain she would be able to cope with the job? She
felt devastated, convinced for one terrible moment that she was
about to be sent home again, back to the village shop and her
warring parents.

'I'm not ill, am I?'

'No, of course not. Fit as a flea. But will you be able to
manage to fell trees and manhandle the poles?'

'I'll manage,' Gracie stoutly defended herself. 'I'm really
quite strong.'

'This is Tarzan, not Jane, you're looking at. She could
take Hitler on single-handed, let alone a piffling little tree,'
Lou put in, hoping to help her friend, and after another
agonising moment while the nurse chewed on her pencil,
Gracie was finally rewarded by a shrug, a smile, and passed
fit for service.

A general scrummage ensued as the girls were sorted into
squads and issued with the remainder of their working uniform:
dungarees, breeches in corduroy for everyday, alpaca for best,
Aertex shirts, a warm sweater, long socks and the famous green
beret.

'What about underwear?' Gracie politely enquired, examining the growing pile.

'Use your own.'

'Thank heaven for small mercies,' Lou murmured, struggling to find a pair of boots which fitted. Gracie wanted to find an oilskin which wasn't so stiff and huge it swamped her tiny figure. The nurse was very nearly proved right as the mere weight of it almost had her toppling over, the whole rigmarole made worse by another fit of the giggles. Once they were all kitted out, it was time to pile into the lorry and be taken off for their first day of training.

'I feel like I've done a day's work already,' Lou groaned, struggling to keep a grip on the side.

This lorry was the same sort as the one which had picked them up from the station and, before they'd got very far, it once again began to rain, the kind of drizzly autumn moistness for which Cornwall is famous. Gracie commented that they'd all be soaking wet before they even got to wherever they were working. 'It's too bad, you know. We're not like the Land Girls who get to work close to a farm. We'll no doubt be out in the woods all day where there's precious little shelter of any kind.' The other girls agreed, admitting that the vehicle was a death trap, far too slippery and insecure for safety. Unfortunately, none of them was prepared to voice a complaint.

'And don't you either, Titch. For God's sake, don't take that woman on. She's poison.'

'Nonsense, I found her most accommodating. Really, Lou, I think you're worrying unduly. We do have rights, you know. And don't call me Titch.'

'Sorry.'

Whatever rights were discussed in Matron's office after supper that evening, Gracie wasn't saying. Lou could only guess from the tightness of her small, pale face as she re-emerged, and from her morose silence as she pulled on her pyjamas and climbed into the top bunk. None of which augured well for the future. Lou knew from her experience of working in a factory that if you rubbed someone in authority up the wrong way, they always got their own back. In the end.

'Don't worry, love. At least you tried.'

Disappointed and alarmed by the blank wall of indifference she'd experienced, the woman absolutely refusing to allow her complaints to go any further, Gracie snuggled down between the coarse cotton sheets. There was generally a reason, she'd discovered in her limited experience, if someone was being deliberately obnoxious. All she had to do was to discover what it was. Matron's eyes might be gimlet bright but there was something behind them, Gracie was sure of it. Despair, loneliness perhaps, almost fear. She'd seen that expression before.

Overwhelmed suddenly by tiredness, Gracie knew she'd be asleep in seconds for all there was still a good deal of chatter going on in the hut, as well as stifled laughter. This had been the bit she'd dreaded most: having to share accommodation with so many other girls. As an only child, she'd always valued her privacy but, contrary to her fears, living closely with others didn't bother her after all. The gossip and giggles made her feel comfortable and secure, seeming to prove she was part of a team, that they were all pulling together. They were a grand bunch of girls, the woods had been magnificent, and at least she'd survived the first day.

If she failed to get round Matron, she might try the Supervisor in a day or two, with or without permission. All she had to do was pluck up the courage. Before she knew it, the bell was clanging in her ear, the night was over, she'd slept like a log and Gracie was up out of bed like a shot, eager to start another new day.

✳   ✳   ✳

In the first week of training the new recruits were introduced to the four main tasks with which they would be faced: measuring and marking appropriate trees for telegraph poles or pitprops, felling with an axe, use of the crosscut saw, clearing and burning the leftover small branches, or brash as it was called. They were also given driving lessons so they would be capable of handling a tractor or lorry. The days were long and tiring, the obligatory hour of physical training each morning followed by a full day working in the woods which, in addition to instruction in the use of tools, involved learning the different types of trees and timber.

'We'll toughen you up,' was the constant cry from the Supervisor, from Matron, and particularly from the old foresters who attempted to pass on to the girls a lifetime's experience in just one month, laughing at their complaints of aching muscles, blistered hands and sore feet.

One of these, called Thomas but known as Tom-Tom by the girls because his shiny bald pate resembled a highly polished drum, took quite a shine to Lou. He was always at great pains to show her how to swing her axe, and took particular care to position her legs safely out of harm's way, whenever she was using the crosscut saw.

'Soppy old man! He must be sixty if he's a day,' Lou would chuckle, but then would flirt outrageously with him, giving him cheeky winks over the heads of the shorter girls.

'You're incorrigible,' Gracie chuckled, but Lou replied that a friend might come in useful one day. In fact, she had a particular day in mind: the very first Gordon could manage to get a pass and come over.

'You won't find me chopping or sawing then, bet your sweet life on that.' Her face softened and she hugged herself in excited anticipation, making her full breasts jiggle enticingly so that Tom-Tom, watching from a few yards away, very nearly walked into a tree. 'Ooh, I can hardly wait. I haven't seen my lovely Gordon for a whole week. It's mortal agony.'

At the end of a long day in the woods, there was still work to be done. The girls were given evening lectures on hygiene, first aid and fire fighting. They were told that timber was a vital munition, providing pitprops used in the production of coal, railway sleepers, even telegraph poles. They learned how the Women's Timber Corps had proved those pessimists and cynics wrong who'd believed women could never replace the young woodsmen and foresters who'd been called up. On the contrary, they were playing a vital role in production.

At first the old foresters did the felling and a huge shire horse dragged the felled trees into a nearby field where it was the task of the timber girls to cut them into carefully measured lengths. They soon learned the importance of well-sharpened saws and axes, how they mustn't ever drop them and must always carry an axe with the cutting edge downwards.

'Too easy,' Lou announced, after a few days of this. 'Why do we only get the boring part? I want to fell trees, not just slice them up.'

Feeling adventurous, she asked Tom-Tom's permission to give it a go herself.

He was doubtful, as was Gracie, but undeterred Lou lifted her axe and made the first swing, missing the tree completely and ending up with the four-and-a-half-pound axe buried in the ground. When he had stopped laughing, Tom-Tom again demonstrated the correct procedure, the stance, the right swing, the angle of each cut, and Lou teasingly plonked a kiss of thanks on his whiskered chin. But even with Gracie's help they made little progress upon the thick sturdy trunk, and he returned some time later to find them both leaning against it.

'What are you two up to now?'

'Trying to push it over.'

Shoving back his hat, he scratched his head and softly muttered, 'Why need England tremble?'

*　　*　　*

Despite the wet weather which continued throughout that week, they were a cheerful bunch. As they bumped along in the truck, chattering happily together, Lou and Gracie were relieved to discover that the other girls came from similar backgrounds to their own. They'd been hairdressers, clerks, shop assistants, typists, many from industrial towns, so working outdoors was a new experience for them too.

Freckle-faced Tess was their blunt talking, oil-streaked, unsympathetic driver. She'd worked in a wool shop before the war but now, at only twenty five, had gained considerable experience driving for the Timber Corps. Her first task each day was to start up the lorry using its winding handle, since it was too ancient to boast a self starter, no easy task. Lou readily took on this job so that Tess could sit behind the wheel and be ready to pump the pedals when the old engine finally burst into life. Woe betide anyone who was slow at jumping aboard before she set off. Tess waited for no one.

Someone would choose a song, '*Off To Work We Go*' being a favourite, and Buttercup, as the lorry was fondly named, would finally cough, lurch forward, and bump along the deserted lanes in time to the rousing singing of its happy occupants. But the journey was not always so straightforward. Sometimes the lorry would splutter to a halt, the engine dying after only a mile or two, and the passengers would have no option but to walk the rest of the way, while Buttercup followed on later, in her own good time.

But walking or riding, there was always time for talk, or a 'bit of crack', as Lou called it, and as they talked, the girls grew closer.

In their particular squad there was Enid, who hated to get her hair messed up and, like Lou, was desperate to know when they might have a bit of free time so she could sneak out to meet her sweetheart. Then there was lean and wiry Jeannie, a talkative Scot who always carried a packet of cigarettes in her dungaree breast pocket, though she only ever smoked half a cigarette at a time, carefully returning the dog-end to the packet with fingers stained yellow from the habit. Another girl, Lena, rarely stopped complaining for more than five minutes together. If the September sun shone she complained it was too hot to work. When it rained, she moaned about the mud – particularly the mud – but also the pay, the hard beds, her aching back, and anything else which displeased her, even accusing people of borrowing her soap without permission.

'Goodness, Lena. You're not accusing me, I hope? Why would I use your lovely lavender soap when I've got me own best coal tar?' Lou said, her face deadpan.

Lena frowned, not quite sure whether her leg was being pulled or not. 'I really do think people should respect other people's property, that's all.' She brushed away a fleck of mud, thrown up by the lorry's wheels. 'One has to have standards and I really can't cope with all this – this –'

'Weather?' A burst of giggles all round.

'All right. Make fun if you must. I'm only saying . . .'

'We know what you're saying, Lena. Now put a sock in it, lassie,' Jeannie tartly informed her. 'Ye're not the only one suffering here. I'd gi'e me virginity, if I still had it, for a guid long soak in a hot tub.'

More snorts of laughter at Jeannie's bluntness, while Lou glanced anxiously at Gracie who was taking all of this in with a worrying expression of concern. 'I hope you aren't considering tackling Matron again? Personally, I'd rather face an enemy tank.'

Gracie merely lifted her pale eyebrows, flicked back her long blonde hair and said not a word. Nevertheless on the fifth day, when it once again poured with rain, an awning for the lorry was indeed provided, as well as wooden benches around each of its four sides. Tired of being blocked by Matron, she'd approached the Supervisor directly who had apparently been unaware of the problem, or so she claimed, and was only too happy to put it right. Flushed with pleasure at this small victory, Gracie was given a rousing cheer and treated as a heroine, though she apologised that she'd got nowhere over the mattresses. Matron was adamant on that. The 'biscuits' would stay.

Lou was astounded and hugely impressed. There was more to this girl than met the eye. However, there remained the danger that in bypassing Matron and achieving her object, she might well have inflamed relations with the woman still further.

At least the food is good,' Lou had remarked on the first day as she'd bitten into a hefty cheese sandwich. 'What a treat! I love cheese. Haven't had any in ages.'

The girls' appetites, already healthy, grew day by day and lunch was always a welcome interlude, a time to find a quiet spot under a tree, occasionally to be warmed by the pale autumn sunshine when there was a break between showers. It was an opportunity for them to put their feet up for half an hour, to get out their packets of sandwiches and thermos flasks of tea.

On the second day Lou had again welcomed the cheese sandwich, and the third. Even on the fourth day, as Lena was loudly complaining and asking for sardines, she'd devoured her lunch without comment. By the end of the week, though, as she opened yet another packet of cheese sandwiches, she began to think that for once Lena might have a point. 'Oh, no, not again!'

'As agricultural workers we're allowed extra cheese,' Tess explained. 'So that's what we get. Cheese, cheese and more cheese.'

'One can have too much of a good thing,' Lou groaned, biting into the thick crust with a grimace of distaste.

At the start of the second week she came to regret her objection to cheese when she opened up her lunch packet to find a kipper, complete with bones and tail, stuck between the two slices of bread. 'Lord, I can't eat this.'

Some of the girls valiantly tried, picking out the bones with painstaking care. Lou tossed hers into some brambles and, grabbing Gracie, made her do the same. 'Come on Titch, I spotted a pub down the road. Let's sweet talk good old Tom-Tom into keeping an eye out for the Super, while we go and get a proper feed.'

Keeping a wary eye out herself for the Supervisor, Lou threaded her way through the trees, Gracie close behind. Reaching the edge of the woods unobserved, the two girls lay flat on their stomach and wriggled through a gap in some prickly hawthorn bushes, squealing in agony every time they were stabbed by the sharp thorns. Giggling uncontrollably by this time, they slithered and rolled down the smooth bank of a high Cornish hedge, lost their footing and landed right on top of a passing bicycle which had just come hurtling around the corner, sending the poor unsuspecting cyclist flying.

Chapter Three

Rose lay on the ground beneath a tangle of bent wheels, arms, legs and prone bodies, Tizz's anxious barking ringing in her ears, wondering how much worse the day could get. Even as the three girls sorted out which limb belonged to whom, her mind wasn't taking in a word of their abject apologies or their offers of a stiff drink. She couldn't even find it in herself to calm the poor dog down. She was too busy examining the extent of the damage to the bicycle, worrying about lunch and how on earth she was going to get home now in time to make it. Worst of all, she worried what Eddie's reaction would be to this further failure on her part.

The day had got off to a bad start already with her being late with his breakfast. He'd paid no heed to her excuses about having overslept because of a prolonged weeding session in the garden the day before, he'd been too busy complaining about his toast being cold and the fact that it was a boiled egg again. Couldn't he have bacon for a change? Rose had longed to remind him that there was a war on and bacon was impossible to find, unless they had a pig to kill, which they hadn't. She'd wanted to say that if he wasn't in such a fortunate position as to keep hens, or at least to have a sister who kept hens, he would have had to get through the war on dry toast and home-made jam with very little sugar just like everyone else. But she'd somehow managed to hold her tongue.

Perhaps she held her tongue too often but such arguments carried little weight. Eddie was far too selfish to care about how other people suffered. He only concerned himself with the war so far as it affected him, which was hardly at all. Apart from being rather old, at thirty-four, for the armed forces, he'd avoided being called up by taking this job as estate manager though he did precious little work on the estate, leaving that to others, in particular his little sister. Nor did he actually do much in the way of managing. Since the major part of Clovellan House had been requisitioned by the government, there was little for him to do beyond act as a sort of caretaker of the west wing; the Clovellan family having retired to Canada for the duration. There were times when Rose longed to speak her mind, to point out that she was a person too, with wishes and dreams of her own, yet she rarely did. Rose knew herself for a coward where Eddie's temper was concerned. He was not a man to cross. It was vital that he be kept in a good humour or she would be the one to suffer.

She noted the familiar hump that was Gertie beside him in the brass bed, huddled beneath the bedclothes. Not that Rose had any objection to Eddie courting the housekeeper, though whether he'd ever wed her was another matter and not her concern. Bored with having too little to do, the pair seemed a good match and were able to keep each other amused for hours, it seemed. No, what Rose did object to, quite strongly, was finding herself waiting on his mistress in addition to her brother.

On this subject she never made any attempt to hold her tongue. Only the other day she'd had call to remind Gertie that it was the housekeeper's responsibility to wash the curtains, and not Rose's job at all.

'Why do it then?' had been Gertie's swift response. 'Nobody asked you to.'

'On the contrary, Eddie asked me to. He's as sick as I am of windows festooned with cobwebs. We can hardly see out.'

Gertie had given a careless shrug. ''Oo is there to do the lookin', 'ceptin us?' On the wrong side of forty, she was plump, bone idle, took too few baths and had the kind of raucous laugh and loud voice which filled Rose with embarrassment every time the woman opened her mouth. On this occasion, as on many another, she'd flounced off in high dudgeon, no doubt to complain to Eddie that his sister was picking on her again.

This morning she stirred, grunted, lifted her tousled head and blinked at Rose, before sinking back under the covers.

'You haven't forgotten about lunch,' Eddie sharply reminded her as Rose slid the tray over his lap, and she flushed bright pink because of course she had forgotten. Entirely. She'd planned to spend this unexpectedly glorious autumn day cutting out the old raspberry canes and tying up the new ones. Now she would have to waste the whole morning sweating over a smoky kitchen stove, cooking for his layabout friends and no doubt cleaning up after them for the rest of the day. He would also expect her to be suitably agreeable, laugh at their jokes, simper and flirt, as he did with all the other misfits he brought to Clovellan House. Rose shuddered at the prospect.

'No, of course I hadn't forgotten. How many did you say were coming? Three?'

'There'll be six of us. For God's sake, Rose, can't you remember a damned thing?' He tapped his egg, growled about its hardness and demanded to know what she planned to cook for them.

'Sorry, but it'll have to be good old Woolton Pie again. We've loads of vegetables at least,' she said, thinking of her empty cupboards. No doubt his guests would also use up the last of the parsnip wine, leaving them bereft before winter had even started. Though that might be no bad thing. Eddie had been plundering Lord Clovellan's wine cellars even more recklessly than usual of late and Rose wondered if something was troubling him. He'd certainly become increasingly iras-cible.

She plumped up his pillows, hoping to keep him in a good mood, thinking he seemed older than his years and tired-looking, hair dark with grease, a stubble of several days' growth on his sunken cheeks and sharply jutting jaw. His eyes bore dark shadows beneath their reddened lower rims.

'Vegetable pie? Not again!' he complained, his voice tetchy. 'It's time you got yourself better organised, girl. I told you to get beef steak or chops. Or a chicken would be nice.'

'It would also be impossible. If you want to continue to have eggs for your breakfast, hard or not, we can't start killing off the hens – we've barely a dozen left.' Rose paused at the bedroom door long enough to offer him her most stunning smile and, as so often before, he was startled by her loveliness. That heart-shaped face, with its olive-skinned perfection framed by a mane of wildly curling blue-black hair and eyes as blue as a Cornish sea, was a sight worth seeing. But if such beauty was wasted on himself, he had plans to put it to good use. She owed him that much at least. He realised she was still talking. 'Don't worry, I shall liven it up with powdered egg and tomatoes, we've plenty of both. Followed by lovely apple dumpling. I'm sure your friends will be very happy with that.'

Eddie felt a stirring of unease as he struggled to imagine the fastidious Dexter Mulligan happily tucking into homely pies and puddings instead of the steak or juicy pork chops he'd been promised. Very particular about promises being kept was Dexter, whether it be a decent lunch, a good hand at poker or a bit of how's your father. On this occasion he'd been promised all three, Gertie always being willing to spread her favours if necessary. But then she knew full well that keeping Dexter happy was vital, or he might start to tot up just how much in his debt Eddie actually was. And that would never do.

Eddie also made sure that Rose knew nothing of these all-night card parties, or how much of their joint wages vanished on the back of a card.

Gertie's muffled voice emerged from beneath the covers though no head appeared this time. 'It's a wonder we ain't all bleedin' clucking. I'll wake up and find I've turned into a flippin' hen meself one of these days.'

As ever, fears for his own skin spilled over into annoyance at Rose. 'Gertie's right. I know I should be grateful when the rest of the world gets only one egg a week but I'm not in the least bit grateful, Rose. I'm simply fed up to the back teeth with your complete incompetence. And they're not my *friends!* How many times do I have to tell you? They're colleagues, business colleagues. Useful contacts. *Associates!*'

'Of course. Sorry, I keep forgetting.' Seeing his face darken with fresh irritation, Rose began to feel hot and flustered, anxious to escape his censorious attitude. And really she never fully understood what business it was, exactly, that he was involved in. Nor dare she ask, her thoughts flying back to the lunch and her urgent need to inspect the kitchen garden for vegetables. It was all very well saying vegetable pie but there was no guarantee there'd be anything exciting in season, and Eddie always expected the very best. The celery certainly wasn't ready, nor the leeks. Perhaps she might find the odd remaining marrow in the glasshouse.

'I just wish you'd try to be more imaginative with the meals you choose to serve, as well as better organised,' he told her crossly, as if all the pantries and larders in Clovellan House were still stacked with the best of fare, and the servants' quarters awash with people to cook it. 'And you're forever on the last minute. How many times have I told you to plan properly?'

'I do my best. For goodness' sake, Eddie, there is a war on.'

'I'm sick of the bloody war.' With one furious gesture he swept the egg to the floor and Rose flew to pick up it before the spilled yolk ruined the rug. Gathering up the remains of his breakfast, she edged towards the door. 'Would you like more toast instead?'

He ignored the question. 'Other people cope, and so should you. Think ahead for once, why don't you?'

It seemed the last straw for he was constantly reminding her to be careful with the budgeting, saying how difficult it was to make ends meet. 'Other people don't have a house the size of Clovellan to manage, even if it is only the west wing, and all *without* the help of a decent housekeeper.' She raised her voice to make sure Gertie could hear beneath the blankets. 'Or a brother who thinks he's Lord Muck and insists on holding grand luncheon parties he can't afford. You should cut down on this socialising of yours, Eddie. What with the war and everything, we all have to make sacrifices.'

'As I've explained to you a dozen times, my little soirées are essential to our survival, to *my* business plans and to *your* future security. Why are you so *stupid?*'

For once Rose stuck to her guns. 'Because I only have one pair of hands. Why doesn't Gertie help more, that's the question?'

'I helps a lot, I do,' came the mumbled response from beneath the bedclothes.

'She has other duties.'

It was as if something inside Rose snapped. 'And we know what those are, don't we? She'll lift her skirt for anyone but never lift a finger to help me. The pair of you are worse than useless. You leave me to do everything and it isn't fair, it really isn't. I never asked to come and live here, in this big draughty house. I would've been quite happy to stay in our old home in Paignton, or to take a smaller house some place if we'd needed to economise. Nor have I asked you to hold luncheon parties for *my* "future security". If I had my way I'd leave this place. I could be doing something far more useful for the war effort than cooking vegetable pie for your *business associates*. I'll tell you that much for nothing, Eddie Tregarreth!'

Rose was breathless by the time she'd finished her tirade, rebellion spent, as this was the nearest she'd ever come to crossing him. Yet she saw at once that her efforts had been wasted, for all she felt some satisfaction at having expressed her feelings out loud at last, for Eddie simply put back his head and roared with laughter.

'*You* help the war effort? Don't make me laugh.' He was enjoying himself so thoroughly that Gertie emerged from the bed clothes, shrieking with gusto as she wrapped her fat arms about his neck and slobbered kisses all over his face. Eddie grabbed the ample breast pressed up close against him, giving it a lusty squeeze as he pulled Gertie back down beneath him, humped up the bedclothes and began to straddle her. 'Now, my sweet maid, what can I do for you?'

Taking advantage of his distraction, Rose made her escape. Experience had taught her that any further argument would only make matters worse.

He came to the kitchen later to offer his apologies, which Rose graciously and lovingly accepted. She understood perfectly that he wasn't quite himself this morning, should have guessed he might have a bad head. Would he care for coffee? Yes, it was only chicory but better than nothing. He wouldn't? Water then? An Aspirin? No? Well, why didn't he take a stroll in the garden? That might clear his head, and she was sorry that she'd forgotten to run his bath but she was having trouble getting the boiler to light again.

'For God's sake, Rose, what have you done to the dratted thing now? Haven't I told you a hundred times not to riddle it too hard? Don't you ever do anything right? You do realise they'll be here in less than two hours? What time will lunch be ready? My God, look at you! What a messy creature you are. I hope you intend to clean yourself up and change before they arrive.'

Tucking back a stray lock of hair that had come loose from the tatty bit of ribbon meant to hold it secure, Rose struggled to decide which question to answer first. She decided her priority must be lunch. 'Don't worry, there's plenty of time to sort out the boiler. Lunch won't be ready till half-past one. You can give them a sherry or something, have your business talk first.'

'Half-past? But we usually . . .'

'I don't care what we usually do, it will be half-past one today. Like it or lump it.' Having offered his apology, she'd hoped that he would go away and leave her to it, or even that Gertie might emerge and help. No such luck in either case. Gertie was, as usual, notable by her absence and Eddie the very opposite. He hovered at Rose's elbow, instructing her on how finely she should shred the lettuce or slice the cucumber, closely watching every move she made.

Out of the corner of her eye Rose could see Tizz cowering in her basket under the table. The old black and tan collie dog always trembled with fear every time Eddie appeared, and no wonder. Even now her brother put out one booted foot and kicked her.

'For goodness' sake, Eddie, leave Tizz alone. She's done nothing to offend you.'

'She shouldn't be here, in the damned kitchen. It's not hygienic.'

'She's doing no harm. You bring more muck in on those boots of yours.'

Even so Rose wiped her hands on a tea cloth, called the dog and led her out to the wood shed. Tizz, understanding perfectly, made no protest, thumping her tail hard on the ground as Rose explained the situation. 'You know how he is when he's in one of his moods. Stay here, there's a good girl. Just till he's found somebody else to bully.' She bent down and rested her cheek against the dog's face while Tizz snuffled a cold but sympathetic nose into her ear. Rose chuckled softly, fondled the dog's floppy ears then bolted the door and went back to the kitchen.

Eddie was still there, waiting for her, prowling around, opening cupboard doors, telling her which dinner service to use, which cruet, reminding her to polish the wine glasses, to clean the silver as he'd noticed it looked tarnished when they'd used it the other day. It clearly didn't occur to him, Rose thought, to pick up a cloth and do it himself.

Cooking in this vast kitchen was a nightmare, with nothing where she needed it. She much preferred the tiny lodge house but Eddie always insisted on holding his lunches in the dining room of the main house, using it very much as his own, just as if he had every right to do so. She rather suspected there were times when he and Gertie actually slept in the master bedroom. Gracie always hoped someone would notice and complain but nobody ever did. The Timber Corps was far too busy with its own affairs to bother, and inspectors from government offices rarely ventured this far west.

She had the sudden frightening thought that she'd no flour left for the apple dumpling and ran to the larder to check. The familiar white bag sat on the top shelf and Rose clambered up on a stool to pull it down, sighing with relief to find it almost full. But in getting down from the stool, she somehow managed to drop it and lose almost half of its contents all over the floor.

'For goodness' sake, what are you doing now? Do you have to be so completely clumsy and incompetent?'

Rose snatched up the dustpan and brush and began to sweep, flour billowing everywhere, covering her hair, face and arms in a fine white dust. She could feel the tension mounting inside her, tears pricking her eyes. She'd be in need of an Aspirin herself in a moment. Or a double brandy. She went back to peeling the potatoes, hands shaking.

'You should use the potato peeler, a knife is wasteful.'

'Why don't *you* use the potato peeler?' Making no attempt now to hide her distress and annoyance, Rose thrust the potato into his hand and, snatching up a pan, crossed the vast flag-stoned kitchen to the low Belfast sink, filled it with cold water then brought it back to the table to toss in the rest of the peeled potatoes. Eddie trailed after her, there and back, still clasping the unpeeled one.

'Are you sure you've done enough? I said six for lunch.'

'For heaven's sake! You've got a potato in your hand. Why don't you peel that, if you're not satisfied?'

He stared at it as if it were alien produce dropped from another planet. He looked so utterly helpless and forlorn, so boyishly perplexed, that she was suddenly filled with a great wash of love and pity for him. Hadn't he cared for her almost half her life? Hadn't he suffered the loss of their parents too? Despite his odd moods, meanness and temper, he was her dear brother after all. The only family she possessed.

True, he'd exhibited jealousy at the way her parents had spoiled her, but then Eddie would have been the age she was now when she'd been born. Just turned seventeen. It must have come as rather a shock to him to be presented with this unexpected sister after being an only child for so long. She always took this into account whenever she felt aggrieved by his lack of patience with her.

More importantly, ever since Rose was ten years old he'd

been the only father she'd known. She'd depended upon him entirely. So of course she loved him. Penny-pinching, selfish, unpredictable and lazy though he might be, she greatly appreciated his care of her, as well as her own good fortune at having lived the last few years in this beautiful place.

Now she smiled fondly and, taking the potato from him, began to peel it with brisk efficiency. 'You really are hopeless in a kitchen but you're probably right, I haven't done enough potatoes.' She peeled, washed and chopped several more and set the pan on the stove to par boil them for five minutes.

She conceded, in all honesty to herself, that there were times when perhaps she should stand up to him more; that he did indeed bully her too much, particularly when he was in one of his sulks or suffering a hangover, as he was today. Yet wasn't she in dire need of someone to organise her? Wasn't he justified in criticising her incompetence? She was indeed inept, and stupid, and ridiculously clumsy. Attacking an onion, she nicked the ball of her thumb in her haste, almost as if to prove her point. Blood seeped out all over the white flesh.

'Drat!' She stuck it quickly under the cold tap, hoping he wouldn't notice or it would only result in yet another lecture. Fortunately, Eddie was too busy offering yet more instructions, reminding her to put the gas fire on in the dining room half an hour or so before the guests arrived. 'The government's paying and they won't notice a bit extra on the bill now and then.'

She tried to ignore him but he even trailed after her when she dashed out to the greenhouses, hastily pulling carrots, cutting lettuce and cucumber, plucking suitably ripe tomatoes which she could quickly heat up and easily skin for the pie.

'Have you remembered to buy fresh flowers? You know I expect the room to be elegantly done out. One can't have a luncheon party without the correct floral arrangements.'

Rose sighed at the idiocy of this remark, biting back a strong desire to remind him that men years younger than himself were dying every day in France, in Singapore, in Italy, and all he could think to worry about was whether there were enough flowers for the table. 'Of course I haven't bought any flowers,' she snapped. 'We grow our own, for heaven's sake, in amongst the vegetables. Oh, no!' She gave a little cry of distress and, snatching up the bowl of tomatoes, forgetting even to search for a decent marrow, flew back to the kitchen. The water was boiling, spitting all over the clean surface of the stove. She made a dive for the pan, grabbed the handle, nearly dropped it again as it burned her fingers, then almost lost the now over-soft potatoes as she drained the water away in the sink.

Rose took a deep, steadying breath, deliberately striving to calm herself, knowing without needing to turn around that Eddie would be hovering close by, watching every mistake she made. She managed to toss him a careless smile and cheerfully announce that the moment Gertie emerged to help, she'd nip down to the village shop and see if Mrs Conley had a bit of cheese tucked away under the counter. Even the tiniest bit grated on top with breadcrumbs would liven up the taste of the pie.

Now here she was with a broken bicycle and a half-demented dog trying to lick her to death. She tried to stand up; cried out as pain shot up her leg. Correction, a broken bicycle, demented dog *and* an injured ankle. Even if there were any cheese left at the village shop, Rose knew she couldn't get it home in time. Her only hope was that Gertie would salvage something out of the disaster zone she'd left in the kitchen. Even so, Eddie would be furious with her and the price she would have to pay for her incompetence would be high.

Dexter Mulligan did not enjoy his lunch. Seated at the long mahogany table in his expensive houndstooth check suit (no utility clothing for him), his trilby hat neatly encircling the plate beside him, displeasure was all too apparent on his bone-thin face.

Eddie hastened to explain. 'Sorry about there being no steak. You know how it is with butchers these days, can't rely on 'em.'

The other guests, the Pursey brothers, never far from Dexter's side, and Bob Carlton and Syd Thorpe who were market traders of a sort, tucked into the pie with gusto but Dexter Mulligan stabbed half-heartedly at the mess on his plate and then, complaining that it was too watery, tipped the whole lot into a cut glass rose bowl standing on the sideboard. Having watched this performance in complete silence, the others picked up their own plates and followed suit.

'Dear me. What are we thinking of?' Mulligan mildly remarked, running his finger around the lip of the bowl. 'That's no way to treat such a beautiful piece of merchandise. Go and wash it out, Syd. You never know what it might be worth.'

'Don't worry, Gertie'll do it later,' Eddie said, and began to sweat. From the minute he'd seen that bloody hard boiled egg this morning, he'd known the day was going to be a disaster. He'd kill Rose, he would, when he laid hands on her. She would choose today, of all days, to let him down when it was vital he keep his illustrious guest sweet.

Dexter Mulligan was king of the streets, a spiv to see off all others who might lay claim to that title. If there was something – anything – one needed, Dexter Mulligan was the man to find it. At a price. Alternatively he could happily dispose of any item at a nice fat profit. He was a useful chap to know, though not one to cross. In Mulligan's opinion, if a man couldn't make money during a war, he wasn't worthy of his trade. They didn't come any sharper and Eddie had done quite a bit of business with him in the past year or two, anxious as he was to make a bob or two himself. He had handed over several items that he'd unearthed out of the cellars, cups and plates and pictures – the Clovellans would never miss.

Unfortunately, Dexter Mulligan also enjoyed a good game of poker, a skill Eddie lacked for all he'd been persuaded into playing long into the night on numerous occasions. He'd enjoyed some good wins in the past but recently had suffered a run of bad luck. He'd hoped today would turn the tide.

Now Mulligan stood up and declared his intention of taking a breath of fresh air.

'Grand idea,' Eddie agreed. 'Do us all good.' By the time they got back, Rose might have arrived and be able to rustle up something decent for them to eat. 'I'll lead the way, shall I?'

'No, no, Eddie. You stay here and look after my boys. Syd and Bob'll come with me. Gertie can show us round, can't you, doll? When we gets back, we can 'ave a nice little chat about that bit of business I mentioned the other day. Awright, mate?' His sharp little eyes flickered from one of his henchmen to the other, causing Eddie to sweat all the more.

'Yeah, right,' he agreed, and swallowed.

Even Gertie looked less than enthusiastic about her role for once, and cast him an anguished glance as she got up from the table. Eddie followed her to the door, all easy smiles and bonhomie. Uncharacteristically, he helped her on with her coat, in order to instruct her quietly to take Mulligan up to the summer house. 'And keep him happy, for all our bleedin' sakes. *Excel yourself!* Give him whatever he asks for. Or he'll have my head on a soddin' platter.'

After they'd gone, Eddie eagerly offered the grim-faced Pursey brothers a glass of port each, but instead found himself pinned to the wall with the point of a knife at his gullet. ' 'Ere, what the bleedin' hell . . .?'

'You do what Mr Mulligan asks, if'n you know what's good fer yer. Right?'

Eddie decided against nodding since he could feel a thin

trickle of warm liquid which must be blood, running down his neck. ''Course. What you think I am, stupid?'

'Mr Mulligan wants his money, right? All you has to do is pay up.'

'But I ain't got . . .' The rest of Eddie's words were choked into silence by the tourniquet grip Syd had on his throat.

Chapter Four

Lou and Gracie insisted, in view of her injuries and their part in them, that Rose join them in a substantial, if not particularly exciting, lunch of corned beef hash and pickled onions. Since she could barely walk, Rose decided she might as well. It tasted delicious, all washed down with a glass or two of cider. They were only permitted in the bar parlour because the publican's wife took pity on them, women not usually being allowed in there at all, WTC uniform or no. Tizz sneaked under the table in the hope of picking up the odd titbit, dropped for her benefit.

It was a wonder that any of them tasted the food, excellent though it undoubtedly was, as they barely stopped talking the whole time.

Lou promised faithfully to fix the damaged bicycle, some-how or other. 'I'm a whizz wi' bikes. I've one of me own back home. Don't know how I could 'ave got to work otherwise. Wish I'd fetched it wi' me.'

'I thought all you Lancastrians walked to t'mill in clogs, so you can spark them on the cobbles,' Rose teased, mocking her accent.

Lou grinned, not taking the least offence at the ribbing. 'Nay, a bike's better but clog clasps allus gets fast in t'chain.

Anyroad up, we youngsters don't wear clogs so much nowadays. We're a bit more fashion conscious than our mams were.'

'Yes, I can see that you are,' Rose said, blue eyes dancing as they travelled up and down Lou's muddy dungarees, turned up socks and heavy boots.

They were, all three, instant friends, comparing notes and anecdotes, likes and dislikes as well as mutual moans about parents and brothers, not forgetting their opinions on men in general of course. Rose said nothing about Eddie's tendency to bully her. She told them what a marvellous brother he was, though she did admit to how tight-fisted he could be with his own money, while happily enjoying the advantages of his position.

'He's forever involved in some scheme or other to make more, though what exactly I haven't the faintest idea.'

'Perhaps it's the black market,' Lou suggested. 'You know, selling things like ladies' nylons, nails and rivets, tea and sugar.'

Rose giggled. 'More likely to be a bit of old-fashioned Cornish smuggling, baccy and brandy. I'm sure there's still plenty of that goes on. 'Course, he could be trading in diamonds or working as a spy, for all I know.' She laughed again, to make it clear that she was only joking. Rose would hate these two to think of her brother as a criminal. He wasn't like that at all.

Anxious to put the record straight she went on to explain how for the past seven years he'd brought her up virtually single-handed. 'When our mother died as a result of contracting scarlet fever caught from me, poor Papa was far too wrapped up in his own grief to pay much attention to mine. I blamed myself, you see, for having brought the infection into the house.'

'Nay, it weren't your fault,' Lou intervened. 'How could you be held responsible?'

'For a while Eddie did imply that I was but I don't know

what I would've done without him because, in the end, Papa died too. From a broken heart they said.'

'Oh, how terribly sad.' Gracie looked near to tears.

'It was a difficult time for Eddie and me. It took a while before we got over it . . . well, learned to live with it anyway. To adjust and get along.' Memories of times when his rage and resentment had frightened her came almost spontaneously into her mind: of endless weeks of furious silence when he would communicate with her only by leaving notes on the dresser; of days when he'd have her washing the windows over and over by way of punishment, even waking her up during the night to do them all over again. And almost worse than all of this, certainly to the child she had once been, was the way he'd make her stand up to eat her dinner, as if she were unclean in some way and not fit to sit at table with him. The harder she strove to please him, the more she seemed to fail.

Rose blinked away the tears, took a swig of cider and dabbed at her mouth with her napkin, just as her mother had once taught her. 'Enough of me, let's talk about something more cheerful.' His behaviour had been caused by grief, of course. Nothing more. Not for one moment did she ever allow herself to forget how much she owed him. She would have been quite alone without her dear brother.

So Lou told the tale of her wedding with suitable embellishments about the antics of three drunken sailors let loose on the Barbican. 'It's a wonder they weren't arrested. Then Gordon and me went dancing on the Hoe, just the two of us, where Drake played bowls when the Spanish Armada was coming. Nowadays the people of Plymouth dance while they wait for the invasion, hoping and praying of course, that it won't ever come.'

She explained how she'd joined the Timber Corps to be near to her beloved husband, and how she was hoping he'd get leave any day now and come to see her. Lou wept a few tears of her own since she ached for him so, admitting that she prayed day and night he'd be kept safe, working at Devonport Royal Dockyard, and not sent anywhere dangerous.

Rose said, 'Plymouth isn't all that safe, not with all the bombings they've had. And isn't Devonport Dockyard the main naval repair establishment? A number one target, I should think.'

'Oh, hecky thump! I thought he'd be safe there.'

'Nowhere is safe, Lou. Anyway, don't think about it. Change the subject. What about children? Don't you want a family? I mean, you might get pregnant, what would you do about the Timber Corps then?'

Lou shook her head. 'I'm making sure that won't happen. Not yet. Oh, aye, we do want a family, one day. There's nothing me and Gordon would like better. But I'm in no hurry to have a kid, not till the war's over.'

The two younger girls exchanged glances, as if silently agreeing that this was eminently sensible and yet curious to know how she could be certain that she'd keep herself safe. Neither of them quite summoned up the courage to ask.

'Go on,' Rose said, turning to Gracie. 'Now it's your turn.'

'Heavens, my life has been dull and boring from start to finish. No excitement in it at all beyond whether Mrs Fishwick would buy Peak Frean biscuits or Rich Tea. Though at least she was prepared to pay full price. Mrs Catchpole, on the other hand, always bought the broken ones, because they were cheaper. She liked to pick them herself out of the tin and Dad, fool that he was, would let her. Not that she ever got away with that trick when I was serving, because I knew she always chose the biggest bits. Wasn't above breaking the odd biscuit either, if it was one of her favourites. What a cheat!' Chuckling at the memory, Gracie went on to explain about her parents' differing ambitions for her. 'They always disagree on every-thing. On principle, I think.'

'Yes, but what did *you* want to do?' Rose asked.

'I hadn't the first idea, not till I saw that poster offering freedom. Though I think I fell in love with the uniform as much as the job.'

'You can see why, can't you?' Lou quipped, flapping a hand at her friend's equally bedraggled state.

'You should have seen me when I turned up for my interview. Dressed to kill, I was, thinking to make a good impression. Fancy hat, silk stockings, high heels, the lot. I could see all these worthy women eyeing me as if I was a complete fool. It's a miracle they let me in since I looked as if I were applying for a job on *Picture Post*, not the Women's Timber Corps. I hope that by the time this war is over, I'll have made up my mind what I want to do with the rest of my life. Who knows? It'll be exciting to find out.'

This set them all off dreaming. Lou predicted that she and Gordon would have gone to live up North by then, and started the family they both longed for.

'What about you?' Gracie gently enquired.

Rose said, 'Heavens, I don't know. Hopefully I'll find myself a husband. Preferably someone excruciatingly rich and with acres and acres of lush green pastures for me to ride my beautiful chestnut mare.'

'Have you got a beautiful chestnut mare?'

'No, my rich husband can buy me one. Mind you, I'll probably get somebody old and crabby, not a penny to his name, who picks his teeth.' And they all fell about laughing, taking great delight in describing what would make the worst husband imaginable.

'Someone who snores.'

'Or gets drunk every night.'

'Reads the paper at breakfast and smokes in bed.'

'Or has a bald head, like Tom-Tom.'

This last suggestion brought them back to reality with a

jerk. Gracie glanced at her watch and leapt to her feet. 'My godfathers, look at the time. It's nearly three o'clock! We'll be for it.'

Rose's face went white. 'Not half so much as I will be. Eddie'll kill me.' And she hastily explained about the lunch she'd been preparing. 'I only wanted a bit of cheese to liven up the Woolton Pie.'

'By heck,' said Lou. 'If I'd known, I'd've fetched you any amount. That's the one thing we're not short of, cheese.'

Eddie had hoped to set up the tables and rig the cards in his own favour before Mulligan and Gertie returned, but by the time he'd calmed down the Pursey brothers with the aid of an extra large port they were back. Secreting the odd card up his sleeve was all he could do in the time he had available. Unlikely to get him out of the quagmire of debt he was in but the best he could manage in the circumstances.

Gertie was oddly silent and, not meeting his enquiring gaze, went to sit in the farthest corner of the room, her face ashen. Mulligan's expression was as benign and inscrutable as ever. Eddie couldn't like to think what had taken place up at the summer house but Syd and Bob were certainly looking pleased with themselves, like the proverbial cats who'd swallowed the cream.

Eddie hastily offered Mulligan a brandy and prayed for luck to run his way for once. The party of six divested themselves of jackets and ties, made huge inroads into Lord Clovellan's best Havanas, opened a second bottle of port, and the air in the library, which was where they were now happily ensconced, soon reeked of alcohol, cigar smoke and bad breath. But, sadly, Eddie's prayers went unanswered. To his growing dismay, as the afternoon wore on, every bluff was countered, every card he picked up was the wrong one. The Pursey brothers were operating on a closed shop principle as usual, and Bob and Syd had more sense than to risk offending anyone as dangerously powerful as Dexter Mulligan by helping Eddie out. As so often these days, the fellow seemed to hold all the aces.

Mulligan smoothed down his oil-slick black hair, leaned back in his chair and rolled the cigar between his teeth. A swathe of blue smoke wreathed his head and, to Eddie's eyes, at least, he could easily have been a dragon breathing fire. With that black beady gaze, fixed so intently upon his prey, he certainly gave the impression that he only had to snap his fingers and a huge pair of jaws would appear out of nowhere and gobble Eddie up.

'So where's that recalcitrant sister of yours, Eddie m'boy?' he blithely enquired. 'Did you not tell her that I'd a fancy to have her sit by me at table today?'

''Course I did, Mr Mulligan.' Eddie always addressed him in a proper fashion, never risked using Dexter's given name as he hadn't been given permission to do so. 'I made your instructions very plain.'

'You can't have much control over this household, Eddie boy, if'n you allow a young girl to flout your wishes quite so blatantly. Women should be trained with a firm hand, I've always found. Don't you agree, boys?' Sniggers and murmurs of agreement all round. Gertie shrank further back into the corner, almost disappearing behind a Victorian scrap screen.

Eddie scowled at her, beckoning her forward with an impatient flap of his hand. 'At least we have Gertie here to entertain you, eh? Would you like another little break perhaps?' Eddie desperately wanted one. All he needed was five minutes alone with the deck of cards that Mulligan held so firmly in his well-manicured hands.

Dexter Mulligan's gaze slid over Gertie's ample figure with undisguised distaste. 'I don't think so.' She reached for a bottle of gin with an audible sigh of relief. 'Pity about your sister though. She's a pretty little thing, your Rose. Pretty as her name. Ripe for the plucking, though just a touch prickly, eh?' He chuckled softly. 'Are you going to stick or what?'

Eddie was staring at the jack, queen and king in his hand, pretending to shrug off his concerns as he desperately struggled to remember what cards had previously been thrown down, wondering if there was any hope of his getting a full house, if he dare risk slipping the ace from his sleeve. And then for no reason Eddie could think of, Mulligan's tone subtly changed and he leaned forward in his seat. 'Aren't you concerned that something might have happened to her? She might have had an accident.'

For a moment Eddie's mind was a complete blank as he struggled to push aside his own fears about how he could possibly hope to settle these latest losses and save his own skin, when it suddenly occurred to him that this could be the answer. If Rose had indeed suffered an accident, he might well be able to use it to his advantage. To buy more time, if nothing else. Turning to Gertie, he barked at her to run down to the village shop and see what the hell was keeping his sister. 'If she's gossiping with that Mrs Whatever she's called, tell her I'll have her guts for garters.'

When Gertie had gone, Dexter Mulligan sank back in his seat with a contented sigh. 'I await her arrival with eager anticipation. In the meantime, let's do a bit of business. What've you got fer me this time? Something tasty, I 'ope.'

'There's not much left, to be honest,' Eddie said, a careful note of regret in his voice. 'Not that's worth anything.'

'You surely aren't going to disappoint me?' Though the words were softly spoken, the tone was menacing and Eddie got hurriedly to his feet.

'Would I do that, Mr Mulligan? No, no, I was simply saying, the choice was getting more limited, that's all. However, I've found this nice picture that might be of interest.' He pulled out a heavy oil painting from behind the screen. It was of a stag on some nondescript Scottish hillside. Dexter Mulligan gazed at it in silence for some seconds.

'We don't have much call for Scottish glens here in Cornwall.'

'Beautiful piece of work, don't you think?'

Mulligan glanced at his comrades and apparently they agreed with him for he turned to Eddie and said, 'I don't think so, Eddie m'boy. Bit gloomy, eh, and we both know you're getting in over your head at the mo'. So, I'll settle for the rose bowl, shall I, and call it quits. Remind me of your Rose if nothing else.'

Eddie could feel the prickle of sweat on his skin like sharp little needles of ice. 'N-no! The rose bowl would be missed. Been in the family for generations. I'd never get away with that. I'd be sacked. Ruined.'

Mulligan chuckled softly, a dribble of spittle at the corners of his mouth, just as if he was salivating with anticipation at some secret joke. He slapped Eddie on the back, rested a comradely arm about his shoulders that was anything but and whispered into Eddie's ear, 'Sacked? Ruined? Well, m'boy, what worse situation can you be in than the one you're in right now, eh? Besides, Lord-Toffee-Nosed-Clovellan is in Canada, ain't he? What would he know about it?'

'He'll come back when the war's over, and if all his good stuff is gone, he'll crucify me.'

Even Syd and Bob seemed to find this amusing and laughed like drains. Mulligan's expression, however, was deadly serious. 'They're laughing because they know you've really nothing to lose. I would've beaten him to it by then.'

Three things happened next, almost simultaneously. The secreted ace chose that precise moment to fall from out of Eddie's shirt cuff and deposit itself face up on the table; Gertie burst into the room announcing that not a soul had seen Rose;

but it was as Eddie looked into Mulligan's accusing gaze that the idea came to him. The perfect solution to get him off the hook.

'Can we have a bit of a chat about this, Mr Mulligan?'

'I'm all ears, Eddie, m'boy All ears.'

'You've upset him good and proper this time.'

Gertie issued this warning with a look of pleased satisfaction on her plump face. There were flecks of egg still at the corners of her mouth, remnants of vegetable peelings still scattered about the kitchen table and a sink full of dirty crockery. Rose concluded that they had eaten pretty much what she had planned for them. No one had thought to clear away or wash up.

'Where is he?'

'With his friends, a'course. In the library.'

Rose went to the sink and turned the taps full on. A rush of cold water filled the stone basin. 'Hasn't he even fixed the dratted boiler?' Gertie shrugged her fat shoulders and moved away, as if it were none of her business. Rose flung a tea towel at her. 'Here, you're the flippin' housekeeper, you do it.' And calling Tizz to heel, she marched off.

Her rebellion was soon quashed, as she'd known that it would be. Eddie found her hiding among the raspberry canes and Rose had never seen him so angry. A white line tightened his upper lip as he berated her for her negligence and lack of consideration. Tizz got up from where she'd been lying in a patch of autumn sunshine and came to stand beside her, leaning protectively against her leg.

Rose quickly apologised, attempting to explain about the accident, the broken bike, the injured ankle, but the unmitigated anger in his eyes seemed to stop the words in her throat. Besides, she would never dare to tell him about the lunch or the treat of finding two new friends. He would only taunt and ridicule her for bothering with people who'd be gone in a matter of weeks, but she needn't have worried. He wasn't listening to a word she said.

He bluntly instructed her to go and clean up the kitchen at once, and then to scrub the floor. Rose hastened to comply, deciding that it would be worth cleaning twenty kitchens for the pleasure of those two precious hours spent in the company of her new friends. She thought Eddie would be content to leave it at that but, as he turned to go, he issued one further instruction.

'My associates are still here. In the library. See that you bring a good bottle of whisky with the tea.'

Rose bridled. 'Whisky? I'll bring the tea, and even a few biscuits, but I'm taking nothing from the wine cellar. That's stealing. If you want whisky, you can fetch it yourself.'

He was back beside her in seconds, grabbed her arm and actually shook her. 'You'll fetch the bleeding whisky and afterwards you'll go upstairs with Mr Mulligan. It's all arranged. And don't bloody argue because you're lucky he didn't finish me off there and then. I owes him a bit o' money and he's not one to mess with, ain't Dexter Mulligan, so you be a good girl and sweeten him up for me.'

Rose listened aghast, not quite able to take in the full implication of his words for all they were clear enough. He'd never actually used physical violence on her, though he generally found other, more subtle ways of gaining her obedience. But this was one step too far for Rose and she could think of nothing to say.

'Do you hear me? Are you taking this in?' Tizz gave a low, warning growl.

She stood her ground unflinching, and glared back at her brother in mutinous defiance. 'I'll do no such thing. Send Gertie. She's your whore, not me.' It was the years of her adolescence all over again. 'And I'm still not fetching any whisky.'

He lifted his hand as if driven at last to strike her and the dog leaped. Rose let out a scream as man and dog wrestled, although it was Tizz she feared for. She knew who would win. Eddie reached for a broom, swung it and there was a yelp of pain. He grabbed Tizz by the collar and began to drag her away.

'Where are you taking her? What are you doing? Oh, no, not the cellar. Please, don't lock her in the cellar! Not again. You know how she hates it in the dark. Put me in the dratted cellar if you must, you great bully, but leave Tizz out of this.'

Struggling to hang on to the writhing, wriggling animal, Eddie was still able to reach out and grasp her wrist. 'Yeah, why not? You can keep the bloody dog company. Mebbe then you'll both learn the value of obedience. And it'll give you time to realise that Dexter Mulligan is the lesser of two evils.'

Tizz did her best to protect Rose but both dog and girl knew their efforts to be futile. Eddie dragged the pair of them along the stone-flagged passages of Clovellan House, down the dark steps to the damp, stinking cellars where once Roundheads had secured their captives. He flung them inside the ice-cold cell and slammed shut the solid, iron-studded door. 'Shout all you like, no one can hear you in there. Soundproof, these doors, so the torture victims wouldn't disturb the master of the house.' He laughed. 'Here's a bit of candle. Use it wisely, it's little more an inch or two long. Mebbe by morning you'll see the wisdom of making Dexter Mulligan a happy man, then he'll cancel my gambling debt. That's not too much to ask, is it?'

'Why should I? It's not my fault. You were stupid to get involved with him in the first place.'

'Sanctimonious little madam! Always so bloody prissy and self-righteous. The one everybody loved to cuddle and pet. Stole my inheritance, my heritage, the love of my parents . . . and now you'd stand by and see Mulligan's henchmen make mincemeat of me, would you? I think not. You cool your heels in here for a while, my girl. I'll get some obedience out of you, one way or another. See if I don't.' The sounds of his laughter echoed back along the empty passage as the ring of his footsteps retreated.

Lou worked hard on the repairs to Rose's bicycle, spurred on by guilt. A few days later, she suggested they return it and Gracie agreed to go with her so that they could repeat their apologies for having caused the damage in the first place, and perhaps make arrangements to meet up with Rose again.

They chose one evening when there was no lecture and slipped out after supper to walk the mile and a half through the wooded estate to the tiny lodge house. A plump woman with shaggy, red-dyed hair, dressed in a grubby jumper and skirt, told them Rose was up at the main house.

'We could leave it here, I suppose,' said Lou doubtfully.

'No, let's find her,' Gracie insisted, acting on an instinct that Rose could be in need of a friend or two.

'You might not find her,' the woman called after them. 'It's a big place.'

'It is indeed,' Lou agreed as they walked into the courtyard, 'and very like the *Marie Celeste*.'

There wasn't a soul in sight. Not in the courtyard, the myriad outhouses and pantries, the stables, nor in the vast empty kitchen. They goggled at the rows of gleaming copper saucepans hung about the walls, at the massive oak table which occupied the centre of the room, the huge range which seemed to fill one entire wall and even sported a spit.

'Golly! You could roast a whole ox on that thing – a pig anyway.'

Lou giggled. 'I expect they do, every Sunday. Pity we missed it, today being Thursday like.'

Only two doors led out of the great kitchen, one back the way they had come, the other presumably being the entrance to the rest of the house. Nervous of being caught where she'd no right to be, Lou crept to this door and peeped through.

'Hello! Anyone there? Rosieee!' No reply. She glanced back at Gracie and, encouraged by her nod of agreement, tried again, taking a few steps along the stone-floored passage. 'Hello!' Somewhere in the gloom ahead Lou thought she heard a faint sound and waited, trying to decide what it was exactly. She jumped when she felt something move beside her, but it was only Gracie and the two girls clung to each other, remaining very still as they listened.

'Sounds like some sort of machine, in dire need of a drop of oil, I should think, judging by that whining noise it's making. Mebbe she's using a Hoover and can't hear us.'

'Could it be a dog?'

'Surely not. No dog would whine so much, would it?'

'What should we do?' Gracie edged along the passage, uncertain, straining to penetrate the gloomy darkness ahead.

'Happen we should just walk in, bold as brass like. What do you reckon? If we saw Lord Clovellan himself, we could say we'd popped in to have a chat with Rose. Back home in Rochdale, folk burst in without even knocking, at all hours of the day and night.'

'Sadly, Lou, this isn't anything like Rochdale. They might think we were trespassing, or trying to steal the family silver.'

'Nay! Why would they think that?' But Lou considered the point in all seriousness and finally conceded Gracie was probably right. She was disappointed all the same, having been looking forward to seeing Rose again, and she somehow felt the need to know that the girl was OK. 'I just thought . . .' Lou began, then became aware of a strange musty odour she hadn't noticed before. It brought her up short, causing a cold, chill prickle of fear to creep down her spine. Then she felt the faintest touch upon her neck. 'What was that? Did you feel summat?'

'No, could be a ghost.'

Lou started. 'Oh, don't even suggest such a thing.' Another sound, higher pitched this time, like an eerie cry, followed by a noise like a door banging. 'Eeh, heck, happen you're right. I don't like this place. Too quiet by half. I'm off.'

So saying she turned tail and ran, Gracie at her heels, chuckling softly, though what she could find so amusing about all of this, Lou failed to imagine. Her own usual droll sense of humour had quite deserted her. She felt chilled to the bone with the creepiness of the place. Nothing would persuade her ever to go near it again. Rose would have to come to them. They scampered back through the kitchen, the pantries and larders, and out into the courtyard where Lou let out a great sigh of relief.

'By heck, that were a rum do. What do you reckon it were?'

Gracie said nothing, merely gazed at her friend out of wide, suspiciously bright eyes.

They left the bicycle propped up in the laundry with a note attached to the handlebars, inviting Rose to come over any evening for a gossip. Then they set off back to camp, Gracie still struggling to stifle her giggles. It was only when Lou finally lost patience and insisted that she explain what was so damned funny that Gracie admitted it had been she who'd tickled Lou's neck with the fringe of her scarf. 'I was the ghost.'

Lou let out a great roar, Gracie squealed in pretend alarm and the pair were quickly racing back down the long drive, their fright and nervousness forgotten and only the fun remaining.

Had they looked back at the house, they might have seen the pale outline of a heart-shaped face in one of the attic windows, watching them go.

Chapter Five

Part of the girls' responsibility was to ensure that the quality of the wood they cut was of the very best. To hammer this home, a day or two later they were woken an hour earlier than usual, loaded on to the lorries and taken to visit a mine. The Supervisor was in charge as usual, though Matron came along too.

'Just to keep you gels in order,' she bluntly informed them as she climbed up front beside the driver in her long brown coat and hat, a remark greeted with subdued groans all round.

The mine was many miles from camp and, as they jumped down from the lorries, Gracie noticed that Matron had remained in the cab. She went over and tapped on the window, thinking perhaps the old dear had nodded off and hadn't realised they'd arrived.

'We're here.'

The window was wound down and Matron's fierce face pushed through the gap. 'Then jump to it, Freeman. You don't need me to hold your hand.'

'Aren't you coming down with us?' Gracie politely enquired.

'Of course she is,' came the Super's voice from behind. 'Aren't you, Elsie? Nothing you'd like better than an underground tour, as we all would. Anything you girls do, we can do.'

But as the Super marched off, calling to the other girls to get in line and be sharp about it, Gracie looked back at Matron, now forever Elsie in her mind, and was quick enough to see the colour drain from her face.

'Don't you fancy it?' she asked, quite kindly. 'Some people have a dread of confined spaces. Claustrophobia. Is that a problem you suffer from, Matron?'

The woman looked as if she would dearly love to deny it. Her face was contorted into tight folds, mouth pursed into a sunray of wrinkles. She made what looked like an attempt to get out of the truck then seemed to lose control of her muscles, as if she were paralysed and simply couldn't bring herself to climb down. She began to shake. There was no doubt now in Gracie's mind, she had indeed found Matron's Achilles heel. The poor woman was terrified of going down that mine.

'Stay there. I'll tell Super you're not feeling well, shall I?' Gracie suddenly realised this was perfectly true. 'Actually you don't look too good. I think you should get out of the truck. Here, let me help you.'

Gracie led her into the mine office and found her a cup of tea which Elsie accepted with gratitude but poor Gracie was now on pins to get back to the others before the Super missed her. 'I'd best go.'

'It was my son,' Matron gasped.

'What?'

'My eldest, Donald. He was sent down a mine though he wasn't a miner. He wanted to be a soldier but they sent him to dig coal instead. One of Bevin's boys. There was a fall and . . . trapped . . .'

Gracie listened, horrified, then put her arms about the huge woman, now a quivering wreck, and held her while tears rolled down the fat cheeks. 'You don't have to say another thing. I understand.'

After a moment Matron pulled out a hanky, struggling for

control. Her eyes seemed suddenly bleak and empty, and her voice seemed to come from a long way away. 'And my other son, David, was killed at Dunkirk.'

'Oh, God, no!' Gracie was struck dumb. It sounded as if this poor woman had lost her entire family. She didn't dare ask if there was anyone left. No wonder she was always in a foul mood with that bitter twist to her mouth. To say she was sorry would sound trite and inadequate, even so Gracie said it, for want of anything else. 'Can I do anything more for you?'

Matron patted the back of her hair, checking it was tidy. 'No, I shall be all right now. Thank you for the tea. I appreciate it. Now you'd best go, Freeman, or you'll be in trouble.'

'You'll be OK?'

'I'll be fine. Pay no heed to me.' Gracie could almost see the drawbridge coming up again, the armour which she'd erected around herself to discourage pity, or worse *self*-pity. 'I'd be obliged if you'd forget everything I've just told you. Make no mention of it.'

Gracie squeezed her plump hand and hurried away.

First they were shown the stack of pitprops at the surface. Many had already been peeled of their bark but some hadn't and the girls were all given a lesson in how to do this task which helped the seasoning process. Each prop was placed on two trestles and, using a sharp knife and firm downward sweeps, the skin of the props was sliced away.

'As is the skin from my knuckles,' yelped Gracie, but her skill improved with practice. It also taught them why it was important for them to remove all the small branches and arms, not only for the safety of the miners, but for the poor soul who had to do this job all day.

After that they were given helmets so heavy Gracie could barely keep her head upright, and promised a ride in a cage that went deep down into the ground.

'Hell's teeth, I'm not sure I fancy that,' Lou whispered. 'Why do we need to go?'

'Because,' said the Super, right in her ear, 'you're the ones cutting the poles which will hold the roof up for the miners. If you've been down a mine yourselves, you'll know how it feels and make sure that you cut strong ones.'

The point was certainly driven home as they were led through the shafts and galleries where the men worked, and the purpose of various pieces of machinery carefully demonstrated. There was electric light for part of the way but they were then shown shorter, narrower passages where the miners were expected to work in difficult and cramped conditions, often solely dependent upon the lamps affixed to their helmets. The atmosphere grew hot and airless, though the ventilation fans were working normally. It was explained to them about the pumps, and how these were constantly at work, preventing the mine from flooding.

Today, being a Sunday, the miners were not working and the silence was profound, broken only by the constant dripping of water and strange creakings that echoed in the empty vastness. Their guide carried a candle and a canary in a cage, both of which he used to test the quality of the air at the head of each shaft. When they reached the coal face, he showed them the pitprops, some of them cracked and bent.

'Don't worry, girls. These aren't any of yours. They've been 'ere a long time,' their guide reassured them. Even so they felt guilty, as if they were responsible for sending the inferior wood.

He offered them all a turn with a pickaxe to cut some coal, which they all tried with great trepidation. On the way back in the lorry, Lou said that the next time they were felling soft-woods for pitprops, she'd make doubly sure that they chose good strong poles with no sign of weakness in any of them.

Gracie agreed. She'd felt quite certain that the great mass of earth above her head had been about to collapse on top of her and press her into the blackness. But despite these fears, she'd learned a great deal from the trip. More than she felt comfortable with.

Gordon was waiting for them when they arrived back at camp. He lifted Lou bodily from the back of the lorry and carried her off to great whoops of delight from the other girls.

'Don't do anything I wouldn't do,' chorused Tess and Jeannie together.

'To the woods!' yelled Enid.

'I think not,' the voice of Matron boomed out and poor Gordon very nearly dropped his beloved in the mud as he instantly responded with a smart salute.

'Have you permission to be on this site, sailor?'

'No, sir . . . er, ma'am. I mean, I've got a late pass. Just for tonight.'

'This is a work area. For women only.' Matron hoisted her ample bosom on to her folded arms and glared at him.

'Yeah, I can see that.' His eyes roved over the beaming faces surrounding him, all filled with curiosity and avid interest at this gorgeous hunk of male they'd discovered in their midst. Lou decided it was time to pitch in with her four pennyworth. The sooner she got her lovely Gordon away from their adoring gazes, the better.

'What he means is he understands all of that but he just popped in to let me know he was here, that he'd be available later like.' Fresh gales of laughter from the audience and a few ribald remarks. 'No, no, I mean on the spot, that he's managed to get a bit of leave. Oh, dear, we'll surely get some free time this evening, won't we, Matron? I can go out with him, can't I? There isn't another lecture, is there? Or could I miss it for once? We're only recently wed, d'you see, and we're so *very* much in love.' She put such pleading, such feeling, into her voice, it would have moved a heart of stone. Matron didn't flinch.

'Your personal affairs are hardly my concern, Mason. But I'm afraid you don't go anywhere without my permission.'

She made to walk away but Lou took a step towards her in her desperation, despite the fact she itched to run away with Gordon that very minute. It was exciting and brave of him to walk right into the camp like this, bold as brass, but she did wish he'd given her notice he was coming. She'd have been more prepared, wangled some time off. 'Aw, go on, Matron. Be a sport. He *is* me husband after all. Can't I go with him to the flicks or summat? Who knows when I might see him again? And there is a war on.' A hard lump filled her throat and Lou swallowed, aware suddenly that this was true. Her plan to be near Gordon could all come to nothing the moment he got his sailing orders.

'I want you off government property now, sailor. And the rest of you girls, about your business. Supper is in half an hour.' Unmoved by Lou's pleas, the woman flounced away, the long green overall beneath the heavy brown coat almost skimming the sea of mud.

Lou was utterly devastated, the disappointment so keen that she felt sick and tears were pricking the back of her eyes. She didn't dare glance at poor Gordon's crestfallen face or she might very well have started blubbing in earnest. There was a sympathetic groan of disappointment from the onlookers but it was Gracie who hurried after Matron and caught up with her. Some sort of exchange took place between them; too far away and much too quietly spoken for Lou to hear what was said but, after a moment, the senior woman suddenly swung about and glared back at Lou.

'You'd still need to be in by nine-thirty.'

'*Nine-thirty*? But . . .'

'That would be fine,' Gracie hastily intervened. 'You understand that too, Gordon, don't you?'

'Sure thing,' he agreed, cap in hand and face alight with eagerness. 'Not a second later, Sir . . .'

'Ma'am. If you can't even work out what sex *I* am, what hope is there for your poor wife? Nine-thirty. On the dot. I shall be standing at the door to keep check. One minute late and you're on report, Mason.'

Lou didn't linger to find out what stratagem Gracie had employed to persuade the old dragon, though it had certainly worked. She was in far too much of a hurry to go before the permission was withdrawn. Within ten minutes, Lou had changed into her glad rags, as she called them, and was sashaying out of camp, her arm tucked into Gordon's, a chorus of whistles and envious glances following them every step of the way.

They didn't go far, certainly not to the flicks. For one thing, Lou hadn't been in the area long enough to have the first idea where to find a picture house, or even how to catch a bus or train to one. For another, all they really needed was each other; to kiss and cuddle, to explore their newly discovered feelings. All of which could as easily be resolved in a corner of some field, beneath a tree, or by wandering arm in arm along the quiet Cornish lanes.

Meandering through a patch of woodland on the outskirts of the estate, they spotted a tiny summerhouse. It had a curved roof, rather in the style of a pagoda, and there were strange paintings of figures and animals on the walls. Although it was dusty and neglected, it possessed four solid walls and a door, thus providing that vital element: privacy. Amazingly, it even had a fireplace.

In no time at all Gordon had got a small fire going and they were stretched out before its bright warmth on a heap of dusty sacking, remaking their marriage vows. He was a generous and exciting lover and, Lou knew, in those precious moments of intimacy, that whatever the future held for them, she would never regret marrying him. Never. Just the caress of his fingers on her bare skin set her alight.

Sated by their love making and entranced by the magical glow of the flickering firelight, they talked as never before, drawing ever closer as they revealed secret hopes and desires, exchanged confidences, dreamed dreams, till finally Lou found the courage to voice her greatest fears. 'You aren't going overseas, are you love?'

There was a short pause before he answered. 'I don't know. There's been no hint of it. Not yet. But things are happening, they must be.'

'Why must they?' She wanted to deny the very existence of war, to hold him safely here in her arms for ever.

'Because there always is something going on. The Germans are in Stalingrad, which I don't suppose is good. And since we lost Tobruk and the Eighth Army withdrew, there've been rumours that Monty will do something by way of retaliation. He's the new British Commander, Field Marshal Montgomery, case you're wondering.'

Lou was nodding, listening intently to every word. 'Are you saying you might be involved?'

'I think I'm saying that there could be a knock-on effect. Pulling all the plugs out, as it were. The big push. And, yes, I dare say I'd be off then.'

She looked stricken. 'I thought, as an engineer, your job was more shore based – that you'd stop on at the dockyard?'

He smiled softly at her, brown eyes gentle with not a spark of their usual mischief as they scrutinised her face, seemingly eager to memorise every small part of it. 'It's just a bit of maintenance work while we're in port, love. If it was a major refit, they'd transfer me to another ship. At sea, I work in the engine rooms. That's my job, second engineer, so they can't go without me, now can they? But let's not worry about all of that now. What matters is that we're together, and you drive me crazy. Come here.'

Melting into his arms once more, she strove to push these concerns from her mind, as Gordon was trying to do, but it seemed strange that some unknown man, commander or not, could hold the power of life or death over her lovely husband.

He was kissing her lips, her eyes, the soft curve of her breast, and if Lou had had another question ready, she quite forgot what it could have been. Afterwards, they fell asleep in each other's arms. Gordon had admitted to being tired after a hard week on maintenance. Lou most certainly was, after the day she'd had, and tomorrow would bring another long, tiring spell in the woods. It always was, particularly since she'd mastered the art of felling, though admittedly nothing very large. As she drifted into sleep, she recalled the joy of bringing down her first tree and calling out '*Timberrrrr!*' to let everyone know they must clear out of the way.

'What's that, a matchstick?' Tom-Tom had chuckled but his teasing hadn't in any way dented her sense of triumph. She'd been pleased with herself. It was a long way from worrying about the warp and weft of parachute silk in a Rochdale factory.

Something woke her and with dawning horror Lou realised it was the stable clock. For a moment she panicked as she counted the strokes, but it stopped at nine so she woke Gordon gently with a kiss and he escorted her back to camp well within their time limit.

'How will you get back? Or how did you even get here in the first place, come to that?' it suddenly occurred to her to ask.

He waggled his thumb. 'I'll get a lift back all right. Don't worry about me.' They made arrangements for him to come again the following week then he was gone, vanishing into the darkness as he always seemed to do, so that it almost felt as if he weren't real, not a proper husband at all, just a ghost who flitted in and out of her dreams. Lou shivered, as her mam would say, just as if a goose had stepped over her grave. Then she crept to her bed and buried her head under her pillow, so that Gracie wouldn't hear her sobs.

Even a day without word from him was an agony. Lou would ring him on the camp telephone, write every day, while Gordon would barter leave with his mates in return for cigarettes or rum, begging his chief to let him pop over for an evening or a couple of hours in the afternoon, anything he could think of to get to see 'my missus', as he called her. But there were occasions when he failed to turn up, despite his promises, and Lou would weep with anguish and fear till he rang or she got a note through the post.

She wasn't the only one to suffer this particular sort of pain. Stifled sobs could often be heard late into the night. Sometimes a girl would simply not be there in the morning. She would have packed her bags and gone home, perhaps out of homesickness or a need to be with loved ones when bad news came. Others decided they couldn't take the outdoor life, the tough routine, endure the uncertain weather or acquire the necessary skills. The squad rather expected Lena to go off one day in a similar fashion but, in spite of her continued grumps and groans, she was still present and correct every morning.

'Has someone pinched my blouse? And who was snoring all night? How can I possibly sleep through that racket. Look at the tide mark you lot leave around the basin. What Mummy would say, I shudder to think.'

Hoots of laughter. 'Good old Lena. What would we do without your cheery chatter every morning?'

On other days she would be 'dying of exhaustion', but the least hint of a dance or a trip to the picture house in nearby Fowey and she'd be the first to the wash basins, eager to freshen up and be off. It was hard to make her out at times but Lena was nothing if not an endless source of amusement.

There were feuds of course. Tempers would grow short and an over-tired girl might flare up and object to an untidy bunk mate or the way she cut her toe nails. There'd be tearing rows, name-calling, even the occasional scrap, but generally the mood of the camp was good.

Sometimes, friends though they were, Lou and Gracie might feel 'a bit scratchy' if things got on top of them. Lou might have received word that Gordon wasn't coming after all, or Gracie might have got a letter from home, forwarded from Timber Corps head office, either of which could put them in a foul mood for the day. At other times it might be Tess having trouble with the lorry, or Jeannie grousing because she'd run out of fags.

'I'll swear someone's smoking the darned things behind me back.'

Gracie was usually the one to give in and go and buy her more, knowing the irascible Scot would be on an ever shorter fuse until she'd got her smokes. But mainly everyone got on well.

Lou and Gracie thrived on the outdoor life, loved the work, and discovered that felling was as much a matter of art as sheer brawn, the use of skill and judgement rather than brute strength, though there was a limit, of course, to the size of tree they could tackle. It was important first of all to decide which way it might best fall, without damaging other standing trees, or itself, as it came down, and then to clear the way for it. The preliminary axe work must cut a mouth in the tree on the side they wanted it to fall. They took great pride in leaving no waste, in cutting so low the stumps could scarcely be spotted, even by the eagle-eyed Tom-Tom.

'You don't cut as much as 'ee should, but it's worth having when 'ee gets it,' he told them one day, in his soft Cornish burr, which they took as a compliment, since it apparently meant that what they lacked in quantity, they made up for in quality.

'What a lark,' Gracie would say. 'Who'd think there was a war on?'

On Gordon's next visit, Lou decided that it would do them all good if the entire squad took a day out in Fowey. They all cheered, Jeannie heartily agreeing that a bit of fun would be most welcome, as well as giving them the opportunity to doll themselves up. 'Wearing the auld breeks is fine, but putting on a dab of powder and rouge will remind me I'm still a lassie.'

Tess drove Buttercup, her favourite old truck. They parked it close to Readymoney beach which, fortunately, had not been mined against possible invasion or sealed off with barbed wire since it was a well-protected cove within the bounds of the River Fowey. Gathering up their swimming togs, they ran giggling down the wooded track, past Point Neptune, quickly changed and plunged into the sea. Lou gasped as she sank beneath the waves. 'Lordy, it's cold!' But Gordon was soon beside her and they wasted no time in swimming a little way out, though still safely within the bay, where they could be alone to kiss and canoodle in the water.

It was a beautiful, peaceful spot, the sun sparkling on the gentle waves that lapped the curve of the shore; the small patch of golden sand fringed with rocks on either side; a row of fisherman's cottages edging the shore. Way above their heads, looking out to sea, were the ruins of St Catherine's Castle set on the point of the headland to guard the mouth of the river as it had done for centuries against likely invaders. It didn't seem possible that any foreign force could ever defeat the brave men of Fowey. The 'Fowey Gallants', as they were once called, had sailed the seas for centuries, and were considered invincible. Certainly the Spanish had become convinced of that fact. So far as Lou and her friends were concerned, the town was still capable of seeing off any modern invaders with equal ferocity.

'Race you to the rocks,' Gordon cried and struck out strongly, Lou squealing in dismay that he'd cheated by setting off before her.

Lena paddled about in the shallows with more caution, proclaiming she was no water baby, until Gracie began to spray and splash her, making her yell with delighted fear and get even more wet in her efforts to escape. For once she didn't object to the rough treatment, being far too thrilled to have been included on this jolly outing, despite her reputation as a misery boots.

Gracie said, 'It's good to see you enjoying yourself, Lena,' her own face shining with happiness, blonde hair flowing in the gentle breeze.

'I think I've been stung by a jellyfish,' Lena groaned and couldn't understand why everybody burst out laughing and began pelting her with more water.

They soon became happily engrossed building a sand castle, nobly defended by a deep moat, just as if they were schoolgirls. 'Wish we'd got a flag to stick on top,' Tess mourned.

'Use my sock,' Enid offered, attaching a multi-holed, soggy green object to the end of a long twig and sticking it in the sand. It looked so funny that they all fell about laughing. Jeannie lit up a dog end and wandered off to sit on a rock for a quiet smoke, her thoughts seemingly miles away, as if wishing life could always be this sweet.

After a session drying off in the warm September sunshine they strolled along the Esplanade, strung out in a line arm in arm, into the tiny town; Lou and Gordon dawdling behind with their arms wrapped tight about each other. They enjoyed a cream tea in the Ship Inn, explored the length and breadth of Fore Street, popping in and out of all the quaint shops, and finally took the tiny ferry boat across to Polruan where they climbed the steep hill to walk out over the headland past Lantic Bay.

With the sun warming their faces and the tang of a salt breeze in the air, they were tempted to walk all the way to Polperro but common sense prevailed and they returned within the hour, again by ferry to the Town Quay, and made their way back to dear old Buttercup. It had been a marvellous day, one filled with peace and happiness, golden with sunshine. Apart from the usual gun batteries and the boom defences that protected the harbours, there might not even be a war on, or so they had fooled themselves into thinking for a little while at least.

'Long may it last,' Lou said, gazing deeply into Gordon's eyes. 'I want you always to come home safe to me.'

'I will, don't worry. You won't get rid of me that easy.' Brave words, full of love, hope and the arrogance of youth, which was all they had to sustain them.

Chapter Six

———◆———

Perhaps to bring them back to reality, they were given some practice acting as air-raid wardens. Groups of them were sent into Bodmin, Plymouth, Truro and other surrounding towns to train with the genuine wardens who had responsibility for those who hadn't escaped the cities for the countryside each night but were weathering the air raids in shelters. It was a sobering experience to see women disguising their own fear while they comforted their children with smiles and happy bedtime stories.

They gathered in the shelters, rich and poor, old and young, huddled together for warmth, playing games together and singing songs in an effort to pass the time. It was cramped and uncomfortable, stank of human sweat and urine, often filled with the sound of babies crying or some domestic dispute, but the sharing and camaraderie somehow diluted the terror when the drone of enemy aircraft passed overhead.

Gracie was thankful that for her, at least, this was not a long-term responsibility. There seemed so much to remember: checking that everyone had their gas masks and their admission cards, that they followed the rules and didn't cause a nuisance to others. But despite the unsavoury nature of her surroundings, she enjoyed making sure that everyone was comfortable. Organising the tea making was one priority, chatting with the young mothers about their babies' needs another. Then she had to make sure everyone had brought their own clean bedding and knew to remove it afterwards, and that the old people who couldn't carry much with them were warm and comfortable. She found a cushion and a blanket for one old lady, who was clearly cold and shivering.

'Are you sure you're all right here by the door? Wouldn't you be warmer further in?'

'Bless you. Call me Maggie, dear. But no, I'll stay here thank you so I can watch for my Percy when he comes, as I'm sure he will. He knows where to find me. And I'm not so mobile these days, so I can't walk far.'

Gracie left her, hoping her husband wouldn't be too long.

Some of the women spent the night knitting scarves and balaclavas, the old men playing dominoes and swapping stories. The children all seemed to be tumbled together in one big heap, oblivious of danger. At long last came the All-Clear and Gracie went back to see how her old lady was getting along, only to find the seat empty.

'Where's Maggie? Where's the old lady?'

'Oh, she barely stayed five minutes, slipped back out before they locked the doors to look for her Percy. We tried to stop her but she'd gone before we got a chance.'

Gracie was appalled. Why on earth had she left her? Why hadn't she gone to look for Percy herself? She was quite certain that Maggie and her poor husband would be goners. Perhaps her house, the whole street, had been bombed while she was helping to fill babies' bottles. But the very next night, in the very same seat by the door, there was Maggie, a great grin on her face, and tucked under her arm was a basket.

'Meet Percy. Naughty boy! Caught him in good time tonight.' Percy was a cat.

* * *

76

They hadn't seen Rose again, despite keeping an eye out for her everywhere they went, so they were pleased and relieved when one bright September day she suddenly emerged through the trees, like a sprite out of the mist, and strolled towards them, the dog at her heels. They hugged each other like long-lost buddies, Tizz jumping up excitedly at them all, ecstatically joining in with the reunion. It took a while before the dog calmed down, and several sticks had to be thrown before she collapsed, tongue lolling, and they were able to talk in peace.

'Where have you been?'

'Didn't you get our note?'

'Was the bike OK?'

'What have you been up to?'

'Why didn't you come and see us?'

'We missed you.'

So many questions which Rose skilfully avoided answering. They sat on a log, since Tom-Tom had just announced the start of their dinner break, and she encouraged them to talk about their work, and about what they hoped to do when the end of the training arrived, as it surely would soon.

Lou answered without hesitation. 'Oh, stay here. No question.'

'I'm not sure you'll be allowed to,' Rose warned. 'There aren't any permanent girls kept here. They come and go. This is only a training camp. No one ever stays very long.' There was a note of wistfulness in her voice that was heartrending, as if she were longing for things to change one day, for the girls to stay so she could have some proper friends. They looked at her closely, seeing the reality of her life for perhaps the first time.

Lou suddenly grasped her hands. 'I've just had a wonderful idea. Why don't you join the WTC too? There's no reason why you couldn't be a Lumber Jill. If I can do it, anybody can.'

Gracie whooped with delight. 'What a marvellous notion! Of course, that's exactly what you must do, Rose. You'd soon

77

catch up with what we've learned so far, then we could be together always.'

Her eyes were shining as she listened to these plans being made, and just for one heady moment she almost believed them to be possible before reality closed in. 'I'm only just turned seventeen. Eddie would never allow it.'

'Don't ask him.'

'I'm only eighteen,' Gracie said. 'What of it? My parents were dead against my joining but I stuck to my guns, if you'll pardon the expression. There's a war on, for God's sake. People aren't asking too closely about what age a person is. Anyway, I believe you *can* join the Women's Land Army at seventeen. It's only the WRNS that need you to be older. So what are you waiting for, girl? Get fell in.'

'And get felling.' They all roared at the foolish joke.

'Rose, there you are girl. I thought I heard your voice.'

Rose started and looked up into her brother's implacable face. 'Oh, Eddie. I'm sorry. Am I late again? I was just talking to my friends. They were wondering if . . .'

He was about to say that he didn't give a tinker's cuss what they wondering when his eye fell upon Lou, or rather upon the fullness of her breasts thrusting forth above the sagging bib of her dungarees. He studied the length of her legs and how her lovely bright chestnut hair was falling down about her face, despite her putting up one hand to tidy her bangs back into place. His gaze slid over Grace's pale, slender figure without interest.

'Well, well, p'raps you'd best introduce me. I'm always happy to meet your friends.'

Beaming with relief, Rose told him their names, where they came from and how they happened to be in the WTC. Had Lou not stopped her, she might well have babbled out their entire life history. Something's wrong, Lou thought. Either the girl barely spoke a word or she talked twenty to the dozen.

'You can spare her for a few more minutes surely?' Lou mildly remarked, eyes flashing provocatively as she responded teasingly to his appreciative stare. 'We're just on our dinner break. Surely she's entitled to one too?'

'Of course. I was only worried about where she'd got to.' There was a brief silence. When nobody attempted to fill it, he went on, 'Perhaps I'll see you young ladies later, back in camp. Or bring them round to the house one night, Rose.'

'Very kind of you,' Gracie began but, turning his back on her, Eddie sauntered over to where Lou sat perched on a tree root. He hunkered down so that his face came to within inches of hers. 'We're always glad of a bit of company out here in the back woods.' His voice was soft, caressing. 'You'll come, I hope?'

'Wouldn't miss it for the world,' Lou whispered back, in the same tone, a beguiling air of innocence shining from her eyes as she carefully kept her wedding ring covered.

The corners of his mouth twisted into a slight smile before he stood up, allowing his gaze to linger upon her for another second or two, then swung about and strode away. The moment he'd gone, Lou caught her friend's eye, wrapped her arms about her waist and doubled up with laughter. 'The old bugger! He was flirting wi' me, weren't he?'

'You were leading him on something shocking,' Gracie chided, 'and he fell for it, hook, line and sinker, poor man.' The pair were soon rolling about, helpless with mirth. Rose looked on, bewildered.

When she'd calmed down enough to speak again, Lou said, 'I must say, he ain't half bad-looking, your brother, though a bit rough round the edges, happen. A decent shave might improve matters but he's not bad, not bad at all.'

Gracie poked her in the ribs. 'Hey, you shouldn't even be looking. Not you, a respectable married woman.'

'I know. Gordon would hang him from the mainbrace, whatever that might be.'

This set them off into fresh paroxysms of mirth and Rose struggled to join in. She'd never thought Eddie could cause such hilarity in anyone. She'd certainly never found him the remotest bit amusing but then she was his sister so he wouldn't chat her up, would he? 'At least you got an invitation to supper out of him. You will come, won't you?'

'Wouldn't miss it for the world,' Lou chortled.

Gracie wagged a finger at her. 'Best ask Gordon's permission first. We can't have Rose's brother thinking he's going to have his wicked way with you and all he gets is a smack in the chops from your husband. Bit of a disappointment for a chap, don't you think?'

Rose said, 'Actually, a smack in the chops from anybody's husband might do Eddie a whole lot of good,' which for some reason put a stop to the laughter as they all looked at her in surprise.

Until that moment, she'd always spoken of him with affection, saying what a marvellous brother he was to her, or at least been at pains to point out there was no real harm in him. Lou had a sudden recollection of their visit to the kitchens of the big house, and the strange sounds they had heard. 'He didn't actually *do* anything to you over that missed lunch, did he?'

Rose was relieved to answer in all honesty that he hadn't touched her.

'We heard this whining sound.'

'Oh, that would be Tizz, making a fuss.'

She made no mention of her own long day and night spent in the cold, damp cellar, nor the further two days locked in an attic room, Tizz in a cupboard on the landing so they couldn't even be together. The dog had indeed spent the whole time, practically, whining and scratching to get out. Rose didn't even glance down at her faithful companion as these thoughts ran through her mind but she was thankful Tizz was beside her now, as usual, leaning heavily and protectively against her leg.

'Lou thought it was a ghost . . .' And Gracie had to relate her own version of that visit which resulted in yet more hilarity.

What with the interruption, entertaining as it was, they'd forgotten all about eating but the mention of that first lunch they'd all enjoyed together served now to remind them. 'See,' Rose said, 'I've brought some sandwiches as my contribution today. "Only egg, I'm afraid. I didn't have anything else."

'*Egg!*' Without another word the trio fell upon the delicacy with gusto.

In no time at all, it seemed, they were into the last week of their training, worrying what was to happen next. It was an anxious time as Posting Out day would soon be upon them; the day when they would be given their first placement. Qualified candidates would be formally enrolled into the Timber Corps and sent to some job or other, which could be anywhere in the country. It might involve felling, doing a census, measuring the girths of trees, driving or haulage, or simply being involved with paperwork. They weren't given much say, but were allowed to put forward their preferences and, encouraged by Lou, who was determined to remain near Gordon, the squad had requested to be posted together somewhere in Cornwall.

Enid too was keen to stay in the county, since she'd met an airman from St Mawgan and was always nipping out to meet him. On at least two occasions both girls had arrived back dangerously late, stuffing their kitbags beneath the blankets to make it look as if they were asleep.

'You'll get found out,' Gracie worried, seeing that the pair were again making preparations to break the curfew.

'Then you'll just have to sweet talk the old goat some more, won't you?' Lou teased. Then more seriously, 'You never did explain exactly how you persuaded Matron to let me go out with Gordon that time, or on so many occasions since, come to that.'

'That would be telling.'

'Aw, go on. I thought we were mates. No secrets.'

'This is one secret that is shared between myself and Elsie.'

'And who's Elsie when she's at home?'

'That would be telling too.'

Jeannie said, ' 'Gi'e over worrying about what's past, girl. It's what happens next that matters. There's some of us might like to move further north. I wouldna mind goin' back to bonnie Scotland meself. Though I'm told there are few billets out in the wilds of the highlands so it'd be more camp life. And a pretty cold one, I'd say.'

Lena pulled a face. 'I'd prefer working for a timber merchant myself, or in a nice warm sawmill. More civilised.'

'Dinna ye believe it. There's some randy buggers run these sawmills.' Which made them all laugh.

'What about farmers? Don't they have a reputation too, Jeannie?' Lou asked, brown eyes shining.

'Och aye, but they're old, so they can't run so fast as me.'

Gracie said, 'Have you got a boy friend back home in Scotland then? Is that the real reason you want to go?'

The Scot began patting and searching in her pockets for a cigarette. Sliding out the packet, she pulled out a dog end and lit it, taking her time to draw in a long, satisfying drag. 'Not any more. I had a fiancé. He was in the RAF but was shot down.' The silence was long and sombre. It was Jeannie herself who broke it. 'Don't say anything. There's nothing to say. Such is life. So, it might as well be Cornwall as anywhere, I suppose. I'm game.'

Lou was out with Gordon on the afternoon that Gracie's parents came to take her home. In fact on this, their last

Saturday, all their plans seemed to go awry. It had been arranged that tonight they would take up Eddie's invitation to supper, then Gordon arrived unexpectedly and Lou begged Gracie to go without her.

'Offer my apologies but say I got called away. A relative came to visit. Long-lost Aunt Mathilda. Anything you like.'

'Relative? Don't you mean husband?'

Lou shrugged her shapely shoulders and pouted her lips carefully to apply a second layer of lipstick. 'Tell him the truth if you like, I don't care. He may appear to be smitten but he'll get over it. Don't worry, I'm a one man girl, me. It's just that I do love to tease. I was only having a bit of fun. I'd've let him down gently.' She patted her hair, smoothing it back from her face and pushing in a couple more kirby grips to hold it in place.

'Playing with fire more like. Why do I feel I'm drawing the short straw here?' Gracie moaned.

'Stop fretting. You're not the one he's after.'

'Thank God.'

'Besides, you'll have Rose for company and get well fed for once. That can't be bad. Anyway, you're probably right. It might have got a bit tricky if I had gone. Charm and good looks he may have in abundance, but I'm taken. Tell Eddie Treverrith that.'

So it was that Gracie was sitting alone on the doorstep of their hut, happily cleaning the mud off her boots, when her parents suddenly appeared before her, their homely faces beaming with delight at their own cleverness in finding her.

'Ah, there you are,' her father announced in his lilting Welsh tones, just as if he'd only momentarily misplaced her.

Gracie was appalled to see them standing there, her mother's best Sunday shoes sinking deeper by the second into the awful mud. She got hurriedly to her feet, a fixed smile of welcome on her face as she invited them inside.

Her mother refused absolutely, almost as if she believed it
would be no cleaner inside the hut than out. 'We'll wait here for
you to change,' she said, shifting her feet to a less soggy patch of
ground so as to make the very opposite point.

'Change?' Dreading the start of a lecture, Gracie momentarily closed her eyes, gathering strength. None came, only the
touch of her mother's hand, removing a speck of mud from her
cheek. From most mothers, Gracie realised, it would have been
a kiss, or at least a hug.

And then Howell stepped forward, proffered a whiskery
kiss and, tightening her resolve not to flinch, Gracie put her
boots back on and laced them up with fingers which suddenly
felt thick and clumsy; taking her time to roll the woollen socks
down while she worked out a strategy. On wet days, the socks
were always turned up, but the weather recently had been fine
and warm with today a bright sun peeping out from behind
scurrying clouds.

'We reckoned you'd have got over this daft notion of yours
and come home long since,' her father continued.

As if such a thing were possible. Gracie protested vigorously
that it wasn't a 'daft notion' at all and, no, of course she hadn't
'got over it'. She was doing an important job of work and would
continue to do so. Yet she noticed the exasperated glance
exchanged between them and knew they weren't convinced. It
was rare for their opinions to coincide but where bringing their
beloved daughter home to their own fireside was concerned,
they were as one.

Brenda Freeman was equally nonplussed, as much by her
daughter's workmanlike appearance as by her blunt rejection of
their misguided attempt at rescue. But she wasn't about to
accept defeat easily. 'I insist that you clean yourself up and look
civilised so that we can at least take you out to tea. Is that too
much to ask?'

How could she refuse when they'd come so far? She was far

from delighted to see them, but Gracie had no wish for another row. Her father settled the issue by proudly announcing that he'd managed to save up enough petrol to bring the car, which was parked at the camp entrance.

'All right, but don't think for one minute this means I'm giving up. I'm surprised, Father, that you should think so little of me that you'd imagine I'd chicken out in less than a month.'

They drove into Bodmin and took high tea at the smartest hotel they could find. Brenda always liked the best, even if she couldn't afford it. They sat in awkward silence for some time waiting to be served. But the food, when it finally came, was certainly a treat so far as Gracie was concerned and she tucked into the plaice and chips with relish, following by bread and butter pudding. What this lacked in actual butter, it more than made up for with a tang of something that had undoubtedly come from behind the bar. The pudding made her father frown with disapproval.

'It tastes like brandy. However could they afford it?'

'This is Cornwall, Dad, with lots of coastline. You'd be amazed what gets in here that the authorities don't know about.'

'Is that why you came so far away? In the hope we'd never know where to find you. We certainly noticed you never put an address on any of your letters. That upset your mother greatly.'

For the next hour and half Gracie was subjected to a grilling which left her weak with exhaustion. She heard how the business was collapsing without her, wages being far too high these days for Howell to afford to take on what he termed a 'proper shop assistant', and it was all getting too much for her poor mother. Brenda Freeman's health was robust but that never stopped Howell from using it as an argument if all else failed. Besides, it would be Gracie's business one day, he reminded her, so it behoved her to help look after it.

'But I don't want it, Father. I don't want to spend my life

working in a village shop.' She wished she had a pound for every time she'd repeated this simple fact. 'And what about Mother's dream for me to be a teacher? I can't do both, now can I? I can't please one of you without upsetting the other, so I'll do neither, thank you very much. I don't want to be either a teacher or a shop assistant.'

'So what do you want to do then? Seems to me that you haven't the first idea. Never did have. Otherwise, why would you get this daft notion into your head to be some sort of Lumber Jack.'

'Jill. Lumber *Jill.*' Gracie felt she might go mad if the meal and the interrogation continued for much longer, and got to her feet, suggesting that it was time they left. If they hurried, she thought, she might manage to salvage some of the promised evening she was meant to be spending with Rose and her brother. She'd have to eat another meal but that was no hardship.

Her mother looked flustered, glancing around to see if they were being observed. 'Sit down at once. You're making an exhibition of yourself.'

'I'd just like to get on with doing the job I have got, which I happen to love.'

'*Nonsense!*' Her father dragged out the word with such contempt in his voice, that Gracie had to clench her fists hard so as not to cry.

'Why do you always put me down? Why can't I choose, for once, what I want to do with my own life?'

'Because we know better, that's why. We have only your best interests at heart. You can't spend your life dressed like a navvy, chopping up bits of wood.'

'I don't chop up bits of wood. It's a responsible job, having to choose which are the right trees to fell for pitprops, or telegraph poles, and taking them down without . . . Oh, what's the use? I'm going. I'll get a lift back to camp.' She stumbled across the room, half blinded by tears yet acutely aware of the other diners watching her with surprised curiosity. By the time Gracie had reached the swing doors, Howell was beside her, his hand upon her shoulder.

'Now then, you've left your poor mother in tears. We'll have none of your tantrums here, thank you very much. Come and sit down like a good girl with your ma and me, and we'll have a nice fresh pot of tea.'

'So where the hell are they, these bloody friends of yours?'

Rose couldn't believe it. Neither girl had turned up. Here they were with supper all ready and not a sign of either of them. She'd opened a large tin of salmon as a treat, one she'd been saving for a special occasion, made a lovely salad from the garden and uncorked the last bottle of parsnip wine. And that's what this should have been, a special occasion. She couldn't remember the last time they'd had friends to visit. But it was past seven o'clock and Lou and Gracie were already more than an hour late. The evening was rapidly turning into a disaster.

'Something must have happened. They would never have let me down in this way, not deliberately. They're my friends.' Nervously, she checked her watch for the umpteenth time, smoothed the already immaculate lace-trimmed tablecloth, straightened knives which were already straight, lit the candles and then blew them out again.

'For goodness' sake, stop fussing.' Eddie was furious. He'd had a hard job coaxing Gertie to go off and visit her mother for the weekend but his juices had been running in anticipation of what the evening held in store. He'd planned to leave the skinny one talking to Rose, while he took the flighty piece for a stroll outside, or rather a quick roll in the hay. He'd even shaved, dammit. Now his plans were in ruins and who else could he blame but this bloody sister of his? Hadn't she spoiled his life from the minute she'd appeared? His parents had worshipped the ground she walked on and scarcely noticed him. 'Of course they're not your blasted friends. Look at yourself – too thin, hair an untidy mess as usual, boring skirt and jumper. You look like a ragamuffin. They'll be off to pastures new any day, like all the rest. Glad to get away from you and your silly fawning behaviour, I'll be bound.'

Rose couldn't have felt any worse if he'd struck her. The fact that her new friends had not only forgotten to come this evening but would soon be leaving altogether, filled her with utter despair. The prospect of being left alone once again with this brother she'd once adored, and had now come to loathe, was more than she could tolerate. Even the woodlands, which she loved, seemed like a cage, holding her fast in their remoteness.

Rose sensed her eyes growing all hot and prickly with her efforts not to cry and, in that moment, all the excuses she usually made for Eddie's selfishness, evaporated. 'They do like me, I know they do! It's all *your* fault. You were pestering Lou and you know she's married. She probably decided she didn't dare risk coming after all because you might try it on.' Tears were raining down her cheeks, despite her best efforts to stop them.

Eddie turned away from her, disgust plain on his rugged features. 'Soddin' hell, not the waterworks as well? Don't think I didn't notice that little tart trying to cover up her wedding ring. She fancied me all right, make no mistake, married or not. She's the sort who'll do anything for a lark, good time girl like her. If she's changed her mind it's because of you and your stupidity. You always let me down. Look at the trouble you caused me when I invited Dexter Mulligan that time. Wouldn't even join us for a glass of something in the evening, but went and sulked in your room.'

'I don't like him, and I'm sure he stole that rose bowl. I

swear I haven't seen it since the day before that lunch when I polished it.'

'Don't talk stupid. Dexter Mulligan's too clever to be a petty thief. I gave him the blasted bowl.'

Rose's mouth dropped open. She'd known he was in some financial difficulty but it stunned her now to learn just how bad it must be. 'You *gave* it to him? But – it doesn't belong to you. How could you give it to him – to anyone? And what on earth will you say to Lord Clovellan when he returns?'

Eddie smirked. 'I'll blame the war. All sorts of stuff goes missing in wartime. And the house is occupied by government riffraff, ain't it? How should I know who's wandering about the place half the time?'

'Because you're the caretaker, for heaven's sake. You're supposed to look after everything. Oh, Eddie, what were you thinking of? Why did you take the risk?'

Despite his bluster, Eddie wilted under her accusing stare. 'Because I was in a tight corner, that's why, and you wouldn't soddin' help me out of it.'

Rose shook her head in disbelief. 'Sometimes I don't know you at all. Why let yourself get involved with the likes of Mulligan in the first place?'

Eddie's face locked tight with fury. 'Who the bleedin' 'ell are you to criticise? Where are your friends when you need them? All you had to do was to be nice to him. Is that too much to ask in return for me putting a roof over your head?'

Rose shuddered. 'I can guess what "being nice" to Dexter Mulligan would have involved. No, thank you very much. I can't seriously believe that you'd expect me to, just because you owe him a bit of money.'

'A bit?' Eddie's laugh was bitter. 'More like a bloody fortune. And since he was threatening to separate my head from my shoulders, somehow it had to be paid back, sweetheart, one way or another. It had to be either your virginal charms or the bloody rose bowl, and cheap at the price. It's your fault I had to give him the bloody thing, not mine. We'll just have to hope we've managed to stave him off for a bit, won't we? Because if I have to use you, Rose, my love, I will. What choice do I have?'

Chapter Seven

Gracie was sitting anxiously in the back of her parents'
Morris 10, driving down miles of unknown country lanes.
She hadn't been particularly alarmed at first when they'd
set off in this direction, as her father had claimed it to
be a shortcut, but after a while she became seriously
concerned.

'Are you sure this is the right way? I don't ever remember the
lorry coming along this road at all. We should surely be at the
camp by now.'

'Stop your fussing, girl. Put your head down and get some
sleep.'

'Sleep? It should only take twenty minutes from Bodmin to
the camp, half an hour at most. How could I sleep?'

She saw them exchange glances and it was then that the
horrible suspicion dawned. They weren't taking her back to
camp at all, they were taking her home. Her own parents
had abducted her. If it weren't so terribly serious, she would
think it hilarious, but this was no laughing matter. Matron
would have her head on a platter. Gracie jerked forward in
her seat.

'You must take me back this minute. I'll be in dreadful
trouble if I'm not back by nine-thirty. Oh, why did I allow you

to persuade me to sit in the bar parlour and have that sherry, listening to your tales about Aunty Phyllis and her back problems, and yours with the shop? Why didn't I *make* you take me back when I first wanted to go?' There were tears in her voice, filling her throat, running down her cheeks. 'Matron will put me on report. They might even kick me out for breaking the rules.'

'Good thing too,' said Howell, in his most forbidding voice.

'Daddy, you mustn't do this to me. It's all wrong.' But even this childhood name she'd once used so lovingly, and now could hardly bear to as it indicated an affection she no longer felt, failed to move him.

'Stop fussing, dear. Father knows best.'

Gracie looked at her mother askance. Back at the hotel Brenda had drawn her to one side and said quite the opposite; saying how much she hated him, how she really couldn't cope, not on her own. She'd pleaded with, nay, begged her daughter to come home with them. Gracie had felt swamped by the bleakness in her mother's gaze, the agonised tone of her voice, yet had held firmly to her own resolve to return to camp. She'd escaped the chains that bound her, and nothing would induce her to put them on again.

'You can't possibly get away with this. You'll have to stop for petrol *some* time.'

'Your father put two Jerry-cans in the boot. And we've plenty of food with us. I brought a hamper specially,' Brenda informed her, her usually gloomy face for once wreathed in self-satisfied smiles.

Why was it that the one time in their lives her parents weren't fighting each other, they were attacking her? 'This is ridiculous. I can't believe this is happening.' But it was. Her own parents had kidnapped her and there didn't seem to be anything she could do about it. In the end, all Gracie could do was to sit back and accept the inevitable, grimly weighing up the possibilities for escape.

An opportunity presented itself on the outskirts of Exeter when Brenda was compelled to stop the car in order to spend a penny. Gracie went with her, of course, and the moment the two women were alone, wasted no time in exploiting the opportunity.

'Mother, I can't do this. I can't come back with you.' Gracie had been away from home scarcely a month but instinctively knew that if she gave in and went back now, before she'd even had the chance to prove herself, she might never get away again. She was young, with all her life before her, and thirsty for adventure. Deliberately hardening her heart she persisted with her argument. 'I *won't* come home. I like what I do! I've made new friends and have the chance of a fresh start.'

'If I thought you were leaving home for some good purpose, I'd be content. You're an intelligent girl. You could make something of your life. You could be a teacher, a woman of importance and independence, as I'd always hoped. Why do you insist on wasting your life? It's a crying shame. I do at least agree with your father about that.'

Gracie well understood that these aspirations her mother held for her originated from her own unhappiness and disappointment with life, yet she felt weighed down by this, knowing that if she succumbed, in no time she would be back in exactly the same situation as she was before. 'I'm not wasting my life. Keeping the country supplied with wood *is* important. Maybe when the war is over this job won't be enough for me, and I might want something different. Who can tell what any of us will want by then? But for now, this is right for me. Can't you — won't you at least try to understand? Why won't you see that I'm happy?'

'Because the war won't last for ever. You must think ahead. And it would help me so much if you came home, Gracie dear. Let's support each other through the duration. After that I'll feel more able to cope. You can't leave me now, I need you.'

Gracie gritted her teeth, determined not to give in to emotional blackmail. 'Whatever problems you and Father have, and I know they must be legion, they aren't mine any more. They never were, not really. You have to find a way to resolve them yourself.'

Panic came into the older woman's eyes. 'I can't, Gracie. You know how he is, how he treats me. So cold and condemning.' She began to cry; desperate, heartrending sobs which tore Gracie in two so that she felt bound to hold her mother awkwardly in her arms as Brenda wept into her shoulder. Never close, yet the bond held. 'I shouldn't have married him. Perhaps I never would have, had it not been for you.'

'Don't be silly, it has nothing at all to do with me.' Gracie turned away to wash her hands which she found to be trembling but Brenda had no intention of stopping now. She grabbed hold of her daughter and swung her round.

'I married him because I was carrying you. I thought I loved him, that it would be all right, that he cared for me, but he was just doing what he thought was right. He always blamed me.'

'For what? Getting pregnant? It takes two, Mother. I always guessed I wasn't premature, as you claimed. It's hardly unusual, is it? What does it matter?'

The tears dried instantly on Brenda's sagging cheeks as if scorched; the mouth so twisted with loathing that the once handsome face became distorted and ugly. 'It matters because it's contrary to his beliefs. He says we might have married, or we might not; that I lured him into breaking his vow of chastity before he'd made up his mind. He sees you as a child born from sin, tainted in some way. He says a child conceived out of wedlock is a child without purity.'

'What a terrible thing to say! Is that really how he sees me, as someone impure? Dear God!' Gracie felt numb, unable to take in the full import of her mother's words.

'That's why he's so determined to keep you at home, to protect you.'

'To protect himself more like, and his precious reputation.'

'That too, I dare say. He's always been fiercely determined to be a "pillar of society". But he means it for the best. It's just how he is. He says that if you come home, he'll forget all about this bit of rebellion, pay you the going rate for your work in the shop, and make you a partner in the business the minute you turn twenty-one. How would that be, love? If you don't want to be a teacher, at least that's better than roaming across the country in the freezing cold cutting trees, isn't it? At least we could support each other.' The tears were flowing once more. Her mother's eyes were puffed up, face blotched red.

'You can't do this to me, Mother. You can't lay the blame for Father's bigoted attitude on me. It isn't fair. I didn't ask to be born and I don't see myself as being in the least bit impure or tainted. I need to make my own life, away from him . . . away from you both.' Despite her brave words, Gracie was still reeling from these revelations, still struggling to make sense of it all. 'He's got worse as the years have gone by, becoming increasingly cold and remote. I could never do enough to please him.'

'Because he's afraid you'll turn into a whore, like me.'

Gracie leaned over the sink, feeling suddenly wretched and sick. 'How can he make such judgements on me, as if I've no control over my own behaviour? It's so cruel.'

'I'm sorry, love. I shouldn't have laid it on you so bluntly. I've kept it quiet all these years and now, out of selfishness, I've let it out and spoiled things for you.'

Mother and daughter looked into each other's eyes with new understanding. Gracie said, 'No, you were right to tell me. You should have told me before. I'm glad I at last understand why he has always seemed to hate me — hate us both in a way. Why do you stay with him?'

Brenda's expression was raw with pain. 'Because at first I loved him and thought he would change. And then because I was weak and couldn't find the courage to break free. Not like you.'

'You have Aunt Phyllis. Go and live with her for a while. I'm sorry, Mother, but I can't ever come home. I've my own life to lead and I'm even more determined to live it to the full now that you've told me all of this.'

Brenda opened her bag, drew out a comb, and with a rock steady hand took off her hat and began to tidy her hair. She freshened her lipstick, powdered her nose, pinned back the hat, then snapping shut the clasp of her handbag, as if in that way she could shut away the pain of her past life, she turned to face Gracie. 'Maybe it's time a few things changed, eh? Time for new beginnings for us all.' Her tone had altered, taken on a harder edge, a new resolve.

For the first time in a long while, she smiled. 'You're absolutely right to leave home. Howell's the one who's tainting you, with his own nasty notions of what's right and proper and his twisted way of thinking. I'm glad you've joined up and that you're happy. You do what you want, love. I reckon I might go and visit our Phyllis as you say. She drives me scatty with her potted plants and endless tales of woe but it can't be any worse than life behind that bloody shop with your father.'

It was the first time Gracie had ever heard her mother swear and it made her laugh. 'Good for you.' They held each other close for a moment, then Brenda patted Gracie's shoulder, tugged her hat into place and winked.

'We'd best go or he'll think one of us has fallen down the

lavatory pan.' Face serious again, she said, 'When you go love, go quick, and don't ever look back.'

As they emerged from the public lavatories Howell was waiting outside, as Gracie had known he would be. He stood, hands in pockets, shoulders hunched, scowling with impatience as rain dripped from the brim of his trilby hat. Hating herself, Gracie threw one last apologetic smile to her mother who was nodding encouragingly to her and, before he'd realised what she was about, turned and ran. She heard his shout but did not pause for a second. She ran as if her life depended upon it. Nor did she once look back.

Matron was standing in her favourite spot by the door on the dot of nine-thirty as usual. Lou was lying beneath the covers fully dressed, having just this second hurtled through the door and taken off nothing but her lipstick. Going to bed this early didn't trouble her unduly, since they'd be up at first light as usual, but leaving Gordon certainly did. It was always hard. Tonight, they'd strolled through the woodlands by the River Fowey, dawdling by Respryn Bridge and then making their way back to the seclusion of the old summer house, which seemed like their own private kingdom.

She closed her eyes and relived those precious moments. The hardness of his body against hers, the hot demands of his kisses, the trail of excitement left by his exploring fingers; such utter bliss, just thinking about it made her stomach tie itself into knots. Whatever would she do if she couldn't see him every week, speak to him every day? It would be purgatory.

'And where is madam?'

The familiar stentorian voice at her side brought Lou from her reverie with a jolt and only at the last second did she prevent herself from shooting out of bed; which would really have given the game away, since she was still fully dressed in her glad rags, right down to her shoes. 'Matron?' Eyes wide in pretend innocence, Lou gazed with trepidation upon the moonlike face before her which seemed to quiver with rage, the eyes glinting angrily.

'I said, where is she?'

'Who? Me? I'm here. As you can see.' Lou offered a tremulous smile of reassurance, aware of the stillness of her comrades in the beds close by, who even seemed to have stopped breathing.

Matron hammered one fat fist on the upper bunk. 'I mean this little madam. Your bossy friend. Where is *she*?' Lifting the large watch which dangled upon her massive bosom, Matron consulted it with a narrowed gaze. 'It is now twenty-one, fifty-seven, which means that Freeman is long overdue.'

Lou lifted her eyes to the bunk above, where she had assumed Gracie would already be ensconced and dead to the world. With great dexterity and no small degree of athletic skill, she held the blanket tightly to her chin while wriggling sideways to gain a better look. It was difficult to be sure but she saw enough to confirm that the bed above was indeed empty of its occupant. Even the blankets were still tightly tucked in. Her heart plummeted. Where on earth could she be? This wasn't like Gracie at all.

Lou looked helplessly at Matron. 'I haven't the first idea where she is. Do you think something could have happened to her?'

Unmoved by this genuine concern, Matron merely made a snorting sound deep in her throat, which wasn't at all pleasant. 'Something is definitely *going* to happen to her, if she isn't back soon. The moment she arrives – the very *moment* she gets back, do you understand? – you send her to me.'

Matron called in at hourly intervals during that long night, each time growing more and more irate. Lou began to hope that

Gracie never would come back; that way she might manage to survive.

When she felt it was safe to stop running, Gracie stood bemused in the empty street, breathing hard, striving to quell the stitch in her side. What now? She bent over till it had eased slightly and she'd got her breath back. She couldn't bear to think about the way her father's narrow-minded attitude had stifled the love his wife had felt for him. For the first time in her life, Gracie felt sorry for her mother. And she couldn't begin to consider how it might have coloured her own view of life. How dreadful to accuse an innocent child of being tainted, through no fault of her own. But now wasn't the time to worry about all of that. Gracie urgently needed to get back to camp, without delay. After that, she could only hope that her charm with Matron still held.

To one side lay the city, row after row of featureless houses; to the other what appeared to be open country but could well have been ruins laid waste by the bombing. It was hard to tell in the darkness. The small, hooded torch, which she'd learned always to carry in her pocket, could pick out few actual features in the blackout and Gracie was afraid to leave it switched on for too long in case she used up the precious batteries or somebody shouted at her 'put out that light'. Deciding she'd no option but to continue along this road until she could thumb a lift from some passing motorist, as Gordon seemed to do with comparative ease, she set off again with fresh resolve.

She walked for miles, or so it seemed, till her feet were hot and tired and her shins bruised from tripping over the rubble that littered the streets. At length her eyes grew used to the darkness, aided by the moon as it sailed out from behind a bank of clouds, and she walked with greater ease. But since she didn't know Exeter, any landmarks that did stand out against the lighter sky were useless to her. Thankful for the warmth of her WTC greatcoat, Gracie felt quite alone in the world, the hollow echo of her heels on the damp pavements the only sound in the darkness. There was an eerie stillness in the air, every door shut fast, the occupants no doubt huddled within the fragile safety of their four walls. Almost as if they were holding their breath, waiting for something to happen.

The next second she knew what it was. It began with the whine of the air-raid siren, quickly followed by that stomach-churning drone of enemy aircraft above. Within seconds, doors were flung open and where there had been emptiness and solitude now came a heaving mass of people, their arms loaded with precious belongings, children clinging to their mother's skirts, all silent and businesslike, all hurrying in one direction, all with one single thought in mind: to survive.

The Baedeker raids, named after the famous German guide-books, had begun earlier in the year, Exeter suffering the first attack in this series of raids, in April. Bath had come next, with hundreds of people dead in just two consecutive raids. York, Norwich, Canterbury had all taken a battering in the weeks following, along with other historic cities. And now, months later, the local residents had grown used to leaving the city night after night to sleep in the open countryside, in tents or barns, or even under hedges. But with the coming of the colder nights and more sporadic raids, many had grown careless or over-optimistic, believing they would be safe. Now they knew different.

As they hurried through the night, Gracie ran with them. If there was to be salvation in the form of a shelter nearby, they would know where to find it.

Even as the thought formed in her stunned mind, she saw that it was already too late. First came the flares, lighting the skies with their deadly radiance. Then the incendiary bombs, followed by the high explosives which dropped with frightening swiftness out of the dark heavens. Explosion after explosion rent the air like a cataclysm, flattening buildings, bursting gas and water mains, pitting the road upon which she ran with smoking holes in the broken stone. She felt that the whole world must be on fire, falling apart before her very eyes.

Gracie saw walls crumple like paper, whole houses collapse like a row of dominoes, burying everyone within; the light of the explosions starkly brightening the grim little streets into a Technicolor vision of death and destruction. In the space of one breath hundreds of lives were blown away on clouds of stinging, suffocating smoke. It made her eyes stream, caught at her throat, making her cough and choke, stumble and fall to her knees. Then it seemed as if the earth split in two, as if the jaws of hell had opened, and Gracie was looking down at a mass of screaming people buried in its dark red belly. Dozens fell into the pit and all she could see was a writhing mass of helpless bodies.

Her last conscious thought was that if she survived this night, it would be a blessed miracle.

'Are you all right, dear? Need a stretcher or are you walking wounded?'

Her head felt as if a thousand axes were splitting her skull. Lights exploded and danced in her head then finally swam together, settled and formed themselves into a kindly face topped by a tin helmet. 'I'm OK. I can walk, I think.'

The ARP warden helped her to her feet, dusted her off, checked her briefly before turning away to the next victim. Gracie called after him, 'I can help. I'm in the WTC.'

'What's that when it's at home?'

'The Timber Corps but we've had air-raid training.'

'Right. Get on with it then. We need all the help we can get here.'

How long the raid had lasted she never discovered, minutes had seemed like hours, and the remainder of that horrific night seemed to drag by in the length of a lifetime.

Gracie had witnessed the worst that man could do, now she observed the best. She saw firemen, Red Cross and auxiliary workers, bleary-eyed and filthy, some cut and bleeding themselves, exhausted yet resolutely determined to stay on their feet and do the job they'd been trained to do. Some plunged into burning houses to carry out lifeless or half-dead bodies, placing them on stretchers to be driven away in an endless stream of ambulances. One man, having gone inside, never returned as he too became trapped by the fires. The devastation was total, yet not for a moment did anyone say as much, or lose the will to salvage what they could.

Gracie held the blue waterproof bags as they slipped in severed body parts. She helped a WVS woman deliver a dead baby as its mother went into sudden, urgent labour, and carried away its tiny, half-formed body in a flour sack. She watched in awe as family members found each other and wept or stared, dry-eyed, at the heap of rubble where their loved one had last been seen before methodically and calmly starting to remove it, piece by piece, endlessly searching, never giving up hope. Others sat in shocked, silent groups, uncertain what to do next or where to go, all the possessions they had once owned now gone, perhaps their entire family with them, yet their dignity and resolve not to weaken remained firmly intact.

When it seemed that the worst of the raid was over, the mass exodus began. As if of one mind, the people got to their feet, gathering together whatever possessions they could find, and began to walk from the city.

Gracie did not go with them. She picked her way gingerly through the rubble and detritus which had once represented the homes and lives of these people. She listened intently for the slightest sound as she had been taught to do, the narrow beam of her torch invaluable as she searched for any sign of life. With every step she feared masonry might fall upon her, that she too might be burned alive or blown to bits by a landmine or unexploded bomb which could choose this precise moment to go off.

She saw a heap of rags, lifted the edge of it and looked into the staring eyes of a child. Head gaping open, blonde plaits matted with blood, one handless arm flung out. For a moment Gracie thought that the girl was dead. Even so she quickly probed with her fingers and found the flicker of a pulse, just below her ear. 'Help! Stretcher here. Quickly!' In an instant the child had been bundled into a blanket and borne away, either to live or die as a result of her horrific injuries, but at least she would have a chance now.

If she'd thought this was bad, minutes later Gracie found a baby, its tiny puckered mouth still clinging to its mother's nipple, but were there any milk left to draw, this baby would suckle no more. She drew a blanket over the pair and walked away, too traumatised even to weep.

'It was a nursery school, love,' said a kindly voice in her ear. 'Took a direct hit. There were thirty-six children in there, plus nursery nurses and mothers.'

Gracie looked about her with closer attention and saw that she was in a school playground. Eerily, a swing creaked as it moved to and fro in the night breeze but there were no children left to play upon it. They would never play anywhere again for they lay buried beneath a heap of black stones that had once comprised the walls of their school, or were scattered in pieces across the cracked playground, respectfully draped in old sacking. There came the sound of soft weeping, while other women screamed as the remains of their children were gathered up and removed. More poignantly, here and there a still figure stood, silently grieving.

Gracie had a natural distrust of emotion, having seen too

much of it in both her parents. But not revealing her feelings didn't mean that she didn't have any. She cared deeply. Sharing the devastation with these people, she felt that their tears were her tears, their sorrow, her sorrow. She desperately longed to do something to help. Yet there was nothing she could do.

'Oh, dear God. Why kill babies? Why?'

'There's no answer to that one, dearie.' Firm hands attempted to draw her away but Gracie refused to go.

'No, no. There must be some still alive. I need to look. I must find them.'

'There's nothing left. I reckon they're all goners.'

She searched for hours, painstakingly examining every broken body, assisting the auxiliaries as best she could, but the woman's guess proved to be correct. Not a living soul remained. It couldn't be right, she thought, fierce in her anger, sticky with sweat and desperation and sickened by the waste of it all. The stink of cordite seared her nostrils. War shouldn't be like this. War was an adventure, a lark. It should be something that took place *elsewhere*, many miles away in the skies, on the seas, between huge armies, trained fighting men. Not in their own back yards. Not on school playgrounds.

Only later did she feel the fear: a paralysing, physical terror which erupted as bile from the pit of her stomach. Shivering as the hot sweat of her vomiting cooled on her rain-soaked skin, she remained where she'd fallen on her knees for long moments, unable to think or move. She felt as if a part of her too had died, as if this night would remain with her forever. Gracie wiped the contaminating filth from her face and drew in a steadying breath, determined to carry on with her work, her attitude clearly stating that you simply had to get on with things, to deal with whatever life threw at you.

Yet suddenly there seemed nothing more to be done.

Her foot caught in a spar of wood and she stooped to pick it up. It was the remains of a poster which had once read: *Save coal.*

Keep your eye on your fuel target! Ironically, all around her was any amount of broken lumber which would serve in place of coal, assuming any one had a fireplace in which to burn it.

'Leave it for the bulldozers now, dearie.' The woman's voice again, coming out of the gloom. 'Come and 'ave a cuppa. Your hands need tending to.'

And so, along with everyone else, the walking wounded, the refugees and auxiliaries alike, Gracie was shepherded into a nearby school where the WVS were providing tea and sympathy in equal measure. Although, she hoped, not too much sympathy, or that would have her weeping; a pointless exercise. The cut on her head was cleaned and dressed; the blisters on her hands, caused by desperately trying to douse the fires, were bandaged and would, in time, recover. Those more seriously injured, or who had lost loved ones, might never do so. Her own problems, of being put on report for being absent without leave, of offending her father and upsetting her mother, now seemed small by comparison.

There was the very same ARP warden who had dug her out of the ruins, still wearing his tin hat and whistle. He came straight over the moment he spotted Gracie. 'You did a good job, girl. Well done! Name's Ted by the way. Here y'are. Get that down ye.' He handed her a steaming mug of tea which Gracie accepted with gratitude. It was hot and strong and black, soothed her parched throat for all it could not wash away the taste of death.

'What next?' she asked, when the tea had done its work and she could speak again.

'Oh, we'll have to stop the looting, I expect, and start the job of sorting out a place for everyone to sleep. Then there'll be matching lost children to their families, if we're lucky. Not pleasant, but nothing is in this business. What about you, where were you off to when the bombs hit? You're not from round here, eh? Where exactly are you supposed to be?'

Gracie told him. Wasting no words, hiding nothing, she quickly put him in the picture. He shook his head perplexed but, to his credit, asked no prying questions, simply told her to hand on a minute and he'd see what he could do.

He found her a convoy of army vehicles which were heading west as far as Dartmoor. 'After that, you're on your own.'

She accepted with alacrity and swallowed the rest of her tea in one. She was on her way.

Their last Sunday of training was drawing to a close and the squad were sitting down to a supper of sausage and mash when Gracie walked in, looking as if she'd just gone five rounds with Tommy Farr, the ex-miner turned champion boxer.

It had taken the entire day for her to get back to camp, travelling in a convoy of army trucks. She'd certainly been well protected by a lively bunch of soldiers but progress was slow. They dropped her near Tavistock, with much back slapping and jokes about how they'd like to meet up with her again some day, preferably in the woods next time. After that she'd managed to hitch several lifts which included a bread van, a vicar's old Ford which insisted on breaking down every five hundred yards or so and the back of a farm truck carrying a load of pigs. Consequently she stank of a rather odd combination of antiseptic, scorched cloth, fresh bread and pig manure.

In addition there were her burns, cuts and bruises, and tears to her uniform. Blood mingled with the dust in her filthy hair and her eyes were red-rimmed and sunken, still staring into horror.

Lou sat stunned, lost for words at sight of her. Jeannie said simply, 'Crikey!'

Gracie barely had time to utter a hasty, 'I'll explain later,' before Matron loomed and promptly marched her off.

Neither Gracie's appearance, nor the briefly told tale of her harrowing night, were enough to save her. Several hours later, the squad were informed that, in view of disciplinary offences, their request to stay in Cornwall had been refused.

Chapter Eight

Since the débâcle of the ruined supper, Eddie had scarcely spoken to Rose. He was in one of his sulks which, as she well knew, could last for days, even weeks. It really was most unfair of him to blame her for something beyond her control but that was Eddie all over. He always had to blame someone, and it was never himself. There were times when Rose felt utterly bewildered by his behaviour, wondering what on earth she'd done to offend him. At one time, she used actually to ask him, to seek an explanation, thinking to put it right. But this served only to aggravate the problem. She'd learned to keep quiet and wait for it to pass, rather like a rainy day.

Now she stood at her usual post at the kitchen sink and watched the lorries drive away, taking her dear friends with them, all belief in herself gone.

Last night it had all seemed quite different. The three girls had wept together, promising to write, to telephone, to visit. Rose had listened to the long and convoluted explanation of why they had not come for supper, and how sorry they both were to have let her down. They would never have done so, they explained, had circumstances not conspired against them. Lou in particular, she could tell, was filled with guilt, for her reason for not coming had been nowhere near as heroic as Gracie's.

She'd simply chosen instead to go out with her husband, and who could blame her? Certainly not Rose, who had eagerly welcomed this as proof of their friendship and unstintingly accepted their apologies.

Eddie simply scoffed, dismissing the explanation as excuses or pure fantasy.

'What a fairy tale. Abduction? Found herself abandoned in Exeter in an air raid? Pull the other one and see if that's got bells on it. I warrant she never left the comfort of her own bed. They didn't wish to dine with us. Never had any intention of doing so. They look down their superior noses at folk like us who they see as the servant classes, the ignorant masses.'

Rose had tried desperately to defend them. 'That's not true. They don't see us in that way at all.'

He shook his head, saying it really was time she learned to understand people properly. Even his voice had a pitying ring to it. 'They could've telephoned or sent a message, as decent folk do. It's only common courtesy.' He sniffed disdainfully, with the air of a man who would never be found guilty of committing such a breach of etiquette. 'They'd never any intention of coming because they aren't proper friends at all. They were only humouring you and laughing at you behind your back. You're well shot of them.'

Following this conversation, Rose went her room and wept in abject misery. Why was it that everyone she loved always left her in the end? Her beloved mother, and then dearest Papa. She'd made few friends after their deaths because Eddie had been most particular whom he allowed her to play with, or else they were constantly moving on to the next job, the next town. Having settled here, at Clovellan House, she'd thought every-thing would be perfect but a whole stream of friends had been found and lost before Lou and Gracie who, somehow, Rose had believed to be special.

But, as time wore on and Eddie's opinions were constantly

drip fed into her consciousness, they came to be her own. The story of Gracie's parents abducting her, and then abandoning her in the middle of an air raid, did begin to seem rather far-fetched. Why would two loving parents do such a thing? And it was quite rude of Lou, she supposed, simply to choose to do something else without even warning them. Hadn't Rose gone to a great deal of trouble to prepare a lovely supper, opening a tin of salmon specially? Admittedly Lou loved Gordon, and was never sure when she might see him again. Perhaps it was dangerous to have any friends at all. Despite the excuses she made to herself, Rose's insecurity was such that she began to wonder, deep down, if Eddie might be right.

It had ever been so. She felt far too fragile and uncertain of herself to believe that she might be correct, and not him.

There was a new set of girls in training now but Rose made no attempt to acquaint herself with any of them. It seemed far too risky. They would leave too, in the end, so where was the point? But she missed her friends dreadfully. Lou and Gracie sent her the odd postcard. One from Dorchester, another of Montecute House, and one closer to home showing a wonderful vista of the Quantock hills. Each gave her tantalising glimpses of their life on the road, although, reading between the lines, she wasn't entirely convinced that all was well with them. She couldn't quite put her finger on what it might be but something wasn't right.

Still, she longed to be with them, to be a part of their team, their lives. Anything rather than the endlessly lonely routine of skivvying for her brother. Try as she might to please him, Rose discovered it to be a hopeless task as Eddie sank deeper into depression day by day. He even blamed her when some scheme he'd devised to sell the vegetables she grew had fallen through, even though it had been the Supervisor of the camp who'd spotted him loading them into a van and had objected, explaining that these were now government property and not his to sell.

'If you'd said they were grown in our own garden at the lodge house, she couldn't have complained about your selling them,' he growled at Rose.

'But that would've been a lie. Anyone with eyes in their head can see that the kitchen garden up at the main house is full of vegetables, and that I work in it every day. In fact, the training camp has started to take quite a lot of what I grow, to use in the canteen. How can I deny such a well-known fact?'

'They don't even pay you.'

'Why should they? They own the place now, in a way. At least the government does. Anyway, I like to feel useful.'

'You – useful? Don't make me laugh.' And he strode away in disgust.

The only friend she had left was Tizz, her beloved dog, who trailed after her through the garden and the kitchens, wherever she went during the day. Sometimes the dog could even anticipate what Rose was about to do next, her inbuilt clock being so finely tuned to the daily routine and to her mistress's every movement.

'Damn' dog should earn its keep, not loll about the house all day,' Eddie would say.

The thought came to her that he was even jealous of Tizz, simply because she preferred to be with Rose and refused to come when Eddie called her, or obey him in any way. At times it was almost amusing to see the dog so stubbornly outfacing him. The louder Eddie shouted, the further Tizz would withdraw and refuse to obey.

'She's as bloody obstinate as you.'

'You have to be more patient. She'd come to you then.' And Rose would laugh and demonstrate. 'Come, Tizz.' The dog would prick up her ears and scoot after her beloved mistress, quick as a flash. Eddie might accuse her of fussing and pampering the animal but Rose really didn't care to think how she would cope without her.

To offset her loneliness over the loss of her friends, Rose allowed herself little time to brood or indulge in self-pity. There was far too much work to do in any case. Gertie had apparently taken umbrage over her banishment and refused to return from the visit to her mother, which left even more for Rose to do. The loss of his nightly comfort hadn't helped Eddie's temper one bit and he would snap and grumble and complain about anything and everything, even to accusing Rose of spoiling his chances, both with Gertie and with Lou.

'You hate it if anyone fancies me, or if anything good happens to me,' he snarled, mouth twisted in distaste as he poured himself yet another finger of his employer's whisky. He always drank it in one swallow and would then quickly pour another, an unmistakable tremor in his hand. 'You always have to spoil everything. You have to be the bloody *favourite*, the one everyone *adores!* Just as it was with Mother. Father, too, for that matter.'

Eddie, in drink, was not a pleasant sight. He became either maudlin or aggressive and Rose didn't much care for either. She always refused to be drawn into an argument, went to bed early and left him to it.

Rose guessed it might all have something to do with this long-standing disagreement he had with Dexter Mulligan. She'd seen Mulligan's flashy Morris car once or twice lately in the back courtyard. The man gave her the shivers so she always made sure that she kept well out of the way.

One morning she failed to do so. She was happily pegging out the washing when the car pulled up. Three men got out in quick succession and Rose suddenly found herself surrounded.

It was so unexpected that she stood there uncertainly, a pile of lace curtains in her arms, experiencing a growing sensation of alarm as she glanced anxiously from one to the other. She wondered whether they intended her any harm, or if the sudden tension in the air was simply a product of her overwrought imagination.

Two of them, who she understood to be the Pursey brothers, hovered in the background as Dexter Mulligan approached. He took hold of her chin between yellow-stained fingers and turned her face towards a ray of sunshine so he could examine it. 'Pretty little thing like you shouldn't be spending your time skivvying for an ungrateful brother.'

'I don't mind,' and she quickly drew away, though it was of course a complete lie. She minded very much indeed.

'I'm sure we could find you something far more appropriate to do with your time,' he said with a chuckle, a sound which chilled her. Mulligan's very nearness gave her funny little prickles between her shoulder blades. Even the smirk on his companions' faces made her want to snatch up her wash basket and run. Instead, she lifted her chin and outfaced them.

'Oh, don't worry, I've no intention of staying here for ever. I've got plans.'

'Have you indeed? I wonder what they might be, and if our Eddie has any say in the matter. We'll have to have words with our Eddie.'

For some reason this made them all laugh but, to her great relief, they strolled away then, laughing loud and long.

Dexter Mulligan had finally run out of patience and sent round his heavies. They were waiting for him in the courtyard the very next evening when Eddie went out to fill the coal bucket; a task normally done by Rose, but she was proving strangely obstinate about such tasks at the moment. One minute he'd been bending down to shovel up a load of coal, the next he was lying flat on his back on the cold stone courtyard, seeing stars. Not giving him any chance to recover, the Pursey brothers set about punching and kicking him in the ribs, in the back, and all about his head, loosening two teeth and leaving him dazed and half-dead with shock and pain. What was more, they made it painfully clear that he could expect much worse next time.

'Pin back yer ears and listen carefully, me 'andsome,' they said in their soft Cornish burr. With one brother sitting on his legs and the other holding his neck in an arm lock, Eddie listened with great attention. 'Mr Mulligan wants you to know that the rose bowl didn't fetch what he'd hoped for, there not being much call for such treasures with a war on. So what're you going to do about it?'

The trouble was, Eddie had been plundering Clovellan House for so long that he was rapidly running out of items which wouldn't be missed. He tried to explain this to the Pursey brothers. 'What can I do? I've cleared the loft and the cellars of anything of value. I can hardly take pictures off the walls, can I? Or clocks off mantelpieces, leaving great, yawning gaps. Folk would notice and the bloody government is in residence now, which makes it more difficult.'

Joe Pursey softly tut-tutted, as if this were all a great pity. 'Well now, you 'as two choices. Either you settle what ye owe, or you get that choice sister of yours to be more agreeable, as you promised, if you recall. Mr Mulligan says he's waited long enough and fancies she's ripe for the plucking. Just make up yer mind which it's to be. But make it damned quick. Then yer life's yer own again. And don't think ye can escape. Mr Mulligan, 'e has friends everywhere, 'e do. Got that?'

'Yes, yes, I've got it. I understand perfectly.'

The clock, it seemed, was ticking. Useless to accuse the Pursey brothers of cheating in those damned poker games. Dangerous to complain that Mulligan himself doubled the interest owed each and every dratted week. He had Eddie by the short and curlies and there was an end of the matter.

The beating left Eddie with an even deeper resentment against Rose, or rather a worsening of the one he'd nursed for so long. He blamed her entirely for his precarious situation. If she'd been doing her job properly, as she should have been, then he wouldn't have needed to cross the yard to fill the coal bucket himself and it might never have happened. The fact that the Pursey brothers could have attacked him at some other time didn't register in his stubborn brain. In Eddie's opinion the entire mess was Rose's fault for not being prepared to pacify Dexter Mulligan's temper with a bit of sweet talk, which would have been no skin off her nose and would have helped him enormously.

Eddie neglected to remember his own constant bullying, or the hours Rose had spent cleaning, cooking and waiting upon him from dawn to dusk over the years. He carried only one thought in his head: self-preservation. If Dexter Mulligan wanted Rose, he could have her. What else could he do? he asked himself self-pityingly. She was the only card he had left to play. In any case, she was an ungrateful little madam. Hadn't he ached for revenge against her all his life? He'd enjoy making her pay, see if he didn't. He would personally deliver her into Mulligan's nasty hands.

Until she'd said those words, no notion of any plan had existed in Rose's head but, following the incident with Mulligan, she could think of little else for she saw that it was indeed true. She did have plans, or at least she could soon make them if she wished. Hadn't it been her very own friends who'd made the suggestion? She could join the WTC, just like them.

Acting on impulse she went straight to Eddie and explained she wanted to do her bit for the war effort. He looked at her for a long moment without speaking, eyes wide, brows raised, as if expressing surprise that she could nurture ambition of any sort. 'You, work for the war effort? Don't make me laugh. Who'd employ you?'

'I'm seventeen. Quite old enough,' she countered, struggling to stop her bottom lip from trembling. 'Don't you think I should at least try?' It was one thing to decide stand up to Eddie, quite another actually to do it. He always seemed to undermine her belief in herself just by the scathing way he looked at her. Today he didn't even trouble to answer her question.

'Dexter Mulligan's coming over this evening. Get to the kitchen and make sure you make him a decent meal this time.'

'Take it in yourself. I'm going nowhere near him.'

Eddie grabbed her by her wild, flowing hair, making her yelp. 'Do as I bloody say, if you know what's good for you, girl. I need a chance to put things right. If I go down for looking after number one, just like everyone else does in this bloody war, then you go down with me. That would mean losing our home as well as my job, and then where would we be?'

Rose wanted to say that she'd be free at last, but the fear and anguish in his eyes was filling her with a sad sort of pity for him. The thought of Eddie in jail was too awful to contemplate and, as always, she began to weaken. Wasn't he her very own brother, whom she loved dearly? Hadn't he provided her with a home for years, even if life wasn't quite as she would have hoped? He'd surely learned his lesson and wouldn't be so foolish as to take anything from Lord Clovellan again. Wasn't he saying as much? The least she could do was to support him when he needed her.

Rose agreed to compromise. She would do her best to be

pleasant to Mulligan, she agreed, so long as she wasn't left alone with the man. 'He gives me the shivers.'

'You won't be left alone with him, I'm sure of it,' Eddie said, not quite meaning what Rose thought he meant. Then he happily went and informed Mulligan that it was all set up. He was welcome to enjoy his sister, in return for the cancellation of all his outstanding debts. A clean start, that's all he needed.

'She'd better be worth it, Eddie lad.'

'Oh, she will be. She will be.'

Rose felt perfectly safe in the dining room as she served the food: pork chops that had taken all their spare coupons for weeks in advance. Mulligan expressed his appreciation by never taking his eyes off her. His hands too seemed to be everywhere. Whenever she brushed past, he would pat her bottom, smooth her hip, fondle her breast as she leaned over to pour the gravy, and once lifted her skirt to check if she was wearing stockings or whether the golden colour of her legs was entirely natural.

'Nice soft skin, though I do prefer suspenders. What a pity that the war has denied us these little pleasures. 'Course, I could always lay my hand on a few pairs of stockings for you, little maid, if'n you make it worth me while.'

Mindful of Eddie's warning, Rose suffered his attentions with a steely resolve, for all she could feel herself blushing scarlet with embarrassment. 'That's all right. I don't have any need for stockings.' But worse was to come.

She brought out the home-made apple crumble and placed it on a mat, preparatory to serving it.

'I rather fancied a sweeter dessert,' Mulligan said, the hard lines of his face twisting into the parody of a smile which ended up more as a nasty leer.

Not at first understanding, and mindful of her promise to

Eddie to keep his friend happy, Rose said, 'I do have some sugar. I could make it sweeter for you, if you wish.'

Dexter Mulligan let out a great guffaw of laughter, in which the Pursey brothers gleefully joined in.

'I meant, little lady, that we'd rather thought you might be on the menu. Now then, boys, who wants the first bite? Would someone like to warm her up for me?'

With dawning horror, Rose saw that one of the Pursey brothers had got to his feet, fat face wreathed in a lurid grin, his hands busily unbuttoning his trousers. In panic, her eyes flew to her brother. 'Eddie?' But he'd got up from the table and moved over to the grand fireplace where he stood with his back to her, lighting himself a cigarette. Instinct told her that this was where he meant to remain, no matter what took place behind him.

Out of nowhere it seemed hands were lifting her and Rose found herself placed on the dining-room table, right next to the apple crumble. Her spinning brain seemed to be offering up a dizzying set of pictures, like snapshots leaping at her from every direction. The gaping trousers; the neglected pudding; the obstinate blankness of Eddie's back; the leering grin of Dexter Mulligan as he rocked back and forth in his chair in what seemed to be delighted anticipation of what was to follow. Without pausing to think of the consequences of her action, Rose lifted the jug of custard still clutched in her hand and poured it into Mulligan's lap, then smashed this treasured piece of Spode china over Joe Pursey's head.

And that's when it all started to go wrong, Eddie recalled, hours later, as he reached for another snort of whisky. In the pandemonium that had followed, Rose had stormed off, head high. He'd been forced to leave the Pursey brothers to mop up the slimy mess as best they could, so he could chase after her to bring her back and make her sorry for this display of temper.

Rose, however, had apparently vanished off the face of the earth. He searched everywhere, even the dratted barns, to no avail. To say that Mulligan had not been best pleased was an understatement. It had cost Eddie several bottles of Lord Clovellan's best claret, not to mention one of his finest pure malt whisky, in order to placate him. Grabbing the bottle now, he emptied the dregs into his glass and gulped it down in one.

Drat the girl. Why did she always have to defy him? It had been a great relief when Mulligan had finally gone, though making ominous threats that he wouldn't forget this insult. He'd be back.

Eddie must have fallen asleep at this point in his recollections because when he awoke his mouth tasted like sawdust and his head felt as if it had been severed from his body. The room seemed to rotate around him, and the first sounds of a dawn chorus echoed in his head like gun shot. How he hated his life. Nothing had ever gone right for him, not since Madam Rose had come on the scene. All his parents could ever talk about was how they must take special care of little Rose. How adorable she was. How Eddie mustn't hurt her; constantly reminding him how young and vulnerable she was, and how she deserved all their love. Maybe it was time he told her all about her precious parents, and the truth about herself. That'd change her tune right enough.

They should never have bloody died and left him lumbered with her.

He'd put a roof over her head, food into her belly, and what gratitude did he get? How did she repay him? By insulting his friends. This show of obstinacy was typical of her. But then she complained all the time, claiming she had too much work to do, objecting to Gertie or any other female he happened to take a fancy to; she scolded him like some sanctimonious schoolmarm if he slept in Lord Clovellan's bed. As if it did any good for rooms to be left idle, or for the cellars and lofts to be stuffed with things that hadn't seen the light of day for centuries. Who would ever miss them and why shouldn't he enjoy a few perks? She even nagged him for drinking the master's whisky. At which thought, he pulled himself to his feet to go in search of a fresh bottle.

She'd no sodding right to insult his friends. And it was highly dangerous to get on the wrong side of Dexter Mulligan.

Dawn was breaking as Eddie stumbled his way through the kitchen, staggered and almost fell over a chair, sending it crashing to the ground. In response there came a pandemonium of barking from the direction of the stables.

'Bloody dog.' That was another creature he hated. Her precious Tizz, bought by 'Darling Papa'. Eddie wove his way over to the back door, picked up his gun which he'd left carelessly lying about after picking off one or two rabbits, and went out. He could stop that bloody racket, if nothing else.

Chapter Nine

Rose's first task each morning was to let Tizz out of the stables and feed her. She would much rather have had the dog at the foot of her own bed, but Eddie had strong rules on the subject which must be obeyed. She didn't greatly mind. She always enjoyed the morning ritual as Tizz made such a fuss of her, as if she hadn't seen Rose for six weeks at the very least. She would jump up and lick her face all over, charge about in excitement and roll over in the dust or the mud, before gobbling up her breakfast in double quick time, eager to face the excitement of the day ahead.

Sometimes she might even leap into Rosie's arms like a demented puppy.

Girl and dog would stand in the morning sunlight, the one laughing, the other yelping and licking, punctuated by short, high-pitched barks; the pair so delighted to be reunited neither was prepared to end the embrace. To the dog, here was the person she would obey without question, follow to the ends of the earth and give up her life for, if called upon to do so. To the girl, the dog smelled deliciously familiar and comforting, the warm, hairy old body wriggling with ecstatic joy in her arms as the long tail batted back and forth. Her one friend in all the world.

It came as a surprise therefore when that morning Rose found the stables empty. After she'd looked everywhere and failed to find any sign of Tizz, she went to ask Eddie if, for some reason, he had already let her out.

She found him in the main kitchen, a newspaper spread out on the kitchen table in front of him, on to which jam was dripping from the thick slice of toast in his hand. 'Eddie, have you seen Tizz? Have you let her out and fed her this morning?'

He ignored her, said nothing at all.

'Eddie, I'm asking you a question in a perfectly civil fashion. Have you fed Tizz?'

'No, 'course I haven't. She's gone.'

Rose went very still. 'What do you mean, gone?'

'I've sold her. Tom Winterton was looking for a new bitch to work his sheep, his last one having died last week. So I sold him Tizz. Gave me a good price.' Turning a page with careful precision, he took another bite of toast and continued with his reading, just as if she weren't there.

'But . . .' Rose could barely speak. Her mind seemed empty of words. The silence stretched as she dragged herself out of the depths of shock in order to respond. 'How could you sell her? She's far too old to work sheep. She's never been trained to do such a thing.'

'Comes by instinct in a collie. She'll be fine. Got a good few years in her yet.'

'I'm not sure why you've done this dreadful thing but it isn't fair. There are few enough people living around here and the girls at the training camp never stay longer than a few weeks. Tizz is the only friend I have.' Rose hated herself for sounding like a tearful schoolgirl, but the thought of getting through each day without the dog was unbearable.

'And whose fault is that?' He was shouting at her now, even if it worsened the thumping in his head. Thrusting back his chair, he stood before her in a threatening manner, his face ugly with temper. 'Who would want to be friends with a nincompoop like you? You always have to bloody defy me. All you had to do was be nice to Mr Mulligan. *Was that too much to ask?*'

Losing patience with him completely, Rose left.

She went first to Ned Winterton and offered to buy back Tizz. The farmer looked surprised. 'I haven't got her, Rose. Why would I buy her for a working dog? She's too old.'

'Eddie told me he'd sold her to you, though he'd no right to do so. She's my dog.'

'Well, all I can say is, I haven't got her. Do you reckon he sold her to someone else? Though why anyone would buy her, I can't think. She's a nice little bitch, Rose, but too soft for a working dog.'

She tried several other farmers, sure she must have misheard Eddie or misunderstood in some way, certain she would find Tizz in the end. On the way she called on the Supervisor at the training camp to enquire where her two friends had been sent but was told that the WTC never handed out personal information of that sort.

'I rather thought I might join the Timber Corps myself,' Rose ventured.

'And you'd be very welcome, dear. You could start your training here, right now.'

The prospect of having to remain in the area hadn't occurred to Rose. The thought horrified her. 'Oh, no. I'd want to go somewhere different. Is that possible?'

The Supervisor frowned at this but offered to look into the matter and let her know. Rose attempted to explain that she needed an answer this very minute, that she couldn't afford to wait, but the woman wasn't listening. 'Now I really must dash, dear. Busy, busy. Do bring over some more of those lovely tomatoes you grow so well. Delicious.' And she marched away, blowing on her whistle to summon the new girls to their lorries.

Rose went to see Matron, since the woman had seemed to

get along quite well with Gracie at one time, in the hope that she might be more sympathetic. No such luck. She took the opportunity to complain at length about Gracie's perfidy; how she'd taken advantage of Matron's moment of aberration in revealing personal details best kept private, to go off gallivanting all night without permission. If she'd got caught up in an air raid, she'd no one but herself to blame. It just went to show, Matron said, that you couldn't trust anyone these days. Rose gave up and left the training camp, with no intention of returning.

It was as she made her way back through the woods that she came across the dog. Tizz was lying in the undergrowth. She'd been shot clean through the head. Rose sank to her knees with a sob and cradled her dear friend in her arms.

Rose found Eddie in the cellar, helping himself to another bottle of wine. She'd guessed he would be there. It was the first place she'd looked. Only the tumult of her rage and the shock which numbed her held the tears at bay. A voice in her head was telling her that it had been a mistake to return, to come back home at all, and yet she couldn't bring herself simply to walk away, not after what he'd done. She had to know *why*. She had to understand. She was his little sister, all he had left in the world. Didn't he care for her in the slightest? 'Oh, Eddie, why? Why did you do it? It was you, wasn't it? You killed my lovely Tizz. How could you? How *dare* you? Was this revenge against me for not agreeing to play your nasty little games with Mulligan? What has happened to you? Why are you behaving like this? Mummy would be so disappointed. She had such high hopes for you.'

Eddie glared at her out of bloodshot eyes. He could hardly focus but he didn't need to. He could guess the look of censure and criticism which would be in those beautiful blue eyes of hers, and hated her for it. 'Don't you bloody tell me what my mother wanted. What right do you have? Just because you wormed your way into her good books and turned her against me.'

Rose gasped. 'I never turned her against you. How can you say such a thing?'

'Because she loved you more than she loved me. Everyone knew it.' he struggled with the cork in the bottle he was holding, managed to yank it free and filled a wine glass till it overflowed, all over the stone-flagged floor.

'That's not true. Mummy adored you. She loved us both and it would have hurt her terribly to see us squabbling and fighting like this. And Tizz was *my* dog. She belonged to me.' Rose had to stop talking as her throat closed up, choking on unshed tears.

Eddie put back his head and laughed, instantly regretting the action as the movement made him wince and he instinctively put a hand to his head. A thousand hammers were beating against his skull and he knew who to blame for that. He certainly wasn't in the mood to be cross-questioned by this little madam. 'Who on earth gave you that idea? How can she be *your* dog? You own nothing, 'cept what I'm prepared to let you have. Never did. Not even your own soddin' name.'

Rose struggled to take in the import of these few cruel words. She didn't understand what he was saying but felt as if something was uncoiling inside her head, as if she'd turned over a stone and found maggots beneath. She felt a sudden need to examine it further.

'What do you mean about my name, Eddie? I think you should explain.'

'I don't need to *explain* anything to you.' He sprayed wine as he spat the words at her.

'Please, Eddie, I want to understand.' And now her eyes did fill with tears. Angrily, she brushed them away.

He picked up a bottle and threw it at her. It missed her by inches, splashing red wine all down the white cement wall. 'Don't bloody lecture me! Right bloody cuckoo in the nest you were.'

Rose stood rooted to the spot, stunned by this outburst, by the entire day's events. Used to his gloomy moods as she was, he'd never before shown quite this level of violence. What on earth was happening? She shook her head, desperately trying to clear it, to think. 'I don't understand. What do you mean by cuckoo in the nest? Why do you call me that?' Had something else gone wrong with these nefarious business affairs of his? Did he want her to leave? This surely couldn't all be because she'd refused to keep Dexter Mulligan sweet? Was that why he'd shot dear Tizz, in retaliation for another ruined supper? Surely not. It didn't make sense.

His burst of energy spent, Eddie suddenly turned maudlin. 'I gave you a home and look what thanks I get. What gratitude have you ever shown me?'

'Oh, for goodness' sake, Eddie. I've spent the last seven years of my life thanking you, showing my appreciation for your taking on Papa's role exactly as he asked you to. We've looked after each other as a brother and sister should. We've both grieved for the loss of our parents, yet it wasn't my fault if Mummy caught that terrible disease from me and died or Papa died of a broken heart.'

He took a slurp of wine, rocked back on his heels, then took a step or two towards her to snort his contempt directly in her face. 'Dad didn't die of a broken heart. People don't, for God's sake, except in trashy novels. He took a handful of pills because he couldn't bear to live without her for another day. 'Course it was all your fault. If you hadn't caught that dratted disease in the first place, neither would she. But then if you hadn't been bloody born, she'd never have wanted you.'

Rose backed away, giving a nervous little laugh, not liking

the direction this conversation was taking one bit, and he still hadn't explained about her name. 'I think you've got that the wrong way round, haven't you? She must have wanted me, else how could I ever have been born in the first place?'

Eddie put back his head and laughed, a harsh, sadistic sound that echoed around the vaulted recesses of the cellar. 'Well, that's where you're wrong.' He waved the bottle at her, savouring the moment. '*My* mother was *not* your mother at all. You were not the child of my parents.'

Rose began to tremble. 'I don't understand. What are you saying?'

'I'm saying that you were adopted. She picked you out from a children's orphanage. You're nothing but a bastard. So, like I say, even your name isn't yours.'

Rose felt as if she were standing outside herself, watching and listening to a conversation between two complete strangers. As if she'd suddenly moved on to a different plane and was no longer a part of the real world. Even the questions were coming from some part of herself over which she had no control. 'Why? Why did she do that?'

'Because she felt like being charitable, I expect.' He burped loudly and then the words just poured out, as if he'd taken the stopper out of a bottle of poison. 'Or maybe she thought a new baby might make her feel young again. She'd been a bit below par for a long while. I was seventeen and didn't want a baby around, did my best to put her off the idea, but Dad would've given her the moon, if he could. The moment my mother held you in her arms, that was that. You were brought home, the papers signed, and from then on she showed no further interest in me. The pair of them doted on you in a quite nauseating manner. I became like an outcast just because I wouldn't join their adoration society. Of course, it was only because you were such a novelty. If she'd lived, I'm sure she'd have grown bored with you too in the end, as she did of everything else, including me. So, I really don't care if you are lonely, whether you stay or leave, live or die. You're not my bloody sister. You're nothing to me. Nothing!'

Rose was staring at him, stupefied, as all her known world crumbled to dust before her eyes. Yet what he said must be true. It explained everything. 'Why didn't you tell me before? Why keep it a secret?'

He chuckled, though with no sign of amusement in the puffy red eyes that glittered with rage. His moment of lucidity over, he staggered towards her, losing his grip on the bottle which fell to the ground and smashed, as he lunged and grabbed her arm. 'Fact is, I put off telling you 'cause I didn't want you to go off in a huff. I liked keeping you here. Beholden! Forcing you to wait on me, hand, foot and finger. I enjoyed anticipating this moment, when I would eventually tell you.' He pushed his face to within an inch of her own. 'You're not my soddin' sister. So I can do what I bleedin' well like to you. D'you hear me? D'you understand what I'm saying?'

Rose was too shocked even to think of a reply. She just gazed back at him, dumbstruck.

'So, if you wouldn't do it for Mulligan, you can bloody well do it for me. Why not?' And grasping the neck of her blouse he ripped it from her body, then he hit her. The blow sent her reeling and Rose fell to her knees some distance from him, jarring and bruising them so badly that for a moment she feared her legs might be broken. But the jolt served to bring her out of her stupor. She knew instinctively what would happen next. He needed to humiliate her, to re-establish his power over her. That was why he'd shot Tizz, out of revenge and a need for power. Yet still she defied him, and there was really only one effective way left to him. Even as these thoughts whirled through her head he was regaining his balance, lurching to his feet and staggering towards her. The one advantage she had over him was that he was drunk and she was stone cold sober.

Rose glanced quickly about her, saw that she was within reach of the door and, gritting her teeth against the pain, pulled herself to her feet and flung herself towards it. His shout rang out just as she reached it. Too late. She was through. Summoning every ounce of her energy, she slammed the heavy door shut, cutting off his roar of anger for the cellar was, as he had so often told her, entirely sound-proof.

She went to her room and packed a few essentials, including her Post Office account book in which were a couple of hundred pounds given to her by her beloved mother. She carefully locked up their part of the house and left before dawn.

Rose walked for miles, through Cardinham, past Dozmary Pool where some said Arthur had retrieved the magic sword, and on over Bodmin Moor. The night was pitch black and freezing cold but then so was her heart. It seemed to be barely beating, lying like a stone within her, but not for a moment did she hesitate, not even to glance back over her shoulder at the life she'd once led. That was behind her, which was where it must stay. If she dwelled upon it too much, or attempted to analyse too closely the dreadful events of this night, Rose knew she might never find the strength to go on.

It was two miles beyond Jamaica Inn that she hitched a lift in a cattle truck and left Cornwall altogether. The only trouble was that because she'd been unable to wait for a reply to her query about joining the Timber Corps, she hadn't the first idea where she was going.

The only towns of any size that she knew of were Plymouth, which was too close to home to be safe, Exeter, which her driver refused to go anywhere near because of the risk of bombing, and London, which was too far away.

He dropped her off sometime after noon in a quiet country area he called the Cotswolds, where he assured her there'd be plenty of work to be found. If, in her distraught state, Rose thought beyond the overriding desire to get as far away as possible, the nearest she came to a plan was to work on the land. Labour was in short supply because of the war. She had gardening skills, knew how to grow tomatoes, keep chickens, and could also cook, make jam and preserve pretty well anything you'd care to mention. Listing these accomplishments gave her courage.

So this seemed as good a place as any.

The truck driver was concerned for her. 'Are you sure you'll be all right? I could take you all the way to Birmingham, if you like. That's where I'm going with this load.'

Rose knew nothing about Birmingham and after hours of jolting in the rattling old truck, longed for fresh air and to stretch her legs. Anything, she decided, would surely be better than the life she'd left. 'I'll be fine,' she said and, hoisting her bag up on her shoulder, gave him a brief nod of thanks and set off valiantly along a narrow road which led into a small village with the homely name of Lower Trencham.

The first farm she tried almost laughed at her request for work. The second shut the door in her face. The third was more kindly and at least gave her a glass of fresh milk, still warm from the cow, but, sadly, although they said they'd be glad of her help, they couldn't afford to pay her anything beyond her keep. Rose was sorely tempted to accept as the farmer's wife had a merry face and a kind smile but common sense prevailed. She should be paid a proper rate for a day's labour, otherwise how would she make any progress? She needed not only to survive but also to save money for her future. She'd no one to rely on now but herself.

Rose plodded on, knocking on every likely door in the scattered village, watching sadly as heads were shaken, listening carefully to any suggestions or advice offered as to who might be in need of a bit of cheap labour. But as dusk fell hope and optimism faded and finally, driven by exhaustion and limbs that protested in every aching muscle, she prised open a loose board and slipped into a barn, desperate for an hour or two of sleep.

To her great disappointment it was not filled with hay but rusty old machinery. A bitter wind whistled around the door and through the many cracks in the walls, and she was forced to put on every item of clothing she possessed in order to keep warm. Rose curled herself up tight, shut her eyes, and willed herself to sleep.

She strove not to think of Tizz, yet it was hard. The shock and numbed disbelief which had kept these images at bay during the day were now wearing off and several times during that long, freezing night, she would wake, heart pounding, and know that in her dreams at least she'd witnessed her dear friend's death. She didn't give a passing thought to Eddie.

A sound seemed to be echoing in her head, coming from some far-distant place. Rose found herself gripped and shaken hard by a hand upon her shoulder, bringing her instantly awake.

'Wot the 'ell are you doing 'ere? 'Oo let you in?'

She struggled to gather her wits, to bring some sense into her sleep-fuddled brain. 'Nobody. I – I came upon your barn quite by chance and didn't think you'd mind if I spent the night here. I had to have somewhere to sleep. I'm sorry.'

The man's glare was unnerving. The ensuing silence as he considered this statement even more so. Rose sat quite still as his eyes roamed over her, though they didn't do so necessarily in the same direction at the same time, there seeming to be a slight cast in one of them. Yet evidently he was taking in every detail of her unkempt appearance, her tousled hair and few pathetic possessions.

He was old, fifty, sixty or seventy, Rose couldn't be sure, with red-brown hair and in dire need of a shave. Perhaps he'd decided to grow a beard or, more likely, the household was short of hot water and he couldn't be bothered to boil any. His clothes comprised a tweed jacket that looked ancient with holes in the elbows and grain spilling out of the pockets. He wore a muffler wrapped about his scrawny neck, tucked into a stained waistcoat, and trousers that were a sort of mud colour; strapped tight to his calves were canvas gaiters. Rose thought they looked decidedly uncomfortable. On his feet were enormous steel-tipped boots which rang on the stone flags as he shifted his feet. She realised this had been the sound which had woken her some seconds before the hand had touched her, almost as if he'd been hard put to know what to do for the best when he'd first spotted her.

Rose wished she looked more presentable, that she'd had time to clean herself up, comb the tangles from her hair and remove some of the odd collection of clothing she'd piled on to keep warm.

He gave a short, ill-tempered grunt and jerked his head in the direction of the door, his aggressive expression having changed to one of bored disinterest as if it wasn't in the least unusual for him to find someone sleeping in his dirty old barn. Rose sighed and began to pack up her few belongings, heart sinking as she proceeded to leave. At the door, she made one last desperate bid for salvation.

'I'm a hard worker. I can cook, clean, hoe, weed, whatever you need. All I ask is bed and board and a few shillings a week to put by. Could you manage twenty? Eighteen perhaps?' She believed she was offering him a bargain as the timber girls got twenty-six.

Bushy eyebrows lifted in surprised unison. 'Is that all? I wouldn't mind that meself.'

'Please. I'd take less. Whatever you think fair, only you won't be sorry you engaged me. Perhaps your wife needs help in the house?' Rose glanced towards the kitchen window where she'd caught a glimpse of a figure hunched over, supposedly washing dishes while trying to see what was going on, as she had used to do.

'You'd have to ask her.'

'Would I?' Hope soared. 'I mean, may I? May I ask her?'

The farmer had already turned away on a half shrug. 'Do as you please. You could have bed and board in the loft over the stables in return for some hard graft but the wife is the one who'd have to pay you to work in the house. She hires and fires girls, not me. Ask Agnes.'

Agnes was, it seemed, perfectly agreeable to some extra help about the place, and offered ten shillings a week. Rose knew it was a pittance but felt desperate enough to take it, a great surge of relief that she wouldn't have to go back on the road washing away any reservations.

Chapter Ten

Summer was a distant memory. The autumn days were growing shorter, the leaves losing their colour and turning brown, rustling beneath their feet as they walked through woodlands. There was a crispness in the air as the warm moistness of a damp autumn evaporated in the chill approach of winter. There remained also a certain chill in the girls' relationship.

Lou and Gracie had been sent on census work. Even though they were sharing a room at their billet, conversation was confined to remarks such as 'Do you want the window open or closed?' or 'It's your turn to be first in the bath tonight'. Their bemused landlady watched her new tenants each morning at breakfast, silently eating their porridge with nothing exchanged between the two of them but the marmalade. Polite, business-like and utterly miserable.

Their task, along with many other teams across the country, was to take a count of all standing timber. This entailed travelling throughout Devon, Somerset, Wiltshire and Dorset, investigating every green patch on the Ordnance Survey map, then taking sample surveys so that reasonably accurate estimates could be made. Heavy inroads had been made into established woodlands and with no end to the war in sight, it was necessary for the authorities to know just how much standing timber there was still available.

Many tears had been shed as the squad had gone their different ways.

Jeannie and Lena made up a second team, working further north in Gloucestershire, Hereford and Worcester. Tess had moved on to driving duties elsewhere. At the last minute, Enid had decided to marry her airman and got a job cleaning nettles and ragwort from a farmer's field close to the airfield. It was dull, back-breaking work but at least she could count the planes going out and coming in again each evening, and see her husband at every available opportunity.

Lou envied her. She had seen Gordon only once since the Saturday before Posting-Out Day. He'd sent her a frantic telegram, saying that he'd got his sailing orders at last and she'd dropped everything to catch the train to Plymouth, agonising over its slowness. They'd had only a few precious hours together before she was standing on the quayside, weeping and waving him off, along with the other wives and sweethearts. The war didn't seem such a lark now.

She'd gone back to the farmhouse where they were billeted with her heart in her boots. Unfortunately, Gordon's leaving did nothing to ease the restraint between the two girls. Their friendship had been sorely tested by the kidnap attempt and its repercussions for the squad. Lou couldn't quite bring herself to forgive Gracie for having been so easily taken in by her parents, while Gracie remained adamant she'd been utterly helpless until her mother's need to visit the lavatory.

'Even then I had to run, with Father shouting and waving his fists like fury at me. He chased after me for a while, until he got out of breath. You can't imagine how awful that was.'

'Nowhere near as terrible as never seeing my Gordon again,' Lou replied, in clipped tones.

Gracie, riddled with guilt, was dismayed by the unfairness of her friend's attitude. 'Do you think I ever imagined, for one moment, that they might do such a crazy thing? It must have been all Father's idea, and Mother went along with it out of weakness. He'd set his heart on my joining him in the shop, and he does so hate to be bested. Goodness knows what they meant to do with me at home. Chain me up in the cellar and feed me on dry bread and water till I promised to obey their every whim, perhaps?' she said, chuckling at the very idea. Gracie had made a mental note never to be as weak as her mother. She would choose a man with greater care, she'd decided, and once having found him, they would be equal, in every way.

Lou refused to be either mollified or teased out of her glums. She was far too worried about Gordon who was even now steaming overseas, right into the line of enemy gunfire. She almost felt as if this were Grace's fault too. 'You *could* have left earlier. You could have stood up to them more. Did you never think of the effect your lateness would have on the rest of us? Just like that time when you fought Matron over the "biscuits" and the lorries, for goodness' sake, as if that had anything to do with her. You put her back up from the start. No wonder she pounced on you when she got the chance. Why can't you consider *other* people for a change!'

'Are you accusing me of being selfish?' Gracie looked at her friend, bemused and hurt. 'Hold on a minute. In one breath you're telling me to stand up for myself more, and in the next not to make a fuss so that I don't offend anyone.'

'So that you don't offend *Matron!* Didn't you realise how much power that woman has? Now she's used it on us. And Gordon has been sent overseas and I'll *never see him again.*' And because she was so very near to tears and hated to be seen in such distress, Lou had stalked off to sob in private.

Relations between them had continued cool ever since. It was going to be a long winter.

Yet they enjoyed the job and found it interesting, and both

girls loved the challenge and the freedom. They had their
bicycles sent from home so they could get about easily. Their
first task was always to check whether the green bit on the map
was indeed woodland and not useless scrub, or had perhaps
already been cut. After that they would map its boundaries,
dividing it into workable portions before they set about
discovering the average volume per tree and the average number
of trees per acre. In order to do this as accurately as possible,
they would select a plot which typified the whole wood. The
larger the acreage, the greater the number of samples that
needed to be taken, so they might spend several days complet-
ing just one piece of woodland.

And as they worked, few words were exchanged. Only what
was necessary and no more.

Gracie would measure the girth of a tree with a tape at a set
point from the ground. 'Thirteen and a quarter inches. Got
that?'

'Of course. I'm not deaf.'

'This is a larch.'

'No, it's a silver birch, can't you tell by the leaves?' The type
and quantity of standing timber was of vital importance, and
careful notes had to be made of the tree's possible age, whether
it were Scots pine, European larch, beech or oak, if it had been
damaged by squirrels, disease or blight, and whether the wood
had any outstanding features or peculiarities. After this would
come further dispute as they attempted to estimate the height of
each tree, and just to make sure they were doing the job
correctly they might be inspected from time to time by their
divisional officer or someone from the Forestry Commission.

Before they could embark on any particular survey, they first
needed to locate and contact the owner of the wood and gain
his, or her, permission to acquire the timber. They'd met some
delightful people this way, including actresses and Members of
Parliament, many of whom were only too happy to donate their

trees to the war effort, though perhaps requesting a few favourites to be left standing, a point on which the team were always ready to oblige. But it wasn't always so straightforward. Old ladies would sometimes stand on their doorsteps with tears in their eyes, declaring it was impossible for them even to consider relinquishing such a family treasure.

'You can't take my wood, my great-grandfather planted it in eighteen fifty. It's always been here, a part of the estate. I know each and every tree individually.'

Or even: 'Where would all the dear little squirrels go?' And they found themselves giving assurances that they were only stocktaking, that others coming after them would make the final decision.

They'd once been chased away by a farmer wielding a cut-throat razor, while another had taken a pot shot at them with his air gun. Fortunately his aim had been wild and they'd already dived into the duck pond. It was a memorable experience.

This morning was proving to be yet another. They were having no luck at all locating the owner of the next piece of woodland they wished to survey, and the frosty atmosphere that still prevailed between the two girls wasn't helping one bit. Everyone they'd asked had either been a stranger to the area or stone deaf, or so it seemed. In the end they'd spotted a man clearing out ditches and he'd told them Colonel Driscoll was the chap they were looking for. Unfortunately, this was his day for hunting or racing or some such, so they'd be lucky if they caught him.

'It's another world,' Lou muttered. 'Come on, we can't waste the entire day waiting for Colonel whoever he is to finish chasing foxes or betting on the gee-gees. Let's make a start and get his permission later.'

More naturally cautious, Gracie thought this risky, and suggested they mention their presence to someone up at the big house. 'Maybe there are other members of the family living there, or even a housekeeper.'

'Fuss, fuss, fuss.' They cycled up a drive that was at least two miles long in Lou's estimation although Gracie thought half a mile a more accurate assessment, only to find the place locked and barred at every door and window. No sign of the Colonel or a single member of his family. Not even a housemaid, let alone a housekeeper.

'Has the old boy taken the whole lot of them hunting with him? Well, that settles it,' Lou declared. 'If we don't get a move on, by the time the inspector arrives, we'll be way behind and then we'll get another rocket. And our reputation is already in ribbons as it is.'

'Thanks to me, you mean.'

'If the cap fits.'

They might well have gone on indefinitely in this vein, despite the fact they were both secretly longing for the feud to end but were too proud to admit it. Salvation, however, was at hand in the form of one small boy, highly inquisitive and full of the adventures he devoured daily in his *Hotspur*. When he spotted two shabbily dressed figures in dungarees lurking in the woods, each carrying maps and clipboards, he ran hot foot to the village bobby to report them as enemy spies.

Constable Wells was bored and in need of a bit of excitement, so he readily agreed to get out his trusty old bike and follow the boy to investigate. A breath of fresh air would do him good, he thought, and you never could tell, it might be his lucky day. It was just as well he did go, he told his good wife afterwards, for indeed there were two strangers in Belmont Copse. 'Though you could've knocked me down with a feather when I saw they were women. Who'd've believed it?'

Whatever the girls said made not a scrap of difference to him. The Constable was so delighted to have something happen in Little Grippington for the first time in heaven knows how long, that he was more than ready to lock them up, on the off chance they were indeed spies. He arrested them on the spot, not believing a word of their tale that they were counting trees for the government. Which government? that's what he wanted to know.

'*Ours*, for God's sake,' Lou cried in desperation. 'We're in the WTC and have papers to prove it.'

'WTC? Never heard of them. Is that your code word then?'

Lou groaned. In vain did she attempt to explain that the initials stood for Women's Timber Corps, a section of the Land Army. Constable Wells knew for a fact that that particular body worked on farms, all open and above board, and didn't prowl about other people's estates in a suspicious sort of way. 'Anyway, you can make papers say anything these days. And who issued them, that's the question? I must say they're getting mighty cunning these Bosch, using women as spies. Whatever next? You could be another Mata Hari, for all I know.'

'Really and truly, we *are* counting trees,' she persisted, as he led them resolutely back to the station, wheeling their bikes.

'We also check how old and what condition the trees are in,' Gracie put in.

'Or whether there are birds nesting in my brain too, I suppose,' Constable Wells sneered, determined not to be taken for a plodding country copper. 'If y'are who ye says y'are, then the Colonel will know all about it. We'll ask him, soon as he gets back.'

'Where is he? Will he be long?' Gracie asked, feeling thoroughly frustrated and anxious about the prospect of a night in the cells.

'He's gone to the race meeting in Newton Abbot. He'll be home tomorrow, sure as eggs is eggs. Not that we've seen many of those lately. Now you two young ladies makes yerself comfortable. My missus'll fetch you over a bit of soup later, if'n she can spare any. Don't worry, the Colonel will sort out all this mess.' Whereupon he closed and locked the cell door, making it clear that was his final word on the matter.

They spent a most unpleasant and uncomfortable night, attempting and failing to sleep on a hard cell bed which, as Gracie pointed out, made Matron's 'biscuits' seem as soft as goose down. The place stank of disinfectant and something they'd rather not put a name to.

'Hell's teeth, this is a right pickle, eh? I see you didn't try to tackle Constable Wells on the subject of mattresses,' Lou challenged, though she couldn't entirely prevent her mouth from twitching a little at the corners, as if itching to smile at the farce of it all.

'Don't think I'd've got anywhere,' Gracie ruefully admitted. 'Do you?'

'Probably not, but it might've been entertaining to watch. More fun than staring at these four walls with only a dish of watery soup for supper. This is all your fault, you know.'

'How is it my fault? What on earth have I done this time?'

Lou pouted but it was clear she couldn't quite put her finger on anything in particular, so simply settled for, 'Well, it generally is. We wouldn't be in this spot at all if you hadn't come in late and . . .'

'Don't start that again, for goodness' sake.' Gracie flung herself off the bunk and began to pace the floor. Five steps in one direction, six in the other. She quickly grew bored of counting and sat down again.

The pair sat facing each other on the two hard benches which served as beds and privately wondered how on earth they were going to get out of this one. Lou was bitterly yearning for Gordon and worrying over her lack of paper and a pen, which meant she couldn't write her daily letter to him.

Gracie was thinking that her career in the WTC seemed doomed to be one entirely of argument and incident, her best friend lost to her. In addition, her parents were more divided than ever before. Her father would be blaming her for encouraging her mother to leave home, while Brenda would no doubt be regretting this rash act every time she listened to the tale of how Aunty Phyllis fell from a trollybus and damaged her back. Could she be blamed for that too, since Gracie had been with her at the time? She would not have been in the least surprised. What on earth her parents would say when called upon to supply bail for their gaolbird daughter, she didn't dare to consider.

Colonel Driscoll considered the two miscreants with undisguised curiosity. 'Prowling about my woods, d'you say? Dashed if that doesn't beat all. Can't quite see them fitting the bill as spies, though, Constable. Bit far-fetched, what?' He put on his spectacles and peered at them more closely through the tiny window in the cell door. 'Open up. Let's take a dekko at them, eh?'

Constable Wells painstakingly unlocked and swung open the heavy door and both Lou and Gracie scrambled to their feet. All they were longing for by this time was breakfast and a hot bath. If being nice to the Colonel could bring either one of those about, it would be worth conjuring up a modicum of charm.

Gracie smiled her most winning smile while Lou quickly tidied her hair, wishing she'd thought to carry a lipstick in her dungarees pocket. 'Good morning, sir,' they said, almost in unison. 'What a relief to see you at last.'

'We've been looking for you for ages.'

'Have you indeed? Why was that?' Thumbs stuck in the pockets of his check waistcoat, he rocked back and forth on booted heels, examining them in detail from top to toe. 'Wanted some pretty flowers to grace your dining table, eh? Or somewhere suitable for a picnic with your young men? Not the done thing, don't you know, taking stuff from a chap's wood without permission. Could prosecute you for trespassing at the very least.'

'Do we look as if we're off on a flippin' picnic?' Lou briskly responded, affronted by his superior attitude, one which reminded her of the tales her mother told of the cotton barons during the Depression. She certainly wasn't having anyone lord it over her. She was a fervent Labour supporter, after all. 'As we tried to explain to the Constable here, we're in the Timber Corps and have permission to inspect and survey any piece of woodland on the Ordnance Survey map, absolutely everywhere. Out of courtesy, we did call upon you but you were out. Everyone was, apparently. So we went ahead without you.'

The Colonel blinked in surprise, as though he were unaccustomed to being so bluntly spoken to. 'I say, bit rich, what? Got some spunk, though, give you that. Quite a peach in fact, eh? Now I come to look at you.'

'Thank you.' Never having been compared to a fruit before, Lou warmed to the compliment, tempering her tone slightly for, now that she looked more closely, he did have quite delightful, twinkling blue eyes. She heard Gracie clearing her throat and knew, instinctively, that she too was beginning to enjoy this encounter. Had they been on proper speaking terms, Lou thought sadly, they might by now have been actually sharing jokes behind their hands.

Gracie said, 'We were only doing an initial recce, you might say, until we found you, sir. If there'd been someone in authority to ask, we would have done so.'

'Hmm, it was Mrs Bradshaw's afternoon off, and the gardener would be, well – dash it – in the garden. Or he'd better be,' the Colonel finished, rather crisply. 'I was – well, I was – otherwise occupied.' He had in fact spent a rather dull afternoon at the races, losing more than he'd intended, but he was perfectly philosophical about that. There would be other meetings, other horses who didn't fall down at the last damned hurdle.

Gracie then produced her identification card. They both showed their badges of crossed axes, even their worksheets and OS maps. In no time at all, the Colonel was satisfied. Even the Constable was reluctantly forced to accept that Little Grippington had held on to its claim of being the quietest village in the South West.

The Colonel took them home to what he described as his 'faded country pile', a fairly accurate description of a granite manor house which seemed as dark and gloomy on the inside as it did out. Every surface seemed to be covered with books, piles of old newspapers and betting slips. There were dog bowls everywhere, and as they entered each room, Colonel Driscoll would launch into a potted history of his ancestors while pretending to search for his spectacles in various cupboards, generally finding what he was looking for in the shape of a glass, always mysteriously half filled with amber liquid.

The absent Mrs Bradshaw, now back from visiting her mother who lived in the next village and had trouble with her rheumatics, happily cooked them a substantial breakfast. The girls demolished the home made sausages, black pudding and fried bread with relish, the best fare they'd tasted in a long time. They were also allowed the use of a freezing Victorian bathroom, where they took it in turns to bathe in a couple of inches of water, naturally disagreeing strongly over who should go in first, while the other stood shivering on the cork bath mat.

After a lunch of bubble and squeak, they walked the wooded estate with the Colonel, painstakingly negotiating which trees would need to be felled and which could be left to form a shelter belt around Belmont Wood, thus giving the impression it remained intact.

Lou took pains to point out that new whips and saplings would be planted in due course, in place of those which the Corps felled. 'They're being grown in special nurseries, though priority at the moment is on acquisition rather than replanting. That'll come later of course.'

'So I should hope, dash it.'

Lou was warming to the old codger and his evident pride in his land, even if the domestic order of his establishment left something to be desired. He invited them to stay on to dine and, since their landlady would by now have been made fully aware of their incarceration behind bars, they accepted with alacrity. Besides, no self-respecting Lumber Jill ever refused a good meal.

'That's the ticket.' He beamed. 'Enjoy a bit of feminine company, don't you know. Quite a treat.'

As they went to freshen up, Lou let out a little squeak and for the first time in weeks addressed Gracie without conscious thought. 'Hell's teeth, the old goat just pinched my bottom.'

Dinner was superb, taken in a cavernous dining room which boasted a fine plaster ceiling and an oak overmantel decorated with carved grapes and vine leaves, beneath which a huge log fire burned. One wall was entirely taken up by an ornate sideboard which held more food than the pair had seen in a long time.

They began with a fruit sorbet, followed by a delicious trout caught from the Colonel's own stretch of the River Exe, and a scrumptious apple pie, all washed down by one of his finest clarets, or so he informed them. After a platter of cheese and biscuits, which the girls left largely untouched, Mrs Bradshaw led them upstairs. She showed them into separate rooms, one in a faded crimson, the other a somewhat wishy-washy blue. Both

were decorated with silk-embossed wall coverings, showing
faded squares where pictures had once hung. And each sported
velvet curtains, gold tassels, ancient gas fittings, and boasted a
vast four poster bed.

'Beats last night's accommodation into a cocked hat,' Lou
murmured, half under her breath. She stood awkwardly at the
door to her room for a moment, feeling suddenly, oddly, bereft.
This would be the first night she would have spent on her own
since joining the Timber Corps and somehow the idea didn't
appeal. Gracie, she noticed, was lingering with equal reticence at
her own bedroom door, her pale grey eyes on Mrs Bradshaw's
departing figure.

They exchanged sidelong glances and Lou experienced a
sudden urge to run to her erstwhile friend and beg her to forget
all their differences; to forgive her for blaming her over the
perceived breach of discipline which had lost Lou so much time
with her darling Gordon, and for them to be as they once were.
Chums, mates, buddies.

Before she could quite find the words, Gracie had said,
'Goodnight then,' gone inside and shut fast the door.

It took so long before sleep claimed her, the bed feeling so huge
and empty, the room an amphitheatre of echoes and strange
creakings, that Lou almost decided to give up trying, to sneak
next door and fling herself on Gracie's mercy. But the mattress
was soft and squashy, she felt quite warm and comfy, so lay
happily dreaming of Gordon, praying with all her strength that
he would be kept safe and well, wherever he might be.

It must have been shortly after midnight that Lou again
became aware of her surroundings, realising that she must have
slept after all and wondering what had woken her. The chiming
of some distant clock perhaps. The room was dark. She
couldn't even make out any rim of light around the curtains

and there wasn't a sound, save for that of a distant barn owl and the rasp of someone breathing. *Breathing!*

Even as this thought penetrated her sleep-befuddled brain, Lou felt the mattress sink as someone climbed into bed bedside her. Gracie, she thought, no doubt feeling lonely too, had come to join her. Lou whispered, '*Gracie, is that you?*'

A large hand closed over her breast, and a rough, whiskery chin scraped across her face, seeking her lips. 'What a little peach!'

Lou screamed. Though afterwards she had no recollection of doing so, she must have hit him, because she was still fighting what seemed like a dozen arms, hands and skinny, hairy legs when Gracie stormed in. Weighing up the situation in a trice, she clobbered Colonel Driscoll over the head with one of his own brass warming pans which just happened to be handy. It barely stunned him, but he got the message.

'I say, just a lark, don't you know.'

The two girls spent the rest of the night cuddled up close in Gracie's four poster, weeping from a combination of sorrow and laughter but all differences between them quite forgotten.

As the days and weeks slipped by Lou and Gracie learned a great deal about the world they inhabited. They watched deer browsing, whole armies of ants going about their business, discovered where rare varieties of orchids could be found, watched kestrels soar and listened to the different sounds of the wind in the trees. Even Lou could now distinguish the song of a blackbird from a song thrush, and could name the different species of owls.

Gracie refused to discuss the air raid, thinking that if she didn't talk about it, she could put the horror of it behind her. But the after effects of it still lingered, so that she alternated between a highly strung nervousness and an almost philosophical fatalism. She did explain about the high expectations of her parents, the bigoted intolerance of her father and the new understanding she'd reached with her mother. 'I think that's why I love this job so much – because I can be my own person. At last.'

'I know what you mean. I was doing useful work in the mill, but I only went into it because it was expected of me. Everyone in our family for generations back has been a weaver, even before there were factories to put us in. Not that I ever knew a world beyond the factory gates. I like this one better. It's grand is this. Hey up, look, there's Mr Fox off on the razzle.'

By the end of November their task was completed and once more Lou requested a return to Cornwall, simply because it would be to Plymouth that Gordon would return and where she must wait for him. Typically their request was ignored. It was decided instead that although they had done their job well, their particular speciality in training had been in felling and no such jobs were currently available in the South West. Therefore, they were to be sent north, to Grizedale Forest in the Lake District.

'But that's more than three hundred miles away,' cried Lou in dismay.

'Don't worry. Knowing your Gordon, he'll get himself transferred to a ship that docks in Liverpool.'

'Do you reckon?'

'I do, and at least we'll be together,' Gracie consoled her, hugging her close. 'But I do wish the others were with us too.'

'Oh, so do I.'

Chapter Eleven

Agnes Sullivan was a thin, well-worn woman who rarely spoke a word, either to her husband or her lodger. It was almost as if Rose were invisible and she fervently wished at times that she was, certainly so far as the old farmer, whose name was Maurice, was concerned. If he wasn't talking to her, endlessly relating tales of his lumbago, his pigeons or how well his leeks were doing, he would watch Rose with avid interest. She would often pretend to be asleep as she sat by the fire after supper so as to avoid those staring eyes, yet somehow his riveted gaze seemed to imprint itself upon her closed lids.

They were certainly an odd couple and even though Rose had been at the farm for several weeks now, she still didn't feel as if she knew either of them very well. Agnes spent much of her time knitting, and had no doubt embroidered the religious texts which adorned every wall. These were the only form of decoration in the bare room which served as both kitchen and living room, there being not a sign of an ornament, picture or piece of bric-à-brac anywhere; not even curtains at the windows, save for the paper blackout blinds.

At seven o'clock Agnes would switch on the old crackling wireless and they would all sit and listen to the news in complete silence. They would listen to Lord Haw Haw's outlandish claims of imminent victory and Winston Churchill's rousing oratories with equal lack of expression. At least Rose learned something of what was happening in the outside world, which was the only way she could since no newspapers ever appeared in the house.

When the BBC announced that the Germans had been 'hit for six' she felt like jumping up and cheering though managed to restrain herself, largely due to Agnes's sour expression of disapproval. 'It will all be over soon, won't it?' she said, thrilled and yet oddly disappointed that this might very well be the case, long before she'd got around to joining the Timber Corps.

Neither Agnes nor Maurice responded and a few nights later the talk was all of American advances in North Africa so Rose could only conclude that Britain was as deeply immersed in the war as ever. She half sighed with guilty relief and continued to dream and make her plans. Occasionally Agnes would allow them to listen to the BBC Light Orchestra but nothing frivolous of any other sort was ever permitted. More often than not, once the news was over, she would reach forward and switch the wireless off.

'Can't we listen to ITMA?' Rose would ask. 'Tommy Handley is hilarious.'

'Hilarity is the work of the devil,' was Agnes's response to this innocent request.

At eight o'clock precisely, Maurice would pick up his bible and the old paraffin lamp, put on his cap and muffler and set off down the garden to 'the petty'. This was the name they gave to the toilet, a small wooden shack situated in a bramble patch at the end of the kitchen garden, which held a tippler lavatory with a wooden seat, shiny from use and with a pungent aroma. Rose had a vision of the old farmer enthroned there while he read his prescribed texts for the day. It almost made her laugh out loud every time he set off, his expression one of deep contemplation. He would be gone for a long time, perhaps an hour or more as he no doubt also went to check on the animals and shut up the hens. During this period Agnes would fold away her knitting and set about getting herself ready for bed.

She would remove her cardigan and blouse, unlace the pink cords of her corset and drape it over the back of her chair. Then she would stand at the kitchen sink in her skirt and plain shift, painstakingly wiping her hands and face with a wet flannel. Next she would roll off each stocking and wash her feet in the enamel basin. Lastly, she wove her hair into one long plait that hung down her back. The first time this ritual took place, she cast sideways glances across at Rose who interpreted these as an indication that she should do the same.

'I'll take my wash after you've finished,' she said, not feeling inclined to make this a communal event.

'You mustn't wait too long. Maurice will be back soon.'

Every evening Agnes would issue a similar remark, yet Rose resisted. At length, when her ablutions were completed, the old woman would riddle the coals, put up the fireguard and retire to her bedroom, shutting fast the door. She never said goodnight, but would hand Rose a stub of candle and admonish her not to use too much hot water. 'And don't forget to shut the kitchen door properly when you go back to the stable.'

'I won't,' she would reply. The moment she was alone, Rose would leap up to shoot the bolt on the back door so that Maurice couldn't accidentally walk in on her. Then she would rush through her wash at record speed and make sure that she'd left the house long before there was any chance of his returning. Crossing the yard each night she'd imagine him prowling about somewhere in the dark. It always filled her with dread and she'd dash up the wooden ladder to her truckle bed.

The loft, which was more like a storeroom for accumulated rubbish, offered little in the way of comfort. Even the huge black spiders that hung from strings of webs festooned below the beamed roof gave Rose the shivers. And the smell was nauseating a frowsty, musty scent of mouldy hay mingled with the ripeness of horse dung, overlaid by an indescribable aroma of dirt, decay and something more, something Rose was unwilling to put a name to. In the end, though, it became unavoidable.

Without doubt there were rats in the stable below. She would lie and listen to their squeals, together with the screams of the horses and the beat of their agitated hooves on the stable floor. One night she awoke with a start, quite certain that she was being watched, that eyes were peering at her through a crack in the trapdoor, though probably it was no more than the wind rattling the old boards, making it sound as if someone were about to creep in. Rose wedged a hoe through the handle, right across the door, just in case.

She kept her few belongings in an old tin trunk which, with the lid closed, also served as a bedside table. Upon this Rose put the night-light, set in a saucer of water for safety's sake. Each night she lay between her rough blankets in the truckle bed and attempted to sleep, unwilling to blow out the candle which alone seemed to hold the unknown terrors of the night at bay.

And as she lay there, in the dark, her thoughts would return to Cornwall on a wave of homesickness. She should never have trusted Eddie with Tizz . . .

She was just a dog, she would scold herself as she once again woke cold with sweat from her recurring nightmare. An animal, who therefore could easily come to grief. Was it not the law of nature? Yet it made not one jot of difference. Tizz had represented far more than simply a dog to Rose. She had been the only creature in the world, other than her two absent friends, who'd cared about her.

If she thought of Eddie at all, it was to remember his bullying. He'd killed darling Tizz because he was jealous, vindictive and cruel, savouring the moment when he could take his revenge. Now that she faced this terrible truth, Rose could recall other incidents in her childhood when he'd often been unkind to her.

He'd once urged her to skate on a frozen duck pond and she'd gone right through the ice. Fortunately the water hadn't been particularly deep. On another occasion he'd deliberately hidden her favourite story book, *Little Women*. When it had finally been found, soaking wet under a tree, her mother had blamed her for being careless with it. Rose had attempted to protest her innocence, to no avail, and been left feeling confused, knowing she was not the culprit. She understood now that she'd been too trusting, too certain of everyone's adoration of her ever to imagine her wonderful brother could have damaged it out of malice.

She'd believed Eddie to be her true brother, difficult, moody, idle and often drunk, yet Rose had thought that he didn't mind looking after her, that he had her best interests at heart — when all the time he'd been plotting in the most damaging and heartless way to tell her the truth about herself. He didn't love her. Never had. But at least now she understood why. Elizabeth and Sam were not her real parents at all, so even their love must have been tempered by charity. Eddie had said that her mother would have grown bored with her, if she'd lived long enough, and although Rose fought to resist this idea, the notion had taken root and grew like a canker in her mind now she was quite alone.

'Can't you do something about the rats?' Rose asked Maurice one day, driven to tears by the terrible fear of being bitten in her sleep. 'Put some poison down maybe?'

He made no reply, just stared at her long and hard, but a night or two later Rose heard an unholy din coming from the stables below. It sounded as if the rats were having a riotous party but whatever the farmer had put down must have done the trick. Thereafter her nights were more peaceful, though how long this situation would last Rose didn't care to speculate, any more than she could guess how long she would stay in this awful place. It worried her to think how she would cope up in the loft when the snow came. It might even fall through the holes in the roof on to her bed. But she must stay until she was paid for the work she'd already done.

One night as she made her way to bed, shivering with cold as winter deepened, Rose heard a rustle in the undergrowth and jumped in alarm. Quickly, she lifted the lamp and swung it from side to side. 'Who's there?'

And then she saw him, crouched by the door.

'Oh, Maurice, you startled me. What are you doing lurking there?' Heart pounding, Rose attempted to sound jauntily cheerful but her voice came out all squeaky and high-pitched, shaky with fear.

'I was waiting till it was safe to go in.'

'Go in? Oh!' Her face cleared and her heart slowed to a steadier rhythm. 'You mean, into the kitchen after our nightly wash? Oh, sorry, I didn't think. Yes, it's quite safe to go in now, thanks. Goodnight, Maurice.'

He didn't reply but stood and watched her walk to the stable door. As she lifted the latch he stepped forward and put out a hand to stay her. 'You're a nice lass. I wouldn't want nothing to happen to you.'

Rosie's heart seemed to cease altogether in its beating, and she instinctively backed away, as alarmed by the compliment and what that might imply as by the veiled warning. With no mother to gently explain the facts of life to her, Rose carried a twisted, cruder version in her head, gleaned from Gertie's snide remarks and innuendo, or from Eddie's more forthright language; made worse by the vile noises the pair made in their enthusiastic coupling. This left her with the impresson that sex was, in some mysterious way, both pleasurable and obscene, which filled her with a strangely aching curiosity. This old man, however, filled her with cold fear. 'What do you mean? Why should anything happen to me?'

'Do you like it here? P'raps you do. P'raps you don't. But a nice girl like you shouldn't be wandering about the countryside on her own. 'T'ain't safe.'

'Why do you say so? Why would I not be safe here?'

'I'm not saying you won't be. Only thought that p'raps you should go – while you can.' Then he vanished into the darkness but his strange remarks, and the urgency with which he'd said them, remained with her like a chilling warning.

Every morning when she woke, cold and aching in her uncomfortable bed, Rose would tell herself that she should leave, this very day. She'd wash her face in the bucket of cold water she kept in the loft, sometimes breaking ice in order to reach it, and think of the small amount of cash that she'd brought with her and kept secreted in the tin trunk. Perhaps Maurice was right and she should leave. She had some more money, safely deposited in her Post Office savings account. She could catch a train and go somewhere different; anywhere would be better than this. But Rose didn't even know where the nearest town was, so couldn't lay her hands on her money quickly, nor where the railway station was.

What a fool she'd been! She should have kept looking for a recruitment office, not taken this job in the middle of nowhere with absolute strangers.

Rose decided that she daren't risk spending any of her precious money, not even on a train fare. She'd already done a great deal of work on the farm for which she'd received meagre return for her labours. No hard cash as yet, only her keep, so each and every morning she would vow to stay till she'd been paid, and not a day longer.

With fresh resolve she set about all the myriad tasks set by the farmer's wife, while Agnes herself did less and less, shutting herself in her room to read or knit a seemingly endless scarf. Rose's first task each morning was to feed the fifteen calves. It was her favourite part of the day. She loved to sit with them, enjoying the warmth of their presence, finding comfort in their satisfied grunts of pleasure as they ate; even the soft sound of their breathing made her feel less alone. It was the only place she allowed herself to cry. Sometimes she felt as if they were crying with her.

After that she would scrub out the dairy; then there were the beds to make, the sweeping, dusting, washing, ironing; the scrubbing and scouring of stone floors. Rose would like to have protested that she'd been employed to work on the farm, not in the house, but dare not.

When she'd finished in the house, she'd make up a sandwich, wrap it in a cloth and set off for the fields, weary before she even began. She'd spend the rest of the day cutting nettles, picking stones, spreading manure on a frozen field, or feeding and tending the few sheep and cows Maurice kept. After that it was back to the house for supper, more often than not something like cold pork and mashed potatoes, though once a week Agnes would make a huge stew which was intended to last them for days. Unfortunately, she always made it in the very same enamel bowl in which she washed her feet, which rather took the edge off Rose's appetite.

However much she consoled herself that the strange warning from the old farmer had probably been no more than well-meant advice, because Rose was so very young and alone, it left her more wary of him than ever. But for all her reluctance not to spend any time alone with him in the house, she couldn't avoid him during the day.

Rose dealt with these somewhat irrational fears by keeping up a line of forced, cheerful chatter. 'Is this how you like the logs chopped, split into two?'

'That'll do nicely.' Sometimes he sounded almost genial, which made her even more fearful. Was he trying to ingratiate himself with her, gain her trust before he pounced?

'I learned to use an axe by watching my friends. They were in the Timber Corps. Part of the Women's Land Army, you know?'

'Women are doing all sorts these days,' he grunted, implying this was not, in his opinion, a good idea.

Rose refused to rise to the bait. 'Yes, isn't it wonderful? Do you know anything about them? About the Timber Corps, I mean. I've thought about joining myself. Do you think I should?'

By way of reply, Maurice gave her a hard, interrogative stare from under bushy brows, which made her shiver. Then, stroking the bristles on his chin, he continued, 'You'd have to ask Agnes 'bout that. She's the one who understands women's business.'

She brusquely told Rose to put any daft notions of that sort out of her head at once. 'You owe me at least another month's work for the food I've put into your belly already, not forgetting taking you in off the road and putting a roof over your head.'

Rose acknowledged this undeniable fact without commenting that the roof in question was only that of a stable, and it leaked. Or that the food was diabolical.

Quite unexpectedly Agnes's thin lips curled upwards into the ghost of a smile. 'I will admit that you've worked hard since you came. I'm reasonably satisfied. I get rid of troublemakers and time wasters pretty quickly but you've been a good girl.

Yes, a good girl. No trouble at all.' She reached out and patted Rose's cheek. 'You deserve some reward for your efforts.'

Rose was surprised and pleased by the kindly gesture. Did this mean Agnes was about to pay her at last? 'Thank you. I'm glad to have been of service.' She would like to have said that she'd enjoyed the work and the time she'd spent with the old couple at the farm, but that would have been stretching the truth a little too far.

'You're a pretty girl too, aren't you? Beautiful, I'd say, with that cloud of dark hair and those magnificent blue eyes. Not to mention those perfect cheek bones.' Again she stroked Rosie's cheek, this time with the tips of her fingers, very lightly caressing the silky skin.

Blushing slightly, Rose mumbled her thanks. No one had ever paid her such compliments before and she clung to these few kind words as if to a lifeline. It seemed some consolation that even if Maurice Sullivan gave her the shivers, at least his wife was friendly enough, despite her old-fashioned ways. It felt good to be appreciated.

Agnes Sullivan's improved mood lasted some weeks and made that first bitter winter away from Cornwall at least bearable for Rose. Agnes would sometimes make her something special for tea, perhaps liver and onions, considered quite a treat, or a corned beef pasty. She would smooth Vaseline into her work-roughened hands, or wash Rose's hair for her. These small attentions, pleasant though they were, did not disguise the fact that she had still not received any pay for her labours, nor was she ever included in the trips out for supplies that the husband and wife took each month.

Rose felt it would soon be time to reconsider her future and make some changes. A fear was growing in her that the war might be over before she'd joined up or found her friends and then she would have missed all the excitement. One morning she took a firm grasp of her courage and asked the all-important question. 'Is the nearest town very far? Would there be some sort of recruitment office there, do you think?'

'For what?' Agnes's eyes glazed over as she looked at Rose, as if she wasn't properly listening to a word she said.

'For the Timber Corps.'

Agnes named some market town which Rose had never heard of, concluding with a shrug, 'It's nine miles away. That's where we go each month, to buy in supplies.'

'Nine miles!' Rose was bitterly disappointed, all too keenly aware that she didn't have the energy to walk so far to an unknown town and all the way back, on the off-chance someone might be able to help solve her problem.

'It's just that I thought I'd like to find these friends of mine. Besides, although it was very kind of you to take me in, and I do appreciate your kindness, Agnes, I feel I should be moving on. It's not too late for me to join up, is it? I might only be young but surely I could be of some value. What d'you think?'

'I think you should peel those potatoes and stop prattling on. I don't pay you to stand there dreaming. Have you scrubbed those pantry shelves, like I asked you?'

'Sorry, I forgot. I'll do them the minute I've finished the vegetables.' Rose cleared her throat. This was the part she'd been dreading. 'Actually, I've been here half the winter already and you haven't paid me a penny. I was wondering about that.'

'End of the quarter, assuming you haven't run off in the meantime,' came the curt reply.

There seemed little else to say. Rose decided that she would just have to be patient. Hands raw from the washing soda, and with the chilblains on toes already sore and bleeding from the freezing temperatures in the stable, she swallowed her disappointment and went back to work. But then why should it hurt that neither Agnes nor Maurice showed the least interest in what she might wish to do with her life? She was nothing to them. Not even her own brother had cared about her, so why should they?

Even so, this didn't prevent a lump from coming into her throat, or her chest going all tight with the pain of it. Perhaps she was fated to spend the rest of her life without a single friend or companion to call her own. She put down her head to hide the spurt of tears that ran down her cheeks, and got on with the scrubbing. Such menial tasks seemed to be her destiny. She longed to find Lou and Gracie and was truly fearful that she never would.

Rose even began to worry that Agnes might never let her go, that she and Maurice would try to keep her here, working like a slave for them, exactly as Eddie had done. That wouldn't do at all. Eddie had used her, kept secrets he should have told her. As had her own parents. Rose didn't like that. She would decide what she did in future. Nobody else. She would do exactly as she pleased.

The very next time her employers went into town to collect their monthly supplies, she would ask to go with them. Except that she wouldn't be coming back. Rose meant to collect the money they owed her, then stay and make proper enquiries about joining up. She resolved to ask at the Post Office or the Town Hall, if she couldn't find any recruitment office. All she had to do was to be patient for a little while longer and see out the quarter to pay day.

Later that night, as usual, Rose was hastening through her ablutions, wondering if she might ever again experience the luxury of a hot bath and of being truly clean. She'd taken off her cardigan, blouse, skirt and woollen stockings, even her petticoat and brassière, and was standing in her French knickers, soaping herself down when she heard the creak of a door opening. Dear God, had she forgotten to bolt it? Had Maurice returned unexpectedly early? Snatching up the towel, she swung about, ready to give him the sharp edge of her tongue for intruding when she saw that it was in fact the inner hall door which had opened and Agnes who'd entered. Candlestick in hand, in her long white night-dress and with a single plait draped over one shoulder, she looked like a figure from a Victorian melodrama, or a child's nursery rhyme.

Rose almost giggled with relief. 'Oh, Agnes, you gave me the fright of my life. I thought it was Mr Sullivan.'

Agnes smiled as she approached. 'Aren't you cold standing about half-naked? You should hurry up or you'll risk a chill.'

'I – I've almost finished now.' A wave of embarrassment washed over her. Rose much preferred to attend to these matters in private. She reached for her discarded undergarments but found her way blocked by Agnes. 'Oh, excuse me.'

Agnes didn't move and Rose felt suddenly trapped, with her employer in front and the sink pressing against her back. There was something in the mesmeric quality of the woman's gaze which brought a sudden chill of unease.

Then in one fluid movement Agnes's hand snaked out and captured one damp nipple, squeezing it between finger and thumb. Rose gasped with shock. But in the seconds it took for her to draw breath to protest she became aware that Agnes's other hand had slid up her thigh, beneath her knickers, and was now pinned between her legs, fingers probing with pernicious purpose.

'Dear God. What the hell are you doing?' Rose pushed at her, desperately trying to jerk away, for all she was jammed in a corner and there was nowhere to go. She slapped at one hand and then the other in her panic to be free but succeeded only in tightening the woman's tenacious grip. The hands seemed to be glued to her, like great red greedy spiders kneading and clawing at her flesh.

'Let go of me. Stop it. *Stop it, I tell you!*' Rose was gasping and crying, pleading and begging and finally erupted into screams as the woman's hold was too strong to break. There was no hope of escape.

For the second time in her short life, Rose ran. She flew up to the loft to collect her precious bank book and few belongings, not even pausing to wash away the blood that trickled down the inside of her leg. Then she rushed down the wooden ladder out into the night, uncaring of the dark, the cold drizzle, or the pain in her groin to find the ever-vigilant figure of Maurice, silently watching her hasty departure. Rose now realised that he'd tried to warn her; that in his odd way he'd been guarding, not stalking her as she'd imagined. Unfortunately, he'd been quite unable to protect her from those intimate female moments before bed. How she'd misjudged him! She'd erroneously believed that in some strange, unspecified way he'd been warning her to beware of himself. How wrong she had been.

'You're off then?'

'Yes.'

'Best thing.' He jerked his head in the direction of the kitchen. 'I'll see to Agnes. I'll see everything's taken care of.'

Rose stared at him, her mind a blank, not taking in a word he was saying. She was shaking too much to think, let alone talk. She turned on her heels and ran for the better part of a mile, a mixture of terror and fury lending her the energy she needed. She developed a stitch in her side, cricked her ankle and was gasping on each painful breath before she slowed to a more sensible pace. The night was cold, the light drizzle having changed into driving, freezing rain yet not once did she look back or think of returning, not even for the sake of the much-needed wages which were due to her. She simply tightened her resolve, hardened her heart and walked on, growing calmer and more in control with each step.

The difference this time, Rose told herself, was that she knew exactly where she was going. She'd seen a signpost to Stroud. That was the name of the town Agnes had mentioned which was nine miles away; where surely someone would know how she could join her friends in the Timber Corps.

Never would she forget the sickening little grunting sounds Agnes had made. Rose felt violated. First she had to deal with Eddie's bullying, and now this. The very fact that the attack had been carried out by a woman somehow made it a million times worse. Agnes should never have attacked her in that way. It was just her bad luck that she'd chosen to do so in the kitchen, and that the carving knife had been so handy.

Chapter Twelve

The cathedral-like serenity of the dark forest was awesome. Not a breath of wind stirred, no birdsong or animal cry broke the stillness, only the sound of their own quiet breathing. Lou shifted one foot and a twig cracked, making both girls jump then smile at their own timidity. Beech, ash and sturdy oak towered above their heads, reducing them to the size of ants on the forest floor. They stood almost ankle-deep in a carpet of last autumn's leaves, the coppery glow glazed by the frost of late winter. A redwing, a winter immigrant in search of softer climes, flew out of the canopy right before their startled gaze.

'Oh, did you see the orange flash beneath its wing?'

'Hush, I see a red stag, over there in the peat wallow. How fine he is.' Gracie and Lou crouched together, not daring to move in case they should frighten some other shy creature in the dense undergrowth, in which they themselves were the intruders. The scent of damp moss and the sharper tang of larch, pine and birch was strong in their nostrils.

Thousands of years before, bears, wild boar and wolves had inhabited this forest. That's how Grizedale had first acquired its name, being Norse for 'Valley of the Pigs', and Satterthwaite, the village quite close to where Lou and Gracie were billeted, meant 'Summer Clearing'. It seemed somehow an appropriate name for it was a pretty village that you happened upon quite by chance, like a shaft of sunlight in the lush green valley of Rusland. It comprised a few Lakeland stone cottages with gardens turned over to growing vegetables rather than the profusion of flowers they had once boasted; plus the usual village ingredients of church, parish rooms, school and the Eagle's Head, the local inn, a popular venue in which to enjoy a glass of beer to wet your whistle after a hard day's work.

The girls were billeted at a small farm, half hidden beneath the beech trees along one of the myriad country lanes on the outskirts of Satterthwaite. Gracie had described it in one of her rare letters home to her mother as clean but spartan. Its floors were of bare stone with not a rug in sight, and freezing cold much of the time. It had no electricity, relying on oil lamps and candles, and could lay claim to only one sink with a single cold tap situated in the kitchen. Each morning she could manage little more than a quick splash from the jug and basin in their room, the water was so cold. In addition conditions were somewhat cramped, though as Lou was fond of pointing out, 'You won't hear me complaining. We've been known to sleep ten in a bed in our house in Rochdale.'

'I'm sure you exaggerate,' Gracie would giggle.

'Nay, I tell you nowt but gospel truth. Not far off anyroad up. There were me and me two sisters in one room, the two older ones at top of bed, me at t'bottom between them. Eeh, it were a relief when our Katy got wed.' Gracie noticed how Lou's Lancashire accent always broadened when she talked about home. She rather liked it. 'Then me three brothers and me Uncle Manny — that's Emmanuel, in case you didn't know — in t'other, and me mam and dad wi' our Dolly, she's the youngest, in t'third. I don't know how they managed to have so many kids wi' all them folk around, pokin' their noses in like. But it never bothered me mam. She allus said we were lucky to get a three-bedroomed house, or we might well have been ten in one bed.'

Lou and Gracie shared a bed, not quite wide enough for two, in the only spare bedroom and took it in turns to turn over. They also took it in turns to bathe in a tin tub before the fire every Friday night. After which they were expected to go to bed early, as the bath was then emptied and a couple of inches of fresh water added for the benefit of their landlady, Irma Cooper, followed by her son.

'Now tha doesn't want to watch me cutting me toe nails,' she would say with a grin. 'It's not a pretty sight.'

'Everyone's entitled to some privacy once in a while,' Lou very properly remarked, and then spoiled it by whispering behind her hand to Gracie, 'Her son Adam, on the other hand, might be worth a dekko at, what d'you reckon?'

'You're incorrigible.'

Adam's weather-beaten appearance, his hard hands, muscular body and long-legged stride from walking the hills, seemed entirely at odds with his bashful reticence. Sometimes Lou caught him casting shy glances in Grace's direction. 'Don't you fancy him then? According to Irma, he could do with a good wife. So how about it? He's rather dishy, don't you think?'

Gracie flushed bright pink but she did pay him closer attention next time she saw him chopping logs in the back yard, or washing his face at the stone sink in the back kitchen. He was a quiet man, saying little unless spoken to directly.

His mother, on the other hand, rarely stopped talking. Irma Cooper was a lively, unfussy soul with no pretensions and, as she herself declared, a light hand with pastry and people alike. Whether this was entirely true or not had still to be discovered but she certainly maintained an orderly household without any sign of rules. She never complained if they entered her clean kitchen without remembering to take off their boots. Nor did she mind putting up their sandwiches at cockcrow, or clearing up after them if they chose to do it themselves. Nothing troubled her. 'Easy going, that's me,' was her constant cry. Or, 'What does it matter? It'll all be the same in a hundred years.'

Irma was a sociable woman, tall and striking with dark hair and a bright, alert expression on a face that many would call handsome. Young enough still to be fond of a knees-up, she enjoyed a good joke and a bit of a laugh. For all she spent a good deal of her time elbow-deep in washing up water or cleaning out poultry houses, she took great pains with her appearance, frizzing up her hair and wearing the brightest lipstick she could find.

Beech Tree Farm had originally been a simple cottage built during the last century in a remote spot, ideal for a young woodsman and his wife. But Irma had found that living alone for much of each day while her husband worked out in the forest made for a lonely existence, so she'd occupied herself by keeping chickens and a few pigs. After he'd died, her predicament had grown worse and she'd bought a bit of land and launched into farming. No more than a few hens and geese, a couple of cows and the odd pig, but it made her a living, just. Her son Adam now worked the farm, having bought or rented still more land and expanded the livestock. But Irma's need for company had increased over the years.

Most days some tradesman or other would call. Bert the fruit and veg man on a Monday, the fresh fish seller on Thursdays, and the butcher's van on a Friday. In between there was the bread man, the knife grinder and the odd gypsy selling ribbons and lace. She could buy all she needed standing at her own front door but that wouldn't do for Irma. She would walk into the village most days, to visit the shop, take part in some meeting or other at the church or parish rooms as she was heavily involved in village affairs, or simply chat with friends, encouraging them to walk out the mile or so to her house every Wednesday afternoon for tea and a bun. And indeed they came in their droves, sitting around the circular table with its plush fringed cloth in the front parlour, pulling everyone to pieces (as Irma herself described it) while they knitted balaclavas or socks for the soldiers, or discussed the quickest and surest way to end the war. Really, if only Mr Churchill had had the good sense to call upon their expertise, it would have been over in no time.

If the two friends ever wished to know the name of a flower, the route up a particular mountain, what the weather would be like the next day or what was on at the pictures in Ambleside, one would say to the other, 'We'll ask Irma.' She was also a mine of information on births (some of them without a husband in sight), marriages and deaths, long before any details appeared in the local paper. Both girls were convinced that she carried in her head the family tree of each and every village resident, past and present.

Irma was a treasure, capable and reliable, who could turn her hand to anything.

'To judge from the meals you provide, Irma, you'd never think there was a war on,' Gracie would say. 'If I go on eating like this, I'll be as a fat as a pig in no time.'

'Nonsense. Look at you. Thin as a drink of water.'

She'd give them creamy porridge for breakfast, with black pudding or home-cured bacon on Sunday as a treat, and lots of home-made bread and jam. The fruit was from her own garden, naturally, as were the vegetables, but with rationing the way it was, it seemed a miracle that she managed to get the sugar. Yet there again they underestimated her. Irma was the secretary of the local WI and was therefore granted extra rations so that they could supply various hospitals and of course 'our boys' with their excellent produce.

'You'll be right as ninepence with me,' she'd inform the two girls as she placed a hot potato pie or steamed roly-poly on the table before them.

'Indeed we will, Irma,' they would agree. And although any Ministry of Agriculture inspector would be hard put to discover more than the regulation twenty-five chickens on her land, the farm never seemed to run short of eggs despite several customers popping to the back door late of an evening. Whenever Lou went home to visit her family, Irma always gave her half a dozen to take with her.

The girls felt sure that they'd landed in paradise.

But even paradise can be flawed. If Irma had a fault, it was her fondness for a choice bit of gossip. The girls had learned, when they were enjoying their nightly 'bit of crack' with her, not to say anything they didn't want the entire village to know.

This was, of course, the main reason she took in paying guests. With a son as quiet and hard-working as Adam, she relied upon her lodgers for entertainment. In this respect Lou and Gracie were something of a disappointment since they tended to nod off during her more convoluted tales due to the fact that they too were exhausted after working all day in the forest. She always forgave them as they were pleasant, well brought up girls, far from home and clearly in need of motherly care.

She was particularly avid for details of their love life. She certainly knew all about Gordon and always handed his letters over to Lou with a wink or a sly grin. On the mornings when there was no letter, which were admittedly few since Gordon was a faithful correspondent, she would shake her head with a sorrowful expression, assuring Lou that it was probably the censor who was holding up the deliveries.

'Have to go through every letter with a fine-tooth comb they do, just in case our boys have let something slip. My friend Madge has terrible trouble getting any through from her son. He's stationed in Singapore, or is it Ceylon? I forget. Anyway, she'll hear nothing for days, sometimes weeks, then she'll get half a dozen all at once. It's very worrying for her. And what about you, my dear?' she asked, turning to Gracie with a questioning smile. 'Have you no young man sailing the seven seas for his country, or dug down in some trench somewhere?'

Gracie shyly shook her head, the silky pale swathe of hair wafting softly against her slender neck. 'Who would want a skinny waif like me? I'm not exactly your pin-up type, am I?'

Irma laughed and told her that some chaps might think pin-ups could be more trouble than they were worth. 'Your day will come, mark my words. Mind you, I say that about our Adam and look at him, twenty-nine and still unwed. I despair at times, I do really.' She studied Gracie with a considering expression as a thought occurred to her. 'How about if I fixed you two up with a date?'

'Date?' Gracie wasn't sure whether to be horrified or amused by Irma's blatant attempt at matchmaking. She decided on the latter. 'I doubt I would suit.'

'Oh, I don't know about that. Quiet, li'le lass like you would happen do very nicely. The ladies' committee is organising a dance in the parish rooms. Our Adam don't usually care for dancing but I might be able to talk him into it, if he could take you.'

'Oh, no, you mustn't talk him into anything. That would be dreadful.' Gracie might well agree that her social life could do with a bit of livening up but not this way. To have a man forced to take her anywhere would be hugely embarrassing and humiliating.

'Well, suit yourself. Anyway, don't decide now,' Irma said, patting Gracie's hand in a kindly way. 'Sleep on it.'

'What's wrong with me?' Gracie asked, studying her reflection in the mirror that night as they got ready for bed. The pale oval of her face framed by straight blonde hair seemed to shimmer in the candlelight; grey eyes wide and questioning, like a child who had been hurt and didn't quite understand why. But was her face beautiful, or even passably pretty? Somehow Gracie didn't think so. It wasn't at all the sort of face to make a man's heart beat faster, even the undemanding Adam Cooper. Which was quite depressing in a way. 'Why is there no man out there pining to be my lover?' Though Gracie didn't begrudge Lou her many admirers, at times a part of her did wonder why she herself never attracted such attentions.

'I'm sure there must be,' Lou said, not noticing her friend's disquiet as she was fully occupied pulling on an extra pair of socks against the cold. 'You just haven't found him yet. They say there's someone for each of us, don't they?'

Gracie blew out the candle and climbed in beside her. For a few moments they lay curled up like spoons, shivering in the darkness, silently reflecting on the possible truth of this statement. 'But if there's only one person for each of us, it's rather a chancy business ever finding them, isn't it?' Gracie mused.

'Well, I found Gordon just by going on holiday to Cornwall. So you never can tell when Mr Right might turn up. He could well be at this dance, you never know. I'm thrilled about the possibility of a dance, aren't you? Time we had some fun.'

'Yes, but what if you hadn't chosen to go on holiday at just that moment, or to visit Brixham on the very same day that Gordon had got leave, then you would never have met him, would you?'

'Oh, no, I'm sure I would have. On some other day, in some other place. We were destined to meet.'

'But how did you know he was the one?'

'I just did. We both did.'

Gracie frowned into the darkness, for this was something which had long puzzled her, probably because she had no experience of observing marital happiness at first hand. 'Yes, but how? I mean, how could you be sure it was love and not just — *you know* — lust! A desire to go to bed with him.' She giggled, having thoroughly embarrassed herself now.

'Gracie Freeman, what a thing to say! You really are a

caution. If I'd said such a thing at home, my mam would've told me to wash me mouth out with carbolic soap.'

'Aren't all men like that?'

'No, they certainly aren't. My Gordon isn't. Now go to sleep and stop worrying.'

And Gracie dutifully stopped fighting her eyelids which were desperately trying to close and allowed herself to drift. Later, she was woken by Lou's quiet sobs into her pillow and put an arm gently about her friend's heaving shoulders to console and comfort her, feeling guilty at having upset her and knowing that there were worse things to worry about in this world during wartime than whether or not she ever found a lover.

The air raid she'd witnessed in Exeter, for instance. There were some nights when she couldn't sleep and memories of that awful day would come back to haunt her. She hadn't spoken of it in any detail to Lou or anyone. She couldn't bear to. Bringing it out into the open would surely make things worse. Gracie preferred to shut the memories away in some recess of her mind, in the hope that eventually they would vanish for good. Each night, as she lay down to sleep, she prayed she wouldn't wake up sweating with fear, recalling every moment in vivid, terrifying detail.

Tonight she deliberately directed her thoughts to pleasanter issues, such as her longing for a boy friend of her own. Then again, where would be the point in committing herself to someone when it could all end in terrible loss and suffering?

Yet somehow, deep in her heart, Gracie knew that she would find someone, one day. As Lou said, she might meet him anytime, next week at the dance, even tomorrow. On this happier thought, and with Lou's even breathing telling her that exhaustion had finally claimed her, Gracie slipped into sleep.

* * *

Irma's friend Madge owned a tiny shop which occupied the front room of her cottage on a quiet lane right in the heart of the forest. It soon became a favourite place for Lou and Gracie to call whenever they were in the vicinity. They would buy liquorice sticks, pear drops or sherbet dabs, just as if they were still young girls, which in a way they were, and enjoy a bit of crack with Madge. A bell clanged as they pushed open the door and went inside, and they would instantly be overcome by the wonderful aroma of Madge's own freshly baked bread.

The first time they'd called, they'd discovered her to be a jolly, round-faced woman in a huge, wrap-around floral apron. 'Anything you're wanting, just keep a look out for our van. My Jim goes round and round these lanes like a Mayfly. Stop us and buy one, that's us.' And she chuckled like a babbling brook as she snipped the correct number of coupons from their ration books; a noisy, happy woman with a brood of wide-eyed youngsters of varying heights and ages, all crowding about her, the smaller ones sneaking jelly babies from the jar on the shelf behind, or peeping out from behind her skirts.

She introduced the three eldest as Sarah, Rachel and Matthew. 'Sarah's the sensible one and Rachel, our little sweetheart, would charm the birds out of the trees. I've another daughter, our Molly, but she's working today, in the bobbin mill. Matthew's a fine young man, don't you reckon? He's waiting to be old enough to join his brother in the army.' Madge waggled her eyebrows in a gesture which clearly meant, "Over my dead body", since she already had one son in Singapore.

'Pleased to meet you.' Lou and Gracie grinned at the two girls, shook hands with the solemn Matthew and gratefully accepted a jelly baby from a fourth child, Daisy.

'You're staying with Irma then?'

'That's right. At Beech Tree Cottage.'

'So what d'you think?'

'About what?'

'About Irma, of course. Who else? Keeps that son of hers on a tight leash, eh? You'll have noticed, I expect. Give her eye teeth, she would, to see him wed. Desperate for grandchildren. That's why she takes in lodgers. I dare say one or other of you two is the next candidate.'

Lou agreed that she had mentioned something of the sort, while Gracie simply blushed.

'Though she'll have summat to say on his choice, make no mistake. But then she allus did like her own way, did Irma. Known her since I was a lass, so I should know, eh? Never underestimate her. Once she has her sights set on summat, there's no stopping her. Make sure you don't allow her to bully you. Think on!'

'There's no danger of that,' Gracie said, determined to stand up for herself, praying Madge wouldn't hear how she'd allowed Irma to talk her into this so-called 'date'.

Madge raised her eyebrows, taking this newcomer's measure. Clearly approving of what she saw, she smiled warmly. 'Aye, you've a sensible head on your shoulders, I can see that much. Well then, if you cycle over here for summat, one of my tribe'll serve you. And if we haven't got what you want, we'll either get it in for you the very next day or you'll have to do without it altogether.' Nodding happily over this dumbfounding logic, quite convinced she'd made a joke, Madge slipped a slab of home-baked ginger parkin and a wedge of cheese into a bag for them. 'There y'are. Bit of summat special for your tea. I know how you Land Girls do love your cheese.'

Lou and Gracie smiled in unison but managed to say nothing to this, not even to correct her mistake over their identity. Land Girls indeed! Once safely outside, they both doubled up with laughter.

When they'd calmed down a little, Gracie said, 'What do

you think she meant about Irma? About not underestimating her.'

'I've no idea, and I really don't care,' Lou gasped, wiping tears of mirth from her eyes. 'She gave us extra rations. I love her already. Madge could turn into a blessing.'

Chapter Thirteen

As so often in Lakeland, the weather was unpredictable: one day mild and blossoming, the bobbing daffodils golden in the sunlight, fresh green grass starred with delicate primroses and wood violets; the next so bitterly cold the buds shrivelled and froze on the trees. Soon the grip of winter would leave the land and a brief spring would pass slowly into the welcome warmth of summer. But no matter what the season, the work of the great forest would continue. Charcoal would be burned, rushes collected, baskets made, woods coppiced, as had been done since Norman times when the monks of Furness Abbey had owned the forest. Ownership might have passed through several hands since but, if now it was called upon to provide wood for a less peaceful role than the local bobbin making, at least the forest itself was unchanging, constant, an endless regeneration of cutting and regrowth.

Out in the wider world, change was very much in evidence. The victory of El Alamein had provided the boost to morale everyone had needed this winter, and if no one fully understood what exactly was happening in Stalingrad, at least there was hope in the air at last. All anyone could do now was to keep on believing in the ultimate victory.

The girls' task most days, when they were not actually

felling, was to measure and mark suitable trees. Any softwood over fourteen and a quarter inches in girth was a likely candidate. Sometimes, like today, when shafts of sunlight pierced the gloom, the work was a joy. More often than not it seemed to be raining, almost as if the trees themselves attracted such conditions. Then everything could go wrong.

The blaze of white marking paint, with which they'd so carefully daubed each tree, would be washed off before it had time to dry, or they'd lose all sense of direction in the forest, walk for miles, probably in circles, and end up marking all the trees twice. Or the measurements they'd scribbled in their notebook in a howling gale would be quite indecipherable the next day. Even if the weather were not at fault, their own incompetence or naïvety could lead them astray. They might run out of paint, trip over the pot and lose half of it in the undergrowth, or get themselves caught up in a tangle of brambles and briars. Nothing, they'd discovered, could ever be taken for granted about this job. Even so, they loved it.

They loved the fresh glow on their cheeks, their bright eyes and the feeling of alertness which came from working outdoors. They loved the freedom of the woods, the scents, the fact that each day, despite the routine, something new or unexpected could happen. They loved it all, even if they did often have to eat their sandwiches standing up, and spend most nights drying off their wet things ready for the next day, or stamping on the tiny wood spiders that dropped from their clothes when they undressed at night. Gracie never minded these as they had such pretty colours and patterns but Lou would squeal and jump about in agitation. Then would follow an hilarious half hour while they chased, located and evicted every spider from their room. Not an easy task in the gloom of candlelight.

'Why am I doing this dreadful job? At least in a weaving shed we never got spiders in our knickers. Have you checked between the sheets, Gracie? I don't want them in my nightie as well.'

'So far as I can see in this light, the sheets are perfectly clear of livestock.'

This would happen most nights until eventually Lou would climb into bed with some degree of reluctance, starting at every tickle, quite certain she wouldn't sleep a wink. Yet because of the fresh air and the vigorous exercise, more often than not they'd be asleep the minute their heads hit the pillow.

The girls weren't always alone. As in Cornwall, they often worked with foresters who were too old even in their late-thirties and forties to be called up for active service. Local girls were bussed in, often from Barrow, to help with the peeling and stacking of timber, and there were the refugees or displaced persons as they were more properly called. These were Poles, Jews, Czechoslovakians, Latvians and the like; cheerful, hard-working young men, eager to play their part in a war which had driven them from their homelands. The lorry brought them by ferry across the lake from a local camp where they were billeted, to work in the forest most days of the week. The Forestry Commission paid the government one shilling an hour for the benefit of their labour, and most of them were ready enough to do their bit.

One young man in particular, known simply as Luc since his surname was unpronounceable, spent much of his time trailing after Lou with dog-like devotion. It was perfectly clear that he adored her, worshipped the ground she walked on.

'We belong together, I think. Lou and Luc. Ees good, yes?'

'It would also be bigamy,' she would cheerfully remind him, wiggling her ringed finger in his face. Somehow this made no impression at all.

'Husband not here. Luc ees here. You need man now. Yes?'

'Oh, yes. I mean — no. At least — not like that.' It was Gordon she wanted, ached for, with a pain in her heart which at times consumed her.

'You no like Luc?'

'Yes, of course I do. You're a very nice man.' He was indeed supremely good-looking, dark and handsome with Rudolph Valentino eyes, and his devotion was really quite flattering. Unwilling to offend her admirer, Lou would hurry away giggling, refusing to take him too seriously for all he continued to pursue her. But she couldn't help feeling sorry for him and, as they ate their sandwiches at dinnertime, she would encourage him to talk of his home, which he did readily enough, often with tears in his eyes.

'In my country, the Russians they come and take our land. They leave us with very leetle. It ees hard. Very hard. Just when we think we might survive, they come and take more. What can we do? We accept or we go to Siberia. Many people go to Siberia in cattle trucks. Teachers, doctors, important people, not poor farmers like us. No come back. My family lucky. We left alone but I join army against the Communists. We fight on the Eastern Front. I get wound and escape with Polish friend through his country to England. I very glad. Ees good in England.'

Lou listened to this tale, not quite able to take in the true awfulness of it. 'What about your family? Your mother and father? Do you have any brothers and sisters?'

For a brief instant his face brightened into a smile filled with pride and joy. 'Two sisters. They very young, stay with my mother. My father, he broken man. Lost his land, his – what you call it?'

'His future?'

'Yes. The hope he had for his family. My elder brother Buca, he join ship. My mother write me. Say it go down. Since then – "He paused, shrugged his shoulders as the tears spilled over. 'I hear nothing.'

'Oh, Luc, that's awful. Dreadful. What can I say? Except, I understand. You're not alone in this pain. My husband is at sea, God knows where. Oh, I do hope he comes home safe.' Now they were both crying and Luc was patting her hand.

'See. We comfort each other, you and I. Ees good, yes?'

And through her tears Lou had to laugh. 'Some comfort I am. Look at us. Like a wet fortnight in Blackpool.'

Luc evidently thought differently since he took to riding a rusty old bicycle over to Beech Tree Cottage and, propping it against the garden wall, would wait for hours on the off-chance that she might come out.

'Hey up, lover-boy's here again,' Irma would chuckle, and Lou would groan.

'Oh, no. I've told him a million times that I'm not available, that I'm married.'

'Happen he thinks that what the eye doesn't see, the heart won't grieve over.'

'That's a horrible thought.'

'Not unusual in these times.'

'I shall go out this minute and tell him to sling his hook. He's getting to be a pain in the rear end.'

Despite her Lancashire bluntness, nothing Lou said made the slightest difference. Luc was infuriatingly persistent. The story of his ardour soon became common gossip and wherever she went in the village, people would nod and wink, exchanging a few mumbled words behind their hands. Lou was quite sure they were saying, 'That's the girl who's having an affair with one of the refugees.'

'Everyone's talking about me, and I haven't done anything wrong,' she would complain, stricken by the unfairness of it. 'How can I convince him to leave me alone? How can I convince *anyone* that I'm trying my best to do just that?'

'It'll blow over,' was Irma's advice.

'But I don't want it to blow over. I mean, I want them to see the truth. I want them to believe me, that I'm not, in any respect, encouraging him.'

'Just being female and looking as you do is encouragement enough,' laughed their incorrigible landlady. 'Would that I still had such a figure.'

Gracie was no help at all on the matter. All she ever did when the subject was raised was to burst into laughter, assuring Lou that she didn't, for one minute, believe Gordon would hear anything of Luc's infatuation. Whenever he did arrive for that much longed for reunion, he'd be far too pleased to see his wife again to listen to malicious gossip. But having been reminded of her beloved husband, this would only reduce Lou to tears of anxiety and concern for his safety, so that Gracie learned to hold her tongue and say nothing at all.

Arrangements were well in hand for the coming dance, and excitement was running high. Adam had been duly persuaded by his mother to accompany both girls. It seemed he had no wish to single one out, which was a great relief to Gracie, for all she suffered yet more teasing from Lou.

'What a pity. I felt sure this could be the start of a real pash.'

'If you don't stop plaguing me, you'll be going on your own. And you know I always do what I say,' Gracie warned. 'Remember the lorries and Matron.'

Lou groaned. 'Don't remind me.'

Preparations began the night before as the pair washed their hair in Lifebuoy soap, twisting it up in pipe cleaners to get a bit of a curl, and then lay about on the rag rug, trying to dry it in front of the fire.

'What a carry on. I'm either scorched or freezing,' Lou complained, 'depending which part of me is nearest or furthest from this blaze. And is it even worth it? The dance will be full of gossipy old women looking forward to a good feed, and farmers who have only come for the whist drive and dominoes.

Besides which, it'll be freezing cold, nobody will ask us to dance and the band will play out of tune.'

'Oh, no, you're entirely wrong,' Gracie demurred. 'It will, I'm sure, be quite perfect. It has to be. Irma is organising it. But even if it isn't, it really doesn't matter. For me, the anticipation and whole process of getting ready is almost more fun than the actual event.'

Lou snorted her derision. 'Speak for yourself. I want to have a good time, war or no war.' Turning around and sticking her head halfway up the chimney, she continued, 'Though I'm not sure how I can manage to do that without my Gordon, not with the irrepressible Luc chasing after me every second.'

Gracie smoothed a huge dollop of Pond's cream all over her hot face. 'You'll have to give him a dance at least. He'll expect it.'

Lou sat up and looked at her askance. '*A dance?*'

They regarded each other in silence for a moment and then as they became aware of how comical they both looked with their faces all hot and red, covered in cream and with pipe cleaner curlers sticking out all over their heads like porcupines, they collapsed with laughter at the idea of anybody wanting to dance with either of them. When they'd calmed down again, Gracie said, 'You'll have to. It wouldn't be polite not to.'

Lou considered her outstretched fingers as she applied a few precious drops of a scarlet nail polish that she'd managed to acquire. 'Maybe I will, maybe I won't.'

'Just one dance. There can be no harm in that, surely?'

Lou rolled her eyes. 'Let's hope not. We could devise a signal. If he gets a bit too fresh, I'll put my hand up to my hair and start to tidy my bangs. When you see me do that, you come right over to rescue me. Agreed?'

Gracie giggled. 'Only if you agree to protect me from Irma's unconscionable matchmaking.'

'What are you bothered about? Adam's rather dishy, and

you're free and single. He'll make someone a good husband, and that someone could be you.'

'Lou.' There was a warning note in her voice. 'I'm not ready to be anybody's good little wife. Not yet.'

Lou sighed. 'Oh, all right. If you insist.'

'I do. Otherwise I shall leave you to the tender, loving arms, and garlic-scented breath, of Luc.'

'God forbid. All right then, pact.' And the two friends shook hands and hugged on it, though Lou seemed far from convinced that Gracie was adopting the right attitude, tried once more to say as much, but caught that familiar fierce expression in her eyes and sadly abandoned the attempt.

On the day of the dance the two girls trotted downstairs and duly twirled a little pirouette on the rag rug to show off their finery, at Irma's insistence of course. Adam stood looking equally awkward in his best tweed jacket and tie but made an earnest attempt to be suitably appreciative, politely admiring each one of them in turn. His irrepressibly curly hair had been slicked down with Brylcreem and his shoes polished as bright as a pair of chestnuts.

'Well, what do you think, Adam old son?' Lou demanded, posing decoratively in a red crêpe dress that fitted where it touched, moulding itself tantalisingly to her voluptuous curves.

Adam cleared his throat, already constricted by the starched collar and tie. 'Very nice, Lou. You look very – bright and lively. I'm sure you'll have plenty of partners.'

'And what about Gracie? Doesn't she look sweet and pretty?' Irma urged, half dragging the poor girl forward for her son to admire.

Gracie kept her gaze fixed floorward as she felt his eyes studying her, acutely aware of her burning cheeks and wishing she'd found something more exciting to wear than a simple blue print dress with a white trim at collar and cuff. The blue ribbon Lou had insisted on tying about her straight blonde hair, Alice band-style, must make her look like some silly schoolgirl.

'Oh, yes, indeed,' agreed the ever gallant Adam. 'Very pretty.'

'There you are, dear,' Irma whispered, 'didn't I say he'd be smitten?'

Gracie fled and buried herself in the safety of her greatcoat, making a private vow to find some corner and hide herself well away so that Adam couldn't find her, let alone feel obliged to dance with her.

They set off together, a slightly subdued and silent trio, though for different reasons. Adam was as quiet and enigmatic as ever. Lou was thinking nostalgically of Gordon, last heard of in a letter she'd received nearly two weeks ago, when he'd claimed to be sailing homeward, though where his tour of duty had taken him, he naturally didn't say. Lou didn't greatly care. She just desperately hoped that he might get a bit of leave soon, though how he would ever be able to find her up here in the wilds of the North, she couldn't imagine.

Gracie felt acutely embarrassed at having been procured a 'date' and she began to see what Madge meant. Irma was becoming quite a problem in this respect. At least she wasn't standing on the doorstep waving them off, which would have been excruciating, having left before them, driven off in Arthur Rigg's old bread van bearing a huge enamel dish of tatie pie, a tray of plain scones, and threatening blue murder if Millie Conroy had forgotten to do the jellies.

The evening began with the traditional whist drive, followed by the hot supper which Irma and her band of stalwart helpers had prepared. Their efforts were greatly appreciated as there had been times during the seemingly endless years of war when good food had been less easy to come by here in Grizedale and the Rusland Valley. Its very remoteness meant that roads were often impassable if winter weather was bad, and locals still spoke of the resentment they'd felt in the early days when their supplies of poultry and eggs had been commandeered for the prisoner-of-war camp at Grizedale Hall, which hadn't seemed right. There still was ill feeling that the POWs were fed the same rations as an active British serviceman, far better than any civilian, so Irma's tatie pie was more than welcome.

After the supper had been cleared away there developed a general air of eager expectation and much giggling as the village girls waited excitedly for the band to arrive and the dancing to begin, each of them covertly eyeing up the enticing array of partners. As well as the refugees, foresters and members of the Territorial Army, there were some soldiers from a nearby Transport Maintenance Unit and a small group of airmen who'd come over specially from Millom.

'Not a bad turn out,' Lou whispered softly in Grace's ear. 'Maybe I should slip me ring off and test the wares.'

'Behave! One of these days, you'll land yourself in deep water with your teasing. Some bloke will take you seriously, then what would Gordon have to say?'

'Ooh, I wish he would walk in right this minute. I'd give him a welcome he'd never forget.' And Lou's eyes filled with ready tears.

The music was to be provided by Bert, a local farmer who played the accordion, or 'squeezebox' as he called it, and his mate Tom, who was slightly deaf and scraped a bow over his fiddle in a manner which might be considered musical. They tuned up precisely on the stroke of nine, starting off with a lively waltz, quickly followed by the Valeta, the Boston two-step and an eightsome reel. And if a few notes were misplaced, at least the music was energetic and well received. The floor had been sprinkled with soap flakes to make it slippy, and every window and door covered with blackout curtains or blinds to ensure that the evening was in no danger of being spoiled by a complaint from the local bobby. Nobody expected to get home much before the early hours.

Already breathless from the exertion of these first dances, Gracie found, to her great surprise, that far from being able to hide away, she was never short of partners and again jumped eagerly to her feet, with one of the airmen, when the band struck up the Buzz-off foxtrot. She was thoroughly enjoying herself, and then came the moment everybody had been waiting for: the Cushion waltz.

The band struck up 'Moonlight Serenade' and a cushion was placed in the centre of the floor, to much giggling and urgent whisperings from the local village girls. Upon this knelt an eager young man who was expected to kiss the girl of his choice before dancing with her. One by one the young airmen, foresters and smiling refugees took their turn. Lou was chosen by Luc of course and, rolling her eyes in comic reluctance, she sashayed across the floor and gave him a smacker. Everyone whooped with delight.

Eventually Irma pushed the bashful Adam on to the floor and one of the local girls shouted, 'Pick me, Adam lad.'

Another protested, 'No, pick me. Pick me. I'll give you a hearty kiss any time.'

To her complete horror Gracie found herself being thrust out on to the floor after him. By Irma, of course, and she heard a groan of disappointment ripple through the watching crowd. The village girls were always a bit jealous of the newcomers and this wasn't going to help relations one bit. Adam was a catch any girl would welcome. Anyone, that is, except Gracie. At least, not like this. She quite liked him but she needed to be chosen for herself, not because Irma had decreed it. The pair knelt awkwardly upon the cushion.

'Lord, I'm s-sorry about this,' Gracie stammered, flushed with embarrassment. 'I never meant . . .'

'Don't worry. That's my mum all over. Never takes no for an answer, not once she's got an idea fixed in her head. Let's just get on with it, shall we?' This hadn't been quite the response Gracie had hoped for, though it was not unexpected. Who would willingly wish to kiss her, plain and thin as she was, with not a sign of Lou's luscious curves?

They dutifully kissed, the barest brushing of lips. Gracie closed her eyes and waited for the bolt of lightning to strike, the one which Lou spoke of so frequently. Nothing of the sort happened. Although Adam's mouth was soft, and his kiss pleasant enough, she was aware only of an overpowering scent of Brylcreem and new wool, and the jeering, laughing crowd all around them. She couldn't help wondering if perhaps this first kiss might have felt different had they been somewhere more private. Filled with acute embarrassment, the pair stumbled to their feet, Adam took her stiffly in his arms and they began to dance. Gracie could feel the hot stickiness of his hand through her thin cotton dress. It was not encouraging. From the corner of her eye she could see Irma standing watching them, hands clasped at her waist, scarlet mouth beaming with delight. Gracie didn't dare even to glance at Adam as they shuffled awkwardly about the floor, and neither spoke a word. They stayed together for the expected two dances, then Adam gave a little bow and escorted her back to his mother. It was the most excruciatingly embarrassing episode that Gracie could ever remember.

Irma was waiting to welcome them back with open arms and seemed highly delighted with her machinations. 'Oh, what a picture you two make together. That was lovely. Aren't you glad you came now, Adam lad?'

'Oh, yes,' he said, without expression. 'Thrilled to pieces.'

Gracie fled to the cloakroom to cool her burning cheeks with cold water.

Lou found her there, moments later. 'What is the matter with you? Didn't you see me frantically patting my hair and redoing my bangs like mad?'

Gracie looked bemused, having quite forgotten the signal for rescue that Lou had concocted. 'Sorry, I was too concerned with my own situation.'

'What situation? You were happily having a ball with lovely Adam, while I had Luc's hot little hands roving all over me like searchlights in a gun battery. Heavens, you were right. I should take care who I tease. He's lethal. Like a bleedin' octopus with ten fingers on each tentacle.' Lou again patted her shining chestnut bangs, teasing stray curls into place while casting sideways glances in Grace's direction. 'So, go on. What situation? How did you get on with lover boy then?'

'I don't want to talk about it, if you don't mind.' And, much to Lou's frustration, Gracie lifted her chin in the air and sailed back into the hall.

Shortly after that the evening ended, with everyone taking their partners for the last waltz as the band struck up 'Begin the Beguine'. Fortunately, at least so far as Gracie was concerned, Adam was grabbed by one of the village girls so she danced happily enough with one of the older foresters which, if not exactly romantic, had the advantage of being safe, with no more expected of her than to keep in time with his rather precise counting of one – two – three; one – two – three.

Irma arranged for Adam to see the girls safely home while she helped with the clearing up.

'Don't worry about me. Arthur will fetch me home in his van. You young ones don't want us hanging around anyroad,' giving Adam a nudge with her elbow and a huge wink before sailing off, well pleased with herself.

Resigned to the inevitable, Gracie allowed Adam to help her on with her coat. It was as they went outside that the trouble started.

Luc suddenly appeared out of nowhere, clearly the worse for drink, and began sounding off about how it should be his privilege to walk Lou home. 'She is my girl. I loff her! Everyone knows I loff her!'

Lou giggled. 'Love, not loff. I love you.'

'Oh, my darlink Lou, I haf at last won your heart.' Taking her words at face value, and not as a correction of his diction, Luc swooped her up in his arms and began showering her laughing face with kisses.

'Give over, you daft 'aporth,' Lou cried, desperately trying to free herself but not taking him too seriously. 'Get off home and put yer head under the cold water tap. Let go of me, there's a good lad.' But either because of the drink or the heat of his passion he didn't let go, rather his embrace tightened, the kissing becoming ever more ardent and intense. Somehow he managed to slip open the top few buttons on the front of her dress and was fumbling inside, seeking her soft, full breasts.

'What the hell's going on here, Lou?'

Chapter Fourteen

Clutched tight in Luc's sweating embrace as he dipped his head into the vee of her dress, Lou jerked her head round and gazed in stunned dismay into Gordon's furious face.

What followed was so swift, so totally unexpected, that no one had the chance to react, let alone prevent it from happening. One minute Luc was muttering undying devotion into Lou's cleavage, the next he was flying through the air. His yell, as he hit the turf, was earth-shattering. It was only as Gordon, fists clenched, flew at him again that Lou came out of her daze. Gracie and Adam did likewise, and the three of them fell desperately upon Gordon to try to pull him off.

Luc was yelling as if blue murder were being done to him, and Gordon was swearing that there soon would be. The noise must have attracted attention because suddenly the place was teeming with airmen, foresters and transport men, all eager to fight they knew not who, over they knew not what. They were determined that if there was a battle going, they meant to be a part of it and the situation gathered a momentum of its own.

Adam and Gracie finally managed to drag Luc out of the fracas while Lou clung on to Gordon. She looked as if she might never let him go again, clasped tight in a smacker of a kiss.

Gracie stood with her hands to her face and looked down at Luc. Curled into a protective ball, he looked what he truly was: a young, desperately unhappy boy. 'Oh, my godfathers, he's dead.'

'No, he'll live, probably a wiser man. Fetch some water to clean him up,' Adam instructed her. 'I'll get him to his feet.'

Lou was crying now. 'He meant no harm. He was just a bit drunk. Oh, Gordon, I'm so glad to see you.'

Subdued, and looking a bit shamefaced, he held her close. 'How was I to know? Seeing someone apparently attacking my wife, I just knocked his bleedin' block off. What sort of a welcome is that for a chap when he comes home?'

The scuffle ended with no serious injuries. Luc was cleaned up and returned to his colleagues, none the worse for his ordeal apart from a black eye and a bruised ego. Lou went with Gordon to the Eagle's Head where they intended to book a room. 'The honeymoon suite,' she declared with a wink.

Gracie and Adam were left to walk slowly home together. Eventually she felt calm enough to talk, as if the incident had united them in some way and drawn them closer. 'I'm sorry you felt in any way obliged to dance with me this evening. It was all your mother's idea. You shouldn't let her bully you, though I wouldn't dream of blaming you for that. My parents are just the same. Always think they know what's good for me.'

'Do they?'

'Oh, yes. That's why I joined the Timber Corps really, for a bit of freedom.' And Gracie explained about her mother's plans for her to be a teacher while her father had intended her to follow him in the business, as well as their misguided attempt to abduct her from the Timber Corps. 'It was farcical in a way, like something out of a Ma and Pa Kettle film. Father with two

Jerry-cans of petrol so he wouldn't have to stop, and me running off the minute Mother was forced to spend a penny. You had to laugh, really you did.' And as she saw the sparkle of humour in his grey eyes, Gracie did at last see the funny side of it herself and they both began to chuckle. Not wanting to dampen their more relaxed mood, she made no mention of getting lost in Exeter or the horrors of the air raid. She was far too thrilled to find that his stiffness was thawing a little, that he might even be warming towards her, if only a little. It almost felt, for a moment, as if he quite liked her.

Adam said, 'Mam's been trying to find me a wife ever since I turned twenty-one. She's in despair because I spend all my time working and never seem to show any interest in girls.'

'You will, when the right one comes along,' Gracie consoled him. 'At least, that's what Lou says and I must believe her. She never seems to have any trouble at all in finding a fella, as you can see, despite the fact that she's already happily married. Some have it and some don't, I suppose.' Gracie giggled but Adam looked suddenly serious.

'Don't put yourself down. You're a really nice girl, Gracie. I'm sure one day some man will be thrilled to have you for a wife.' She managed to smile and thank him for his kindness before rushing upstairs to bed. It was the most charming put-down she'd ever received.

Luc made a point of calling at the cottage to apologise to Lou for his unseemly behaviour. 'I am sorry your husband choose that moment to arrive. This is bad luck for us, yes?'

'No, it wasn't,' Lou protested. 'It was just as well, considering the state you were in.' She then proceeded to lecture him, very kindly but firmly, so that he stood before her, red-faced and hunch-shouldered, hands in pockets, like a naughty schoolboy.

He looked so pathetic and so sorry for himself that she couldn't be too cross with him. Besides, she was far too excited by the fact that Gordon had succeeded in transferring to a ship that docked in Liverpool and would be there for at least a week. He'd even wangled a twenty-four hour pass to visit her. Determined to see as much of him as she could, she begged some time off as they'd arranged to spend the following weekend in Southport together. The prospect of a further two precious nights together before his next tour of duty filled Lou with joy. She was ecstatic.

When Friday came, she persuaded Irma to let her have the zinc bath tub all to herself for once, and drenched herself in Lily-of-the-Valley talcum powder with a liberal dab of the same scent behind each ear. Dressed in her best navy blue suit, the one with the zigzag buttoned jacket and a skirt that just skimmed her knees, which seemed entirely appropriate for meeting a sailor husband, she bribed Arthur Rigg to give her a lift to the station at Ulverston.

Once Lou had gone, Gracie settled down for a quiet evening in with Irma, one in which she would no doubt be destined to listen to another of her convoluted tales. Instead, as the clock struck seven, Irma reached for her coat. 'I did mention that I was going over to Madge's, didn't I?'

'I don't remember your saying anything about that, no. But I don't mind, Irma. I'll be quite happy here on my own.'

''Course you will.' She began to button up her coat quickly. 'Not that you'll be entirely on your own, will you?' Irma pinned on her hat, picked up her bag and gloves and made a dash for the door, as if she were suddenly in a tearing hurry. Just before she disappeared from view, she put her head back round the door and beamed cheerily at Gracie. 'You won't mind just popping that minced beef pie in the oven, will you, for our Adam's supper? There's plenty for you both, of course. He'll be in about half-past, as usual.'

Gracie looked surprised. She'd forgotten about Adam. Of course he would still be here. He rarely went out, except perhaps later to the Eagle's Head for his regular Friday pint. 'All right, Irma. I'll do that.'

'Thanks, love. What a treasure you are. Just right for my boy.' So saying, she vanished into the night and Gracie closed her eyes in despair.

Irma had done this deliberately. She'd left her here alone to see to Adam's supper and to sit with him all evening, just the two of them. What on earth would they talk about? No doubt Irma hoped he'd feel obliged to take Gracie with him to the pub. She groaned at the embarrassment of it. Could she perhaps just pop the pie in the oven on a low light and then go off somewhere herself? But where? She didn't know anyone well enough to barge in unannounced. Drat Irma. Why didn't she realise that she was actually doing more harm than good with this stupid subterfuge and matchmaking? Adam wouldn't take kindly to being manoeuvred into spending time with her, any more than she herself had taken to her own parents organising her future career. It would be another disaster, just like the dratted dance.

The back door slammed and Gracie flew into the kitchen, anxious at least to do the right thing by him. He would be hungry after a long day working outdoors. Adam was standing at the sink. He'd stripped off his pullover and thick check shirt and was sluicing himself down with cold water. She watched as the soap suds slid over the rippling muscles. Lithe, young and fit, Gracie could imagine the tension in them, the smooth wet skin beneath her hands, were she to offer to scrub his back. She did no such thing. Instead she mentally shook the image away and began to babble.

'Sorry. I – I just came in to make your supper. N – no, your mam made your supper 'Course she did. I mean, I'm supposed to put it in the oven.' Gracie snatched up the pie from the larder shelf and, as she reached to open the oven door in the tiny scullery and Adam moved to get out of her way, they did a sort of two-step from side to side before finally colliding. The pie slid out of her hand and would have dropped on to the stone-flagged floor had he not managed to catch it most adroitly.

'That was a close shave. Good job I was always a fielder.' He grinned at her and Gracie flushed. In that moment Adam realised, for the first time, that she was indeed pretty. Very pretty. 'So,' he said with a smile, 'there's just the two of us for supper tonight then?' And having safely set the dish on the oven shelf, Gracie shut the door on the blast of heat, her cheeks more flushed than ever.

'Afraid so. Hope you don't mind?'

'Not at all,' he said, his smile deepening as he too appreciated that this was yet another situation of his mother's devising. 'I can't say I mind in the least.'

To be fair to Irma, the minced beef pie was delicious, as were the stewed prunes and custard to follow, and the two of them got on much better than either might have expected. Not for a moment would Gracie have termed it romantic, but they chatted happily enough, becoming quite friendly as they ex-changed details of their respective and decidedly different childhoods; shared hopes, dreams and aspirations for the future, once the war was over. All told, it proved to be a surprisingly pleasant evening. So pleasant, in fact, that as they washed up the dishes together in the intimate closeness of that tiny scullery, Adam expressed surprise that he'd forgotten all about going to the pub for his usual pint.

'Oh, dear. I didn't mean to spoil your evening.'

He laughed. 'That's not what I meant. I thoroughly enjoyed our chat.' Then he asked if she'd like to go to the picture house in Ambleside with him one night. 'It's not too far in the van. We could do a matinée one Saturday, if you prefer, and have high tea somewhere afterwards. Tomorrow perhaps? What do you reckon?'

'Well,' said Gracie, suddenly at a loss for words. 'Well . . .'

'It makes a change to go out, don't you think?'

'Yes. Yes, it does indeed. That would be very nice. Thank you.'

The very next day, since Gracie had the afternoon off, they went to see Noël Coward's *In Which We Serve*, and she wept, thinking of poor Gordon and how on earth Lou would survive if his ship went down too, just as HMS *Torrin* had done during the evacuation of Crete.

'It's only a film,' Adam said, offering her a hanky to dry her tears.

'But it isn't, is it? Not really. This sort of terrible thing happens all the time. It's so easy to forget there's a war on when we're in the forest and the sun is shining, and we're happily felling or lopping the trees. But then something happens to remind me, like this film or an air raid I was in once in Exeter, and I remember. It comes back to me, all in a rush, why we're doing what we're doing. It's all so awful.' And the tears flowed faster than ever, so that Adam felt bound to put his arm about her shoulders and comfort her.

'There, there, it's all right. Don't take on so. We'll win, see if we don't.' And she gave him such a lopsided, watery smile that he put his mouth to hers and kissed her. It was only meant to make her feel better, of course. And it did. It was a soft, sweet kiss and although there were still no fireworks, as Lou had predicted, she managed to dry her tears, accept the ice cream he bought her and relax sufficiently to enjoy the rest of the picture.

After the film, as they sat and enjoyed spaghetti on toast in a nearby café, he asked her about the air raid and Gracie told him. She related the full horror of that night in Exeter for the first time, freely admitting how badly it had affected her, how she'd suffered nightmares for weeks afterwards, waking in a sweat as she saw again the dead baby, the children sprawled across the playground. Even now, she wept as the images replayed in her head but he didn't interrupt. He let her talk and when she was done, she felt cleansed, as if a weight had been lifted from her shoulders. She hadn't even realised how hard it had been pressing her down, like a great black shadow. He was so kind and sympathetic, so easy to talk to, that Gracie wondered why she'd ever felt shy with him.

'We must do this again some time,' he said, as they drove back to Beech Tree Cottage.

'Yes, I think I'd like that,' Gracie said, and right then, at that precise moment, she truly meant it.

The following Saturday, Adam again offered to take Gracie to the pictures. She accepted despite a lingering reluctance that refused to disappear. Why this should be, she didn't wish to investigate too closely.

This time it was Ronald Coleman and Greer Garson in *Random Harvest*; a wonderful love story of a music hall star marrying an injured ex-serviceman, and love among the cherry blossom in a wonderful English spring, so that Gracie didn't object when Adam put his arm about her shoulders. Could she fall in love with him? Did love feel like this – a nervous, heavy feeling, almost of foreboding, deep in her stomach?

On the drive back to Satterthwaite, Adam stopped the car by a gate and turned off the engine. Gracie sat absolutely still, saying nothing, wondering what he might do next. Would he kiss her? Did she want him to kiss her? She wished that she knew how to flirt with a man, as Lou seemed able to do with such confidence. Of course, Lou was older and had more experience. She was also safely married, so nobody took her teasing and flirting too seriously. Except for poor Luc, who'd soon learned the error of his ways.

'Would you like me to kiss you?'

In all of Grace's romantic dreams, and she'd experienced plenty of those in her young life, she'd never imagined being asked this question. She'd always believed that kisses should be stolen. Nor could she think of any proper response. If she said yes, that might sound too forward. If she said no, too discouraging. Her mind whirled. 'Um, well, I don't think I'd mind,' she said. There, that left the decision to him, didn't it?

He pulled her into his arms, placed his mouth firmly against hers and began to kiss her. Gracie held her breath, half wondering how she should respond, and half hoping the kiss would be over soon before her lungs quite exploded. She was almost grateful when it did end and he began to nuzzle her neck. She supposed this was all part of the rigmarole of courting as well. Gracie wasn't sure whether she liked it. His chin felt rather rough and scratchy and she had to concentrate very hard so as not to giggle. If only she'd asked Lou for some advice on what one ought to do. Should she stroke his hair perhaps, or put her arms about his neck? She could smell grass on him, the cigarette he'd just smoked, and animal feed. Not unpleasant exactly but not quite as she would expect Ronald Coleman, for instance, to smell.

Nor did she recall Ronald Coleman bothering to ask Greer Garson, come to think of it, before he'd kissed her. They'd just seemed to melt together. Gracie felt far from melting. She felt cold and awkward in the car. The gear lever was poking into her knee and something even colder was pressing against her breast. With a slight shock she realised it must be Adam's hand. Somehow he'd slid open the buttons of her blouse, eased up her brassière and was kneading her breast as if it were made of dough. She felt her cheeks start to redden. This wasn't at all what she'd expected. So methodical and detached, clinical almost. Not in the least bit romantic. And Gracie felt frighteningly vulnerable, as if she were pinned against the leather seat by that hand, the skin so hard and rough she was quite sure she'd be bruised by it. He must have felt her stiffen because he suddenly jerked away from her, as if he'd been stung, and abruptly sat back in his seat.

'I'm sorry. I didn't mean to cause offence. I thought – I thought you wanted – would expect me to do that. Most girls do, don't they?' Gracie had no idea what most girls did, so she said nothing. Some part of her stunned brain noticed that he didn't seem particularly excited. Not like Ronald Coleman at all.

Finally she gathered her wits and said, 'I'm afraid I don't know what I want. I'm not very experienced at – these sort of things, you see.'

'Yes, I see. Of course, I do see that.'

They both straightened their clothing and sat staring out of the misted windscreen. Abject misery settled heavily around Gracie's heart. What had she done wrong? Why couldn't she relax? She'd ruined everything now, by being stupidly shy and girlish.

'Perhaps we'd better get back,' Adam said, reaching to start up the engine. It refused to fire on the starter and he had to get out and crank it. It had started to rain and he was soaked through by the time they set off. Gracie sat hunched in her seat and wished herself invisible.

On this same Saturday, Lou and Gordon were enjoying a blissful weekend in Southport. The boarding house where they stayed could hardly be called classy but it was clean and the landlady not the interfering type, which was just as well since they spent most of the weekend in bed, where Gordon thrilled his wife with his kisses and his love making, as he always did.

'You'll have me up the spout if we go on like this,' she gasped, and insisted they take a brief spell of fresh air. They walked along Lord Street in the sunshine, dreaming of one day buying the carpets and furniture they could see through the taped up windows of the expensive shops, when they had a little house of their own. They kept well away from the wide expanse of sands where coils of barbed wire could clearly be seen so that they could pretend there wasn't a war on at all.

On Saturday night they went dancing in the Winter Gardens, which cost three shillings for the pair of them. They swayed in each other's arms to the strains of 'We'll Meet Again,' and Lou wept on Gordon's shoulder, overcome by the prospect of yet another parting. Then he blew another five bob on fish and chips in one of the National Restaurants. He talked very little about the war apart from having once been involved in 'some tricky stuff around Crete', and commenting on the huge tonnage of shipping consumed during the Africa campaign the previous year. Then, quite bleakly, he said, 'This spring saw the worst losses of the war so far. We need more bombers on escort duties. I'm lucky to be here,' after which confession he fell silent for a long time.

Lou asked no questions, partly because he wasn't allowed to say much, but also because hearing the details frightened her. She preferred simply to post her letters to the same land base and have the authorities forward them on to him, and not think too clearly about where exactly he might be when he received them or what he might actually be doing. She didn't want to know about bombers, torpedoes and battles in the Atlantic, or the threat of U-boats. She just hoped that Gordon blasted them all out of existence and came home safe and sound.

Chapter Fifteen

Grizedale Hall was set deep in the forest. Once the home of Harold Brocklebank, a Liverpool ship owner until his death in 1936, it was an ideal location in which to accommodate high-ranking U-boat and Luftwaffe officers. Surrounded as it was by barbed wire and guarded by sentries, there had been one or two escapees but even the most daring rarely got far. They faced walking over miles of rugged fells before reaching the north-west coast and generally ended up lost, wet and cold, happy to be recaptured. Since it housed generally high ranking German officers, locals had dubbed it 'Hush-Hush Hall' or 'U-boat Hotel'. They spoke of a darkly brooding, strangely sinister air about a place which still boasted fine oak panelling, billiard room, library, drawing room, and all the other accoutrements of country life that a wealthy gentleman had once enjoyed, as well as glorious stained-glass windows bearing mottoes, one of which read: 'The whole world without a native home is nothing but a prison of larger room'.

This Monday morning, as on many another, the girls rode their bicycles along the quiet, winding country road, singing 'Wish Me Luck As You Wave Me Goodbye'. Lou was smiling and singing, while tears dripped off the end of her chin. The cans containing the white paint they daubed on the trees rattled and clanged on their handlebars, not quite in time.

She broke off mid-song to ask Gracie if she'd told her all about her weekend in Southport. Gracie confirmed that she had, several times in fact. 'But don't let that stop you.'

It didn't. Within seconds, the tears had been wiped away and Lou was happily chattering twenty to the dozen, describing in detail the excitement of her 'blissful' weekend. She was still talking as they approached the post box where she meant to pop in her latest letter to Gordon, written only last night, just hours after they'd parted. Beside the post box stood a wooden sentry box, one of several in the locality. Another stood by the barrier close to the hall itself. The soldier inside was usually a veteran from World War I who knew every villager by name. Nevertheless, even posting a letter meant identifying oneself.

'Halt, who goes there? Friend or foe?'

'Friend,' Gracie automatically responded, struggling not to smile. She guessed that the old soldier quite enjoyed it whenever someone happened along, as carrying out sentry duty for hour upon hour in this remote spot must be exceedingly boring.

'Advance, friend, to be recognised.'

Lou instantly halted her tale as Gracie provided the necessary identification. She rarely said a word during this ritual, for no matter how many times she came close to the high perimeter fence around the compound she always felt a chill between her shoulder blades. The men were here because they'd been captured attacking our boys. Every night when she went to bed Lou silently prayed for Gordon's safety. It was wonderful that, for once, she knew her prayers had been answered, even if he was expecting to be leaving for some undisclosed destination within the next few days. As always she'd made up her mind not to think too closely about this, but simply to pray all the harder.

A detail of prisoners-of-war marched past, boots ringing on the rough stones of the lane as they headed down the road, no doubt on their accustomed exercise drill to the village and back. One of them called something out to the two girls but the guard in charge barked at him in German, probably to order him to behave or to keep his 'eyes front'.

'You're even getting propositioned by the enemy now,' chuckled Gracie, and Lou rolled her eyes in despair.

'Never!' The very idea filled her with horror.

The girls wheeled their bicycles on, well away from the high gates of the grey stone mansion where other prisoners would be playing football, strolling on the terrace, digging the garden or taking part in some form of drill.

It didn't seem right, somehow, that these men, the enemy, should be free to play games while Gordon could, at this very moment, be steaming back into danger. Lou averted her eyes from the marching POWs and started up her story again. 'Soon as he left me, he was off for a quick visit to his mam. "Don't worry, love," he says, "the war'll be over in no time, everyone says so. This is the last push, then they'll hang up their hats and surrender." Do you believe that, Gracie? Do you think the war will soon be over?'

Gracie wasn't listening properly. Her head was filled with thoughts of the surprising turn her own life had taken this weekend. The trip to the cinema with Adam had been an eye opener in so many ways. She felt as if her depression over the air raid had finally lifted, as if she had found a friend. But was it the kind of friendship that could grow into something more, something special?

'Are you listening to me?'

'Sorry. I was miles away, worrying.'

'Worrying about what?'

The last thing she wanted was to talk about her afternoon with Adam. 'Oh, I don't know. The war, I suppose. My parents. People back home. Everything really.'

'Oh, me too. Isn't war a sod?' They got back on their bicycles and continued gloomily on their way.

Parting with Gordon had been like having a limb torn away.

They'd stood locked in each other's arms, weeping, before he had got into his train to go in one direction, and Lou had crossed to the other platform to go in the other. It had seemed like the end of the world. Just recalling that moment brought a rush of fresh tears to her eyes and she dashed them quickly away, not wishing Gracie to see her weakness. She was turning maudlin and she really mustn't. Hadn't she promised him that she would be strong and brave?

No matter what, they'd both do their bit to the best of their ability. She could still hear his words, so full of courage and conviction: 'The sooner we beat the bloody Nazis, the sooner you and me can get started on married life proper.' Lou could hardly wait.

'I've no idea when I'll see him again. Oh, lord, I can't bear it.'

Gracie reached over and squeezed her hand where it gripped the handlebar of her bicycle, causing a dangerous wobble for them both. 'Yes, you can. You'll bear it because you must. Anyway, he'll be back before you know it. And you're right, the war *will* be over soon. I'm sure of it. Now we have to find Alf, so look sharp about it. We mustn't be late.'

Alf was a forester and, since he'd been put in charge, was known as their ganger. He claimed to be long in limb and short on patience. Lou declared him to be also lacking in a sense of humour but, with forty years' experience under his belt, he didn't take kindly to being kept waiting or having his word thwarted. He tolerated girls working beside him with resigned forbearance except that if he asked them to perform some job or other in a certain manner, that was the way it must be done.

'Morning, Alf,' Lou jauntily remarked as she sauntered up. He didn't answer at once as he was bending over, fiddling with his boot laces. She pinched his rear end, making him jump and swing about, brows beetling furiously.

'Hey up, you. It's time you were taught some manners, madam.'

'Eeh, me mam's been saying that for years. Go on, give your face a holiday. Laugh.'

Instead he glowered, as he always did, his moustachioed mouth clamped firmly shut over what remained of his yellowed teeth. He stiffly informed them that a small group of the junior officers from the camp were to help with the task of clearing undergrowth today. This was unusual, as few were ever required to take part in physical labour, partly because of the security aspect but also because they considered it beneath their dignity to involve themselves in manual labour and, in line with the Geneva convention, were never asked to do so. It was said that some even objected to the machine guns, mounted at strategic points on the surrounding hills, claiming they had given their word not to escape and, as men of honour, would keep it.

Gracie smiled and accepted this information with a nod of agreement. Lou, on the other hand, was outraged. 'How can we be expected to work with POWs? They're our enemies.'

'Happen they are,' Alf agreed, an edge to his voice. 'That's because theer's a war on and they got caught. So what? They were paid to carry out orders, as are you.'

'I know that, Alf, but . . .' Gracie kicked her ankle and Lou yelped.

'That's fine,' Gracie said with a smile. 'We'll show them what to do.'

'How can you be so obliging?' Lou hissed fiercely under her breath.

'It isn't their fault they've got caught up in this war, any more than it's ours. Or your Gordon's, for that matter.'

'How dare you compare these German POWs with my Gordon?'

'Oh, Lou, put a sock in it.' Seeing her friend's eyes fill once again with ready tears, Gracie softened her tone. 'Gordon will be fine. I promise you.'

'I know, I know. I just can't help comparing . . .'

'Well, don't.'

There were five of them, young men little older than themselves. Wearing regulation uniform, they looked to Lou remarkably well-fed, clean and fit. 'At least they're out of it, and can no doubt see out the rest of the war in perfect safety here. Having the time of their lives, I shouldn't wonder,' she grumbled.

Before Gracie had time to say anything to this, one of the guards, who must have overheard the comment, stepped closer to mutter, 'Aye, life of bleedin' Riley some of 'em lead, I can tell you. But don't be fooled by this lot's air of youthful innocence. Tek yer eye off 'em fer a second and they'll be off like rabbits over the fells.'

Gracie hid a smile and quickly explained, via an interpreter, what would be required of them. The group set to work readily enough, clipping and cutting back the briars and brambles. It seemed strange to be standing so close to people classed as the enemy. They didn't seem in the least combative, aggressive or even resentful, merely mild and compliant as if relieved to have a proper task to do at last. Watching them work, she felt a surge of curiosity, almost pity, for these young men. What had their jobs been before the war? Teachers, doctors, students perhaps, or even farmers. She didn't expect, for one minute, that they'd welcomed this war any more than she had. What had they suffered before arriving here in Grizedale? And did they miss their families, their wives and sweethearts?

She found it hard to imagine that any of them would want to risk being sent back into the maelstrom of combat. Even the watchful presence of the guards seemed unnecessary.

Two of them in particular, who worked closely together,

appeared almost pleasant. One was short and stocky, though quite dapper with his close-cropped brown hair. His companion was taller, with fair hair brushed straight back from a broad, square face and high forehead. She supposed he was quite good-looking in his way, with brooding eyes and full-lipped mouth, and then blushed – for she'd really meant – for a German, of course. He didn't seem too well as he kept pausing to bend over and cough for a moment before valiantly going on with the task. Gracie thought that he shouldn't have been detailed for an outdoor job if he wasn't well.

She could tell that all the young German officers were suffering from the unaccustomed manual work as they kept blowing on their hands.

Gracie had grown used to having an aching back and shoulders but she sympathised. The blisters that had once pitted the soft skin of her own hands had given her great pain and discomfort, but they'd grown tough and would no doubt remain so, forever scarred by the work she'd done. She'd toughened up, too, in many other ways since joining the WTC. She loved the freedom and fresh air, the comradeship and fun, but best of all she loved the fact that her father wasn't around to tell her what to do all the time; that her mother wasn't here to whine about a more suitable career for her brilliant daughter. Gracie had no wish to be brilliant. She just wanted to be young and alive, independent and free. She thought freedom must be the most important, most precious, possession in all the world. She gazed thoughtfully at the POWs, wondering how they could bear to be kept locked up, and if they considered it their duty to try and escape?

The work was monotonous and they were glad enough to stop for a mug of tea at ten o'clock. As they stood drinking it, a fine drizzle started.

'Great, that's all we need,' Lou muttered.

The prisoners hunched their shoulders against the rain,

warming their hands on the tin mugs of tea, it being a typically cool Lakeland day though it was early June. The tall, fair-haired young man began to cough even more. Gracie fumbled in her pocket, then hurried over and handed him a peppermint.

'Try that. Might help.' Even as she held out the sweet, the guard snatched it from her grasp.

'No fraternising,' he barked.

'Sorry, I just thought he needed something to help stop that cough.'

She glanced across at the young man where he stood, hunched and miserable, struggling not to lapse into another fit of coughing and, for a second, looked directly into his eyes. It was a moment like no other. His expression did not in any way alter and yet she read so much in that gaze. There was a smile there, and curiosity. But mostly it was a look of recognition, as if each was saying to the other, Ah, there you are. What took me so long to find you?

Gracie backed away on legs that felt suddenly weak and uncoordinated. The incident had unsettled her. She felt dazed and confused by that look which had passed between them. It was quite unlike anything she'd experienced before. Afterwards, it was hard to concentrate on her work. She found herself listening for the slightest sound of his cough. She kept glancing across, watching, waiting, willing him to look in her direction, but he seemed determined to concentrate on his work. At twelve-thirty they stopped for another break and the two girls settled down to eat their packed lunch beneath the shelter of a nearby beech tree: a delicious cheese and potato pasty prepared by Irma. The POWs sat a short distance away, flanked by their two guards. Alf came over to Lou and Gracie and started to tell them about some new Lumber Jills due to arrive soon.

'Oh, goody. Time we had a bit more female help round here,' Lou said, thrilled to hear this bit of news. 'More use than a chap any day of the week.'

Alf snorted. 'Not in my book. Women are nowt but trouble. I wouldn't let one anywhere near this work, if I'd my way.'

'It's fortunate that you don't then, isn't it?' Lou responded, giving a cheeky wink when he glowered at her all the more.

Gracie asked when the new girls were expected to arrive.

'How should I know? Nobody tells me nothing,' he irritably and quite inaccurately complained since everyone knew that Alf believed in 'keeping his ear to the ground'. The newcomers, whoever they were, were to be billeted at the village pub. 'So let's hope they're not teetotal. Otherwise they might find that rowdy rabble a bit hard to live with.'

It was as they were chiding Alf for his rude comments about the regulars at the Eagle's Head that they suddenly heard a shout go up. Gracie saw that some sort of scuffle had broken out among the prisoners. What exactly was taking place, she couldn't quite make out but then one of them jumped apart from the rest, holding something in his hand in a threatening manner.

Lou gasped, 'Crikey, he's got a stick.' Alf cursed softly under his breath while they all heard the ominous click of a rifle being cocked.

'*No!*' The agonised cry came from one of the other prisoners, the tall, fair one with the bad cough. The one brandishing the stick was his friend.

Without pausing for thought, Gracie rushed forward and put out a hand as if she might actually grasp the arm of the guard with the gun to restrain him, even as he stared along the line of fire. The air rippled with tension and menace; the presence of war suddenly seeming very real and frighteningly close. The fair haired one said something in rapid German, obviously in defence of his friend. Then two more guards appeared out of nowhere and the next instant the stick had been dropped and the troublemaker was being marched off back to camp, hands clasped behind his head. The guard beside Gracie slowly lowered his gun and shouted some order in German at the diminished party, followed by what could only be a string of swear words, before marching them back to camp too. Clearly, guarding the POWs had broadened the man's vocabulary considerably. Fortunately for Gracie, he offered no response to her attempted intervention beyond a furious glare of disapproval.

'By heck,' Alf said in her ear, 'that were a reet daft thing to do.'

'I suppose it was, but I couldn't just stand by and see him shot.'

'Aye, well, he'll have a few days in the cellars to cool his temper. Like a bloody dungeon it is down theer. I know, I went down once when Mr Brocklebank lived here.' Alf spoke with relish, as if the prospect pleased him. 'And I'd recommend thee adopts a bit more caution in future an' all, lass. Thoo can't tackle this war single handed, tha knows. Even a spunky lass like theeself.'

A couple of days later when they were again working on clearing undergrowth with the same group, save for the miscreant who was presumably still incarcerated in the cellars, Gracie found a note tucked inside her coat which she'd left lying on the grass. It read: 'Thank you for saving my friend. My name is Karl Meinhadt.'

Gracie stuffed the note quickly into her pocket. Emotions in turmoil, she couldn't believe what was happening to her. For the first time in her life she had attracted attention without actually seeking it. No over zealous mother, as had been the case with Adam, had instructed this young man to look at her in that searching, openly admiring way. Uncalled for, inappropriate, undeniably rash if not actually treasonous, a German POW had not only noticed her but clearly liked what he saw. She knew, without a shadow of doubt, that he found her attractive. But he was her enemy. Gracie had a vision of a pair of pale blue eyes that carried a hauntingly benign, oddly familiar, expression. The memory made her shiver, as if with anticipation.

It was several days later and Alf had instructed Gracie and Lou to wait at the end of the lane for the lorry to pick them up, as they'd be working in a more distant part of the forest today. It was late and they sat on the grass verge to wait.

Lou glanced curiously at her friend. 'You've been rather quiet of late.'

'Have I?'

'Seems so to me. Anything wrong?'

'Why should there be?'

'Hey love, this is me you're talking to, not some blind idiot. Come on, tell me. What's up?'

Perhaps it was the sympathy in her voice, or the warmth in her northern tones but suddenly Gracie found she wanted to talk, to share her problems and worries with someone. She began by explaining how she'd enjoyed her trip to the pictures with Adam, but then how he'd tried it on and she'd stopped him. 'I was sorry about that, because we'd come to be quite good friends. But I didn't feel happy about letting him. It wasn't quite right, d'you see? Can you understand that?'

Lou guffawed with laughter. 'With lovely Adam? No, I can't understand at all. I wouldn't throw him out of bed on a dark night.' But seeing Gracie's troubled expression, she sobered and squeezed her hand. 'So why didn't it feel right? What was troubling you? Did he do something he shouldn't?'

'No, I don't suppose so. At least I don't think so. I dare say it was all – well, perfectly normal. I wouldn't know, would I, not having your experience?'

'You make me sound like some cheap hussy.'

'Oh, sorry, Lou. I didn't mean to. Only – it's just that I can't help thinking about – about the other day. You know.'

'Other day? Why? What happened the other day? Here, you haven't got another secret admirer, have you?'

Gracie met Lou's questioning gaze and remembered, with a shock, her complete antipathy towards the German POWs. What should she say? How could she begin to describe the turmoil inside her own head? How every night when she closed her eyes, she could see his face swimming in the darkness. His clear blue eyes smiling into hers. Karl Meinhadt. Even his name sounded like music to her.

Yet he was the enemy.

Gracie was still struggling to find a way to put all of this into words when she heard the hoot of the lorry's horn. Lou jumped to her feet.

'It's here. Come on. We'll have to leave this heart to heart till later.' As Lou started to scramble aboard, she chanced to glance up and saw an unexpected, grinning face, dearly familiar.

'Are ye still struggling to climb aboard, Mason? It's lang past time you learned to be a bit more athletic.'

Lou let out a great squeal of joy. '*Jeannie!* I don't believe it. What are you doing in this neck of the woods?'

'Och, what d'you think we're doing here, girl? We're the new Lumber Jills. Didn't they tell you we were coming? Gi'e us your hand, or we'll be all day waiting for ye to get a leg up.' Jeannie and Lena each took one of Lou's arms and hoisted her aboard, much to the amusement of the refugee work party who were doing their best to understand what was going on.

'Oh, crikey, I don't believe it! Lena too. I'll go t' bottom of our back yard wi' clogs on. I never thought to see you two here.' They were bouncing about in the back of the lorry, hugs, tears and laughter all round.

Gracie stood in the road, staring up at them, bemused but grinning from ear to ear. 'Perfect. Just perfect. You are staying, I hope?'

'Away wi' ye, lassie. 'Course we're staying. Didn't I say you wouldna get rid of us that easy. We found out where ye both were, put in a request – a very forceful one I'll have ye know – to join you, and here we are. End of story.'

Lena turned up her coat collar, shivered and asked in her most plaintive tones, 'It felt like summer down South. What's the weather like here in the Lake District?'

'Awful!'

'And the mud?'

'Even worse than Cornwall.'

'Oh dear. I'm not sure I shall be able to cope.'

'Good old Lena. Don't ever change, will you? We love you just the way you are.' And they were all laughing and hugging each other all over again.

'All we need now,' Gracie said, as she was hauled aboard alongside them, 'are Tess and Rose. I think of Rose often. I wonder how she is, and if she's still in Cornwall. I miss her. Tess too, of course.'

'Och aye, Tess would soon sort this driver out, the way he rolls into every ditch and pothole on this damn' road. I swear he nearly pitched us in the drink before we ever got on that dashed ferry. As for Rose, open yer eyes, girl. What d'you see?'

Gracie glanced into Lou's grinning face, and then from behind the group of grinning refugees emerged a familiar figure. 'I don't believe it. Is it really you?'

'Last time I looked it was,' said Rose. 'Same old me.' But the moment she stepped forward into the light, Gracie saw at once that it was not the same old Rose at all.

Chapter Sixteen

The squad were delighted to be back together and worked all the harder as a result. Their first task was to plant larches and Scots Pine close to Esthwaite Water. They'd measure one spade length plus one foot then put in a sapling, three acorns placed in the gap between the trunks. These would take longer to get established but the faster-growing soft wood would shelter them through the early years.

For Lou and Gracie, planting was a welcome change from all the measuring and felling they'd been doing of late, and it felt so good to be with the other girls again. There was much joshing and joking, and they all sang happily as they worked, just as they used to do in Cornwall. 'Yankee Doodle Dandy' was this morning's favourite as they'd all been to see the picture starring Jimmy Cagney. They also sang more patriotic songs like 'There'll Always Be an England', or one of Vera Lynn's numbers. Lou swore that Jeannie could sing 'Bluebird' every bit as well.

'Dinna talk so soft,' she would say, flattered nonetheless.

The sound of a car on the road below made them all lift their heads, curious to see who it was. It was large and military, all the windows blacked out. The girls recognised it at once as one from the POW camp.

'Some poor bugger being taken to London for interrogation,' Lou said. 'Should've kept his nose clean though, shouldn't he?'

Gracie felt a stab akin to fear in her heart as she stopped work to watch the progress of the vehicle. Could it be Karl? Were they taking him to another camp for being so brazen as to look her in the face, or because she'd given him a sweet for his cough? His cough! Perhaps he was ill and being taken to hospital. She almost wanted to take issue with Lou over her lack of sympathy for the prisoners. Instead she said, 'Why would they want to interrogate anyone? What secrets could any of them possibly be privy to, locked up in that place?'

'Somebody planning an escape maybe. The state of the enemy submarines. Who knows?' Lou shrugged her shoulders, tucked up a lock of hair that had fallen loose and, with a weary sigh, hunkered down to plant a handful of acorns. 'I hope nobody's counting these blooming things, because I'm not.'

Alf wandered over to check why they'd stopped working. 'You lasses short o' summat to do?' he asked, in his usual pithy way.

'We work because we want to,' Rose rejoined. 'Not because you order us to.'

'Hoity-toity!'

Not for the first time since she'd arrived, Gracie cast an anxious glance over in Rose's direction. She was every bit as beautiful though she'd ruthlessly tamed her long black tresses by cutting them all off. Now, curled close about her head, her hair had a wild, tousled quality that, far from detracting from her beauty, made her look even more alluring. Yet she seemed somehow more fragile; the lines of her young face were harder and more finely drawn, the sea blue eyes smouldered with a brittle edge to their piercing brightness. Rose had said little since she'd arrived, but it was clear, to Gracie at least, that something had occurred which had damaged the innocent young girl she had been.

Drat this war, she thought. That was the real enemy. Not Karl, simply because he was a German and therefore on the opposite side, but the war itself.

Alf was certainly not oblivious of Rose's undoubted sensual appeal and didn't in the least seem to mind her cheeky response. He was actually chuckling, as if he found the remark amusing. 'Nay, thoo lasses'd not last long wi'out a man to call the tune. Just like them POWs, thoo needs watching.' Jerking his head in the direction of the departing car, he continued, 'That fool'll be sorry he ever crossed 'em. Like that other one, a year or two back. He rattled 'em good and proper. Stepped out o' t'military vehicle what'd fetched him, and not only told his guards wheer he were but how far it were to Windermere and Kendal, which lakes provided steamer trips and even how much it cost for a cream tea in Grasmere. He'd been in the holiday business afore the war. Worked for some big hotel or other.' Alf let out a great guffaw of laughter. 'Mind you, he should've kept his trap shut. They bundled him back in t'car and took him off someplace else. Silly bugger.'

All the girls had a good laugh at this, enjoying the tale. Gracie and Lou exchanged a speaking glance. It wasn't like Alf to be so chummy. Could it really be Rose's smouldering new look which had loosened his tongue, or did he have some other purpose? All was made plain with his next words.

'It's happen part of a search patrol. They say theer's one getten loose.'

'Loose?'

'Aye, an escapee. So afore thoo gets into thee bed toneet, mek sure thoo teks a good look under it. 'Oo knows what thoo might find lurking theer.'

'Do you think Alf was serious?' Lou wanted to know, as the pair of them prepared for bed later.

Gracie was standing at the open window, shaking her dungarees outside to make sure she'd brought no more spiders home. 'Who can tell? He was certainly in a more jovial mood than usual. Perhaps it was just his warped idea of a bit of fun, to scare the living daylights out of the new girls. He'd get a lot of satisfaction out of doing that.'

Kicking off her slippers, Lou scrambled into bed and pulled the sheets up to her chin, stretching out her aching muscles with a long moan of relief. 'Lord, I'm tired. We worked damned hard today. No doubt tomorrow Alf will be calling himself a hero, claiming to have caught the blighter single-handed.' She chuckled.

Gracie climbed in beside her then quietly asked, 'What do you think about Rose? Does she seem – I don't know – different to you?'

'In what way?'

'I'm not sure. She just seems harder somehow, and yet . . .'

'More fragile? Yes, I do see what you mean.' Lou was thoughtful for a moment. 'Almost as if she's been badly hurt. Do you think she has? She's not said much to me about where she's been, or what's happened to her since we last saw her. Has she told you anything?'

'Not a word.'

'You don't think she's found a fella, do you?'

'Not Rose. She's too young and innocent by far.'

'She'll be eighteen before too long, surely. You were young and innocent yourself once, and look at you now, being courted by our lovely Adam. Oh, what was it we were talking about the other day? Something about some other secret admirer . . .'

'Don't be silly. You must have misheard. I've no admirer, secret or otherwise. And Adam isn't courting me.' Gracie kept her face turned well away as she carefully filled her glass with water, so that Lou couldn't see the colour which came into her cheeks. She'd regretted that remark, ever since she'd made it,

and had no intention of attempting to describe the unforget-
table look which had passed between herself and Karl, or how
much she'd dreamed about him since. She always thought of
him by name now, never as simply a POW. 'You're the one
who pulls in all the talent. Though a chap might soon change
his mind if he was forced to sleep with you and listen to your
snores night after night, as I am.'

'Cheeky bugger! I don't snore.'

'Really? Can you hear yourself while you're asleep then?'

'Anyroad, chaps who share a bed with me don't get much
chance to sleep.'

'Chaps, is it now? Plural. Oh, I see, you make a habit of it,
do you? Wait till I see Gordon. There will be fisticuffs then.'

'Only joking, only joking.' And, giggling, the pair finally
settled down, said their good nights, and were instantly asleep.

Gracie wasn't sure what had woken her. She was certain that her
alarm clock hadn't gone off, and it was still pitch black outside.
But something must have disturbed her, as she still felt heavy
with sleep. Then the sound came again, a great clanging noise,
strangely familiar.

Lou's voice came to her out of the darkness. '*My God!* That
sounds like someone has just knocked the tin bath off the wall
in the back yard.'

'Who d'you think it is?'

'It couldn't be the missing prisoner, could it?'

'Oh, my godfathers.' Gracie was out of bed in an instant, her
feet searching for her slippers, boots, anything, while her hands
floundered about seeking matches to light the candle on the
bedside table.

'You're not going out to look?'

'I must.'

'Wake Adam. Let him go.'

'I'm not scared of an escaped POW. He's probably even more frightened than me.'

'Don't you believe it.' By this time Gracie had her greatcoat on over her nightie and was making her way along the landing, Lou right behind her. The pair crept downstairs, each clinging tightly to the other.

'Don't step on the creaky floorboards,' Gracie instructed in a low, hissing whisper.

'Whyever not? For heaven's sake, if it wakes Irma, don't we need all the help we can get? She'd soon set about any intruder with her rolling pin.'

'If there is an intruder, we mustn't alarm him or he might do something stupid and dangerous. We don't want any trouble. Besides, I want to get a good look at him first. See who it is.' Gracie needed to see if it was Karl. She hoped and prayed that he wasn't the one who had escaped. She wanted him to stay safe and well, even if it was in a POW camp, though it was entirely ridiculous for her to even care.

Heart pounding like a sledge-hammer, Gracie didn't pause to explain any of this. She lifted the sneck of the scullery door and stepped out into the yard. Lou blundered after her. Unfortunately, the candle she was holding blew out in the night breeze and she at once tripped over the tin bath which lay sprawled across their path. Then, as a ghostly apparition appeared before them, Lou let out an almighty scream of terror.

In response, out of the darkness came another sound, even more familiar than the clanging of the tin bath. '*Baaa!*'

'It's a bloody sheep!'

'Oh, Lou!'

And as the two girls fell about laughing, all the lights went on in the house, Adam came bursting out of the kitchen door waving his rabbit gun recklessly about shouting, 'Who goes there?' to be swiftly followed by Irma who switched all the lights off again, sounding very cross as she scolded them for breaking the blackout and making an unholy din.

Gracie was quite incoherent with laughter while Lou could only say, 'Don't shoot. The sheep isn't armed,' whereupon she hooted with glee once more and rolled backwards into the upturned tin bath.

Two days later, having discovered that Alf had indeed simply been playing a joke upon the new girls, and no prisoner had in fact escaped from 'Hush Hush Hall', Gracie and Lou were informed that a small detail of POWs would be made available on a few selected farms, including Adam's. Like many of the other local farmers, he was short of labour and had recently asked for help with hedge layering, as well as a crop of potatoes that needed earthing up.

'Why can't *you* work alongside our Adam, help him with these foreigners?' Irma demanded of Gracie, not entirely happy about having POWs on her land.

'I'm not sure I'd be allowed. Alf organises our work rota.'

'There's no harm in asking. It would be good for Adam to have you around more, love. Give you both a chance to get to know each other a bit better.' And Irma gave a conspiratorial wink.

Gracie made no comment to this but nevertheless agreed she could at least ask. Deep down, she knew her motivation was entirely different from the one Irma assumed; that she'd no intention of putting anyone off the idea of allowing POWs to work on the farm. She wasn't in the least against working with them. If only there were some way she could make sure they were the *right* POWs.

In the end it was all very simple. Adam was keen on the idea and Alf had no objection at all to her request, agreeing without hesitation and even asking her which prisoners she'd be happiest working with. 'Thoo's a nice li'le lass. Quiet and sensible. I don't want you upset by any roughnecks.'

Gracie named the POWs she'd be happy to work with. 'What about those two who helped us on the hedging before? The one with the cough, and his friend?'

'Wasn't the friend him what wielded that stick?' Alf frowned.

Gracie crossed her fingers against the lie. 'I'm not sure. Besides, I think it was someone else in the group who caused the trouble and that trigger-happy guard. The stick chap seemed harmless enough.'

'Aye, well, I might not have any say,' Alf said, which they both knew to be unlikely. 'I'll see what I can do.'

When she informed Adam that his request for POWs had been granted, and that she would be in charge of the party, he seemed delighted. 'That's great. Mam said you'd sort it all out for me.'

'Irma seems to think I'm the solution to all her problems. I'm afraid that's not the case.'

Adam chuckled. 'She's an optimist.'

Gracie thought 'interfering old woman' would have been a more appropriate, if less kind, description of her. But then felt instantly guilty for this uncharitable thought. Irma had done her best to make them welcome, and gave them good country fare to keep their strength up, war or no war. Adam interrupted her thoughts by inviting her out to another Saturday matinée. Gracie politely declined.

'You're still angry with me?'

'No, I'm not angry. I just don't feel ready for whatever it is you want from me.'

'I don't want anything from you. I like you, Gracie, that's all. I enjoy being with you. I thought we were getting on well. Mam's right about that. You're exactly my sort of girl.'

'Because she says so?'

'No, because I say so. Might you feel different in a week or two, if I give you a little time to get used to the idea?'

Gracie did worry slightly about working in such close proximity to Adam and felt a genuine reluctance to become too deeply involved with him, or indeed with anyone. She didn't wish to appear to be encouraging him. She'd made a big effort to cool things between them and he seemed to be both hurt and puzzled by her attitude. He tried apologising, saying he was sorry if he'd gone a bit too fast for her and couldn't they please start again?

'I really don't know. I'm not sure what I feel. I suppose I may change my mind, in time.' She saw his face light up with pleasure and hastily attempted to dampen his enthusiasm a little. 'But don't bank on it. We'll have to wait and see.' Gracie hated the feeling that she was letting him down in some way, letting Irma down. Irma certainly thought so.

'So what's wrong with my lad then? Why won't you go out with him? Is he not good enough for you?'

'Don't be silly, Irma.' It shook Gracie that every detail of this friendship seemed to be closely monitored by her landlady. Did he have to tell his mother everything? 'You can't just order someone to fall in love. It has to happen naturally, of its own accord.'

'Aye, but you've got to provide the right environment in which love can flourish. If you don't go out with him, how will you ever find out what you feel? Give him a chance at least, lass. He's a good lad. You and him are meant for each other. Any fool can see that.'

Gracie stifled a sigh. 'I've promised to think about it. That's all I can say.'

She found it hard to concentrate on Adam's needs, she was far too confused by her own.

Later that day she manufactured an opportunity to call in on Madge, but it was young Matthew quietly serving behind the counter so she bought two ounces of dolly mixtures and left. But then, who could help her to deal with Irma? Nobody.

When the detail arrived, Gracie's heart skipped a beat. Her request had been granted, including the prisoner who'd been incarcerated in the cellar which was surprising in a way. His name, apparently, was Erich Müller. He had an arrogant, almost superior air about him, but then he was a Lieutenant, a higher rank than Karl who was an NCO. Gracie didn't even dare to glance in his direction. Her lungs seemed to be squeezed so tight, she could barely breathe.

There was a guard with them, as expected, but not the difficult one. This one seemed more lax and easy going, perhaps because he had only two prisoners in his care. He propped himself on the stile beside the farm gate, pulled out a newspaper and settled for a spell of quiet reading, glancing up only occasionally to check that all was proper and above board.

While Adam demonstrated the task of how to cut part way through the long woody stems and weave them in to form a layered hedge, Karl's gaze kept sliding over in Gracie's direction. She tried to pretend that she hadn't noticed but, despite all her efforts to ignore him, she was acutely aware of his every movement. She longed just to gaze and gaze at him. She felt the need to absorb every detail of his face, to examine the way his blond hair sprang back from that broad, strong forehead. A film of fair whiskers grew across his upper lip. The mouth itself, full and sensual, curled upwards slightly at the corners. A strong, square chin. Wide flared nostrils. And, most bewitching of all, those pale blue eyes which, when they weren't seeming to look into the depths of her soul, were fixed on some far-distant place, as if constantly searching for something. Freedom perhaps.

Gracie found herself edging closer, so that she was standing no more than a few feet away from him, as close as she dare without alerting the guard.

Dear God, what was happening to her? This man was one of the enemy. If he'd been at sea, lurking in the cold depths in his U-boat, he may well have fired at British ships, killed British sailors. Hadn't she read in the newspaper only the other day how the U-boats were maintaining their crippling attacks on Allied ships? He could easily have torpedoed Gordon's ship, for Christ's sake. What was she even thinking of, gazing at the enemy in this moonstruck way? Gracie knew she should be ashamed of herself, yet all she felt was breathless excitement, the rapid beat of her heart as the blood seemed to pump around her body at a record rate.

Somehow she knew, by the appeal in his unflinching gaze, that he was as overwhelmed by circumstance as she was. In another time, another place, he would have walked over and spoken to her, perhaps asked her out. She would have smiled, willingly accepted, and they would have become instant friends. She knew all of this with a certainty that shocked her. Just as she knew that they would, without doubt, have become lovers. Did this mean that her father was correct? That she was impure?

The morning wore on and, as they worked, the two POWs were kept well apart from herself and Adam. Only once, as the guard ordered them to march to a quiet corner of the field to eat their lunch, did Karl come anywhere near her. Even then he made no attempt to speak, as this would have been against the rules, but as he passed by, he brushed against her hand. It was the merest touch, the slightest butterfly kiss of flesh against flesh, but for the briefest of seconds her fingers curled naturally into his. When he moved on, Gracie had to steel herself not to cry out and call him back to her. Even her fingers felt bereft.

Despite the terrible odds against them, it was clear to her and, she believed, to Karl, that they were destined to be together. The only question was, would the war and his enemy status be too great an obstacle for them to surmount?

The next time Karl and Erich Müller came, Gracie was ready. She'd persuaded Irma to make extra cheese and onion pasties and, wrapping three of these in napkins, she took them over to the guard. He was so pleased at the prospect of good food instead of dry sandwiches that he raised no objection when she asked if she might give the other two to the prisoners. Waving a hand at her, as if telling her to get on with it, he sank his teeth into the rich hot pastry, soon so engrossed in savouring the tasty cheese, he paid little attention as she hurried over to the two young Germans.

'Guten Tag, wie gehts?'

'Danke, gut.'

Having exhausted the extent of her schoolgirl German, and feeling suddenly overcome with shyness, Gracie dissolved into an embarrassed silence. It came to her that she only had to reach out one hand to touch Karl, which made her cheeks redden at the thought, almost as if she had actually done so. Inwardly scolding herself for her inadequacy, she gave an apologetic smile and quickly reverted to English. 'Sorry, b-but I thought you might enjoy these. My landlady made them and she is an excellent cook.'

Gracie held out the two pasties wrapped warmly in their napkins, with hands which weren't quite steady. It was Karl who took them from her, his eyes, fringed by thick blonde lashes, never leaving hers. 'Thank you. That is most kind of you.'

'You speak English.' She was stunned, and also thrilled. 'How did you learn so quickly?'

'I learn before the war. I visit England many times, with my mother.' His 'w' came out all wrong, more like a v, but Gracie found his accent charming, and without stopping to think, said so. It was his turn now to fall awkwardly silent, and she could have kicked herself for making such a fatuous remark since she wanted him to go on talking; she wanted to soak up the sound of his voice so that she could replay it later in her head. But then she needed to know everything about him. Why had he come to England before the war? What was his mother like? Was she concerned and and worried that her son was now a prisoner, or was she content that he was safely out of danger? And how did he feel about it all?

'What is she called?'

'Pardon?' He frowned slightly, a crumb of pasty caught at the corner of his mouth as he smiled. He licked it away and Gracie felt her heart contract.

'Your mother.'

'Ah, she is Margaretha. You like?'

'Oh, yes, that's a beautiful name.'

'And your friend?' She jerked a chin in Erich's direction. 'The incident with the stick when he nearly got shot. What was his problem?'

'There are people in the camp who don't like him. Now he has cooled off his hot head.' Karl shrugged and grinned at her, and her insides seemed to melt.

Gracie became aware that she was the one staring now, her gaze having been riveted to his for several long moments. So long, in fact, that his companion was starting to chuckle. He said something in German to Karl which Gracie didn't understand. Nonetheless she blushed because she could guess the inference. She was making a complete fool of herself, leaving her emotions completely exposed as she stood transfixed before them both like some lovesick schoolgirl. Spinning on her heel she began to walk quickly away, and then to run. She heard his voice call after her.

'Please. Don't go!'

And then a sharp reprimand in German from the guard who, having wiped the last crumb of cheese pasty on to his sleeve, had thought to return to his neglected duties.

Gracie didn't stop running until she'd gained the sanctuary of her room, where she slammed shut the door and leaned against it. It was some time before her heart slowed down enough for her to breathe normally again.

Chapter Seventeen

Rose made no mention to anyone of her stay on the Sullivans' farm, or what had occurred there. That was something best forgotten, in her opinion. She felt as if she'd fought her own private war, never mind the one raging world wide. First against Eddie's bullying, and then having to deal with Agnes's vicious attack. Even now, months later, she would start to shake whenever she thought of that woman's hands clawing at her.

It had crossed her mind to wonder what Maurice's reaction would have been when he went back into the kitchen that night and found his wife. Rose had worried about this for a little while but then she remembered his words. '*I'll see to Agnes. I'll see everything's taken care of.*' Had he known? Did he see something through the window? Perhaps he was glad to be rid of her. They'd never seemed a happy couple. And who would be curious about one old woman? People went missing all the time in a war. He could easily dispose of the body on his farm, and must have done so. Otherwise, someone would have come to arrest her by now. And even if they did come, how could they blame her? If Agnes hadn't attacked her it wouldn't have been necessary to use the knife. Rose didn't believe, for one minute, that she was in any way responsible.

But she'd discovered two things as a result of the various

traumas she'd had to deal with. That she was a stronger person than she'd realised, and that she could look after herself. Rose had no intention of ever again being thought weak or stupid. She absolutely refused to be a victim. She'd found the recruiting office, hadn't she? Joined the Timber Corps and successfully completed her training in Thetford. She was reunited with her friends and was determined that from now on her life would go from strength to strength. She was free at last, and meant to have some fun. She was still young, after all, not quite eighteen.

'Not going out again?' Jeannie asked as she watched Rose apply lipstick in front of the dressing-table mirror they shared. 'Who's the lucky blighter this time? Och, not that *terrible* old Geordie you took up with in the bar parlour the other night?' She rolled her rrr's with such emphasis, the word somehow sounded far worse. Rose only pouted her lips, applied a second coat of scarlet lipstick, and shrugged her shoulders, indicative of her free-and-easy approach to life these days.

'I simply can't stand being stuck up here in this cramped little bedroom the whole time. So what if I do like to dress up a bit when I sit downstairs in the bar? It's better than looking as if I've just been dragged through the proverbial hedge backwards.'

'You mean, as we do?' Lena complained, sounding wounded. 'Aw, that's not fair, Rose. We're too exhausted to bother about paint and powder. Anyway, what chance is there of our getting enough hot water for us all to get ourselves properly cleaned up every night? None.'

Rose fluffed up her hair then lifted her skirts to reveal long, smoothly golden legs. 'Which of you has the steadiest hand tonight then?'

'Och, for goodness' sake, where's the point in drawing lines up yer legs when yer only going to be sitting doon all night?' Jeannie protested. 'Who'd notice?'

'Depends who's there. You never know, I might meet someone exciting one of these nights.'

'Fat chance.'

'OK, forget it. I'll do it myself.' Taking an eyebrow pencil, Rose twisted round and started to draw a line from her heel up the calf of her leg. Her hand quivered slightly and the line wove perilously off course.

'Gi'e it to me, lassie. The way you're managing, it'd look like a drunken snail after a night on the razzle.'

The imitation stocking seams in place, and a final dab of powder on her nose, Rose declared herself ready. 'Are you coming with me or not?' When she got no response, beyond a shrug from Lena and a sound rather like 'Pschaw' from Jeannie, she told them that if they wanted to behave like old women they were welcome, and flounced downstairs to 'test out the talent', as Lou would say.

She'd grown fond of trying out Lou's phrases, though sadly, from Rose, they didn't carry quite the same note of teasing good humour. Her version sounded far more like a sexually provocative challenge.

Tonight she soon felt nothing but gratitude for the fact that her room mates had refused to accompany her for she did indeed spot some new talent: an airman seated at the bar. Rose sauntered right over, climbed on to the stool next to his, crossed those wonderful legs of hers and asked if he'd care to buy her a drink.

He took one look and choked on his beer. 'Sure. Happy to. Josh Wilton's the name.' Later, as they sat together in a corner by the fire, he explained he was stationed with a crew at Silloth and had come down to the Lakes for a few days' break. 'Not having any family over here, I have to take my leave where I can.'

'And what family do you have back home, Mr Wilton?'

'Hey, call me Josh. We don't have to be too formal, do we?'

*　　*　　*

From the start Rose was captivated by his wide, teasing smile, his beautiful white teeth and witty remarks. Being a Canadian, he seemed taller, smarter, better looking and far more romantic and cosmopolitan than any of the village lads she'd seen thus far. He was also more sincere than the Yanks she'd met while on training in Norfolk, who'd been over-opinionated and thought only of themselves.

He called her 'a little honey' and asked if he could see her again.

The next day Rose pretended to be too sick to work and lay groaning in her bed, impatient for Jeannie and Lena to leave while they both fussed over her, offering various pieces of advice and lists of instructions as to what she should do to get better. By seven-thirty they had gone. By ten o'clock she was dressed in grey slacks and a summer blue sweater, seated beside Josh in his Jeep and careering along the empty lanes. He took her to lunch, then to a movie as he called it. After that, he drove still further north through Borrowdale where they walked, hand in hand, savouring the utter silence. The summer day was hot and sunny, cooled by a gentle breeze on the high fells above Buttermere. The craggy spines glinted like silver along the ridges, broken by darker patches of heather and trees.

He somehow managed to find a quiet little inn where no one seemed to have heard of the war, let alone coupons. They ate spicy Cumberland sausage by a roaring log fire, washed down by several glasses of frothy beer. It was the most wonderful day of Rosie's life.

And Josh proved to be great company. He talked about life back home in Canada, about how much he missed it, and how Rose too would just love living out there. Perhaps this was why she knew she could trust him, could believe everything he told her, because he was already making plans, and she was very much a part of them.

'You know, I've been waiting for a girl like you all my life. You're a real honey.'

Rose loved it when he called her 'Hon' or 'Honey'. He said it would be his pet name for her from now on. Nobody had said such things to her before. When he kissed her, she felt weak with longing, burning with need, as if she had a raging thirst which demanded to be quenched. So when he suggested that maybe they should stay the night, as he'd drunk rather more than he'd intended and wasn't really safe to drive back along those narrow roads just yet, Rose simply looked at his gorgeously beseeching, little boy smile and thought, Why not?

There was a war on after all. Every film she'd seen, every newspaper she'd picked up, seemed to be filled with stories of young people like themselves falling instantly and passionately in love, many of them getting married within days of meeting. Look at Lou. She'd met and married her Gordon within a week, and they were blissfully happy. There was absolutely no reason why it couldn't happen for Rose too, and why the hell not? Who knew what could happen tomorrow? He might be killed. They might both be killed. What did she have to lose, for God's sake? What had being a goody-goody all her life ever achieved? Nothing but bullying, jealousy, resentment and abuse. Now Rose fervently believed that you had to snatch at happiness while you could, and look after number one.

Josh was her chance of happiness. At last. If he wanted to make love to her, didn't that just prove how very important she was to him, how much he loved her?

It would also prove that she was a proper woman, no longer an abused child. She would finally be able to banish all the haunting pain of her past.

Their love making had been every bit as exciting and thrilling as she'd hoped. Lying next to him in bed as he slept contentedly beside her, she couldn't resist kissing him and teasing him into wakefulness again. She wanted his hands in her hair, smoothing her naked flesh, his lips upon hers. The very thought made her ache with fresh desire. When he didn't immediately respond, she straddled him, nipping at his mouth with her sharp little teeth, smiling to herself as she heard him groan.

'You little witch!'

He rolled her over, pinning her down with one hand clamping both her wrists against the pillow, nudging open her legs with his knee although she needed no such persuasion. Rose arched her body, lifting herself to him. She wrapped her long golden limbs about his thick, strong body so she could hold him close, the intensity of their passion making her oblivious of everything but the sensations he was stirring within her. When, in the exultation of the moment, he finally released her hands, she grasped at his shoulders, holding him fast, clawing at his back in her determination to keep him inside her; giving him all of herself with a sensuality which was both startling and wondrous. Rose felt as if she had discovered herself at last. And discovered true love. As if to prove it, before they finally got ready to leave around lunchtime, she urged him to make love to her yet again, and once more gave herself to him unstintingly.

Later that day, his leave over, Josh dropped her off at the Eagle's Head with promises that he'd be back. He certainly wouldn't forget her, he assured her. He'd come to see her just as often as he could. 'The minute I get another pass, Hon, I'll borrow the old jalopy and come tearing right back to you.'

'You'll write?'

'Every day.' He kissed her long and hard with another of his ravenous kisses. 'God, I could eat you all up. You bring me out in goose bumps just looking at you.'

Rose chuckled softly, revelling in this sensation of power. It was such a new, and unexpectedly exciting emotion, she asked nothing more. Heady with these delirious new delights, Rose believed every word he'd said.

'That's the last you'll see of him,' Jeannie warned, when she'd heard a carefully edited version of events.

Lou told her she was a damned fool and Gracie was even more condemnatory. 'I do hope you didn't do anything you might regret, Rose?'

Annoyed by her friends' negative attitude and by the anxious query in Gracie's compassionate gaze, Rose flounced over to a chair to sit there in sulky silence. She crossed her legs, the silk stockings so generously provided by Josh giving off a sensuous sort of squeak, making her smile at their remembered passion. He had enjoyed putting these very same stockings on for her. And then taking them off again. 'God, what a load of puritans you all are. Can't a girl have a bit of fun in her life for once?'

'It's only your welfare we're concerned about,' Gracie said.

'I can take care of myself, thanks very much. I've had loads of practice.'

On the Wednesday morning she triumphantly wafted a letter before them all. 'Eat your hearts out, girls. Listen to this. "Never had such a great time in all my life. Hope you're OK, Honey . . ." Ooh, better not read that bit, it's private. Here you are, what about this? "Hope to see you again in the not too distant future. Keep yourself ready for action."'

'Aye, but ready for what sort of action?' Jeannie wanted to know. 'He's not taking advantage of you, is he, *Honey*?'

'*Shut up! Shut up! Shut up!* If all you can think to do is criticise, I'd rather not discuss it, thanks very much.' Rose stalked away, chin high. Later, she secreted the letter under her pillow and each night, as she snuggled down in bed, she would draw it out and re-read it. It was just as well that it gave her so much pleasure for it was many weeks before she felt as happy.

Each day while Erich Müller assisted Adam to earth up the potatoes, Karl continued to work with Gracie on the hedge. The summer days were long and hot, the work strenuous, and yet, despite few words being exchanged between them, her relationship with him grew and strengthened. As they cut and interlaced the branches, it was as if they wove their love for each other into each strand.

Although in theory Gracie wasn't allowed to go too near him, needing approval from the guard if she had to check that he was doing the job correctly, they seemed able to communicate by each lingering glance or brief brushing of fingertips. Sometimes, Gracie would find a note tucked into the pocket or sleeve of the sweater she'd left lying around for this very purpose. These began, innocently enough, by thanking her for her kindness, progressing to more complex messages, telling her he hoped he could work with her tomorrow and the next day and the one after that, and how he would miss her when this task was completed. Finally he spoke openly of his affection for her, of how he dreamed of her every night and couldn't wait to see her smiling face each morning. Gracie kept every one, secreting them in her handkerchief box, only bringing them out to read when Lou and the others were busy elsewhere. This was her own private world. Her terrible secret. One she dare not share with anyone, not even her closest friend.

What might happen to him, to herself, were these ever to be discovered, she didn't dare to consider. Nevertheless she understood the dangers in what they did, the risks they took. Despite her better judgement, she wrote notes in return. She kept them short and, fearful of discovery, as vague and ambiguous as possible. Neither names nor places were mentioned but there was no denying that they were love letters. Nothing less. And she longed to be alone with him with a pain that was acutely physical.

She was thankful that the field was a large one and the hedge verging the lane high and long, but knew the task would be completed soon. Perhaps it was this thought which made her act with greater boldness.

'*Would you be punished?*' she whispered as she walked over to check on whether he'd snicked the thick stem correctly with the billhook, her fingers catching his for the briefest second as she helped him carefully to bend the branch over, making sure it didn't break. She didn't say: If it were discovered that we're in love, because she knew he understood this without her needing to say it.

Then she moved on to check on Erich. 'No, no, be careful to cover every bit of the potatoes or they'll go green.' His fingers were clumsier than Karl's, and he was less patient, so he'd been given simple spadework to do. She demonstrated how to earth up correctly, since he had no English, and he winked at her, as if he knew all her secrets. 'When you've finished this job, Adam wants you to help plant some leeks.' She knew he didn't understand a word yet, strangely, felt less concerned about spending time with him. Always with one eye on the guard, who kept an increasingly casual watch on his charges while lolling about reading his newspaper or smoking, she remained careful, maintaining a brisk and businesslike approach with the prisoners before returning to her own section of the field.

The next morning Karl left a note with his answer. 'They might send me away to another camp.'

'Oh my godfathers, I couldn't bear that.'

Their conversations were always like this, broken up and spread out over several mornings. But as the prisoners gained the trust of their guard, and he became more lax, the two lovers would exchange short bursts of conversation, each desperate to learn as much as possible about the other.

'Where were you born?' she asked.

'In a small town on the northern plains. I volunteered for the navy in 1939 when I was a boy of seventeen, in a fit of patriotic passion. I was too young to understand what I was doing. I should have stayed home and become a saddler, like my father. Listening to your parents is perhaps the wisest thing.'

Gracie disagreed. 'If I had listened to mine I would not have joined the WTC. If you had listened to yours, you might not have joined the navy and then we might never have met.'

She learned that he'd been forcibly transferred to the U-boat Arm in 1940, despite the fact that the service was supposed to be for volunteers only.

'*Freiwillig zur U-boot Waffe!* the posters declared. But although I did not volunteer, as instructed, nor did I dare object as it was my patriotic duty. Following the basic three-month induction period at Stralsund, I underwent a course in telegraphy at the Naval Signals School. First I was made Leading Telegraphist, *Stabsfunkgast*, then Junior Petty Officer, *Funkmaat*. Following this, I was promoted to senior telegraphist.'

He was telling her this as they stood at the hedge, not too far apart but each pretending to be absorbed in their work, as if oblivious of the other, while in fact they were desperately, achingly aware of every nuance of movement, every breath the other took. Their conversation was whispered, questions issued and answered in short, breathless sentences, interspersed with frequent glances across at the lazy guard.

'How did you come to be captured?'

'In the North Atlantic in May nineteen forty-one. One night at about nineteen hundred hours, not long after the *Bismarck* sank, a torpedo jammed in the tube on our boat. Then we are hit by a depth charge. It was like being hammered with a giant's fist. I shall never forget the expressions of fear on the men all around me. There was no panic, just that cold, sweating fear. So this is how it feels to die, I think. But only for a moment. There was no time. There were shouts that we would hit the bottom. I do not know where he found the engine power to move that crippled boat. I shall never know. I thought us done for. But I heard him shout, "Surface!" Just once, very calm. And so we did. Then I was busy with signals from the other boats in the convoy. Each one I take down, decode, enter into the signals log and place before my commander. I must write his response, encode and Morse it out but there was no time. We were captured though considered ourselves fortunate to survive. Most U-boats sink with all hands.'

'You could have been killed and then we . . .'

'*Ruhe! Sprich nicht. Arbeit!*' The guard had noticed them talking and was ordering Karl to be quiet and to get on with his work. Gracie hurried guiltily away.

Throughout all of this, work was progressing well. Too well. Soon it would be finished and Karl and Erich would have no further need to come every day to Adam's farm.

'I won't see you again,' his next note said. 'How shall I live?'

Gracie went to discuss the matter with Alf. 'I think the POWs enjoy having some proper work to do. What will happen to them when this hedge is finished? Can they work on some other project? In the forest perhaps?'

He gave a noncommittal shrug, his eyes narrowing as he looked at her more keenly. 'Any special reason why they should?'

'No, of course not. I just wondered, that's all.'

'Not for me to say. No doubt we'll get us orders, along with everyone else, when the time comes. When will thoo be done?' he asked.

'One more week,' she said, wondering how she could make the work last so long.

Perhaps it was the thought of having so little time left which

provoked them to take a risk. Thursday proved to be wet with
the kind of relentless rain a mountainous area such as the Lakes
is only too accustomed to, even in summer. When Irma brought
out flasks of hot soup for their lunch, she suggested they drink
it in the barn.

'No point in catching pneumonia.'

The shelter was welcomed by them all: Adam, Gracie, the
guard and, of course, the two prisoners. Adam and the guard
exchanged a little small talk. Gracie and the two young Germans
ate their hot soup and bread in silence. She didn't even risk a
glance in their direction, in case the expression in her eyes
should give her away.

It was when their break was over and they set off to return
to work that the chance they had most longed for finally came.
Adam was leading Erich back through the potato field, while
Gracie and Karl moved off in the opposite direction, around the
perimeter towards the section of hedge where they were
currently working.

'You two all right for a second?' the guard asked. 'I need to
pee.'

'Fine,' Gracie agreed with a casual nod, and he disappeared
round the back of the barn in order to answer the call of nature.
The moment he'd gone, each turned instinctively towards the
other. Karl grabbed her hand and pulled her behind a nearby
beech tree. 'I cannot believe that we have found each other. It is
too wonderful!'

She laughed, dizzy with love for him. Gracie longed for him
to pull her into his arms and kiss her but he held back, perhaps
fearful of his own feelings as well as of being discovered. He put
out a hand, traced the outline of her lips with one tremulous
finger, then, as if unable to resist her any longer, he drew her
close and with infinite tenderness put his mouth to hers. Now
she understood exactly what Lou had meant by fireworks. She
would not have been in the least surprised if indeed a whole

cascade of colour had exploded around them. The rain was washing over their faces, plastering their hair to their heads, soaking them through, but they didn't even notice. Not until the guard emerged, doing up his trousers, did they break away and continue on their way as if nothing untoward had taken place.

To Gracie, it seemed as if her heart were trembling with love for him.

The kiss had ended far too quickly but to the two lovers it felt as if they had shared a lifetime of emotion in those precious seconds. Few words had been exchanged between them. There was neither the time nor the need for such trivialities. Their lips, their hands, their bodies had said everything which needed to be said. But Gracie knew that it was not enough. The kiss had only made their hunger worse, not better.

Irma was waiting in the kitchen for Adam that evening, the moment he came in from the fields. 'It's time you asked Gracie out again. And don't take no for an answer this time. I know she's fond of you deep down, she just won't admit it. She's afeared of committing herself because of the war.'

Adam sighed. He was beginning to lose heart, to think that he was wasting his time pursuing her. She'd changed recently, had been behaving rather oddly, sometimes jumpy and nervous, at other times serene and smiling, as if nursing a secret. 'I'm not sure, Mam. We're good friends, true enough, but Gracie gives no indication we could be any more than that.'

'Utter tosh! You give up too soon, that's allus been your problem. She's just playing hard to get, lad. Stand up for yerself.'

And so he asked her, and was bitterly disappointed when she refused. 'But you said you'd come out with me, if I waited a little while.'

'I said that I might,' Gracie apologised, hating herself for letting him down though in fact she'd never truly promised to go out with him again, only said she'd consider it. 'Some other time perhaps.'

'When? Next Saturday?' he persisted, mindful of his mother's words.

A part of her was growing irritated and concerned by his persistence, and yet she found it impossible simply to give him the brush-off. Loving Karl was too dangerous even to contemplate. It was complete madness and filled her with shame instead of the joy that being in love should bring. It would be far more sensible to accept Adam's offer and try very hard to fall for him instead. Perhaps Irma was right. She simply needed the opportunity to allow love to flourish. Wouldn't that be far more sensible?

But she'd needed no such opportunity to fall in love with Karl, her inner voice reminded her. It had simply happened, quite out of the blue. She'd needed only to look into his eyes at that very first meeting to know he was the one for her. But that didn't mean she had to act upon it, did it? Except that she *had* acted upon it. She'd kissed him. Just as her father had predicted, she was born with sin on her soul. Didn't this prove it?

Raw with pain, Gracie felt herself weakening; thinking that she really must put more effort into *not* loving Karl, into *not* wanting him, instead of planning how they might find a means of escape from prying eyes so they could enjoy more of those wonderful kisses. She should remind herself he was the enemy; that it could never work between them. The situation was utter torment. Loving Adam would be so much simpler. She really should give him a chance.

'I'll let you know.'

Chapter Eighteen

Hurt and puzzled by her refusal, Adam nevertheless welcomed the help that the POWs provided. Government regulations, with all the extra ploughing and digging for victory they imposed, had put more pressure on the owners of small farms. He was even more thrilled and delighted to have Gracie working with him, yet still felt that something wasn't quite right. He couldn't put his finger on exactly what it was. She'd carefully explained that she couldn't stay for long; that she wasn't a Land Girl but a Timber Girl, so must soon return to working in the forest.

'Really, we were fortunate that my ganger let me off normal duties for a while,' she said.

Yet when Alf had suggested that the project was taking rather a long time and perhaps she could leave the POWs unsupervised now, apart from Adam and their guard, she'd protested that this really wasn't feasible.

'Adam needs me for one more week,' she'd said. 'Don't you, Adam?' And of course he'd agreed that he did. He needed her for much more than one week. He was perfectly sure he wished to spend his entire life with Gracie.

He read into her decision to stay an indication of an eagerness equal to his own, which filled him with fresh hope. And yet she wasn't entirely herself.

Sometimes when he chanced upon her, quite by accident, she would start and flush, an almost demented fever in her lovely eyes. On a couple of occasions she'd pushed a piece of paper hastily into her pocket, as if she didn't wish him to see it. When he'd asked if there was anything wrong, she'd said it was just another letter from her parents.

'But it has upset you.'

'No, no. Well – only because they don't really get on. They each write to me, complaining about the other,' she'd explained, with a brittle little laugh. Later, this struck him as strange, since he hadn't noticed the postman coming by any more often. But then old Jack, the postie, might have called while he'd been out back with the cows. And if she did have difficult parents, Adam felt sorry for her. His own mother, widowed though she may be, had spent her entire life putting him first, had always taken the greatest care of him. Sometimes it irked him that Irma was perhaps a bit too overprotective, but he understood. She knew that he'd missed out on so much, not having his father around, and was only doing her best to make up for that and be both parents to him. That was why she'd suggested Gracie was the girl for him, because she wanted him to be happy. And what was wrong with that?

Adam told himself that Gracie surely wouldn't be spending so much time here at the farm if she wasn't growing fond of him. She was always up early every morning, eager to start work, watching with him for the POW detail to arrive. 'Ah, there they are. I'll just see that everything's all right,' she would say, dashing off down the field path in search of the two prisoners with their guard.

'Wait, I'll come with you,' he'd call after her retreating figure, so slight and lithe and lovely as she ran through the field, her fair hair flying in the breeze. 'I'll just finish up the milking,' or cleaning out the byre, or whatever task he was engaged with. But, ever in a hurry to help, she never could wait. Filled with

energy and enthusiasm she would dash off, telling him not to
worry and to join her later when he was ready, which of course
he desperately strove to do, often skimping on his work in order
to chase after her. That was Gracie all over, so considerate.

And when he did reach her, she always showed concern for
him. 'You work far too hard, dear Adam. You really shouldn't
abandon your cows. Leave all of these mundane tasks to Karl
and Erich. They're doing a marvellous job. We'll make farmers
of them yet.'

Though sometimes he had difficulty in catching up with
her at all. She was like quicksilver. One moment Adam
could see her in the distance, perhaps talking to the guard,
happily digging alongside Erich or working on the hedge
with the other prisoner. Then when he reached that spot
she'd be in quite a different place altogether, or else nowhere
in sight, the guard often asleep in the sun, lazy blighter that
he was. Then suddenly she would be beside him again,
cheeks flushed, eyes bright, slightly breathless with the
excitement of discovering him there, and his heart would
lift at the sight of her.

'I've come to walk you back to the house, Gracie. Mam says
it's time for tea.'

'How kind. Then I'll come, of course.' And she would let
him take her hand and lead her back along the path, moments
alone with her which Adam treasured.

Slowly it began to dawn on him what the reason was for her
odd behaviour. He could tell, by the way her pupils dilated and
darkened into a glittering gaze, by the tremor of her hand when
he took it gently in his, that passion raged within her. She was
in love. By, Christ, his mam was right. No doubt about it. She
wanted him. That was why she was taking so long over the
hedge layering. She was playing hard to get.

He thought that the time was drawing near for him to risk
asking her a more serious question. She was hot with love, and

all he had to do was pluck up the courage to declare himself. So what was it that made him hesitate?

The risks Gracie ran even to exchange a few words or slip Karl a note filled her with terror, yet she couldn't seem to help herself. More dangerous still, they would hide between the hedge and the hen coop for secret kisses, burying themselves in old sacks and dead leaves to explore their passion further. To be fair, Erich proved to be a boon in this respect, frequently keeping the guard occupied in idle chatter, or sharing a cigarette with him, so they could enjoy a few moments' privacy. And it was here that they made love for the first time, a hasty and furtive coupling while the guard dozed in the hot summer sun and Adam tended his animals.

Gracie knew that if they were ever discovered in one of their trysting places, at best Karl would be sent away to another camp. At worst, he could quite easily be shot. He only had to be found in the wrong place, at the wrong time, and it could be assumed, not unreasonably, that he was trying to escape. She did not think of the danger to herself but she did begin to worry about putting his life at risk. Yet neither could she stop herself from showing how much she loved him, at every and any opportunity. Their love was completely and utterly irresistible.

In every way it was a dangerous game they played. Even finding a moment alone to read her precious letters was difficult, since Lou or Rose or one of the others always seemed to be around. Not for a moment dare she let anyone guess her dreadful secret. Karl was an enemy of war. Her sin was to love him.

Each night she tossed and turned in her bed, barely sleeping, so that Lou asked what was wrong. Gracie frequently made the excuse of a headache, or of being too hot or over-tired, till she feared that even Lou was growing suspicious.

'For goodness' sake, girl, relax. You've been working too hard. Why don't you ask Adam to take you to the pictures on Saturday? Do you good. Wish I'd a lovely chap to take me out. I miss Gordon so much it hurts, and I haven't had a letter for ages. I'm trying not to worry but it isn't easy.'

Inevitably the day came when the hedge was finished. The final note Karl left for her was heartbreaking in its simplicity. 'This isn't the end,' it said, and Gracie told herself that this must be true, else why would God have allowed them to fall in love in the first place? Even this war couldn't last for ever. Peace was their only hope now.

The squad were measuring and marking trees suitable for felling near Esthwaite Water on a beautiful day in late-August. The small lake shimmered in the heat and even the moorhens were too hot and sleepy to swim about very much, although the girls were longing to strip off and join them in the cool water, when two visitors arrived: the Divisional Officer, who'd come to check that they were doing their job properly (so it was just as well they were), and her driver. More freckle-faced than ever, Aertex shirt and breeches looking as if they'd never seen an iron or coat hanger, at least for once she looked clean, with not a streak of oil in sight.

'Tess!'

They fell upon her with open arms. 'You got here at last. Oh, how wonderful! Now we're a team again. Yippee!' Even the Divisional Officer was laughing as they wrapped arms about each other's shoulders and did a little circling jig of jubilation.

After they'd provided their visitors with tea and cheese rolls, the Divisional Officer beckoned Lou to one side. 'Can we have a private word, Mason?'

They strolled along the path, the quiet of the woodland broken only by the occasional trill of a blackbird or the crack of a twig beneath their feet. Lou was frantically searching her mind for something she might have done wrong, some rule she'd inadvertently broken. She was quite certain that the DO had come to tear a strip off her for something, so the woman's next words came as a surprise.

'I've been very pleased with your progress here, Mason. You have the right attitude, the sort of spunk the WTC likes to see in its members. And it's plain to us that the rest of the squad look up to you. They view you almost as their leader, in point of fact.'

'That's only because I'm older than most. It'll be different now Tess is here. Assuming she stays, of course.'

'Oh, I think she'd be quite happy to give up driving boring officials like me around and return to the old lorries, which she much prefers. But I don't think Tess's being back with the squad will detract from your authority in the slightest. In fact, we mean to make sure it doesn't.' She then informed Lou that she'd been promoted to forewoman; that she would be sent on a training exercise which would last five days where she'd learn about health and first aid, book keeping and the necessary form filling, and of course even more about tree identification, the uses of wood and being responsible for the girls in her care.

For the first time in her life, Lou couldn't think of a thing to say. She was struck dumb. In the beginning, joining the WTC had merely been a ploy to stay close to her beloved Gordon. The war and events beyond her control had put paid to that dream, but she knew now how much she loved her job and wanted to do her best. At least until the war ended, Gordon returned, and they could take up life together as a proper married couple, this was where she wanted to be. Doing her bit. She couldn't wait to write and tell him about her promotion. He'd be so thrilled for her.

She managed a stammering thank you. 'Don't let on. I'd like to tell the squad myself, if you don't mind.'

The Divisional Officer grinned. 'Of course. Your privilege.'

Later, when their visitors had gone, Tess promising to return with all speed, Lou invited them all out to tea the very next day, but refused absolutely to give any reason.

Saturday dawned warm and pleasant, if rather cloudy. A perfect day, Lou declared, for some brisk exercise. The sun broke out from behind a bank of cloud at the very moment they breasted Red Bank on their bicycles. 'Just look at that view!' Gracie cried. 'It quite takes your breath away.'

Everyone felt bound to pause and examine the panorama laid out before them. They were quite out of puff from the climb anyway, but it was indeed breathtaking, hard to believe so much beauty could still exist in wartime. Plymouth, London, Exeter and other famous cities were still suffering from intermittent bombing raids. Over in Warsaw, Jews and Poles were fleeing for their lives. Lancaster bombers were bouncing bombs down the Ruhr and Eder Valleys, and the Allies were finally making inroads into Italy by taking Palermo, capturing thousands of enemy troops. Yet here, in Lakeland, Rydal Water glistened benignly in the sun, and the green vale in which the slate cottages of Grasmere nestled seemed to promise nothing but peace in its lushness.

They left their bicycles by the roughcast walls of the small church, named after the Northumbrian King St Oswald, and the venue for the customary Rush Bearing Festival which took place every year in early-August, though perhaps, Gracie thought, the war had put an end to this too, as it had to so many other innocent pleasures. Oh, Karl, will it ever be over? Will we ever be free, she wondered.

Lou treated everyone, as promised, to a substantial tea of toasted tea cakes and the famous Grasmere gingerbread, accompanied by several cups of strong tea and much noisy chatter.

'We need more of these outings,' she said, reaching for another tea cake and spreading it thickly with the rather tart damson jam. 'It's good for us to get out and about together.'

'Och, dinna ye think we see enough of each other all week?' Jeannie said, fumbling in her pocket for a cigarette.

'Not lately we haven't,' Lena pointed out. 'What with Gracie working with the POWs, and Rose sick again. We've missed you both. We could have done with a few more hands on the felling this week. It was jolly hard work.'

Lou said, 'I should think you're glad the hedging is over, aren't you, and the POWs back in camp? It was obviously quite a responsibility for you, judging from the several bad nights' sleep it gave you.'

Fortunately Gracie managed to avoid answering this question by turning to Rose and asking what had been wrong with her, and if she was feeling better.

Before she had time to answer, Jeannie chipped in, 'She was no doubt having secret trysts with her Canadian boyfriend, and not poorly at all.'

Rose's mouth curled into a secretive little smile. She raised her eyebrows provocatively as if saying they could choose to think whatever they liked.

'Ye see. She's no' denying it.' Jeannie blew out a puff of smoke in disgust.

Lou frowned. 'You don't get paid for loafing about with fellas,' she said in stern, no-nonsense tones, which finally forced Rose to protest that she wasn't loafing about at all but truly had been sick. To her great concern this was no more than the truth.

On several occasions this week, particularly when she'd got out of bed in a hurry, she'd felt the urge to vomit, even if sometimes she'd managed not to. And she didn't need to visit any doctor to guess the reason. What else could it be? A small kernel of excitement burned deep within her at the prospect of having Josh's child. Wouldn't he be pleased? And Rose could think of no surer way of keeping him. He meant to take her home with him to Canada anyway, so it would only mean bringing forward the date of their wedding. Not that he'd actually proposed yet, but Rose knew this was only because of the uncertainty of war. She knew in her heart marriage was what he wanted, what they both wanted.

Lou's announcement broke into her thoughts. 'It seems that Divisional Office has decided that this squad needs bringing into order, and I, apparently, am the girl for the task.'

'What?'

'I've been promoted. Meet your new forewoman.'

This news was greeted with whoops of delight, many hugs and kisses of congratulation and much thumping on the back, all mixed up with noisy protests that they didn't need anyone to keep them in order, thank you very much.

Lou steadfastly disagreed. 'I reckon it's time we all tightened up a bit, worked harder, put in some extra training. We're getting slack.' Voices were raised in argument yet again, but she stuck to her point. 'No, no, look how long it took Gracie to finish that bloomin' hedge. Far longer than it should, despite having POWs to help. Because of the hot, sweltering summer days, we're all slowing down. Well, our boys can't slow down, can they? They can't say they're not going to fight today because they feel a bit off colour.'

Gracie struggled to come up with an excuse but could think of nothing. Her mind was filled with longing for Karl and worry over when she might see him again. Not even the guilt she undoubtedly felt for the sin of loving the enemy could eradicate her need to be with him. She made a private vow to tackle Alf one more time on the possibility of a POW detail working alongside them in the forest. Why on earth shouldn't they? She came out of her reverie with a start, momentarily concerned that someone might have noticed her distraction.

Fortunately, everyone was far too busy looking equally guilty. Even Rose was hanging her head with shame.

Lou continued, 'So I've decided, some time in September, once I get back from this course, we'll all go off to camp and do some serious training of our own. There's some logging going on over Loweswater way. I'll try and get us a spell of work up there. At least it will be a change, and give us the opportunity for a good shake up. What d'you reckon?'

Not surprisingly, Lena was the first to object. 'But it's a *proper* holiday we need, not another project or training camp. I, for one, am quite worn out.'

'I'm sure you are, love, but as I say, "our boys" can't have a proper holiday, can they? We can't ask the bloody Germans to stop dropping bombs so that you can pop off to Blackpool or Brighton or whatever. Nor ask the miners to stop digging for coal so we don't have to cut any more pitprops. Do right, girl. You'll survive, as you must. After all . . .'

'There is a war on,' they all chorused together.

Rose pulled a face. 'I can see Lou's going to get even bossier now she's in charge.'

'Nay, that's not fair,' she protested. 'If I were that side out, you wouldn't all be sitting here, would you, enjoying this tea I've bought for you all? Though what we need now is to walk it off, so come on, finish your cuppa and we'll just have a gentle ramble up Dunmail Raise before cycling home again.'

Refusing to take no for an answer, Lou, in her new rank of forewoman, led them purposefully up a quiet by-road to Easedale, then, skirting the hump of Helm Crag, proceeded to Gill Foot and along a track which led them to the vale of Greenburn. Turning left by a pair of cottages, they made their way across the smooth southern ridge of Steel Fell, passing a pillbox put there in case of an invasion which they all hoped would never come. The sun shone in the sky with only a streak of pink cloud to mar the blue, the day being hazy with heat, and in no time at all they were all breathless and sweating with the exertion.

'How long does this track go on for? I shall need another tea after this,' Lena groaned, ostentatiously nursing a supposed stitch in her side. Since she was the tallest, and had the longest legs of them all, nobody took much notice.

'Not much further,' Lou cheerily responded. And as they could now clearly see Dunmail Raise smoothly rearing up before them, it encouraged even Lena to walk a little faster.

'We must be gluttons for punishment,' Jeannie groaned, as they collapsed flat on their backs on the summit to catch their breath.

Lena sat gazing at the awesome majesty of the view, the panorama of the Lake District stretching out before her like a huge green map. Even the grazing sheep lay about, too lethargic to graze in the summer heat. She hugged her knees to her chest with delight. 'Isn't this marvellous? Smell the grass. Look at the folds of those mountains. Oh, I just love being here, outdoors all the time. I could never work inside again. Never.'

Everyone looked up at her in astonishment. Lou said, 'By heck, Lena love, are you feeling all right?'

'Better than I've ever felt in my life. Oh, I know I find the work physically hard and enjoy the odd moan, but I love being here with you lot. When I think how I used to spend ten hours a day working in a shop, from dawn to dusk, never seeing a minute of daylight, I still pinch myself at times to think how free I am now, enjoying all this beauty and fresh air.'

There were murmurs of agreement all round, and much chatter about how life had changed for them all. But when the talk moved on to what they hoped to be doing after the war, Gracie couldn't bear to listen. It all seemed frighteningly impossible, so painfully hopeless. Where would Karl be then? Sent back to Germany? Perhaps they would never have the chance to be together. She got to her feet, urging them all to do the same.

'Come on. It's getting late. We should be making tracks.'

But no one really wanted to go home. Everyone was enjoying the day out too much. Jeannie suggested they take a swim in the lake to cool off and, as one, they scrambled to their feet and set off like giggling schoolgirls.

Dusk was falling and the light over Rydal Water was deepening to deep cobalt, the sound of crickets loud in the stillness of evening. They'd got a small fire going to warm themselves up after their swim and were all laughing and chattering, sunkissed faces glowing from the heat of the fire.

'We're like the witches from *Macbeth*, all sitting around in the moonlight, chanting our wee spells. All we need is a cauldron, and for Banquo's ghost to appear out of the bushes.'

They all heard it then, a rustling of leaves and branches just beyond the circle of light cast by the fire. 'What the hell was that?'

'It must be Lou, playing a joke,' Gracie said, anxious to keep everyone calm.

'Wrong,' Lou said at her elbow. 'I'm right here beside you.'

Rose said, 'Everyone's here. Oh, lord, now I'm scared!'

A twig snapped, a branch creaked, and then a shadowy figure stepped forward into the clearing. As one, the girls screamed. The sound seemed to scare the intruder every bit as much as it did themselves.

'Christ, don't do that! You frightened the life out of me. Sorry! But thank heaven I've found you all at last. I've been looking for you for hours, then I spotted your bikes on the grass verge.' It was Adam.

They all stared at him in utter disbelief, then everyone started laughing, teasing and shoving each other, saying they hadn't really been scared at all, only pretending. They seemed to think the whole thing absurdly funny, an absolute hoot, except for Adam, who remained where he was in the shadows, as if too unwilling or uncertain to speak. He was looking over towards Lou and Gracie who were now clinging on to each other, helpless with laughter.

Wiping tears of joy from her eyes, Lou said, 'You should go on the stage Adam. You'd do well as Banquo's ghost, you really would. You certainly scared the pants off us.'

'Lou, I'm sorry . . .'

'Stop saying that. We forgive you. Sit theesel' down and have a sup of tea.'

Gracie was examining his expression with closer attention. 'What is it Adam? What are you sorry about exactly?'

Then he held something out towards Lou. It was a telegram. The scream that went up this time chilled them all to the bone.

Chapter Nineteen

Gordon's ship had been listed as missing. Lou left with Adam that very night. He drove her straight to Ulverston railway station where she caught the next train to Liverpool. Whether the ship had been sunk or was simply hit and limping home, nobody had any idea at this stage. Gordon's mother was in Liverpool and wanted Lou with her, for support.

'I'm sure he'll come home safe and sound in the end,' Adam said, handing up her overnight bag and closing the carriage door.

Lou didn't answer. Something had happened to her throat. Not a sound would come out of it. A shout went up, a whistle blew, the train jerked, rattling all the carriages together as it puffed out great clouds of steam, just as that other train had done, so long ago. A lifetime it seemed. Gordon's face was emerging out of the smoke. Lou could see him waving from the platform, shouting something to her.

No, it couldn't be Gordon. He was still at sea. It was Adam. She really must close her eyes for a moment and get some sleep. Maybe then she could sort out her jumbled thoughts into some sort of order. Make sense of them. The carriage was packed but she found a gap and wedged herself between a woman with a baby on her knee and a sleeping sailor, his mouth gaping open in a loud snore. Poor lad must be exhausted to sleep through all this din. Gordon must be pretty exhausted too, she thought, after all these months at sea. He'd be glad to be home again. Lou closed her eyes, certain that when she woke, and found his mum waiting for her on Lime Street Station, they'd dash over to the Pool and find Gordon's ship would already have docked.

Later that Sunday afternoon Rose was expecting a very important visitor, one for whom she had some rather special news. She felt quite happy about it, even excited. She couldn't wait to tell him.

As usual, Josh took her for a drive into the heart of the Lakes, found a quiet country inn and booked them in as Mr and Mrs Brown. It seemed to amuse him to use such an obviously fake name.

Rose held on to her secret until after they'd made love, nursing it as a delightful surprise which she meant to offer him as a treat, like dessert. As she spoke the words, she smiled softly, the all-knowing smile of a maturing woman on a face which still held the sweet innocence of youth.

He stared down at her where she lay, wild dark curls haloed about her lovely, childlike face, her lustrous skin gleaming like gold against the white sheets. Then he pushed himself away from her, stunned dismay clear on his ruggedly handsome features. 'Hey, you're joking, right?'

Rose blinked, and a small frown creased her smooth brow. 'You are pleased, aren't you? I mean, you don't mind, do you, Josh?' A worm of uncertainty unfurled in her stomach. As she reached out to smooth one hand over his cheek, he jerked his head away. She still couldn't quite believe he was truly angry. 'I know it's a bit of a shock at first, but these things happen all the time, and it's not as if we weren't planning to get married anyway.'

'Married?' Even Rose couldn't be unaware of the surprise in his tone.

She swallowed the painful constriction which had come into her throat and ploughed on, remorselessly optimistic. 'You've said over and over how much I'll enjoy Canada. Maybe I could go out there now, stay with your parents or other relatives till the war's over? Not that I mind if it isn't possible for me to go. I can wait for you here. At least I'll have something of you when you have to go overseas again.' She knew she was babbling, but didn't seem able to stop.

He flung back the sheets and, leaping from the bed, began to pace about the room. He looked so strong and athletic in his white shorts, Rose felt her stomach clench with fresh need. She couldn't keep her eyes off him. 'Josh?'

He was flapping his hands at her, as if he'd really like to waft her away and make her vanish. 'Hey, I never expected this. I thought you used something, a sponge, a douche. God, I don't know. *Something!* Hell, why didn't I use something? I must've been mad. Bewitched. All that talk about you liking Canada. Sure, anybody would. It's a great country. But marriage? Naw, I don't recall saying anything on that subject, Hon.'

Rose became very still, then slowly sat up in bed so that she could give her full attention to this puzzling response. Josh didn't seem to understand. She told him, quite calmly, that there was really no need to panic, she would be perfectly all right. 'I'm not in the least concerned, and there's no reason why you should be either.'

He stood by the window, his manly body, which she loved so much, appropriately framed against the majesty of the mountains beyond. As she smiled at him, he seemed to sag with relief. 'Hell, I'm sure glad you're gonna take this attitude. For a minute you had me real worried. Marriage just ain't gonna happen, Hon. It can't.' He came and sat beside her, stroking her arms, her shoulders, her breasts, as he carefully explained. But the words didn't make sense. Rose was forced to ask him to repeat them, to make sure she'd heard correctly.

He playfully tweaked her nose. 'Hey, you know I *would* marry you, if I *could*. You and me have had fun, right? I love you, sweetheart. You're a doll. But back home, I gotta wife already, OK? And three kids. So there's not a damn' thing I can do about it, Hon, not with the best will in the world.'

Summer was fading and September was almost upon them but Rose told no one. The shame of it was too enormous. Nor did she cry or feel sorry for herself. She longed to hate him but couldn't seem able even to manage that. She'd fallen in love. Where was the sin in that? Josh Wilton just happened to be unavailable. She'd stupidly assumed he was free without properly checking. It was all abundantly clear to her now, of course, that no promise of marriage had actually been made. She'd simply taken it for granted, in her youthful naïvety, that it would naturally follow their lovemaking. How stupid could you get!

Sometimes Rose hated being so young. Why couldn't one be born old and wise at birth, and then grow into youth when one was ready for it? That would be much more sensible, and so much less painful.

She'd held on to her pride at least. She hadn't shouted, or screamed, or cried. She'd remained amazingly calm, simply got up, dressed and insisted that he take her home right away, which he'd gladly done, driving quickly back along the lanes to the Eagle's Head as if he couldn't wait to be rid of her. They'd parted as friends, at least on the surface. All the way home, Josh had continued to be as full of good cheer and bonhomie as he normally was. He'd offered her money which Rose had accepted. She was no fool, she told herself. Not entirely anyway. She would need cash when the baby came and, in her estimation, taking it wouldn't in any way threaten her independence.

But then he'd said, 'You do what you think best.'

'Are you suggesting I use this money to get rid of it?'

'Use it however you like, Hon.'

'But that's what you'd prefer?'

'Hey! Not my decision. I'll send you some more, soon as I can. You keep in touch, right?'

Rose had managed to nod, even gave him the smallest glimmer of a smile as he'd jumped back into his Jeep, and, with a screech of tyres, driven off up the lane and vanished in a cloud of dust. She very much doubted she'd ever see or hear from him again.

In that moment, Rose realised that her calmness arose from the fact that she wasn't in the least surprised by the way he'd reacted. It was almost as if she'd been half expecting this to happen; as if she'd known all along that something always did go wrong for her. First her parents dying, just when she needed them most, then her brother bullying her and telling her how she really didn't have a family of her own. Her precious Tizz being killed and, last but by no means least, that assault by Agnes, whom she'd admittedly found slightly odd but had automatically trusted because she was a woman.

But I can cope, she told herself. I shall survive this problem as I did all the rest. No matter what. She'd trusted too many people in the past, all of whom had let her down one way or another. Hadn't she resolved to be utterly ruthless; to think only of herself? She should never have been so foolish as to fall in love or trust in anyone, ever again. She really must learn to protect herself more, to use people to her own advantage as people had used her, then she would be safe. And so would her child.

As the days passed, although Rose felt stunned by Josh's revelation, in no time at all she'd forgiven him. She'd given the matter a good deal of thought and now fully understood why he'd so heartlessly abandoned her: simply out of a sense of guilt and misplaced loyalty to his wife; because at heart he was a kind man. And there were his children to consider, of course. He couldn't truly love that wife of his, not as he loved Rose or how could he have made love to her with such passion? He hadn't meant to be deliberately cruel, he'd simply acted out of thoughtlessness.

She'd explained all of this in the letter she now popped into the post box, an imprint of her pink lipsticked mouth firmly pressed to its seal, carefully addressed to him at his station in Silloth. Rose could only hope he was still there, though she felt certain they would have some means of forwarding his mail on to him if he'd been relocated.

Having done all she could on the matter, for the moment at least, but still feeling sorry for herself and rather at a loose end, she decided to call upon Gracie and see if she had any news of Lou. They could perhaps go out for a walk, or sit and chat in their garden. Anything would be better than being alone with all these private worries weighing her down. She knew the cottage where the two girls lived, a mile or two from the village, although she'd never, so far, called in. This lovely summer evening seemed as good a time as any and the walk might do her good.

As was the custom in these parts, she went around to the back door of Beech Tree Cottage, knocked and, without waiting to be invited, walked straight in. She was surprised to find the kitchen occupied, not by Irma or Gracie but by a half-naked man.

'Gosh, I'm so sorry! I didn't think. I should've waited . . .' But she didn't retreat. She watched with fascinated interest as Adam reached for the towel and began to rub it over his face and chest. Rose closed the door behind her and fluttered her eyelashes provocatively up at him. She really couldn't resist flirting, and he was quite dishy. 'Though I don't mind, if you don't.'

Laughing, he shrugged into a shirt. 'You're one of Lou's squad, aren't you? I've seen you around. It's so hot and dusty, it's a real nuisance not being allowed to bathe more than once a week.'

'And no more than two inches, don't forget.'

'What good is two inches to anyone? Government regulations are fine for those who work in offices but for those of us who do physical labour, or work on the land, it's a nightmare, don't you find? I never feel clean.'

'You look fine to me.' Rose was taking in the glistening beauty of his muscled torso and imagining how much more entrancing it would have been if she'd interrupted him lathering himself in the tin bath. Now that might have been very interesting indeed. In her misery, it hadn't occurred to her that she might fancy other men besides Josh. Now, out of the blue, it did. What's more, she could tell by the way this man was looking at her that he found her attractive too. Rose suddenly saw that life for her might not be so awful after all. That even if Josh did intend to stay married to his dull wife in Canada, there might be other possibilities worth exploring. One of which could be turned to her advantage.

There was a short silence then Adam said, 'Were you wanting Gracie? She's out with Mam. They've taken some salvage over to the parish hall. You know the sort of thing, battered saucepans, kettles, tin cans and jelly moulds. If you've anything metal, Mam'll have it off you. They'll be back soon, I expect.' He paused as if to catch his breath. 'Assuming she doesn't send Gracie off to pick rosehips or blackberries for more jam. For the Vitamin C, you know.' He laughed. 'You never can tell what scheme my mam has in hand.'

They both laughed and the tension between them lightened a little. Adam had buttoned up his shirt. Now he turned around so that he could tuck it in his trousers, then swung quickly back again with a small smile. Rose grinned. 'I can always call again.' Yet she didn't move. She simply stood there, gazing boldly up at him, waiting.

He cleared his throat somewhat noisily, and then surprised himself by saying, 'I was about to make myself a bit of supper. Only Spam fritters, I'm afraid, but I'm rather partial to them. Would you care to join me?'

'Love to. I adore Spam fritters.' Rose had never had them in her life.

'Great!'

They worked together on the dish, Rose slicing the Spam nice and thinly, Adam mixing the flour and water into a thick batter, tossing in a bit of powdered egg for extra flavour. In no time they were laughing and joking together, flicking flour off Rose's nose and splattering globules of batter all over Irma's clean cooker. Rose cut bread and spread it sparingly with margarine. Then she searched out a freshly laundered tablecloth and laid the table by the window of the tiny living room, brewed a pot of tea and even brought a few Michaelmas daisies out of the garden to put in a jar as a table decoration. And all the while, Adam set her mouth watering with the delicious aroma of frying fritters, hissing and spitting in the pan.

They sat facing each other, a shaft of early-evening sunshine lighting Adam's fair hair, already bleached by the sun to a pale gold. Rose knew that he'd been seeing Gracie, taking her out to the pictures, and fancied her rotten. But all was fair in love and war, wasn't that what they said? You had to watch out for number one in this world. Hadn't she learned that much at least? She gazed upon him for a long moment, fork poised, studying the perfection of his profile, the way his light curls fell forward over his brow, before sliding the food thoughtfully into her mouth. 'This is delicious. I've never tasted anything quite so good.'

Adam returned her gaze, studying her piquant beauty as he wiped a dribble of fat from her full soft mouth with the heel of his thumb. He smiled. 'My pleasure.'

They talked little as they ate, but when each plate was empty they sank back with contented sighs, feeling bloated and replete. 'I shall never be hungry again,' Rose intoned, imitating Vivien Leigh's southern drawl from *Gone With the Wind*, and they both burst out laughing.

'I've seen you around. From a distance, of course. But why have we never met properly before?' Adam asked, his gaze warm and admiring.

'I don't know. Why haven't we?'

He reached for her hand and Rose let him clasp it in his own. His grasp was firm and strong, which she rather liked. She gave him the other and he pulled her gently towards him across the table.

The kitchen door burst open and Irma breezed in, basket dangling on her plump arm. 'Hello, love. I'm home. What do you think Mrs . . .' She stopped short, taking in the scene in one swift, appraising glance. Rose, so comfortably ensconced at the table; her best Irish linen cloth, upon which Irma had personally embroidered every stitch, lying stained with crumbs and spotted with fat beneath their joined hands. Her son's gaze riveted upon that little madam's face – and Irma could tell, by the brazen way in which she returned the poor boy's besotted glance, that she was no better than she should be. A brazen hussy if ever there was one.

Unable to disguise the expression of startled disapproval which she knew to be compressing her own mouth and turning her rouged cheeks a deeper pink, Irma floundered uncomfortably for something sensible to say which wouldn't alarm Adam or put him on the defensive. Young men could be tricky.

The last thing she must do was to be openly critical or he'd start to champion the lass. 'Oh,' she said, adopting a pseudo-pleasant tone. Her social voice, as Adam termed it. 'I didn't realise we had company.'

'This is Rose.'

'Ah, yes, I've heard all about Rose. One of the Timber Girls who work with our lodgers, Gracie and Lou. Isn't that right?'

'That's right. We're old friends. I knew them back in Cornwall.' Rose somehow felt the need to make this claim, perhaps due to the hostility she read so plainly in Irma's gaze which she couldn't quite comprehend. 'I hope it was all good, whatever it was they told you about me? A girl's got to watch her reputation these days.' She gave a bright little laugh, then winked at Adam.

Irma acknowledged this gesture as confirmation of her worst fears.

A small silence followed, during which Adam and Rose didn't move from their places at the table while his mother stood stolidly beside them, saying nothing but glaring with such astonishing severity that even Rose could take no more.

'I'd best be off. See if I can find Gracie.' She jumped up and reached for her cardigan which she'd slung over a chair. Adam got there before her to drape it tenderly about her shoulders.

'I'll walk you to the door,' he said.

'I'm sure she can find her own way out,' Irma tartly remarked. She'd still made no effort to unpin her hat or put down the loaded basket. Adam took it from her, set it carefully on the table.

'I'm sure she can, but I'll walk with her anyway. In fact, I might walk along to the village with her. A breath of fresh air would do me good after all that food.'

'I don't think so, son. I was wanting you to do a job or two for me.'

He hesitated. 'Can't it wait? I won't be long. An hour or so at most.'

Irma flopped down into her chair with a weary sigh. 'Oh, well, if you've no time to spare for your tired old mam, I understand. It was only that I've all this stuff to collect and sort out. But don't worry, I shouldn't imagine there's anything too heavy for me to carry. I can manage.'

'But does it have to be done right now? Tonight? I mean, it isn't being collected tomorrow, is it?'

'Huh! Just like a man to think it can all be done at the last minute. Salvage takes time to sort through, you know. And all the rubbish they give you, well, it makes for a lot of work.' Irma sighed heavily again, and with a plump hand that noticeably trembled with fatigue began to unpin her hat.

Adam's face held the expression of a man cornered. Turning to Rose, he offered his heartfelt apologies with a regretful sigh. 'Sorry. Some other time?'

'Sure. Good night all.' Determined not to react to Irma's self-satisfied smile of triumph, Rose twirled on her heel, a positive swagger to her walk as she made her way down the garden path. But despite outward appearances, inwardly she was fuming, furious that he hadn't stood up to his mother. But what could she expect? Adam was still living under the woman's roof, though it wouldn't necessarily always be the case.

'You will call again?' he asked, as he held open the garden gate for her. 'Or we could go out some time. To the pictures maybe. I like going to the pictures.'

'If you were to ask me,' she said, with an enticing smile. 'And if I'm free,' thereby giving the impression that she was hugely popular, with a busy social life, so he'd have to look sharp about it.

'Right,' Adam said, his usual attack of shyness suddenly closing in upon him as he realised how beautiful she was, and what little hope he had of catching her, of catching any woman. 'Right then!'

Rose strolled away with a genuine smile on her face because

she'd actually enjoyed herself. She'd even eaten a decent meal for once without feeling the need to throw up afterwards. And from what she could see at first acquaintance, Adam was really rather sweet, an ideal candidate for what she had in mind, should the need arise.

While Lou was away, all the girls agreed that Gracie should take her place. They'd grown used to someone being in charge and telling them what to do, and were happy to continue in that fashion. 'You're the best one to act as deputy,' Jeannie had said, tears in her soft brown eyes. 'Till our lively Lou returns.'

A small silence had fallen upon them all. Would she still be the same lively old Lou when she did return? Or would everything be different? Gracie decided there was little point in worrying about that until it happened.

'Let's get back to work,' she said, gritting her teeth, and so they did, if not exactly in high spirits, at least as a united group.

One morning in early-September they were joined by a small detail of prisoners to help with the peeling of bark from the poles and general labouring. Erich and Karl were amongst them. Gracie's heart leaped at sight of him but then she felt compelled to keep her gaze averted, in case anyone should read the naked love in her eyes.

'We need to talk,' he whispered, as he began to slice off a section of bark. Gracie's hand was shaking so much she could hardly use the billhook properly.

'Not here. It isn't safe.'

She deliberately walked away from him, ostensibly to check on whether Lena had ordered the lorry which they needed to transport the pitprops to the station.

'It'll be here shortly,' she agreed, rather tetchily. 'Don't nag.'

Gracie checked on Rose, lingered a little chatting to Jeannie, but then Alf shouted across to her, scolding her for wasting time before sending her back to the sawhorse, and Karl. As the morning wore on she almost wished Alf hadn't set them to working together. It was worse to be so close to Karl and yet have to maintain an air of indifference. It was a different guard this time, but he soon struck up a friendship with Alf and evidently considered his detail of charges to be trustworthy. In a way this made it easier for Gracie and Karl to talk, yet somehow a thousand times more difficult, as the smallest mistake, the merest glance, could so easily arouse suspicion.

'It's Erich. He has been called in front of the *Altestenrat*.'

Gracie glanced over to where Erich was working with Alf. But as no one seemed to be paying herself and Karl any undue attention, she said, 'What on earth is that?'

'It is a council, like a court, run by the highest ranking German officers in the camp.' He was speaking quickly now, rushing the words out under his breath although, watching him, anyone would think he simply had his head down and was working hard, peeling away the bark. 'They have made his life unbearable. They say he has anti-Nazi views. Erich has protested but they do not believe him. They bully him, play tricks on him. Call him a coward. They say he must go.'

'Go? Go where?'

'He must try to escape. Or take the consequences.'

Gracie gasped. 'What sort of consequences? I don't under-stand.'

'It is his duty to escape. He has no choice. The Luftwaffe officers will kill him if he refuses. And he needs my help.'

Chapter Twenty

Tess chose that very moment to drive the lorry on to the site, and the next hour or so was fully taken up with exhausting, difficult work. Two poles had to be placed on the ground leaning against the back of the lorry to form a ramp, then the logs were rolled up and stacked on to the bed of the lorry. Rose and Jeannie stood on the back of it to receive the logs, with Lena and Gracie rolling them up from the ground. When the bottom of the lorry was full, Gracie shifted the poles higher for the second layer. She strove to concentrate, for all her gaze kept straying over to where Karl and Erich were working together on the peeling. Were they even now planning their escape? The thought was terrifying. Escape was impossible from here. Everyone knew that. This was the reason the high-ranking officers were brought to Grizedale in the first place, to this grade one prison. Even if they found their way out of the forest, they had at least twenty miles of mountains to cross before they reached the coast. And if they were caught?

They'd be shot.

Gracie's hands slipped on the pole she was attempting to push up the ramp and it rolled back down, knocking Lena flat.

'Oh, I'm sorry, Lena. I lost concentration for a moment.'

Alf shouted something pithy at her but Lena seemed none the worse for her battering. She didn't even complain, simply laughed, got up and brushed herself off. Gracie glanced up and for one brief second caught Rose gazing down at her, a thoughtful frown on her face. Gracie felt her cheeks grow warm with guilt. She hurriedly turned away and bent again to the task with renewed vigour.

Once the lorry was full, with four or five layers of pitprops, Alf shouted to Tess to take it away. 'You go with her,' he told Gracie and Lena.

'Let Rose go instead of me. I don't mind getting on with the peeling.' This was a job they all hated.

'I'm the ganger, lassie. Thoo'll do as I say.'

And so, reluctantly, Gracie climbed on to the lorry beside Lena. Perched on top of the pile of logs, she was acutely aware of Karl watching as Tess drove away, but somehow, by dint of enormous will-power, she managed not to look back.

Concerned about the possibility of Rose upsetting her plans, Irma again took her son to task over his lack of action. 'Stop dithering and get on wi' it. Faint heart never won fair lady. Ask her now. Strike while the iron's hot.' And before that other little madam gets her claws into you, she thought. Though was careful not to say it out loud.

Adam made a half-hearted protest. 'It might not be appropriate, not with Lou away. They're all worried about her and Gordon.'

'Don't talk soft. There'll be just the two of you out in t'garden. I'll see you aren't disturbed. You'd be daft to let this chance slip. There aren't many girls as nice as our Gracie. She's smashing.'

'Yes, yes, I know she is.' Adam was confused, marvelling at his own hesitancy. Not so long ago he'd been desperate for just such an opportunity, to be alone with Gracie for half an hour, ten minutes even, but always there had been Lou not far away, or else Gracie would refuse an invitation to go out with him. Now he came to think of it, those refusals might simply have been out of regard for her friend. Gracie was kind. Not the sort to let a friend down.

'But how do I know that she'd accept?'

'You don't, not till you ask, ye daft ha'porth.' Irma chuckled. 'Anybody with eyes in their head can see she's mooning after you. Off her food, moody and depressed, mind always drifting off some place. Been wandering about like a lovesick calf for weeks, she has, and who else could it be for but you? Get on wi' it, lad. Now's yer chance.'

Adam's heart gave an odd little thump. It was true, hadn't he noticed her odd behaviour himself? It thrilled him that she could feel this way, that any girl could love someone as awkward and shy as himself; a country bumpkin. And he'd fancied Gracie from the start, hadn't he? He was heartily sick of living alone with his mam. He'd every respect for the way she'd coped on her own, bringing up a child, developing this farm. She had guts, did his mam, but no one could deny that they'd led a lonely, somewhat restricted life. She'd be the first to say so, always going on about how he needed to take a wife, to bring some new blood into the place. Irma wanted grandchildren, and Adam wasn't against the idea. Not at all. If he didn't do something soon, the two girls would be packing up their bags and leaving Rusland, then where would he be?

'You must leave me alone with her, Mam. I can't be doing with any of your interfering. The last thing I need is you at my elbow while I'm doing the asking.'

'As if I would! No, no, I've every faith in you.' With a smile of gratification, Irma pinned on her hat, picked up her basket and declared she was off up the lane, to pay a call on Madge. 'I'll not be back till late,' she called cheerily and, giving a saucy wink, sailed out through the front door.

Adam stood gazing out into the back garden where he could see Gracie wandering about among the flowers, scenting the roses, plucking a few chrysanthemums to bring indoors later. She looked lovely, her long pale hair glowing in the golden light of evening. A chap would be lucky to get her.

He asked himself why he hesitated; why he wasn't eager to dash out and join her and say those all-important words? Was it because their friendship had developed slowly, because he'd been a bit gawky and taciturn with her at times? He knew he wasn't good with women, particularly young pretty ones; hadn't had near enough practice, he supposed. And he did desperately want to get it right. Didn't he?

An image of Rose came unexpectedly into his head. The curve of her laughing mouth, that shining halo of ebony curls, those bewitching blue eyes. He'd felt quite relaxed with her, strangely enough. But then Rose was sweet and good fun, less serious than Gracie. They'd enjoyed a good laugh while making the Spam fritters. But she would never make a farmer's wife. His mam had said as much a dozen times, and she was usually right. It was important, Irma had explained, that he choose somebody quiet and sensible, somebody who'd be content to live in this remote backwater. Rose would be forever itching to go to dances, or to visit Carlisle for a spot of shopping. Light-minded and flighty, that's what his mother had called her. And she was usually right his mam, Adam repeated, as if by rote.

You have to think long-term, she was constantly reminding him. As a farmer, Adam understand such a philosophy.

He put on his tweed jacket, not his Sunday best but reasonably respectable nonetheless. He should look clean and decent for this important moment in his life. Then, allowing himself no further time for reflection, and before his shyness overcame him yet again, he went out into the garden and, like a good obedient son, blurted out his proposal.

Gracie was utterly taken aback. 'I can't quite take this in,' she said, fumbling for the right words. 'You aren't seriously asking me to marry you, are you?'

Adam instantly regretted his impulsive act, wanting to retract the offer forthwith, to say it'd all been a dreadful mistake. But that wouldn't have been polite. 'Aye,' he said, giving a slow, thoughtful nod.

'Oh.' A small pained silence. 'Well, I really don't know what to say. I really don't. It's so – so unexpected.' Gracie was dumbfounded, wondering how on earth she could possibly let him down easily without hurting him. She didn't love him. Not the least little bit, though she'd tried, oh, how she'd tried for it would have been the answer to everything. But she'd absolutely no wish to be his wife, to be anybody's wife. No, that wasn't true. She ached to belong to Karl, but he was a German, a prisoner-of-war, so how could she marry him? Oh, what a mess! If only she could just turn to Adam with a smile and say that she loved him too and would very much like to be his wife. But she couldn't. She simply couldn't get a word out. Her tongue seemed to be stuck fast to the roof of her mouth.

'You don't have to answer now,' he told her, his face serious. 'There's no rush. I mean, you can have time to think about it.'

'Thank you.' It was still there, that awkwardness she sensed between them, as if he were always mindful to be on his best behaviour with her, fearful of causing offence. She found her voice at last. 'We'll talk again. Perhaps tomorrow?'

'Yes. Fine. Like I said, there's no rush. I could ask you again in a day or two.' Adam suddenly experienced an awful certainty in the pit of his stomach that he wanted her to say no. He wanted her to say, thank you very much but no, she couldn't marry him. Hell's teeth, what was wrong with him? This was awful, and getting worse by the minute.

Gracie stood up, anxious suddenly to put an end to the embarrassment. She indicated the flowers, still held tightly in her hands. 'I'll put these in water, shall I? Then I think I'll be off to bed. Good night!'

'Good night!'

And without looking back, she walked quickly away.

When Lou returned, a day or two later, arriving very early in the morning as she'd caught the milk train from Liverpool, she walked past Gracie who'd rushed to the garden gate to meet her and straight into the house. She didn't say a word and, appalled by the bleakness of her expression, neither did Gracie. Moments later she was back, changed into her dungarees, her face now a mask of stubborn determination.

'Right, let's not stand about looking gormless. There's work to be done.' And jumping on to her bike, she pedalled away down the lane at a great lick, leaving Gracie to dash back into the house, pick up their snap tins, fling them into the basket hooked over her handlebars and pedal like mad to catch up with her.

The day passed like many another, in marking, felling and clearing, with not a word about what had gone on in Liverpool. Gracie didn't dare enquire what the news might be or whether Gordon were safe. It seemed clear to her that he wasn't or else that there was no definite news of any kind. Deciding that Lou would talk about it when she was good and ready, Gracie got on with the job.

They proceeded as usual, entirely professional, studying each selected tree, deciding which way they would bring it down, bearing in mind that it mustn't fall against the others. Serious damage could be done to all the stock if one came down in the wrong place.

'We'll put the dip here,' Gracie said, indicating a place on the trunk where she would make the first cut. Lou gave an impatient nod of agreement as if telling her to get on with it. The September day was warm and both girls were being plagued by flies and midges. Enough to make anyone bad-tempered, Gracie conceded, even if one wasn't filled with concern for a loved one. She set about making the wedge-shaped cut with her axe, as close to the bottom of the trunk as she could put it. The secret was to know how deep to make the cut. Not far enough and the tree could split; too far and it could rock over and fall in the wrong direction, which was dangerous.

Lou was usually meticulous, exercising faultless judgement. Today her expression was grim, body tight with tension. 'Leave it, leave it. That's enough, it'll go now.'

'No, I think not.' Gracie reached for the crosscut saw. 'Let's give it a bit more help with this. A little careful sawing should do the job nicely.'

But Lou didn't wait. She picked up her axe and, ignoring Gracie's shout, swung it at the tree with such ferocity that the trunk actually shuddered. Then, with an ear-splitting crack, it rocked, tipped, and began slowly to fall. At that moment Jeannie walked out into the clearing.

Lou sat on a fallen log and cried. She cried with such deep anguish, such utter desolation, it was as if she held a whole well of tears in her heart that she'd never reach the bottom of. The pain was so terrible she couldn't see how she could possibly bear it. It sliced her in two, clean through her breast bone, just like her axe through that damned tree. It would send her mad. 'I could've killed her,' she sobbed. 'I could've bloody killed her.'

'Och, never. I'm far too nifty on me pins,' Jeannie said, exchanging an anguished glance with Gracie who was sitting with one arm about her friend, holding her close. It was a relief to them both that she'd finally spoken.

Gracie said, 'Would you like to talk about it?'

The hush of the forest was deep and calming, broken only by the occasional trill of a song thrush, the flutter of a busy sparrow going about its business. Jeannie leaned over and whispered in Gracie's ear, 'I reckon it would be better if I left ye to it. She might open up more. Tell her not to fret. She's got enough on her plate right now. I'm fine.'

As Jeannie crept away, leaving a trail of blue cigarette smoke in her wake, Lou gave a great, shuddering sob, a quiver of pain rippling through her. 'She said I should stay.'

'Who did?' Gracie gently enquired.

'Gordon's mam. "You're his wife," she says. "You should stop here, wait for news with me." But I couldn't. I couldn't stay any longer. I couldn't bear to stand on that quay with all the other wives, just waiting and waiting. "I've a job to do," I told her. "Oh," she says, "and that's more important than our Gordon, I suppose." How could she say that? How could she think such a thing?'

'She was upset. She probably didn't know what she was saying.'

'As if I care a tinker's cuss about anything but Gordon. I don't want to live another second without him. Why doesn't she know that?' Lou looked up at Gracie, her eyes blotched and red with weeping, fresh tears even now welling up and spilling unchecked down her pale cheeks.

'You've had no definite news then?'

Lou shook her head. 'Not a word. They say that the powers that be, the Admiralty or whoever, probably know summat but they're not saying. Not till they're sure. Gordon's mam says no news is good news. "I'm not moving off this bloody pier till I see my son." And she expected me to do the same. Oh, but I couldn't, Gracie. I'd've gone mad. I have to do something. I have to work. Not because I want to, but because it's the only way I can deal with this – this terrible waiting.'

Gracie did her best to soothe her, to assure Lou that Gordon's mother would come to understand how she felt, once she was in a fit state to think at all. 'We all have to deal with these things in our own way.'

'What will I do if he doesn't ever come back? How will I live?'

'Don't,' Gracie said, wiping the tears from her cheeks, smoothing back damp tendrils of chestnut hair. 'Don't even think about that. He'll come back. You must believe it, Lou. Gordon will expect you to have faith, to keep up your courage. You must be strong.'

Lou thought about this for a long time, then pulling out her handkerchief, blew her nose, determinedly wiping away the sniffles. 'You're right. I must be strong. For Gordon.'

'Yes, for Gordon.'

'We'll face the future when it comes, eh?' And looking bleakly into the glittering brilliance of Lou's eyes, Gracie nodded, fighting back her own tears.

'Right then. Let's see if we can bring the next tree down in the proper place, shall we?'

Rose waited in breathless anticipation for Josh to respond. She jumped every time she heard the postman's cheery voice in the saloon bar of the Eagle's Head then she would hurtle downstairs. 'Any post for me?'

'No, love. Sorry.'

Nor did Adam call. She even went along to the parish hall one evening after work, to help Irma sort through the salvage, in the hope she might see him there, but only succeeded in getting roped in to pack clothes which were to be redistributed to some evacuees in Ambleside.

At the end of the evening, just when she was in despair, Adam arrived in his van, presumably to drive his mother home. She gave him her most dazzling smile, leaned through the open window to remind him of the pleasant supper they'd enjoyed together, and then, catching Irma's fierce glare, strolled away before the woman could accuse her of being too forward. Rose consoled herself with the thought that it would be a mistake for him to think her cheap or easy to win over. Nonetheless she was disappointed when, two weeks later, he still hadn't asked her out.

Then one morning, to her great distress and surprise, she had a bit of a show. Nothing much, not what you could call a proper period, but it alarmed her and, desperate not to lose the baby, she cried off sick and stayed in bed all day. Depression sank over her, like a huge black cloud.

Adam had not forgotten about Rose but he was feeling thoroughly confused. Gracie had come to him one evening as he'd been shutting up the hens and told him, hesitantly and with profuse apologies, that she really couldn't marry him; that she wasn't even sure she loved him. A part of him wanted to say that he understood and it really didn't matter. But he realised, in a flash, that it did matter. It mattered a great deal. He saw that if he didn't find a suitable wife he would be chained to his mother for life; tied to her apron strings like some idiot schoolboy. These traitorous thoughts were creeping more and more often into his head, filling him with guilt. Even as he and Gracie talked he could see her peering through the lace curtains, secretly watching them through the window. He couldn't go on like this. He really couldn't. Fond as he was of his mam, he had to find a way to break free. But she'd be dead against Rose. She'd make his life hell on earth if he chose anyone other than Gracie.

'Perhaps you need more time,' he told her.

'No, it isn't that.'

'Of course it is. Don't decide anything yet. I've said there's no hurry. What with the war to worry about, and Gordon missing, now isn't the time for decisions.' And he hurried away to tend to the cows, anxious to avoid any further explanations or excuses from Gracie, and the prying eyes of his mother.

The next day, at her wit's end to know what to do for the best, Gracie spoke to Rose about her problem. 'He's a very sweet, quiet man and I really don't want to hurt him. I never meant to give him the idea that — well, that there was anything at all between us. It's been difficult right from the start.' And she explained about Irma persuading Adam to take her to the dance and then contriving to leave them alone together.

Rose snorted with derision. 'That woman rules his life with a rod of iron.'

'Oh, she means well. Thinks she's doing the best she can by him but . . .'

'It's none of her business who he goes out with or wants to marry. You should've seen her face when she caught me having supper with him that time.'

'When was that?' Gracie was surprised but listened with interest to the tale and soon both girls were giggling. 'Maybe it's really you he fancies, and he only asked me to marry him to please his mother.'

'Surely not? No man would be that daft. Unless he's just confused and doesn't know what he wants. After all, that supper was just a one-off, a chance meeting in a way, because I was really looking for you. Adam and I haven't had much time to get to know each other.' Rose looked at her, wide-eyed with innocence. 'I wouldn't go after him, you know that, Gracie. Not if you wanted him.'

'Oh, but I don't want him. I mean, if you like him – you go ahead. Do you like him? You do, don't you?'

Rose's pretty mouth curved into a provocative smile. 'I wouldn't mind having a shot at it. I took rather a fancy to him the first moment I set eyes on him, stripped off and having a wash in that back kitchen. Very nice, I thought.'

Gracie's eyes were merry with laughter now. 'Oh, Rose, what a muddle. You fancy Adam, Adam fancies me, and I fancy . . .'

'Who? Who do you fancy?' Rose was instantly alert with curiosity. It seemed at times that everybody had someone to love them. Everybody that is except her. Lou not only had Gordon but also the adoring Luc. And everybody was fond of Gracie because of her long pale hair, pretty face and gentle manner. It really wasn't fair.

'Nobody!' Gracie was shaking her head, laughing as if the very notion were ludicrous, though not too convincingly, Rose noticed. She'd keep an eye on Gracie. Didn't they always say that still waters run deep? 'I simply meant that I don't fancy Adam. Oh, dear, what am I going to do about him?'

Rose fluttered her lashes. 'Leave it to me. I'll sort our Adam out. With your permission, of course?'

'Oh, you have it, Rose. Indeed you do.'

Chapter Twenty-one

Rose realised that she would need to make her move with care. No blundering in or trampling over his feelings. No Mata Hari-type seduction. The last thing she wanted was to scare Adam off. She chose a Wednesday evening when Irma was entertaining her friends to one of her regular supper parties. Gracie had told her that Adam usually stayed out in the fields till quite late, anxious to keep out of their way, but in recent weeks had taken to popping round to the Eagle's Head later for a swift half with his friends, perhaps because winter was drawing on. This evening when he called Rose was waiting for him. He seemed flatteringly pleased to see her.

'I'd forgotten you said that you lived here.' It was a lie. No real drinker, normally coming only on a Friday to play darts with his mates, Adam had become quite a regular at the Eagle's Head recently. 'Can I get you a drink? What'll it be?'

Rose, mindful of the child starting to grow within the safety of her still flat abdomen, smiled. 'A lemonade would be nice.'

'Aye. Right.' He approved of that. Even his mother would've approved. She never had a good word for lasses who drank. He brought her the lemonade and a half shandy for himself. They sat and sipped their drinks contentedly together.

'It must be hard work for you, running that place by yourself,' Rose said. 'It's a mixed farm, isn't it?'

'Aye. Sheep, a bit of dairy, and a few fields of crop vegetables, as decreed by the government in these troubled times. It's quite mild here in the Rusland Valley, and we plough every corner these days. Anyway, it keeps me out of mischief.'

Rose sipped at her lemonade. 'I used to do a lot of vegetable gardening myself when I lived in Cornwall. Tomatoes were my speciality. We had huge glass houses that ran the length of one wall. Grew cucumbers, lettuce, marrows, the lot. Fed the entire WTC training camp with my veg, I did.' She was suddenly stricken with panic, wondering what on earth had prompted her to reveal so much about herself. Yet he seemed pleased that she had. He was listening with rapt attention, his expression intense.

'By heck, I never realised that. Was it a big place then?'

'A large estate, yes. Oh, it wasn't ours. My brother . . . 'She paused, corrected herself. 'My ad-adoptive brother worked there as estate manager, but then it was requisitioned, of course, for the Timber Corps and Eddie stayed on as caretaker. I helped a bit.' An understatement if ever there was one. Even the mention of his name brought a chill to the back of her neck, as if he were breathing on it.

Adam picked up on her hesitation on that one stammered word. 'Were you adopted or him?'

'Me.'

'That must've been tough.'

'It shouldn't have been but you're right, it was in the end. I didn't know, you see, not until after my parents, my adoptive parents that is, were both dead. So I couldn't ask them whether it made any difference, my not being their own child.'

'I'm quite sure it didn't,' Adam said kindly. 'They must have wanted you very much to have chosen you and taken you into their lives. They no doubt loved you just as if you were their own.'

Rose looked up at him, eyes filling with a rush of tears. 'What a very sweet thing to say. And you're right, they did love me. I tend to forget . . . after . . . after the things Eddie said and did. They spoiled me rotten, in fact. It was he who . . . well, he was jealous. I can understand how he must have felt, having his nose pushed out of joint by this little squirt who'd suddenly been foisted upon him.'

Adam said nothing. After a moment, Rose took a deep breath and went on, 'He wasn't very kind to me, you see.' And suddenly it all came spilling out: the resentment Eddie had felt towards her, the constant criticism and bullying, the way he'd made her do all the chores, waiting on him hand and foot. 'Even had me waiting on Gertie, who was supposed to be the housekeeper, for heaven's sake. I worked my socks off in that place, without a word of gratitude.' And before she could stop herself, she'd launched into the tale of Dexter Mulligan.

'Are you saying the man tried to . . . That he actually attempted to – to rape you?' Adam was filled with horror at anybody doing such a terrible thing, particularly to Rose, who seemed so young and fresh and innocent.

'Oh, he tried right enough. Not that I gave him a chance. I poured hot custard all over his ardour. That cooled him off, I can tell you.'

'*Custard!*' And Adam put back his head and roared with laughter. Rose laughed along with him because suddenly she saw that it was funny as well as a waste of good custard. This was the point in her mind where she always drew the story to a close. 'By heck, Rose love, you're a one, you really are. A proper card.'

She looked quickly down at her clasped hands. Now was the moment, her best chance. 'I heard you'd asked Gracie to be your wife. Is that right?' When he didn't answer immediately, she sneaked a sideways glance up at him from under her lashes.

'Did she tell you?'

Rose nodded. 'I was surprised. I never realised you and she were, well — you know — close.'

Adam experienced a sudden urge to agree, to say that she was quite right, they weren't in the least bit close. But how could he say that? She'd think he'd run mad. Not even a daft lump of a farmer would propose to someone they weren't close to, or at least imagined they were. He cleared his throat, desperately struggling to find an answer to his dilemma. He couldn't ever remember getting himself into such a pickle, and all because he'd acted on impulse. You should never rush at anything. Hadn't he said that all his life? And he shouldn't always listen to his mother. She didn't know everything. 'It was a mistake.' There, he'd said it. The words just spilled out of his mouth of their own accord. 'I should've given it a bit more thought like, afore I asked her. I weren't thinking clearly.'

Rose was nodding sympathetically. 'You've changed your mind then?' Her voice was soft and gentle, coaxing him to confide in her.

'Aye, you could say so.'

Now he was gazing at her with such fervent appeal for understanding, such adoration in his eyes, that Rose found herself actually blushing. 'Is this because . . . because of what happened the other day between you and me? We were rather cosy at that supper, I suppose. I thought, for a minute there when you were holding my hand, that you might be about to kiss me. Not that I'd've minded. Was quite looking forward to it, actually. But then your mam came in. Never do have good timing, do they? Mothers.'

Adam grinned, relishing her sense of humour, feeling a surge of joy at those simple words: *quite looking forward to it*. He had definitely wanted to kiss her, which at the time had surprised him since he'd already made up his mind that Gracie was the girl for him. It amazed him that Rose had felt the same way. Now he knew with a certainty that excited him that it was Rose he wanted. She was different. Exciting. Irreverent almost. 'I'd made up me mind to ask her, you see, so I did. But even as I said the words, I kept thinking about you. Only it was too late.'

'It's never too late,' Rose said, edging closer to him on the wooden settle.

Adam fell silent for a long moment, staring into the fire as he considered the problem from all angles. Even if he managed to explain it to Gracie, which would be embarrassing, there was also his mother to consider. He'd have to talk her round, and she wouldn't like it. Irma had set her heart on having Gracie as a daughter-in-law, even to the extent of offering to give up the front bedroom so the pair of them could move in once they were wed. Adam doubted she'd be so ready to give up her bed for Rose who she still insisted on calling 'that little madam'. Yet what did his mother know? She wasn't the one getting wed, was she?

Rose rubbed her cheek gently against his shoulder, reminding him she was still there, and he felt a surge of excitement spear his loins. He could actually feel the blood pounding in his member. By heck, but he'd never felt this way about anyone, certainly not quiet, dreamy Gracie who'd always seemed to be streets above him somehow. Cupping Rose's face with one hand, relishing the softness of her skin against the hardness of his, he put his mouth to hers and kissed her. She didn't cringe away, or stiffen, as Gracie had once done. She seemed to melt against him. He could feel her pert little breasts pressing up against his chest and himself growing shamefully hard. He let her go as if she'd scalded him and, breathing hard, looked earnestly into her eyes. 'What d'you reckon I should do about it?'

Rose said, 'I think you should tell her how you feel.'

'I can't do that. She'd be insulted.'

'No, I don't think so.' She thought quickly then added, 'It's true that Gracie might be a bit disappointed, but you'd just have to let her down lightly, wouldn't you? Use a bit of tact. Which wouldn't be hard, not for a nice, kind chap such as yourself. You'd just have to tell her, Adam, that we've fallen in love and there's nothing we can do about that, now is there?'

'Oh, Rose. It's true. I do love you, I do.'

'And I love you,' she said, lifting her mouth readily to his again as she slid her hands beneath his sensible tweed jacket so she could run them over his chest. 'We'll have to get married quickly, don't you think?'

'Why?' He couldn't leave her mouth alone: those soft pouting lips opening like a flower, that little pink tongue flickering against his. Christ, he could feel the reason they needed to get wed by the way the excitement was so quickly mounting in him – and that was before she'd slid open one or two of his shirt buttons and begun surreptitiously kissing the bare skin she discovered there. 'Eeh, Rose lass, give over. You'll have me undone.'

'Why don't we go for a walk, and you can undo me? That would be even more fun, don't you think?'

'No, no, I wouldn't take advantage of you. Never. I'm not like Dexter flippin' Mulligan.' He was panting now, desperate to get her alone and yet afraid of doing so, for fear of losing control. 'I'll talk to Gracie first thing tomorrow, when she gets home from work. How would that do?'

Rose laid her cheek against his rough lapel with a blissful sigh. 'And you'll speak to your mam?'

'Aye, her an' all. Then I'll go and see the vicar. Put up the banns. We don't have to wait long, Rose lass. We've somewhere to live, after all. You can move in with me. Mam'll give us front room.'

'Lovely. And Gracie and Lou can move in here, at the Eagle's Head. Irma could go and live with Madge, her best friend,' Rose decided. 'That would be perfect, don't you think?'

He was so dazed by the notion that this pretty young

woman actually loved him, his loins aching with lust, that Adam would have agreed to anything. 'Aye, happen that'd be for t'best. I'll have a word with her. Don't worry. I'll make it right, Rose. I promise.'

And as Rose kissed him again, she let him slide his hand very slowly up her skirt. It was as far as he was prepared to go but she'd got his promise. She knew he wouldn't go back on his word. What if he wasn't her lovely Josh? At least he was sweet and kind, and her baby would be born in wedlock, with a father, a roof over its head and good prospects in life.

'Is your mother in?' Rose faced the solemn-faced child behind the counter. 'I'd like a word.' Young Matthew turned and yelled through the door that led into the house behind the shop, and the plump figure of Madge emerged through the bead curtain.

Rose said, 'I hope you don't think I'm interfering but I'm concerned about Irma.'

'Oh?' A flash of curiosity from Madge then, as she noticed the interested group of children gathering about her, she shooed them all away, closing the door on them. 'Drive me mad, they do. So, what's up?'

'Well, I think she gets very lonely living out in the forest, all on her own.'

'She isn't on her own.'

'I mean with Adam out all day working on the farm and the girls in the forest. It isn't easy for her.'

The woman's eyes narrowed, looking like soft black raisins in folds of doughy flesh. 'So what are you saying?'

Rose smiled her angelic smile. 'It's none of my business, of course, but I know how much she loves children and I wondered if – well – if you don't mind my saying so, you look to be in need of another pair of hands, with all your brood.

Could she help out a bit, perhaps, in the shop? It would do her so much good to get out of that cottage more.'

Madge's face cleared. 'Oh, aye, she was always one for gadding, was Irma. In her day, that is.'

'Really?'

'Oh, aye. Allus enjoyed a good time, her and that lovely husband of hers. He died far too soon, poor man. Losing him so sudden made her rely too much on young Adam. Always a mistake. Fusses over that boy too much, in my opinion. Eeh, but I'd be glad of a bit more help round here, that's for sure, with this lot round me feet all day. Tell her to call in any time and we'll fix it up.'

Rose beamed. 'Thanks, that'd be lovely. I'm sure it would do her a power of good.'

As she made for the door Madge stopped her, fat fingers fastening on her arm. 'How come she didn't ask me herself? We've been friends for years.'

Caught off guard, Rose floundered for a moment. She'd got what she came for, somewhere to send Irma for a good part of each day in order to leave the field clear for her and Adam. The next step was to oust the old battle-axe from the cottage altogether. She knew Adam wouldn't find it easy to persuade his mother to leave. Rose believed that getting Madge on her side might help. But how to achieve that? She decided that honesty was the best policy in this instance. She allowed a small smile to curl the corners of her lovely mouth, and glanced shyly at Madge from beneath her lashes. 'The truth is, Adam and me, we're walking out.'

Madge's plump face broke into a wreath of smiles. 'So that's the way the land lies. And don't want Irma to queer your pitch?'

Rose laughed. 'Something of the sort.'

A plump fist thumped her in the shoulder. 'By heck, you should've said. Send her round. I'll keep her out of your hair. Everyone deserves a bit of fun in this bloomin' war.' And before

Madge could launch into her latest concerns over her own son, Rose thanked her, made her excuses and fled.

Adam was pleased, if a little nonplussed, by how well Gracie took the news that he was retracting his proposal. She didn't seem in the least surprised, even confessed that she'd guessed there was something between him and Rose, and wished them both every happiness. This made him feel better as it eased his sense of guilt.

'You'll come to the wedding then?'

Gracie laughed. 'That's quick. Is it all arranged?'

'It will be, just as soon as I've spoken to the vicar. There's no reason to wait, not with the war on and me already set up here.'

'Well, I'm delighted for you both, really I am.' And she kissed his cheek. Just a friendly peck but it confirmed to Adam that he'd made the right decision. He felt no surge of excitement with Gracie, nothing like he felt for Rose.

'Thanks for being so understanding,' he said. In fact, this whole interview had gone much more easily than he'd hoped. His mother was another matter.

'*You've what?*' Irma gazed upon her son as if he'd suddenly grown two heads. 'You've asked that little madam to be your wife instead? Have you lost your reason? She'll run rings round you, great gormless lump that you are.'

'It's no good you talking like that, Mam. I love Rose.'

'Love!' Irma said the word on a loud snort. 'Remember Tim Benson, poor man? He thought himself in love with that Dora what came over from Barrow. Right piece of fancy goods she was. Ruined his life, she did.'

'Oh, Mam, don't start. I'm not Tim Benson, and Rose isn't Dora or a "piece of fancy goods". She's not what you think, she's not a city girl at all. She used to grow tomatoes and cucumbers, all sorts of vegetables, on a big estate in Cornwall.

Even fruit for her own jam. She'll settle on the farm grand, I know she will. Anyroad, like it or not, we're getting wed, and there's an end of the matter.'

'Well!' said Irma. 'Well, I never did.' It was the first time, the only time in her recollection, he'd ever defied her. She pursed her crimson mouth to show her disapproval, and when that failed to move him, wagged an admonishing finger. 'Well, when it all goes wrong, don't come crying to me. You'll rue the day, m'lad. See if you don't. You'll rue the day you ever clapped eyes on that little hussy.'

'Don't call her that!' Adam's patience snapped and in a tone which brooked no argument he told his mother that he'd not hear another word against his fiancée. 'She's to be my wife, and I'll have her treated with proper respect. I'll not have you make trouble for her. I'll not have Rose upset, Mam.'

Irma's eyes filled with a rush of quickly manufactured tears as she realised she'd overstepped an invisible mark. 'Eeh, I'm sorry, love. I'd not fall out with you neither, not for the world. You're me only son after all. All right, I'll admit it, she's not what I would've chosen for you but if she's what you want, I'll not stand in your way, lad. I want you to be happy.'

'We will be. I just don't want any trouble, that's all.'

'There won't be any, I promise.'

Adam nodded, appeased by what he saw as this display of contrition. 'And I shall expect you at the wedding. We both will.'

'I wouldn't miss it for the world,' Irma drily remarked.

Satisfied that he'd made his point; had in fact dealt with an emotionally tricky situation which, without the prospect of Rose's love to look forward to, would have been quite beyond his ken, Adam, whistling softly to himself, went happily off to see the vicar, quite forgetting to mention that Rose expected his mother to move out of Beech Tree cottage.

✳   ✳   ✳

Gracie was heartily relieved to be free of Irma's matchmaking as well as Adam's painfully awkward courtship, but she felt desperate to see Karl. The POWs hadn't worked with them for a week or two and she was in an agony of frustration; her mind in a turmoil, filled with questions, busily devising persuasive arguments against why he must not get involved in any reckless escape plan. She had to make him see that waiting patiently for the war to end was their best hope. If only they could have the chance to talk, like other couples, how simple life would be. But then, if they were like ordinary couples they wouldn't have this problem.

Whenever she and Lou wheeled their bicycles along the lane to post their letters, Gracie would be constantly scanning the prisoners on their exercise drill, searching for a glimpse of his familiar figure. She was always fearful Karl might simply have gone, without even a goodbye.

At last he came, with Erich as usual. One day the pair simply turned up, with a guard, and got on with their work. Gracie struggled not to reveal the rush of pleasure she felt simply at the sight of him, yet felt oddly conspicuous, as if people were watching her. She was almost sure she saw Rose glance curiously at her and make some remark to Lena, but no, it was probably only her fraught imagination.

She couldn't take her eyes off him and almost didn't care if people did notice. A part of her wanted the world to know of their love, as if in some way it might protect him. Desperate to snatch a few moments alone with Karl, she was thwarted by Alf who kept the two men working with him on the felling. There was no opportunity for a single moment alone. Only once, when Gracie was handing out cheese sandwiches, did she risk a comment, as bland and inconsequential as she could make it since the others were sitting close by and could easily hear.

'I was in a terrible rush this morning and chose boring old cheese yet again. Always a mistake to take the easy option. One should never make decisions in a hurry, don't you agree?' Gracie stared hard at Karl as she held out the sandwich, willing him to understand that she wasn't just talking about choosing her lunch.

He glanced up at her, the love that shone from his eyes carefully veiled by half-closed lids. He grunted something noncommittal as he politely took the sandwich from her, though she saw he'd brought his favourite black bread with him, which his mother sent him from home. '*Dankeschön.*'

Only once after that did he glance across in her direction, his eyes telling her to have faith and courage, to believe in his love. Blinded by a sudden rush of tears, Gracie got the crosscut saw caught in a knot on the wood and wrenched at it impatiently. Blood spurted and she looked blankly at her hand, stunned by the sight of an open wound where the blade had cut deep.

'Stupid girl! Thoo shouldn't be using that saw on yer own.' As if it wasn't bad enough that Alf had again spotted her behaving carelessly, Lou insisted she get on her bike right away and head straight for the doctor's surgery.

'It might need stitches. You can't take any chances. That cut looks deep.'

She tried to protest but it was no use. Gracie was forced to leave and the next day was put on to paperwork until the wound healed a little. She gave up all hope of ever seeing Karl again.

Though the squad still worked well together on the surface, Lou could sense a deep undercurrent of gloom and unease running beneath. People were growing short-tempered, making mistakes and growing careless. Gracie was either a bag of nerves or falling into long silences, not at all her usual placid self. As for Rose, the bright and cheerful girl who'd once seemed so keen to be a part of their team, she tended to burst into tears at the slightest provocation. Tess and Lena spent far too much time sitting playing cards in their room above the Eagle's Head, and even Jeannie had been a bit below par in recent weeks, clearly affected by the general mood of depression.

It was this evidence of low morale which brought Lou out of her own doldrums. Here she was, a newly promoted forewoman, and her team were falling apart before her eyes. What good would that do? Either for themselves or for poor Gordon, wherever he was. There was nothing she could do about her husband, except wait and hope for the best. But there was something she could do about her friends.

The autumn days were golden with sunshine, warm and sweetly scented with woodland bonfires, although they were growing ever shorter and soon another winter would be upon them. Lou decided that a change of scene might be the very thing to buck everyone up, before it was too late. She didn't announce her decision until she'd made all the necessary arrangements.

Fourteen days working on a logging project up at Loweswater. They'd sleep in an old army tent, cook on an open fire, swim in the lake, have a lovely time in the back of beyond, she told them. 'It'll be just like old times. Porridge for breakfast, sardines or cheese sarnies for dinner, and sweaty socks put out to air each night. But no singing in the morning, please, a dawn chorus really gets on my wick.'

Nobody cheered or smiled or welcomed the proposal. And no one expected to have the energy to sing or was in the least fooled by Lou's counterfeit brightness, but they admired her courage and agreed to give it a try.

Only Gracie openly objected to the idea of two weeks away and suggested that perhaps one would be sufficient.

Lou said, 'Fourteen days. That's the agreement. We'll still be working, don't forget. It's not entirely a holiday.' And that was an end of the matter.

Chapter Twenty-two

They drove out on the coast road. To the right rose the folds of the Lakeland hills, climbing ever higher to frost-bleached mountains dappled by purple heather. To the left lay lush green pastures that swept down to the slate-grey Irish Sea. They passed through mining villages, rows of stone cottages stoutly facing the open fells and the harsh winds that blew across them. Then the lorry rattled on over an empty landscape broken only by the solid dark shapes of Herdwick sheep with the distinctive blaze of white on their regal heads.

They parked the lorry by the side of the lake and only then realised they would have to transport everything across by boat or, since they didn't have one of those, would be forced to trek all the way round, following the woodland path. There was a strong scent of resin in the air, smoky blue hills in the distance. The rocks and roots underfoot were slippery with moss. The sighing of the wind through the trees and the gentle chuckle of waves lapping on the shingle made Gracie shiver. The sense of loneliness seemed suddenly acute, as if they were balanced on the very edge of the world.

Would this be how it would feel without Karl, without even the hope of seeing him again? This aching emptiness, as if a part of her were gone for ever? She shook the notion away. Being morbid wouldn't help one bit.

In the smooth flatlands at the foot of the lake lay a white-walled building which they learned later to be Watergate Farm. It was here, each morning, they would come to collect milk and even the occasional egg, if they were lucky and the farmer's wife was feeling generous.

They pitched their tent in Holme Wood, far enough away from the water's edge to avoid flooding, well away from the logging chute, yet safely within the shelter of Carling Knot which rose up behind the woods, a dark hump on the landscape. Lou announced that each morning they would climb or race each other up this hill, for exercise.

'Not *every* morning?' Lena said, eyes widening in dismay.

'No, of course not,' Lou agreed. 'Not every morning. Some days we'll swim in the lake or go up that one instead,' indicating Darling Fell, the hill on the opposite shore, below which they'd parked their lorry.

The beauty of the spot alone should help to heal their wounds, Lou thought, as she said her usual prayers for Gordon's safety that night, tucked deep inside her sleeping bag. She prayed, too, that the silence and peace of this place would do the same favour for her.

In a way it did feel as if they were raw recruits again, back in Cornwall. They half expected Matron to storm in at any moment and shout 'Stand by your beds'. Except that this was worse.

Here, there was no morning queue for the wash basins because there weren't even any bathrooms. Tess and Jeannie dug a latrine, while Lena and Gracie filled water buckets, at least on that first morning. For lighting they had a hurricane lamp. There was neither table nor chair, nothing more than an old wooden bench upon which three people could sit, at a squeeze. They took it in turns. There were no bunk beds, only blankets pinned together to use as sleeping bags on the hard ground. Gracie had already learned to scoop out a hollow in the compacted earth in order to make it more comfortable and she'd been so tired by nightfall, she could have slept on a washing line. But the autumn dawn had a sharpness to it and she'd woken early to lie worrying about Karl and the proposed escape plan.

How could he even consider helping his friend? Why take the risk? Fear swelled in her like an unstoppable growth, destroying the last fragile traces of her happiness. She felt as if she must fight to claw her way up from some dark place where she'd really rather stay with her head under a pillow. It would be warm and safe, and she'd wait there until the war was over and Karl would be free to love her. In the beginning, the war had seemed like a game. Now she saw only the tendrils of its evil, spreading and poisoning everything in its path. Once she'd been young and thirsty for adventure. Now she felt like an old woman who had lived too long.

Tess's voice came out of the cold grey dawn. 'God, this is awful. Why on earth did I give up my nice cushy post driving officers around in classy Jeeps for this?' And since everyone shared her dismay at their living conditions, nobody had a reasonable answer.

'Some holiday,' Jeannie groaned, burying her head deep beneath the blankets.

Tempers grew ever shorter in the overcrowded sleeping conditions and there was none of the friendly chatter or the sharing of confidences that they'd enjoyed at the initial training camp. The girls took to avoiding each other, spending more and more time out in the open although slowly, bit by bit, the chores got done, the camp was set up and a routine established. Flour and oats, tins of Spam, powdered egg and sardines were all stowed away safely under a tarpaulin, where hopefully they wouldn't get nibbled by marauding red squirrels or other wildlife. Tess built a fireplace for cooking with a crane to swing over it, upon which she hung a large billy can.

'Now we can brew a cuppa,' she proudly announced.

'Home from home,' Rose tartly agreed.

'Well, I think it's great.' This, surprisingly enough, from Lena. Everyone froze her with a quelling glare. She was really getting far too agreeable.

Steadfast in her determination to hold everyone together, Lou refused to become embroiled in any further argument. She pinned up a duty rota, listing who would be responsible for cooking, disinfecting the lats, or cleaning out the tent each day. To her great disappointment, instead of easing relations, this seemed to create even more ill feeling.

'You've got me on breakfasts twice in the first week. That's a bit much, don't you reckon?'

'Dinna ask me to light a fire with two matches.'

'But I thought you were in the Girl Guides?'

'Aye, but they drummed me out.'

'How can I tidy this tent if there's bedding and clothes scattered all over the place? It's not my responsibility to clean up after other folk.'

'I'm not stripping off and washing out in the open. We might get Peeping Toms. Or spiders in the wash basins. I hate spiders.'

'And I'm going nowhere near those lats. That's a stinking job.'

Lou cajoled and pleaded, persuaded and coaxed, explaining that everyone had to take their turn at each and every job. 'That's the only fair way.' And finally she sat everyone down and gave them all a good stiff talking to. This calmed tempers considerably but relations continued to be scratchy. Her ambition to lift spirits and give them all a break didn't seem to be going at all according to plan.

Somehow they got through that first weekend, and on Monday morning were introduced to their new ganger, a rather desperate-looking old man in flat cap, muffler and waistcoat, who might have been more at home at a city football match than standing knee-deep in reeds with only a gang of Timber Girls for company. He was clearly even more unused to working with women than poor Alf, who was only slowly growing accustomed to the idea and was probably quite relieved to be rid of them for a week or two.

'Have thoo done owt like this afore?' he asked, a plaintive note in his nasal voice.

'No,' they said, almost of one accord.

'Victory is ours.'

As the days passed, the work became a refuge for them all. It demanded all of their attention so that conversation became confined to the barest essentials.

The felled larches, destined to be telegraph poles, were brought down by chute from above, through the oak woods which bordered the lake, each falling into the water with a satisfying splash. From here they were towed across by boat to the road on the opposite shore where the logs were then winched on to the back of a lorry and taken to the sawmill. Tess, for one, was relishing the prospect of driving a boat. 'Make a nice change, and it's another new challenge,' she said brightly.

Rose objected, declaring it would make her seasick. She didn't tell them she felt sick most of the time these days, and her stomach ached, partly due to the baby, she supposed.

Nobody took her remark too seriously but simply laughed, as if she'd made a silly joke. Then nobody ever did take her seriously these days. They even seemed to think it amusing that Adam should change his mind about who he intended to marry.

As if the very idea of anybody loving silly little Rose was utterly ridiculous.

In reality, she'd much prefer to have married Josh but since she hadn't heard a word from him in weeks, beggars couldn't be choosers, as they say. Rose had decided that he'd either been relocated or else was unable to help her because of his clinging wife. Nobody understood or even cared how hurt she'd been by his defection. They saved all their sympathy for Lou and her agony over a missing husband, or for pretty Grace with her long pale hair, classical good looks and lovely grey eyes. No wonder Adam had thought her the perfect wife; she was so fragile and winsome there were times when Rose almost hated her. She'd even noticed that German POW – what was his name – Karl? – watching her with covert but very real interest. But then she was a dark horse, was little Gracie. Who knew what went on in the secret recesses of her agile mind, or when nobody was looking? Everyone seemed to forget how well she could stand up for herself, and how determined she could be to get her own way when it suited her.

Perhaps, Rose thought, she should make herself more noticeable. She should do something truly dreadful, then they might all start listening to her for a change. Something like trying to drown herself, for instance. That would make them all feel thoroughly guilty for ignoring her. Though perhaps death was a touch drastic. She was young; had a lot of living to do yet. But she did start to wonder how long one could hold one's breath underwater. The notion of sinking beneath those sparkling, rippling waves became so strangely tempting, she found herself mesmerised by their beauty.

Their new ganger, known simply as Bill, directed them in the skills of rafting with a benevolent hand. He was a kindly man, if somewhat taciturn, with far more patience over their blunders than Alf had ever exhibited.

As the timber came down the chute, Tess and Lena would wait in the motor boat while the others stood, thigh-deep in water, ready to direct and position the logs. These were fastened together by means of a long chain, 'dogs' or long pins hammered into the butt end of the trees. A strong rope was then looped around the centre log of the raft and fixed to the stern of the boat which set out across the lake, pulling the raft behind it.

It was precarious but exciting work, particularly when, as now, the logs were bobbing and crashing about. The girls had to take care not to skin their hands on the rough bark or, worse, get trapped between poles while struggling to fix on the chains. But everyone was putting their utmost into the job, desperately trying to prove that the squad could still work well together. And it certainly made a welcome change to be out on the open water in the sunshine, instead of in the depths of a forest.

But would it lift everyone's spirits and improve morale? Since there was little sign of that happening so far, Lou began to feel inadequate, as if she were failing them in some way. As new forewoman she was the one responsible for the health and happiness of these girls, and she'd wept many a silent tear into her pillow in the dark of night, not only for Gordon but also worrying over whether she could cope with her new responsibility. Their health and well-being seemed to be entirely in her hands. Was she doing things right? When the girls came to her with their problems, could she supply the answers? This was the hardest job she'd ever done. Would they come out at the end of the two weeks recovered from the glums, or would they all have murdered each other by then?

Lou's thoughts again turned to Gordon. She always thought of him as steaming across a beautiful blue sea rather than in the thick of an unknown battle. Never one to dwell on gruesome details, she absolutely refused to imagine his ship sunk or blown to smithereens. If she didn't see it in her mind, then it couldn't possibly have happened. So long as she kept believing in him, Lou knew he would come back to her. One day.

'It's good fun, isn't it?' she called out, a determined brightness in her voice as she turned to address Rose standing close behind her in the water. At least she had been there, only a moment ago. 'Rose?' Lou turned her gaze all around. It took seconds to realise that the girl was nowhere in sight. Lena and Tess were in the boat, Gracie and Jeannie by the chute, she and Rose were . . . 'Rose!'

Without pausing to consider the consequences of her action, Lou dived underwater and began to search frantically about. It was frightening to swim in the green gloom beneath the logs. She felt trapped, as if her lungs were bursting, and was finally forced to come up for air, though only for a second before again she dived. The others by this time had noted her alarm, and they too were in the water, searching, diving and swimming everywhere in a desperate bid to find their friend.

'She's here. I've got her,' Tess called out, bursting from the depths in a spray of sparkling water to begin towing Rose's limp body to the sanctuary of the boat. She clung on to the edge of it with one hand while Lena and Gracie struck out strongly towards her, anxious to assist.

Lou wanted to ask what the hell had happened, had she hit her head, what on earth had caused her to fall under the logs, but now wasn't the time for interrogations. Rose was deadly pale, coughing up half the lake, but was at least alive.

Rose seemed to be none the worse for her ducking, though perhaps a touch more subdued. This wasn't at all what Lou had had in mind when she'd arranged to bring them all on this logging camp. She'd hoped it would lift spirits, not deepen their gloom. Cheer them all up, like a sort of busman's holiday. At least caring for Rose gave everyone something else to think about instead of grumbling among themselves.

She was fussed over a good deal that evening; supplied with endless cups of hot cocoa, extra pillows and blankets throughout the night, checked hourly as the girls took it in turn to make sure she hadn't caught a chill or wasn't about to sink into concussion. When she vomited, just before dawn, it was Gracie who mopped her face with freshly warmed water and lent her a clean night-dress.

'It's swallowing all that lake water,' she consoled her. 'You'll feel better soon.'

Rose had half hoped to be relieved of her problem as a result of the 'accident'. Unfortunately, not a spot of blood had shown itself during the night. Yet instead of being cast down by this, secretly she felt relieved, almost taking pride in the fact that her baby was safe and well; as much an unresolved secret as ever. 'I can't think how it happened. I must have slipped and bumped my head,' was the only explanation she could offer.

The incident proved to be a turning point. It seemed to make them all realise how much they depended upon each other, how they must all pull together to win through, and how fragile and short life was. As a result, over the following days the atmosphere lightened considerably. It was as if a weight had been lifted and the odd chorus of 'Off to work we go' could at times be heard, drifting across the glistening water.

The evenings too grew more lively. Lou would bring out a pack of cards and they'd play poker or something silly like Snap or Happy Families, shouting, laughing and being thoroughly noisy and loud, since there was no one within miles to hear.

'I never knew you could get this merry on a mug of tea,' Tess chuckled.

'It's the smoky flavour that does the trick,' Gracie quipped. 'Beats alcohol every time.'

Lou looked around at her dear friends with pride in her

heart. It was all turning out fine. She should have had more faith in them, more faith in herself. Everything was going to be OK.

On the last evening they lit a camp fire and toasted their cheese sandwiches over the hot embers and talked. They discussed the sense of independence wearing the Timber Corps uniform had given them; how they loved the job and how intense life seemed because of the war. Friendships seemed to be far more important, something to be cherished and enjoyed, for nobody knew quite how long they might last. Even this squad, they realised, could be split up and posted to different destinations at a moment's notice. The best of times, the worst of times.

'At least I don't have my parents hanging around, telling me what to do all the time,' Gracie said. 'Or blaming me when things go wrong.'

'My brother was always good at picking fault,' Rose put in, and glanced over her shoulder, as if she half-expected him to emerge out of the shadows. There were nights when she woke in a cold sweat, when she still heard his shock and fury as she'd locked him in the cellar. That sound had haunted her for months.

'Have you ever heard from him?' Lou wanted to know, but Rose only shook her head and said that she'd no wish to hear, thank you very much; that he was nothing but trouble.

'Aren't you going to invite him to the wedding?'

'No.'

'Oh, he can't be all bad. Nobody is. He has his problems, no doubt, like the rest of us, but most men are softies at heart.'

'Not Eddie.'

Lou chuckled. 'Even your Eddie will have his weak spot, if we could but find it. You really must invite him, then he can give you away.'

'You talk as if the world is all sunshine and light, but it isn't. There's a great deal of nastiness in this world, and evil, in both men and women. I've certainly seen plenty in my short lifetime. I don't want to talk about Eddie, not ever again, if you don't mind.'

Lou shrugged. 'What about Adam? Do you think he's weak or just a nice, quiet man? He certainly allows Irma to rule the roost. It'll take a strong woman to stand up to her. Question is, are you up to the task, girl?'

Rose gave a short laugh, a slight curl to her upper lip. 'I'm quite certain I am. I'll stand no nonsense from that old besom. Look how well I handled Gracie here, sidelining her nicely for all she thought she could have both men. Quite a charmer she is on the quiet, our Gracie.'

There was a sharp intake of breath, puzzled glances in Gracie's direction, followed by a curious, drawn out silence.

'Both men? What are you talking about?'

Rose broke the silence on a soft chuckle. 'She hasn't told you then about her prisoner of love? Her passion for a German?'

Gracie could feel her cheeks start to burn, her heart start a slow, hard beat in her chest. 'Rose, I really don't think we need go into all of that. Not just now.'

'Why not? You encouraged Adam only as a cover for your real feelings. Isn't that the truth of it? I know you and Karl are having a secret love affair. I wasn't born yesterday. It's written all over his face whenever he looks at you. It's written all over yours now. Besides, I've seen you talking to him in that intense way and sneaking off into the bushes when you think no one is looking.'

Again everyone turned to look at Gracie and she knew she was flushing bright crimson. Lou said, 'Is this true? Are you having an affair with that POW?'

Gracie looked into her friend's shocked face and thought of Gordon, perhaps even now lying dead beneath the waves from an attack by a U-boat, the kind that Karl had once served in. She said nothing for a whole thirty seconds, then she nodded. 'It's not our fault. It just happened, right out of the blue. We can't help it.'

'But that's terrible! A betrayal of all we stand for.'

'I don't see it that way. We just fell in love. Where's the crime in that? Are you going to tell on us?' She waited with trepidation for their response.

Nobody answered. In a way it would have been easier if they'd argued with her, saying that he was the enemy and she'd no right to love him. Then she could have defended Karl, told them how lovely he was, how sweet and kind, how he had only been doing his duty as they were; how he was the one man in the whole world she could spend her life with. But they said nothing, simply looked at her with varying degrees of shock and disapproval. Even Lou seemed determined to say no more, her mouth buttoned tight in uncharacteristic condemnation. At length Gracie could bear it no longer. With a little cry of distress, she stumbled to her feet and fled. When the others crawled into their sleeping bags later, nobody spoke a word and Gracie pretended to be asleep.

Chapter Twenty-three

Nobody spoke to her the next morning either. Breakfast was made and eaten in an uneasy silence. Gracie detected some subdued murmurs between the other girls but no one, not a single person, addressed her. All the way home in the lorry they chatted quietly among themselves. Gracie was ignored. It was almost as if she were not there, or as if it would contaminate them to speak to her. It was perfectly clear that they'd sent her to Coventry. They were treating her as if she were a traitor.

She attempted to console herself that perhaps it was because they believed she'd been leading Adam on, using him to cover up her indiscretion. Maybe that's what had upset them. She decided to seek his help.

Gracie found him in the cow shed as she'd expected and told him, quite bluntly and without preamble, what the problem was. 'Normally I wouldn't have said a word about this, because of the risks to Karl and to myself, but the others know all about it now and they won't say how they are going to react to the knowledge. They seem to be accusing me of leading you on, of using you as a cover for this illicit affair, but that's not true. I wouldn't do that to you, Adam. You know I never encouraged you in your fancy for me. And if it appeared as if I did, I'm sorry. I never meant that to happen. Will you please explain this to them? Will you? It would mean so much to me if you would. They might think less harshly of me.'

He stared at her, eyes narrowed as he struggled to digest the full import of what she'd told him. 'You love Karl Meinhadt? A German prisoner-of-war?'

'Yes.'

'And he loves you?'

'He does. You mustn't say anything. Nobody must know.' She was filled suddenly with fear that she'd done the wrong thing by being so open with him.

'And he was the reason you stayed to help me on the farm?'

Gracie drew in a sharp breath. 'That's true but I never, ever gave you the impression that I loved you. At least, if I did, I never meant to. I constantly refused your invitations to the cinema, your offers to go for a walk in the evening. Does that sound like someone who was deliberately using you?'

Adam seemed to be considering all of this with his usual deliberation and the fear inside her escalated. Was he going to agree with the girls' assessment of the situation? Had she made a terrible mistake in confiding in him? Would he now go to the authorities and tell them of her secret love? She felt her control start to waver and pressed a hand to her mouth.

He recognised her distress instantly and setting aside the feed bucket came towards her. 'It's all right, Gracie. I won't tell. If you truly love this man, you have my deepest sympathy. It isn't going to be easy for either of you. And you're right, you didn't lead me on, not in any way. I was the one doing the pursuing, at my mother's dictation.' He smiled in his self-deprecating way and Gracie smiled too, even though there were tears rolling down her cheeks.

'I did actually try very hard to love you Adam. You're such a nice chap, and it would have been . . .'

'Much more sensible?'

'Yes. Certainly safer.' She gave a little hiccup of near-hysterical laughter and again put her hands to her mouth. She felt as if she were balancing on the edge of a cliff and might, at any moment, fall off it.

Adam reached out, placed his great rough hands on her shoulders and pulled her into his arms. 'I didn't just court you because Mam told me to. I did like you, Gracie, only not as much as I like Rose. You know she's the girl for me, and she loves me too. It's because of how I feel about her that I can find it in my heart to feel sorry for you. Come on, chin up. The war can't last for ever.'

His kindness was too much and Gracie began to cry in earnest while Adam held her tight, cradling her in his arms, patting her gently, kissing her soft hair and making soothing, comforting noises. It was at this moment that Rose discovered them. She walked into the shed and, seeing Gracie in Adam's embrace, stood stock still for a moment before slipping out again, unobserved.

Following this distressing conversation with Adam, Gracie felt the need for air and took a stroll down the lane. The hedgerows were filled with rose hips and blackberries, elderflowers and sloes. Their sweet, fruity scents lingered in the air after a recent shower of rain. Irma would soon be bullying them all into another picking and jamming session, as if they didn't have enough to do already. Gracie smiled. Irritating as Irma was, she certainly believed in doing her bit for the war effort. On top of all her work with the salvage, the WVS and the WI, she was now helping Madge three days a week in her little shop. An amazing woman.

Normally, Gracie would have asked Lou to walk with her but her erstwhile friend was clearly avoiding her. Gracie had never felt so alone in all her life, utterly abandoned by her friends. She wondered if they were having a meeting, trying to decide whether to tell the authorities about her transgression. If they did, then Karl would probably be moved to another camp. Sorry as she would be to lose him, Gracie realised that such a move might be no bad thing. It might at least spare him from getting involved in this crazy escape plan of Erich's.

Oh, why did there have to be a war? Why must their respective countries be so at odds? Why couldn't they have met at some other time, a time of peace? Yet she'd read in the paper of women who had been married to Germans for years, living quite happily and peaceably here in England, who were now incarcerated in a camp on the Isle of Man simply because of their husbands' nationality. War surely didn't make every German into an enemy just because of Hitler and his Nazis?

She knew well enough what would happen if their love were ever discovered. Karl would appear before a tribunal or court martial. He would be moved to another camp where he would be kept under close confinement for a long time, perhaps even separated from fellow prisoners. It would be awful for him. And she had seen already the attitude she could expect, even from her best friends.

Could they ever hope for a normal future together? Surely everything must change soon when the war ended, but what then? Gracie understood perfectly well that if she married a German she would automatically lose her British nationality. They might not even be allowed to stay in this country. Loving Karl, she risked everything. In the end, though, even allowing for any lingering recriminations following the end of a bitter world war, the government couldn't keep them apart for ever, and then she would indeed risk anything, everything, to be with him.

Gracie was so engrossed in her hopes and fears that she didn't hear the approach of stealthy footsteps behind her, the soft breathing or the swish of a rope. Only when it swung around her, bringing her down, did she realise and cry out. Far too late.

'What the hell . . .?' She lay, winded, in the ditch, desperately trying to free herself from the strands of rope being swiftly lashed around her arms and legs. She recognised one of her assailants as the girl who had begged Adam to choose her as his dancing partner. The other proved to be Madge's eldest daughter, Molly.

Failing to fend them off, Gracie was reduced to begging them to stop, pleading with the pair to stop this madness. And then Molly produced a pair of scissors. They were large and shiny, the kind used by the village women for cutting up old coats and skirts to make patchwork blankets and clippy rugs.

'There's no need for those. Just untie the dratted rope for God's sake. What is this? Some sort of game?'

Two pairs of eyes glittered with menace. Molly said, 'We never play games.'

Gracie could feel a cold panic tightening her chest for she could guess the reason for the attack. Rose must have spoken to Madge at the shop, or to Molly, about her suspicions. God knows who else in the village knew by this time. The prospect turned her blood to ice.

The other girl yanked on the rope, making Gracie yelp as the cords cut into her flesh. 'Don't think you can just walk in to this village, steal Adam from under our noses then two-time him with a bloody German. You're a traitor, that's what you are. You nasty little cow!'

'Who told you? How did you find out?'

'We saw you canoodling behind the hedge.'

'I wasn't canoodling, we were . . .'

'Shut up!' She lunged at Gracie and, grasping a lock of her hair, chopped it off, quite close to the crown. 'Never leave a stump. Isn't that what you Timber Girls say? Cut as close to the root as possible.'

Gracie screamed, though this far from the house she held little hope of anyone hearing her. Nevertheless, she struggled frantically to free herself, knowing her efforts to be fruitless for the more she resisted, the tighter the rope bit into her wrists and legs, and the more terrified she became that the scissors might slip and cut more than her hair. And all the while her two attackers simply laughed.

When they were done, fronds of pale blonde hair lay scattered in the grass all about. Molly untied the rope and dragged it from Gracie's inert body. 'There'll be no danger of anyone loving you now, not looking like that,' she sneered. 'Not now you resemble a porcupine.' Shoving the scissors back into her pocket, the pair strolled away arm in arm, still chuckling.

Gracie made no attempt to move. She simply lay in the ditch and sobbed.

How long Gracie lay there she couldn't rightly have said but eventually she got shakily to her feet, brushed the grass and mud from her clothes and ran her hands over her head. All she could feel were bristles, standing out stiffly at odd angles. She couldn't begin to imagine how horrible it must look. She supposed she should be grateful that the two girls had only vented their wrath by cutting her hair and nothing worse. After she'd scrambled up the sides of the ditch, Gracie fell to her knees on the stony path, her legs giving way beneath her. Even when she finally managed to get to her feet, she felt so weak and shaky, she wondered if she could even walk. Somehow she managed it, stumbling along the lane towards Beech Tree Cottage, blinded by tears.

When she walked into the kitchen she found Lou and Irma making the evening meal. Gracie saw the flicker of shock in both pairs of eyes. Lou said not a word, simply stood unmoving, staring at her with that mournful, condemning expression. It was Irma who flew to Gracie's side, asking who on earth had done such a terrible thing.

Mindful of the fact that this could be but the beginning of local recriminations against her, Gracie simply shook her head, brushed Irma aside and went up to her room. If her friends had no wish to speak to her, then she wouldn't give them the satisfaction of asking for their sympathy.

Rose and Adam were married, without delay, in the parish church. It was a short, practical ceremony and Rose knew she looked beguilingly sweet and young in a blue velveteen frock which almost exactly matched her eyes. Afterwards they all went over to the parish rooms for sandwiches and cakes, naturally provided by her new mother-in-law ably assisted by her friend Madge. Rose even chose two of Madge's daughters, Rachel and Sarah, to be bridesmaids rather than any of the squad, thereby avoiding having to include Gracie. It was just as well, since nobody felt much like celebrating because of Gordon still being missing.

The only real disappointment was that there wasn't going to be a honeymoon. Adam was even against the idea of a couple of nights at the Eagle's Head because he couldn't leave the farm just now, he explained. Not that Rose minded too much. What need had she for champagne or an expensive honeymoon, or even the good wishes of her friends? She felt drunk with power. She'd got what she wanted, a husband and a father for her child. Rose knew how to stand up for herself, oh dear me yes.

She had, however, forgotten one thing. In all her careful planning and scheming, she'd given no further thought to Irma. When Rose and Adam returned to Beech Tree Cottage after the modest celebrations, it became startlingly clear that her new mother-in-law considered it still to be her home too, new wife or no. What's more, Gracie still occupied the same room with Lou, though as there was no longer any sound of happy chatter coming from it, Rose doubted this situation would continue for much longer. One or both of them would soon move out as relations between the two girls were dire.

But Rose hadn't bargained on sharing her new marital abode with anyone, least of all Irma. For the moment she must make the best of it, for the sake of her unborn child whose very existence she still secretly nursed below her heart. But if Rose had learned one thing in life, it was that nothing stayed the same for long. Things would change. It was only a matter of time.

Rose gazed upon her new husband in despair. 'Why won't you come to bed? What's wrong? Why won't you sleep with me?'

'I didn't say I wouldn't sleep with you. I said I can't sleep in that bed. It's too soft and there are too many blankets.'

'But it's a lovely bed. Big and wide with lots of pillows and a feather mattress. Gorgeous! It was very thoughtful of Irma to give it up for us.' Even if she is only sleeping next door, in the box room Adam previously occupied, Rose thought.

She'd been aware that he was a shy, quiet man, but this was utterly ridiculous. 'Come on Adam lad,' she teased, using the word as a term of endearment as it often was locally, particularly by Irma, thinking to please him. To her horror he stiffened and shrank away from the hand she reached out to him. She would have to tell him about the pregnancy eventually, of course, but not until she felt it safe to do so, when he could be fooled into thinking the baby she carried was his. Not for a moment had Rose imagined there would be any problem with this plan. Now she faced a huge obstacle. She first had to persuade her husband to make love to her, and since he refused even to get into bed, this was proving to be strangely problematic. Feeling thoroughly wretched, she lost patience and tossed the pillow and Irma's best pink eiderdown on to the floor. 'Sleep on the floor then. See if I care.' It wasn't an auspicious start to their marriage but then life seemed to be full of disappointments and Rose was quite incapable now of appreciating any problems beyond her own. Losing Josh had been painful but even if she didn't exactly love Adam, in the last few weeks she'd found herself growing quite fond of him. She certainly wasn't averse to a bit of a cuddle, or to them living a perfectly normal married life together as man and wife. What on earth could be putting him off? He thought her a virgin after all, ripe for the taking, and had seemed keen enough before they were wed. So what was his problem?

Annoyingly, he seemed to be taking her at her word, tucking the pillow under his head and wrapping the eiderdown around himself. He'd even lit up a cigarette and was just lying there, drawing hard on it; staring up at the ceiling with an expression of complete misery on his face.

Rose nibbled on her lip, biting back tears of frustration. She couldn't let this go on. She must do something. Losing patience with him wouldn't help one bit so she decided on a different tack. Reaching down to where he lay stretched out on the bedside rug, she tickled the end of his nose with the ribbon of her new nightie. 'It's not much fun up here by myself. Why don't you at least start off in the bed? See how you go on. How can we – you know – do it long distance?'

Adam gazed up at her, looking a bit sheepish, but made no move to join her. How could he? He didn't seem able to get it out of his mind that this was his mother's bed. Not only had she slept in it with his father in years gone by, but Adam himself had cuddled up to her in its vast softness when some childish ailment or bad dream had kept him awake. Making love in it, even to his adorable Rose, didn't seem quite – struggling for the correct word, he came up with an old-fashioned one – quite seemly.

'Don't you love me any more?' The words came out on a hiccup of misery, illustrating her utter wretchedness. Finally, moved by the tears in her sea-blue eyes, Adam put out the cigarette and climbed into bed beside her.

Rose snuggled up to him, delighted that he had finally succumbed to her charms. 'I thought for a minute I was going to spend my wedding night all by myself.' A thought came to her. 'I suppose you have had some experience? I mean, you have done it before? That isn't why you . . .'

' 'Course I have. What do you take me for? I'm no young boy or naïve fool. It's just that it's been a long time, Rose, and this bed is . . .' It was no good, he couldn't explain how difficult it was to make love to his lovely new wife in his mother's bed. It was too daft for words. It would make him look effeminate, a real weed, a mother's boy. 'I wouldn't want to disappoint you.'

'Oh, shut up, you talk too much. Let's start off with a bit of a cuddle and see what happens, eh?'

He certainly seemed eager to love her; tenderly kissing her, stroking her silky soft skin, caressing her firm young breasts. But nothing else happened. Rose made a valiant attempt, forcibly pushing the excitement of Josh's love making from her mind and concentrating entirely upon Adam. And if his striped pyjamas didn't excite her quite as much as Josh's sexy white shorts, what of it? They could still 'do the business', couldn't they? She nibbled his ear, ran her fingers through his hair, stroked his neck, unbuttoned the flannelette jacket and helped him to take off her nightie. But she might as well have been lying there in three layers of woollen combinations for all the good it did. She could actually feel his body trembling from head to foot, and it wasn't with passion.

'Don't be shy. Relax, it'll be fine.' Rose pulled his hand to her breast; gently nibbled at his mouth, easing it open with her tongue. He groaned, deep in his throat, and, sensing a shudder of excitement ripple through him, she felt a wild surge of exultation that he was about to go the distance. 'Ooh, that's nice,' she said, meaning to encourage him. 'Now we're getting somewhere.' But a little investigation proved they weren't getting anywhere at all. Limp as a wet lettuce, Rose thought, her heart plummeting to new depths of depression. Then, as if he couldn't bear for her to witness his failure, he suddenly jerked away from her, left the bed and abandoned the room altogether.

Rose stayed where she was, blinking back tears of hurt surprise and bitter disappointment. Why did it always have to go wrong for her?

Rose was deeply afraid. How could she tell Adam about the baby when, after two weeks, they still hadn't consummated their marriage? She was at her wits' end to know how to deal with the matter. Nor dare she seek help from her friends, all of whom seemed to think they were a perfect couple, happily married and enjoying a protracted honeymoon.

She continued to work with the squad in the forest, needing still to be a part of the group. Relations between Gracie and the other girls remained the same with her being cold shouldered, cut off entirely from their friendship and treated like some sort of pariah. The attack on Gracie had caused Rose some mild amusement. Serve her right if one or two village girls had got wind of her carryings-on and taken their revenge. She deserved it after the way she'd used Adam to her own advantage. Now Gracie went everywhere with a bandana tied around her head beneath the wide brimmed hat which she'd taken to wearing in place of the green beret. Irritatingly, it looked quite dashing.

Rose felt too tired these days to care about how she herself looked, newly wed or not. Her days of philandering with officers and socialising in the Eagle's Head were very much a thing of the past. She and Adam rarely went out in the evenings. More often than not they spent them sitting around the wireless, an unlikely trio; Adam, herself, and Irma. There were moments when Rose felt as if she were back with Agnes and Maurice Sullivan, a frightening thought. At least Irma liked ITMA, and Tommy Handley was one of her favourites. And, of course, there was no threat of an assault of any kind. Adam never touched her.

Nevertheless, she made a valiant attempt to be a good wife to him. Calling upon her neglected culinary skills Rose cooked him delicious meals using Irma's home grown vegetables. She dug and weeded a whole new patch of ground ready for the winter planting, even got Adam to fashion some sort of greenhouse so that she could grow tomatoes next spring, and perhaps the odd marrow.

Irma watched all of this activity with tight-lipped disapproval. It was perfectly clear that she couldn't bear to see anyone but herself caring for her beloved son. 'Anyone would think you weren't satisfied with the way I've looked after him,' she said, scrutinising an apple pie Rose had made with a critical eye.

'I'm not saying any such thing only, as his wife, cooking Adam's dinner is my responsibility now.'

'It's still *my* cooker. *My* house.'

'I never said it wasn't.'

'I expect you wish I weren't here at all.'

'I never said that either,' Rose lied.

'Two women in one kitchen never works. Best way for us to get along, is for you to carry on with your job in the woods and I'll see to my lad, as I always have. I know best what he likes, after all.'

From then on Irma wouldn't allow Rose to lift a finger. She insisted on doing all the cooking and cleaning herself, even to tidying up their bedroom, which made Rose feel as if their most intimate moments were being picked over and put under scrutiny; their privacy invaded, checked out and criticised. It meant that every morning before dashing off to the woods on her bicycle she must remember to remove the pillow and eiderdown from the floor where Adam still slept and return them to the bed. She dreaded to think what her mother-in-law's reaction would be if she ever learned the truth about what went on between these four walls.

In every way, Irma was in control. Adam conceded entirely to her stubborn determination to continue as usual. She sewed on his buttons, told him when to visit the barber's, washed and ironed his shirts, polished his shoes, set the tin bath on its mat each Friday evening for him and probably scrubbed his back for all Rose knew. It seemed ironic to Rose, who'd once complained of having too much housework, that now she felt useless, of no value at all.

Perhaps because of all this worry and stress, she'd had a small bleed on her night-dress the other night. For a moment Rose thought she was about to lose Josh's baby and had felt a surge of fear and disappointment. If she lost his precious baby as well as him, what would she have left? Nothing. Josh would be gone from her life completely.

Chapter Twenty-four

'It's on!'

'What's on?' Gracie gazed into Karl's face, noting how pale and drawn he looked even as she recognised the glitter of excitement in his pale eyes, and realised with a terrible sinking of her heart what he was referring to. The escape, of course.

The squad was working, as usual, deep in the forest, save for Lou who seemed to spend more time on the telephone to Divisional Office these days, or else involved with endless paperwork, working on records, pay lists and time sheets back at the Eagle's Head.

'Just because I'm not wielding anything heavier than a pencil doesn't mean I'm not pulling my weight,' she would say. But this was addressed strictly to the others. She hadn't spoken to Gracie since that day at the camp when Rose had spilled the beans about her love for Karl. None of the squad had. It was far worse than the spat she and Lou had had when they'd been transferred from Cornwall because of Gracie's being late back. This cut deep to the heart of their friendship, had split it in two.

If Gracie asked her a direct question Lou's mouth would clamp shut and she'd turn away in total rebuff, even avoiding eye contact. It broke Gracie's heart. She felt isolated and nervously fearful over possible repercussions, not for herself so much as for Karl.

The stress of it all made her feel desperately tired, the trees seeming to grow bigger before her eyes and harder to bring down. The October rain seemed somehow more persistent, every bruise and blister more painful, every splinter in her hand a major crisis. She knew she wasn't coping well.

Now, while everyone was distracted handing out cheese rolls and thermos flasks, Karl drew her to one side, out of sight of the others, pressing her up against a tree so that he could kiss her quickly and lightly full on the mouth. It was a crazy thing to do, the act of a desperate man, but for a moment Gracie couldn't resist him. Even the barest touch of his flesh upon hers sent her senses spinning.

Within seconds, though, she'd pushed him away and deliberately strolled back to the saw horse to smile across at the guard, who stared back impassively by way of response. 'Stay away from me. We're being watched. We really shouldn't be seen together like this. It's far too risky.'

'Life is full of risk and I can't help it. I love you.' They saw Alf walk over to the guard and the pair were soon deep in conversation. Taking advantage of his distraction, Karl caught hold of her hand and pulled her back into the bushes to kiss her again and, unable to help herself, Gracie melted into his arms, revelling in the ripples of desire that cascaded through her body. It was terrifying, exciting, nerve-racking and utterly blissful just to be with him like this. The next moment it was as if he had doused the fire in her with iced water. 'The plans for the escape have been finalised. It will take place on the first Sunday in November.'

'Oh, my godfathers, no. *No!* Karl, I don't want you to go. I don't want you to take such a risk. You'll be killed, I know you will.' She was breathless with fear but he only smiled at her and stroked her cheek, endearing himself to her and infuriating her all at the same time. Why wouldn't he listen? Why did men always have to be so damned heroic? 'How can you hope to escape? What is this plan?'

He shook his head. 'Better you do not know. I do not want you involved.'

'And I don't want *you* involved. You mustn't go – I won't let you. They'll realise you're missing and call out the guards, perhaps even bring in the bloodhounds. Even if they don't catch you right away, you'll never find your way across the fells. You'll get lost trying to reach the coast. You'll freeze to death, sink in a bog, be attacked by the dogs . . . You'll never survive.' She was speaking rapidly and breathlessly, pumping the words out in these few precarious seconds while they were momentarily unobserved.

'My lovely Gracie, what a catalogue of disasters you predict for me. Do you think I have no courage, no skill? I plan carefully and will keep us safe. Do not worry, little one.'

'But I do worry,' she murmured, yet melting against him and lifting her face for more kisses. Then just as swiftly she drew away and, snatching up the billhook, began to peel sections of bark off a pole in fierce stabbing movements, as if she needed to attack something as an outlet for her fears, 'How can you possibly keep yourself safe?' The words came out in an angry whisper. 'You're a POW, for heaven's sake. The guards won't stop to ask questions. When they find you, they'll shoot you.'

She stopped hacking at the bark to turn and gaze at him, appalled by her own words. They stared deep into each other's eyes, seeking a way out, perhaps attempting to read hope and a possible future in the love reflected in the other's gaze.

Karl spoke softly. 'It is a risk I must take. Erich needs me. If I do not go with him he will tell about us. There is nothing I can do.'

By way of reply she knocked the pole off the saw horse to

the ground, kicked it with her booted foot as if it alone were responsible for their plight.

Karl calmly lifted another in its place. 'Are you angry with me?'

'Oh, no, no, with the war, the world, everything which comes between us. What does it matter if Erich does tell? Everyone must guess how we feel. All my friends know by now.'

For a moment he looked stunned and then his gaze narrowed. 'What will they do?'

Gracie shook her head, eyes filling with tears. 'I don't know. For now they are content to take their feelings out on me personally.' She whipped off the hat and scarf, revealing her devastated hair. She'd attempted to trim the roughly cut clumps of bristles in a more even fashion but there was nothing she could do to disguise their shortness. Gracie resembled nothing so much as an American GI. Karl stared at her for half a second then gave a low moan.

'My poor darling.' He ached to pull her close in his arms but now he dare not make a move towards her. If her friends could do such a terrible thing, what risks did she run from others, from the authorities? He glanced across at the watchful Alf, still mindful of his duty to help keep a close eye on the prisoners in his charge. Karl knew himself to be fortunate to be allowed to work in the forest. Most of the other prisoners were only allowed out in groups to collect wood for the fires, all under close escort. Only a few of the NCOs, like himself, and those who were more of a problem inside than out, like Erich, were allowed to work with civilians and, having gained trust, be less strictly supervised. But he must never take advantage of this situation, or it might put his beloved Gracie's life at risk. That was why he didn't want her involved. He needed her to be safe. If only he could be with her to protect her all of the time.

He vented his frustration by slamming his first against the bark of a tree. Beads of blood sprang up across the knuckles.

'What have they done to you? What have *I* done to you? I should never have come into your life. It would be better if I were gone.'

'No, no. Don't say that. I love you.'

Alf shouted over to her, 'Aren't you coming for your dinner, girl? It's lovely cheese again.' He came a step or two nearer, though not too close, and for the first time Gracie wondered if he guessed about herself and Karl. Perhaps Alf was more tolerant than he made out. There was an anxious frown etched on his old face and he jerked a thumb in the direction of the guard seated under a tree. 'Everyone else is eating. For now. But thoo'll have me in bother for not keeping a better watch on this beggar.'

'Yes, of course. Sorry!' As she hastily wiped her hands on a cloth, Gracie whispered fiercely under her breath, 'Tell me that you won't do it, that you won't really attempt to escape?'

'I must, Gracie. It is my duty. I have my orders. Erich has rank over me and I must do as he says. Would you have the *altestenrat* call me a coward too?'

She threw down the cloth in despair and, when she looked at him again, her eyes were glittering suspiciously brightly. 'Then I shall help you. I'll bring you food and warm clothing. I'll wait for you. Tell me where to meet you and I'll be there.'

'*No!* I will not have you involved.'

'I'm already involved. I shall wait for you.' And she named a spot in the forest they both knew well. Then, before he could make any further protest, Gracie hurried away to collect her lunch.

She ate alone under a beech tree. None of the other girls spoke to her or came anywhere near. Only Alf wandered over.

'Summat up?' he asked in his quiet, country tones, raising an eyebrow in the direction of the rest of the squad.

Gracie smiled at him. 'Nothing I can't deal with, Alf. Nothing that won't resolve itself, in time.'

333

'Nothing you want to talk about, thoo means?'

By way of an answer, she dropped her gaze and took a bite out of her sandwich.

Alf fingered his moustache, a thoughtful expression in his old eyes. 'Thoo can allus call on me, lass. If thoo ever needs a friend.' And on this surprising statement, he ambled away.

It had been a tiring day in the woods and Rose was glad to be home. Pregnancy was proving to be a most joyless experience. The sickness had never left her, and more often than not she felt worn out and jaded, with an odd sort of ache in her belly, which was swelling and puffing out like a pouter pigeon's breast. Despite these discomforts, she felt excited at the prospect of having a child of her own, Josh's child; happier than she'd been in years. If only she and Adam weren't drifting further and further apart, and his dratted mother wasn't under their feet the whole time, then life would really be quite tolerable.

And she rather thought pregnancy suited her. It was a wonder no one had remarked upon how much she'd changed.

Rose stood in front of the dressing-table mirror, examining her naked body with a curious detachment. She smoothed a hand over the soft curve of her stomach, lifting each breast to see if they were heavier, trying to calculate just how far gone she was. This was difficult as she'd had a little show, on two or three occasions actually, but then this was common, she told herself. She remembered the gossip in the corner shop back in Cornwall when Mrs Clements had given birth to a child with a strawberry birth mark. The village women had explained how this had been caused by bleeding during pregnancy. At first it had troubled Rose to think that Josh's baby might be marred in some way but she had now dismissed it as some foolish old wives' tale. So long as the child was perfectly healthy, what did anything else matter? She smiled at her reflection. It was strange the way she felt quite certain that she was carrying a boy, Josh's son, who she could hardly wait to hold in her arms. With a baby of her own to love, it would make losing him more bearable.

She dreamed of one day taking the boy to Canada and saying, Here you are Josh, this is your son. Wouldn't that give his frigid wife a jolt? She smiled at the thought. It might even make him realise what a terrible mistake he'd made, then he'd come back to her. This was a favourite dream in which she loved to indulge. She wasn't quite clear over the details of how they would get together in the end, but she knew that it would happen. Perhaps she would divorce Adam, or simply run away. The dream wasn't clear on specifics. But until that magical moment arrived, she would at least be safe here, and well taken care of.

Rose stood staring at herself in the mirror, turning this way and that. She marvelled at how the baby growing inside her made her body even more womanly and beautiful, yet wondered how long she could keep her secret before it became obvious, even to a new husband. As if somehow aware of the train of her thoughts, the door opened and suddenly there he was.

'Rose?' He seemed surprised by the sight of her nakedness, and quickly closed the door behind him. 'What is it? Aren't you well?'

She turned to him, her face alight with happiness. 'I'm very well, thank you. Never better. Don't you think I look well? Even beautiful perhaps?'

Adam couldn't take his eyes off her. Parts of her body were milky white but her legs, arms and the slender beauty of her throat were golden from the sun. Even as he drank in the glorious sight of her, she pushed her fingers into her hair and did a little pirouette before him, pert breasts thrusting provocatively forward as she turned. He was indeed fortunate to have such a beautiful wife. For the first time in weeks he felt a stirring in his loins. He wanted her. Dear Christ, how he wanted her. He moved closer, touched one breast with a tentative hand. His fingers looked clumsy and rough against the pale velvet of her skin, the nipples dark, even now hardening beneath his touch. He placed his mouth where his hand had been, feeling the need in him swell and start to throb. With sudden urgency he pulled her towards him, covered her mouth with his. In an instant they were lying entwined on the rug and the heat of his passion was pulsing through him as if he had a fire in his belly. Rose was moaning softly, opening up to him, and with a burst of joy and pride he knew he could enter her this time; he could pierce her sweetness and make her his own.

'Adam! Where are you, lad? Supper's ready and waiting on the table.' His mother's voice, her step upon the stairs. Dear God, she was coming up! 'Don't let it go cold now. We're all ready and waiting.'

'Soddin' hell!' Adam rarely swore but as he felt that glorious passion shrivel and die, he slumped against his wife and felt closer to murdering his mother than any good son should.

Irma observed the progress of her son's marriage with close attention. Something wasn't as it should be. She couldn't put her finger on exactly where the problem lay but there was one, of that she was certain. She could sense an awkwardness between the young couple, and little sign of the affectionate lovey-doveyness one would expect from newly weds. No doubt the poor lad had realised, too late, what a terrible mistake he'd made. Well, he couldn't say that he hadn't been warned. He couldn't lay the blame on her, Irma told herself firmly, if he'd now seen the error of his ways. She'd dropped her objections to the wedding, hadn't she? Once she'd realised he was determined. She'd attended the ceremony, trimmed up her best hat for the event, given up the front bedroom and moved into the back after more than forty years. You would think they'd appreciate such thoughtfulness but not even a thank you had crossed madam's lips.

Apart from being a flighty piece, shoving her nose in where it wasn't wanted and soon getting her feet under t'table in more ways than one, she was a lazy tyke. Never lifted a finger in the house if she could help it, Irma thought, forgetting how she'd repeatedly denied her daughter-in-law the opportunity. The girl didn't fit in, which was exactly what Irma had predicted in the first place. But she wouldn't see her only son suffer, oh, dear me no! After a long day working in the fields he deserved a few home comforts, and who better to provide them than herself, his old mam? Nobody, not even that little madam, could accuse her of being a burden. She'd more than earn her keep.

It hadn't escaped her notice that she'd heard very little in the way of creaking bed springs which was surely unusual, them being newly weds. And there'd been one occasion when Irma had been tidying up in what was now their bedroom, when she'd noticed that only one half of the bed looked as if it had been slept in. The bottom sheet on the other half had been as smooth and neat as a new pin. Now that struck Irma as odd. She decided to investigate.

She chose one morning while Rose was having a good wash in the kitchen, Adam having already gone out to do the morning milking, and Irma felt it was perfectly safe to push open the bedroom door and peep inside. There, on the bedside rug, a testament to all her worst fears, lay a pillow and eiderdown. And as if that didn't speak volumes, tossed casually across both were her son's discarded pyjamas.

Irma was appalled. 'Heaven help us, he's sleeping on the floor.'

Hurrying to listen at the top of the stairs, she heard the unmistakable sounds of vomiting. So that was how the land lay?

She should have guessed. The little madam had made a fool of her boy, like many another in this dratted war. Oh but his mam would be here to pick up the pieces when it all fell apart. He could depend upon that. As always.

She waited, arms folded, for Rose to return. The look on the girl's face was more than enough evidence of guilt.

'So that's the way it is,' Irma announced, unable to disguise the triumph in her voice. 'You managed to wed him and wheedle your way in here but now he knows the truth, he won't sleep with you, is that it?'

Rose gritted her teeth, determined not to be lured into a confrontation; thankful at least that Adam wasn't present to hear what his mother had to say. If she could just keep her wits about her, she might throw the woman off the scent. Lifting her chin, she strode straight past Irma without a word.

'Don't think I don't know that you've got a fancy man. You were seen in the bar parlour at the Eagle's Head regular with one of them Yanks. I can put two and two together with the best of 'em.'

Rose whirled about, her hand on the door knob shaking with rage as she met her mother-in-law's interrogative glare. 'He was Canadian actually, and it was all perfectly innocent. Just another serviceman missing his wife.'

'Ah, so that was the problem, was it? He was already married. Well, whatever he was, it's quite obvious the pair of you weren't simply talking about the weather. Nor was he thinking much of his wife when you got up to heaven knows what mischief.'

Rose wanted to slap the old woman's face, knock her down the stairs for even insinuating Josh's love was somehow unclean and sordid. For Adam's sake, she took a deep steadying breath and resorted to the kind of ice cold countenance she'd developed over the years when dealing with one of Eddie's tantrums, drawing a rock hard shell of protection about herself, as she had learned to do. 'Think what you like. An eiderdown tossed on the floor proves nothing.'

'I heard you throwing up.'

'A stomach upset.'

'Oh aye, and I'm the Queen of Sheba.'

'You never wanted me here in the first place and you've done your best to make sure I'm not welcome. What you don't seem to appreciate is that there's nothing you can do about it. Adam and I are married now. You certainly can't hurt me. I'm impervious to hurt. Didn't you know that?'

'I know you're a hard little bitch.'

Rose put back her head and laughed. It was a harsh, brittle sound which chilled Irma to the bone. She moved threateningly towards her mother-in-law who backed away on to the landing. 'True, very true. But then I've been trained in a hard school.' Whereupon she slammed shut the door in the woman's face.

Irma was mortified to think she'd actually persuaded her son to look for a wife. Now she saw those efforts as misguided, interfering in the laws of nature. However, she did not view an attempt to resolve his marital difficulties in the same light. Irma saw it as her motherly duty not to stand idly by and see that little slut destroy her boy. She cooked Adam his favourite liver and onions for dinner, which they usually shared. Irma enjoyed this time alone with him while Rose was out in the woods. Today it would be the ideal opportunity to get everything out in the open. Not that she'd say anything about her suspicions. Better to let him find out about the Canadian himself, then he couldn't accuse her of poking her nose in where it wasn't wanted.

'You have to tread warily with our Adam,' she murmured to herself. Best she get him to do the talking. To start with anyroad. After that she'd see how much of the truth she could drip-feed into his ear.

She set his plate before him, settled herself in the chair opposite, an expression of intense sympathy on her face, then launched into her plea. 'I can see you're not happy, lad. Whatever it is that's wrong, you can tell me. I'm your mam after all. You can tell me owt.'

Adam set down his fork untouched, pushed aside the copy of *Farmer's Weekly* which he'd been about to read quietly and gazed bleakly at her. The last thing he wanted was to discuss his marital problems with his mother but nor did he wish to appear ungrateful. Besides which he was at his wit's end to know how to put things right. Rose and he were barely speaking these days, and he was still sleeping on the bedroom floor. Could he use this show of concern to persuade his mam to move out and stay with her friend Madge, if only for a little while? They seemed to be getting along all right working together, and she never stopped talking about those kids. He cleared his throat, determined to give it a try.

'I was wondering if perhaps we should have a bit more time to ourselves like, to be on our own more?'

'Time to yourselves? On your own more? Goodness, don't I try to make sure of that? I do all the housework round here after all. Madam doesn't need to do a hand's turn around the place. I'm sure I haven't asked her to lift a finger.'

'I'm not talking about housework, Mam. I'm talking about us needing to be on our own more.'

'Well, of course you need to be by yourselves at times. That's what I'm saying. She comes home from a long day's work in the woods. You come back from the fields and the pair of you are able to sit in here, all cosy together, while I'm in the kitchen making your tea.' She very nearly said 'slaving away', but that might have upset him and made herself seem too much the martyr, which wouldn't do at all. 'What more can I do? Haven't I made enough sacrifices for the pair of you, giving up the front room and not making any objections to your marrying her? I couldn't help but notice you haven't been sharing a bed.' Irma's face took on an expression of pure tragedy. 'You poor boy. I don't blame you for sleeping on the floor. Do you want me to fetch the Put-U-Up from the loft?'

'*No!*' Adam was squirming with embarrassment, hating the direction this conversation was going. 'It's not what you think. I'd just put me back out, that's all, and sleeping on a hard floor helps. It's nearly better now.' Deciding this was the best opportunity he was going to get, he ploughed on relentlessly. 'Look, Mam, we're very grateful for what you do for us, it's just that – well – it would be easier if there were just the two of us in the house like.'

Irma looked at him as if he'd run mad. 'Just the two of you in the house? Nay, lad, wouldn't we all like a place of our own but there is a war on. We're not the only family having to squash up a bit and make the best of things.' And then, quite suddenly, her eyes were awash with unshed tears. 'You're surely not expecting me to move out, leave me own home after all these years, just because you've getten wed? Where would you have me go? I don't think there is a workhouse any more, is there?'

And before he could stop himself, Adam was telling her not to talk daft, assuring his mother that of course no such thought had entered his head. He wasn't asking her to leave, that's not what he meant at all. Perhaps it was having the other two girls here as well which made the cottage feel a bit overcrowded.

Irma's face cleared, and she dabbed at her eyes with her hanky. 'Oh, well, that's soon sorted. I only let them two come in the first place for a bit of company. Now you're wed, things have changed. We'll ask them to move out. There, is that better? Lou and Gracie are reasonable girls. They'll understand perfectly that a honeymoon couple need a bit more privacy.

Lou's mentioned the possibility of moving to the Eagle's Head already, matter of fact, so there'll be no trouble on that score. I could have their room, then you can put the bairn in the box room. Make a lovely nursery, that will.'

Chapter Twenty-five

Adam stared at his mother, enraged suddenly by her inter-
ference. 'Bairn? Nursery? Aren't you jumping the gun a bit,
Mam?'

'Not from what I've noticed. They didn't bring me in with
the milk float.' Irma, annoyed by her son's intransigence in
refusing to marry the girl she'd selected for him, and forgetting
all about her resolve to remain cool and calm, began to spit out
her venom. 'She's no better than she should be! A harlot, no
less. The lass only married you because she's pregnant, as
anyone with half an eye could see.'

Adam gaped at his mother, eyes and mouth wide with
disbelief and dawning horror. 'Pregnant? You're saying Rose is
pregnant? But she can't be. How dare you suggest such a thing?'

'Can't she indeed?' Adam rose to his feet, a gesture which
suddenly gave Irma pause to recall her decision to tread
carefully. He might seem pliable and soft on the outside, this
boy of hers, but he could be stubborn. Hadn't she proof of that?
Changing tack completely, she pinned a smile to her face and
began to clear away empty plates. 'Well, you're probably right.
Happen it's a stomach bug, unless you're a fast worker, lad.' She
winked broadly at her son.

'You wouldn't be the first to think they'd taken enough

343

precautions and found they hadn't. Nature has her ways and means. I take it she's not got round to telling you yet then? Shame on her, and you the child's father.' She gave these last words the very slightest emphasis and cast a sharp glance at him, to see if she'd struck a chord. He'd sunk back into his seat and seemed to be in paralysis now, staring into space. She risked repeating it, despite her vow of caution. 'There's no doubt you are the father, I suppose?' When still he didn't react, Irma continued with carefully adopted indifference, 'Aye, well, I'm sure she'll get round to telling you in the end. Can't keep quiet for ever about a thing like that, now can you? Anyroad, don't worry, I'll not let on. It'll be our little secret.'

'How do you know? How can you be sure?'

Irma was not about to confess to listening at bathroom doors so merely laid one finger against the side of her nose and smiled. 'A woman knows these things. Put it down to female intuition. I just wanted to say that I allus wanted to be a grandma. You must be very proud, lad.' It sickened her to have to say such words, in the circumstances, and she cast him a sly sideways glance to test his reaction to them. She recalled a similar situation over Ulverston way, of a young woman who'd married in haste and then confessed she was carrying another man's child. He was a Yank too, if she wasn't very much mistaken. The girl had run away in the end, out of shame. Nobody had seen her since. Pity this little madam didn't do the same. Good riddance, would be Irma's view.

Adam was simply looking bemused, evidently lost for words. He sat staring blankly and Irma felt like shaking him. Instead, she refilled his mug to the brim with hot, strong tea, and added a couple of spoons of sugar. To hell with the rationing, the poor boy was in shock. Not only had he no idea about the bairn but, if she was any judge, he didn't seem any more convinced he was the father than she was. Bad back, my Aunt Fanny. Happen he'd got suspicious and they'd had a row or, more likely, the wench had simply refused to carry through her obligations. What would happen now? That was the question. It would be interesting to find out.

Adam did nothing. Having seen already what came of making impulsive decisions in life, he wasn't about to make the same mistake twice. He made up his mind to bide his time. He was a patient man, good at waiting.

'You can't spend the winter on the floor,' Rose told him. 'You'll catch your death. Come on, we'll just cuddle up and hold each other close. We don't have to try to make love.'

'I'm not cold, I like it here.'

'Shall I come down there on the rug with you then?'

'No!' He was afraid to go close to her now. The near success of their love making when he'd found her naked had revealed all too clearly that he still desired her with a ferocity that ate into the heart of him. Adam knew himself capable of making love to his wife anywhere at all save in his mother's bed.

But as the October days grew colder, so did their relation-ship. Each and every day he prayed that she would tell him about the baby and explain. He needed to know why she'd been so cruel. Presumably she'd tricked him into marrying her simply in order to provide her child with a father and save her own reputation. He'd believed every word when she had sworn that she loved him. Yet she couldn't have done at all, could she? She'd used him. Too late to realise all of this now. They were man and wife and there wasn't a damn thing he could do about it. Perhaps, deep down, Adam hoped her reasoning hadn't been out of malice at all; that she'd married him because she truly was fond of him, that she regretted her liaison with the father of her child, whoever he was, and needed a fresh start. It certainly wasn't an unusual state of affairs, not with a war on.

As he waited, he felt as if he were caught between the two of them, between Rose and his mother. The one urging him to behave like a normal husband and, if he did, who would ever know whether the child were his or not, except him? The other demanding he be a loyal son and dispose of a wife who had cheated and tricked him. He strove to ignore the problem, even to disregard Rose herself, but it wasn't easy. She was his wife and no matter what she'd done, even if she had used him, he still loved her. He adored her and, pregnant or not, she was still utterly entrancing.

She was never shy about undressing before him and he observed her body with increasing interest and curiosity. He saw very little evidence of a thickening of her waistline or any swelling of her abdomen. She remained as slender and beautiful as ever. She looked wonderful. His greedy gaze couldn't have enough of her. There were times when he very nearly challenged her with his knowledge, when he longed to confess that his mother had told him, yet always he backed away from the confrontation and hardened his resolve to wait for her to tell him of her own free will.

Was she afraid to confess? Why? He would never hurt her, surely Rose realised that? He'd fallen for her, great soft lump that he was, and still worshipped the ground she walked on, for all she was carrying another man's child. At least the waiting would give him time to decide whether he could accept the baby as his own.

And to decide what to do about his mother.

Lou was sympathetic when Rose expressed her dismay over Irma's decision that they should leave as she helped her friend pack. 'No, no, it's right that you should be on your own. You're still newlyweds, after all,' Lou insisted.

Gracie had risen early, packed and left already, saying that since it was a Sunday she wanted to get settled into her new billet quickly then have some time to walk on the fells. Being the first week in November and the weather good, there would be few enough opportunities left for walking before winter set in. Neither Rose nor Lou had responded to this comment.

She'd seemed to be in a terrible hurry and an unusual state of anxiety. But then the reason for this seemed obvious to them both. No one would offer to help Gracie to pack and settle in because she was still very much in Coventry. Serve her right, Rose thought. It was all her own fault for getting involved with a German officer and trying to hang on to Adam at the same time. Rose was delighted to be rid of her and only in these last few days had it occurred to her why. She still felt threatened by her, jealous and afraid that Adam would come to regret not having chosen Gracie instead. It didn't really trouble Rose whether or not her one-time friend was in love with a POW. That had simply been a convenient excuse for taking revenge on her.

Rose had come to realise that, despite her own constant declarations that she was impervious to hurt, this wasn't strictly true. The more Adam turned away from her, the more she needed him. She'd hated the celibate state of their marriage; now she realised it was because she loved him. During these first weeks of marriage, she had come to see her mistake. Josh was the one who had used and cheated her. He no doubt made a habit of taking vulnerable young women to bed. Whereas Adam had always been kind, gentle and supportive, a real gentleman, and yet he excited her. Given half a chance they'd be good together. When their love making had been interrupted by Irma, the time that he'd very nearly taken her on the rug, she'd wept bitter tears. Not simply out of frustration but from a need to show him how much she truly cared.

Rose was furious that Adam hadn't insisted Irma move in with her friend Madge. Hadn't she done everything she could think of to make that happen? And to think he'd actually broached the subject of privacy with her and then chickened out at the last minute.

These thoughts burst out of her now in a rush of self-pity. 'The real problem is his bloody mother, not you. I know Irma is a lovely lady in many ways, a stalwart of the community and all that, but living in her house, sleeping in her bed . . . it's doing my marriage no good at all.'

Lou recognised in the rising pitch of Rose's voice that all was not sunshine and roses in the Cooper household. There was a storm brewing. In fact she noticed for the first time that her friend looked decidedly peaky. She was immediately sympathetic. 'Are you all right, love? You look a bit green about the gills.'

Rose had never felt more unwell in all her life. If Irma had said nothing further to her about the pregnancy, nor had she offered to help in any way when her sickness and debilitation continued. Didn't a mother-to-be usually glow and bounce with new vitality? Wasn't her hair supposed to be lustrous, her skin translucent? Rose hadn't found this to be the case at all. More often than not she felt weak and sick, even faint at times. She found it hard to get out of bed in a morning and the continual cramps in her stomach seemed to be growing worse. Now she strove to shake the nausea off. 'I'm fine. It's that bloody woman, she'd make anyone ill.'

'Dampening your ardour, is it? Knowing his mother sleeps next door?'

'She never leaves us alone. Sits with us every night. Interferes the whole time. She still makes all the meals, does everything for him while I do nothing. I feel useless, as if I'd no right to be here.'

'Have you told him all of this? Have you explained how you feel?'

'Adam knows how I feel. I think he feels the same but he does nothing about it. Hates to hear a word said against her.'

Seeing that her friend was actually trembling, Lou urged
Rose to sit down for a moment on the edge of the bed, and gave
her a comforting hug. 'You look as if you're overdoing it,
actually. Are you sure you're all right?'

Perhaps it was the sympathy in her tone, or because Rose
was anxious to prove that there really was nothing at all wrong
with their marriage, or simply needing to break the news before
her mother-in-law did, but the next words just seemed to fall
out of her mouth of their own accord. 'It's just that with the
baby coming, it'll be even more important . . .'

'Baby? D'you mean . . .' Lou let out a squeal of joy,
snatching Rose to her in a fierce hug of delight. 'No wonder
you look like death. You don't mess about, you two, do you?'

Rose could actually feel the blood draining from her face.
What had she done? 'You mustn't tell anyone. You mustn't let
on that I've told you.'

'Why not? Haven't you told him yet?'

Rose shook her head. 'How can I, with Irma sitting between
us like the Angel of Doom the whole damn' time?'

Lou said, 'Grasp the nettle, love. Oh, don't fret, Irma will be
pleased as punch at the prospect of being a grandma. Give it to
her straight. She's used to a bit of straight talking, is Irma.
Though I'll admit the hard part is getting her to shut up long
enough to listen to what you have to say. Be firm and stick to
your guns though. Right?'

Rose looked unconvinced but then, how could she explain
to Lou that she was unable to tell Irma she was about to become
a grandmother because she'd guessed about Josh, and already
suspected that husband and wife weren't sleeping together? Oh,
what a muddle! Nothing was turning out as it should.

She longed to tell Adam the truth, to confess all, but he
tensed whenever she approached, as if he couldn't bear her to be
near him. On the rare occasions when he did allow her to kiss
his cheek or hug him, Rose recognised a restraint in him, as if

he were straining to pull away from her and be free. There certainly hadn't been any repetition of those few magical moments on the rug.

Sometimes she'd catch him looking at her when he thought himself unobserved. These were the most frightening moments and she would worry that perhaps Irma had told him of her suspicions. If her mother-in-law hadn't done so already, there was always the risk she eventually would. Rose knew that she'd told no one else herself about the pregnancy, until now, not even consulted a doctor yet. It was her secret and only when she was sure of Adam would she dare to share it with him. She needed to throw herself upon his mercy. He was kind and sweet, a good man. In the end, Rose was perfectly sure she could manipulate him into accepting the baby as easily as she'd persuaded him into marrying her. But she had to make her move before Irma put her own poisonous slant on things. And it might already be too late.

For the first time since sanctions had been put into place against her, Gracie actually felt grateful for the fact everyone was avoiding her. The landlady at the Eagle's Head gave her a tiny room of her own at the back, which meant that as she fretted, made sandwiches and gathered a few items of warm clothing which might be useful for Karl and Erich, there was nobody around to witness her preparations.

Today, the day she had hoped would never come, her intention was to leave the pub at around two o'clock, knapsack on her back, ostensibly to walk over the fells but in truth to hide away at the arranged spot and wait for darkness when Karl would eventually come to her. It was going to be a long day.

Then she realised that in her haste to pack and leave Beech Tree Cottage she'd left her thermos flask. Outside it was a cold, bitter day. It was vital Karl should have a hot drink as they made their escape. The greatest risk to survival was the cold, particularly on Lakeland mountains. Gracie decided it wouldn't take more than twenty minutes or so to dash over to the cottage on her bike and fetch it.

It was around noon when the pains started. Rose couldn't believe it was happening. She was little more than three months gone. Did this mean she might lose the baby? She felt utterly devastated and, as the pain sharply escalated, screamed long and hard, certain it would slice her in two. The noise brought Irma pounding up the stairs like a stream train. The older woman took one glance at the young girl, still as slender as a sapling but arched in agony on the bed, and in her coldest voice said: 'You can't have started. It's too soon. Have you told Adam yet?'

Rose barely had the strength to shake her head.

'Just as well I did then. Don't think losing it will save your marriage.'

Rose gazed up at her out of wide, shocked eyes. 'You told him? Why – why didn't he say?'

Irma didn't answer but took one look at the girl's ashen face and lifted a corner of the blanket. She blinked at the sight of the spreading pool of crimson on her best linen sheet. 'Have you seen a doctor, girl?' She snapped out the words as if to emphasise it was really all Rose's own fault. But even as she drew breath to lecture Rose on what she ought or ought not to have done, and what she thought of her for keeping her husband in the dark, her words were drowned by another ear-piercing scream.

The door burst open and Gracie flew in. 'What is it? What's wrong?'

Irma turned to her in panic, genuine fear in her eyes now. 'I reckon she's losing it. The bairn, I mean. I doubt she's even seen a doctor.'

'I've got my bike outside. I'll go and ring for an ambulance. Hang on, Rose, we'll get you some help. Look after her, Irma, for God's sake.'

'No. *No!*' Rose was almost incoherent in her terror. 'Don't leave me. I don't want Irma interfering. She always bloody interferes. *Leave me alone!*' The rest of her words were lost in a gabbling, incoherent scream of terror.

Rose's grief was heartbreaking to witness. She lay in her hospital bed listening to the doctor carefully explain to her that there was to be no child. She'd been suffering from a medical condition called an ectopic pregnancy which meant that the baby had been growing in the wrong place. When she asked if this would prevent her from having children in the future, he told her that it was difficult to say for certain, at this stage, but she was lucky to be alive. Had her mother-in-law and friend not acted so swiftly, she certainly would not have been.

Rose cried. For the loss of her dreams and hopes: not in fact those of one day presenting Josh with a son, or of having revenge on the wife who'd stolen him away from her, but for the loss of this child she would never hold in her arms. She cried out of self-pity, for not getting exactly what she'd wanted, and because Adam would probably hate her now.

Later that afternoon when he came to visit her she was afraid to look him in the eye, to face the contempt he must feel for her. But as he approached her bed, pulled up a chair and gathered her cold hands in his, he gave no sign of it. He seemed subdued, sad almost, but the love he felt for her was still there, shining out of his eyes. It came to her in that moment, for the first time, how very much she'd hurt him. It nearly broke her heart.

'My lovely Rose, you're looking so much better. Thank God! I thought I'd lost you.'

'Adam . . . I've been wanting to explain.'

'Don't say anything. There'll be time for all of that later. What you have to do now is to get well, then I can take you home.'

'She's not coming back to my house, I can tell you that for nowt.' Coming to the other side of the bed, gloved hands clasped tight on her handbag over her corseted stomach, Irma said, 'I reckon it's too late for explanations, don't you? You should've been honest from the start. You made a right fool out of my boy, getting him to wed you when all the time you were just looking for a father for the bairn you were carrying. Someone else's child. What's worse, even when you'd caught him, you wouldn't share your bed with him. Selfish, unfeeling slut! No doubt you were still seeing your fancy man – your *married* fancy man. Hussy and a harlot, that's all you are! Didn't I tell you, lad, right at the start, that she'd be nought but trouble. I should've put my foot down, insisted you . . .'

'Mam! For Christ's sake, *shut up!*'

'What did you say?'

I said, shut up! I've heard enough of what *you* think and *you* want. Do you never stop to consider what *I* think, what *I* want?' He got to his feet and faced his mother across the bed, his expression tight with controlled anger. Now he voiced all the thoughts that had tormented him for months, years even. 'You never give me the chance to make my own decisions, always have to charge in and make them for me. And if ever I don't agree, there's hell to pay. Well, I chose Rose, not Gracie, and I'm glad I did. And if I'd got on with things in the normal way, as a proper married couple should, without being afraid of you listening at walls or keyholes, which I'm quite sure you did, we might not have ended up with all these – problems. Rose might have confided in me like I'm sure she intended to. It's just that she was afraid to, weren't you, love?'

Utterly bemused and startled by this *volte face*, she nodded. 'I thought you'd hate me, and I realised – I realised that I did love you after all, Adam. And I thought if you knew about the baby, I'd lose you.'

Irma gave a loud snort of contempt. 'If you believe that, you'll believe that pigs fly!'

'Mam, I've told you to keep quiet. I'll stand for no more of this back biting and nastiness. If you're to stay with us at Beech Tree Cottage – and I'll not put you out, not even to make Rose happy because it is, as you rightly say, your home and accommodation is tight, what with the war and everything – I'll no longer tolerate you speaking of my wife in that derogatory way. Is that clear?'

'But . . .'

'I said, *is that clear?*'

A pause then during which mother and son glared long and hard, each taking the measure of the other. It was Irma who looked away first. 'Yes, Adam. I understand.' She found she was shaking, realising she'd been beaten not only by that little madam but also by her own son. Rose had won.

'What's more,' Adam continued, more calmly, 'you can have your own room back. It doesn't suit us. We'll take Lou and Gracie's room now they've moved out.'

Once again Rose's tears began to flow. 'Oh, Adam, can you ever forgive me? I never meant to hurt you, really I didn't. I thought it would all turn out for the best, and we'd be happy.'

'We will be happy, if you, Mam, give us half a chance.' He was holding Rose's hands again, wiping the tears from her eyes, kissing her cheek.

'I'm sure it's nothing to do with me,' Irma said as she watched this display of affection with a face like thunder. Pressing her crimson-painted lips together she tucked a few straying strands of hair tidily beneath her best brown hat and began to tug on her gloves in a businesslike fashion. 'I really have far more to bother about than standing here watching you two billing and cooing. I've promised to organise a War Weapons Week in the village. That will take all my time and energies, thank you very much.'

'Good,' Adam said, smiling. 'I'm glad we've got everything settled. I knew it would all come right in the end, if I just had patience. Before you dash off, Mam, will you sit with Rose for five minutes while I go and fetch us both a nice cup of tea?' Leaning over the bed he pressed a loving kiss on Rose's pretty mouth. 'We're going to be very happy, no matter what. Just you see.'

'No matter what,' she agreed, eyes shining.

When he'd gone, the two women sat in silence for some moments. It was Irma who broke it. 'Just because you've won this battle, madam, don't think you've won the war. I'm not done with you yet. You'll never make my lad happy, not in a month of Sundays. And I'll have you out of my house or die in the attempt, see if I don't.'

Rose simply smiled. 'I believe you will.'

Chapter Twenty-six

At around the same time as Gracie set off on her bike for an ambulance, a group of prisoners were allowed out, as usual, on gardening detail in the charge of their guards. This stretch of ground was furthest away from the Hall, an ideal spot from which to make an escape.

The plan had begun to take shape back in the summer when a group of prisoners apparently developed a passion for gardening, Karl and Erich among them. In fact, working in the garden gave them closer access to the forest. The idea was for the guards to grow used to their daily routine and think nothing of them being there. Even before the details of the escape had been finalised, everyone was certain it could be successfully achieved. Karl had felt nervous about the whole enterprise from the start but the *Altestenrat* had condemned Erich as a coward with anti-Nazi views and his presence in the camp would be tolerated no longer. In theory, the council had no official powers, in practice it acted as an escape committee, censored mail and held a court to try fellow prisoners for alleged offences. Its powers were draconian. Erich had been instructed to prove himself by attempting to escape, or be killed for a traitor. Either way they would be rid of him.

Perhaps if Karl had never met Gracie, he too would have

been eager to escape with him and return to his duties in the fatherland. Now all he wanted was to survive the war so that they could be together. This dereliction of his patriotic duty weighed heavily upon his conscience.

Today their task was to clear all the yellowed and dead leaves, to consign all the remains of the summer crops to the compost heap. After that would come the digging.

'You'll need to put some lime in there to sweeten the soil,' the guard in charge told them. He was quite friendly and conversation was always amicable between them. 'It's not enough to just turn it over.'

The last thing they wanted was to put lime in the soil today. Their intention was to dig one extra deep trench and bury the two young men in it with a light covering of soil on top. Karl, keeping well out of sight, heard one of the other prisoners say, 'We shall put in the lime tomorrow. Today we clear. We double dig. We like to make the work last long time, OK?'

'Suit yourself.' The guard wandered over to chat with his colleague, still keeping half an eye on his charges. The prisoners started work.

Karl's nervousness increased as the afternoon wore on. It took far longer than they had anticipated to clear the weeds and dead vegetable matter and now it must be nearing tea time and the digging was still not completed. He could see Erich looking tense and grey faced. The air seemed to crackle with tension, everyone much quieter than usual. Erich was eager for action, excited about the adventure ahead. He'd been given a hard time by some of the other officers who had accused him of having anti-Nazi views. He was anxious to put this bad experience behind him and couldn't wait to get out. For weeks he'd talked endlessly of how he would run through the forest like a deer, keeping undercover and out of sight. 'Then we will cross the open fells with all speed, making a beeline for the Irish Sea. Speed is essential. We have to get far away before they bring out the dogs, following streams and the edge of a lake where possible, to put them off the scent.'

'We must remember to take our compass,' Karl would say, fingering it in his pocket. Many of the officers had compasses which generally speaking they'd made themselves and kept hidden under their bedding or behind skirting boards, together with home-made maps. The plotting and planning of escape attempts filled the monotony of the long days from morning reveille till they were locked in their dormitory bedrooms at lights out.

Everyone had heard of the famous von Werra, who had attempted to escape in 1940 at around this time of year. Erich always cited him as a shining example of what could be achieved whenever Karl appeared to be having doubts.

'But he didn't make it,' Karl would protest.

'He very nearly did, and would have succeeded had not the weather been against him. We will do better. The weather is good. Von Werra took shelter in a small stone hut where two farmers spotted him and gave chase. That was a bad mistake, to stop,' Erich insisted. 'He should have kept going. No time to rest.'

'But they say the fells are high and cold and dangerously remote,' Karl protested. 'We cannot keep running indefinitely. We must stop and rest somewhere.' He'd said nothing yet of Gracie's plan to meet them in the clearing. Best he keep that information to himself for as long as he could. He'd warned her there could be no lingering farewell. He would take the food and warm clothing she brought, a kiss and a swift embrace and then they must part. She'd made a half-hearted attempt to persuade him to take her with him but he'd soon put a stop to that idea, urging her to stay safe and well in England so that when the war was over he could return to Grizedale and find her.

Erich was still telling his tale. 'They say he was captured

high up on Bleak Haw overlooking the Duddon Valley, half-submerged in marshland when they found him. But von Werra was a great hero.' Erich's eyes shone. 'From here he was transferred to a POW transit camp in Swanwick, Derbyshire, and again escaped, this time getting as far as Canada. Can you imagine the courage he must have shown? The dangers he faced?'

'His story is a lesson to us all,' Karl said in a flat, toneless voice, hoping to calm his more excitable friend. 'But I have heard that after he got back home to Germany, via South America, he crashed in a Messerschmidt flying over the Channel. Tragic to lose his life in such a way after all that heroism.'

Erich shrugged. 'I do not believe that is true. It is simply British propaganda.'

'Well, whether it is or not, he was a brave man.'

'And we must also be brave, and more cunning. Von Werra is our hero and yet we must learn from his mistakes. No stopping until we see the Irish Sea. Yes?'

Karl had sighed and agreed, yet had grown ever more fearful of what they faced as the weeks of waiting dragged by. Now here they were, about to put this undoubtedly harebrained plan into action.

'It is time,' a voice hissed in his ear, and he came out of his reverie to find himself being urged to lie down in the trench. 'Hurry, hurry, before the guard looks this way.'

A cloth was put over his head and, seconds later, Karl was lying on his side in the trench while soil was being quickly flung over him. As daylight was gradually blocked out from his hiding place, the pounding of his own heart sounded like a big bass drum in his ears. He stretched out a toe to see if he could touch Erich, who was further along the trench, also being hastily covered with soil. Karl thought this must be the craziest thing he had ever done in his life. He could only pray it didn't bring him to a swift and brutal end.

As he lay there beneath the shroud of cloth, he strained to tune in to the sounds above ground. He heard the men move away, heard the clatter of their boots as they lined up for roll call. In his mind's eye he could see them, the officers at the front, the ratings at the back. Someone would slip from place to place, making it seem as if the correct number were present. He imagined he could hear the counting, the orders barked out in German. Shortly after that came the clump of marching feet, followed by silence. This, he discovered, was the worst part. Only he and Erich could judge when it might be safe to move.

At first Karl had argued they should wait for as long as possible, until dusk had fallen when they could slip away under cover of darkness. But then Erich had expressed a fear that their absence might be noticed before that, once everyone was inside or when they were sitting down for the evening meal, and the alarm be called before they'd had a chance to move. In the end they'd decided to take their chances immediately. Now Karl welcomed that decision. He hadn't realised how very hot and uncomfortable it would be beneath the soil, however thin the layer that covered him. He felt overwhelmed by claustrophobia, as if he'd been buried alive. He could bear it no longer.

As one they burst out of the trench, scrambled under the fence where one of their number had already dug a tunnel for them and, without pausing for breath, raced up the slope through the forest. They were clad only in their work overalls. As they crashed through the undergrowth with as little noise as they could make, Karl breathlessly related to Erich how they must aim to reach the clearing where he knew Gracie would be waiting with food and warm clothing.

Erich grinned. 'She is good, your woman.'

'Yes, she is. I just hope she manages it. We're going to need all the help we can get.'

*   *   *

Dusk had fallen by the time Gracie reached the clearing. She felt breathless with anxiety. She took off her knapsack and flopped to the ground beside it. The greenness of the forest all around her seemed lush and peaceful, deceptively safe. High in a tree she spotted a red squirrel, busily eating its fill in readiness for winter. Would it have enough food to see it through, she wondered. Would it survive? Life was so uncertain, so filled with dangers. Who would have thought, when she and Lou had first arrived here in Grizedale, that it would come to this. With the pair of them estranged, and Gracie risking her very life to save a prisoner-of-war, the man she loved.

Would Karl and Erich survive? Would they come soon, or had she missed them while she was seeing to Rose? She desperately hoped not. Gracie dreaded the parting from Karl, yet the prospect of being robbed of those few precious moments of farewell was even more devastating.

She'd brought a couple of sweaters, scarves, gloves and hats she'd managed to unearth from Irma's collection of salvage; the thermos flask of tea and a large packet of sandwiches. Gracie hoped it would be sufficient to keep them going and give them the strength to reach the coast. It would not be an easy journey. Just thinking of the stretch of mountains they had to traverse made her feel ill.

Carron Fell was bad enough, so often swathed in mist, but that was nothing compared to what they must face later. They must somehow circumnavigate Coniston Water and head west over Dunnerdale, Thwaites and Bootle Fell. All desperately remote, high and dangerous places with precious little in the way of shelter to provide cover. Two scurrying figures could easily be spotted on an exposed mountain top. And what of dogs? How far could they follow a scent? Gracie didn't care to think.

Even if they reached the coast safely, where would they find a boat? Whitehaven? Maryport? Both were busy towns occupied by troops, dangerous ground for two German POWs to be on the loose. But, she argued, perhaps it was easier to lose oneself in a crowd.

Then again, she decided, more likely they would seek to be picked up by a fishing boat on that empty stretch of coastline, though it would have to be by someone who asked no questions. Was such a thing possible? Questions, questions, questions were burning into her own brain, searing her with fear. She really must stop this endless worrying, breathe deeply and calmly, be patient. Wait.

The minutes crawled by like hours and the hands on her watch never seemed to move. The wind changed and a cold night breeze sprang up, the shadows seeming to close in with threatening malevolence. She felt frighteningly alone, vulnerable and afraid. Nevertheless, perhaps because of expending so much emotional energy with worrying, Gracie must have drifted off to sleep for she woke with a jolt, knowing she had heard a sound, strangely familiar and yet alien in the peace of the forest. She couldn't at first decide what it might have been and then she heard it again. A siren. Surely not an air raid, not now? And then her heart seemed to cease in its beating as she recognised the significance.

'My godfathers, their absence must have been noticed!' Her own voice seemed to bounce back to her with terrifying loudness in the dread silence of the forest.

Jumping to her feet Gracie peered through the trees, desperately hoping and praying for a sight of their hurrying figures. She saw nothing, was barely able to penetrate the gloom. The sky seemed to light up and she whirled about, letting out a small cry of alarm. Someone had switched on the searchlights. Not simply the normal floodlights which illuminated the entire compound and surrounding area but the twin swivelling lights with which each sentry box in the valley was equipped. These now raked the sky with their long probing beams. Gracie even imagined that she heard the sound of dogs barking in the distance, growing ever louder as if they were drawing nearer. *Where in God's name were they?*

'Please come to me, Karl. Please!' And then she heard the shot.

Epilogue

1957

Lou walked slowly along the weed-covered drive, her gaze taking in the overgrown grounds, the cracked terraces with their broken masonry and collapsed walls where the prisoners had exercised, the once lovely green lawns a tangle of docks and thistles, the broken remnants of former huts a sad testament to a war long gone if never forgotten. Gone too were the rolls of barbed wire, the high perimeter fence, the sentry boxes. In her mind she could still hear the cry: 'Advance and be recognised.'

Lou smiled at the host of memories this recollection provoked. She loved to remember the old days because memories never let you down. They never died but triumphed victorious over all problems and difficulties; lived with you into eternity.

Her gaze moved on to the startling contrast supplied by the expensive cars, farm tractors, battered old vans and even bicycles that were arriving, lining the drive and filling the stable yard which had served as barracks for the guards. Dealers with bulging wallets, farmers with an eye to a bargain, treasure seekers and the plain curious were crowding into Grizedale Hall today. They'd all come to investigate this prestigious monu-

ment to the success of a Victorian businessman, to witness the
demise of this once famous mansion which stood at the head of
one of Lakeland's loveliest and most tranquil valleys, and whose
location had awarded it a unique place in history.

Most poignant of all were the former prisoners themselves
who came: middle-aged men bringing their families to see
where they had spent so many years of their youth during a
seemingly endless war; to show their loved ones the messages of
hope and faith they had carved into the oak panelling which
today was to go under the hammer as the hall was taken apart,
stripped of its glory and sold, piece by piece, before being
demolished and razed to the ground.

As, for the first time, Lou walked into this building which
had played such a part, albeit in the background, of her own
youth, she felt overwhelmed by sorrow at the waste of it all. For
the loss of young lives who had once fought so bravely; the
destruction of what had once been a fine mansion, degraded
and despoiled by the passing of years. Stained-glass windows
broken and open to the weather, priceless gold damask wall
coverings ripped to shreds, fine oak floorboards and panelling
filthy and scarred. What hadn't been broken or smashed had
been ruined by damp and neglect. Rather like friendship, came
the sudden, chilling thought.

The auction was already under way and Lou searched the
crowd of eager faces for any she might recognise. A bright
smile, a frantic wave of a gloved hand. 'Over here! We're over
here.'

Lou joined Rose, nodded a greeting to Adam. 'I couldn't see
you in the crush.'

'We've just bought some tongue and groove flooring at
fourpence a foot. Adam is thrilled.'

'Aye, and if I'm lucky, I'll get them window frames an' all,
for a knockdown price.'

Lou glanced over to the windows, many still boasting the

mottoes put there by their once proud owner. *God sends grace.* She read the inscription twice, a sense of deep sadness fluttering like a shadow over her heart. 'I wish He would send Grace,' she murmured, half to herself.

'What did you say?'

Lou stifled a sigh and smiled brightly at Rose. 'I said it's such a tragedy, this place. Such an utter loss. They're giving it away. Doing more damage to the house than the Germans did. But don't tell my boss I said so. The Forestry Commission wants no one else to own freehold property in the middle of their forest.'

The fifteen-foot-high stone chimneypiece of the great hall, complete with arched stone fireplace, metal canopy and dogs, ornamental pilasters and carved overmantel depicting the four seasons, went for only seven pounds. It was the best that the disappointed auctioneer could squeeze out of his buyers. It wasn't so much that money was tight as that they disapproved strongly of the sale in the first place, and had no intention of putting money into the pockets of those responsible. Not that anyone could be entirely sure who exactly was responsible, whether it be the local authorities or the Forestry Commission. The debate had raged for months and would no doubt continue to do so. The only good thing to come out of it would be that so many of its treasures would turn up later in other proud Lakeland homes and hotels.

Lou had seen enough and made her excuses to Rose and Adam. 'Meet you in the Eagle's Head later.'

Outside, the bright sunlight half blinded her, bouncing off flashy cars where once had stood armoured vehicles with windows blacked out, bearing prisoners to some unknown destination for interrogation.

'Lou? It is you, isn't it?'

She swung about, shading her eyes, and then, suddenly, there she was. Dear Gracie, neat as a new pin and slender as ever, pale blonde hair swept up beneath a smart, fashionable hat. The sweet, oval face no longer bore the imprint of youth but had matured to one of serene loveliness, presenting a picture of calm contentment, apart from the big grey eyes which were, as ever, fiercely challenging, daring anyone who crossed her path to be anything but entirely scrupulous and fair. She greeted Lou wreathed in happy smiles, just as if she had last seen her only yesterday and not twelve years ago. 'It's so good to see you again. I rather hoped you'd be here.'

Lou said nothing, finding herself at a loss for words. Gracie only laughed at her confusion, then gathered her close in a warm hug. Unable to help herself, Lou hugged her just as fiercely in return, holding her lost friend tight for several long moments before disengaging herself and quickly wiping away a tear. 'I was thinking about you in there.'

'Happy thoughts, I hope.'

'I was remembering you and me on our bikes, riding up this lane, chopping down our first tree – or not as the case may be.' She grinned. As one they turned and began to walk away from the house. 'And I was thinking of Matron and those dratted biscuits you hated so much.'

Gracie put back her head and laughed, a musical, joyous sound. 'Heavens, yes, and the lorry. Do you remember the lorry? And that awful kipper complete with bones, and sneaking out for lunch to the local pub, and the *cheese rolls*.' They spoke these last two words in unison and both burst out laughing, holding on to each other as they used to do.

After a moment Lou said. 'Rose is inside. Adam farms in quite a big way these days so has an eye for a bargain. We're meeting up at the Eagle's Head later.'

'Good, I want her to know there's no hard feelings over her spilling the beans about Karl and me at the camp that night.' For a moment the big grey eyes looked troubled but Lou chuckled.

'Oh, she understands now that you'd never have tried to win Adam back, and that she owes you her life for calling the ambulance that day. They never did have any more children but they're happy and, in the end, that's all that matters, eh?'

'What about Irma? Is she still with them?'

'Sadly she died, in that bad winter of nineteen forty-seven. She must have gone outside for something, kindling perhaps, and was found frozen to death in the farm yard the next morning, in a huge drift of snow. It's believed she was suffering from confusion or some sort of senile dementia, or perhaps had a stroke, fell and banged her head. No one is quite sure. The sad part was that Adam wasn't home at the time, or he could have gone and looked for her. He'd been moving his stock on to lower, safer ground. Rose was asleep upstairs so didn't realise there was a problem until too late. That was a bad time.'

'I'm sorry. Poor Irma.'

'Yes, poor Irma. And you?' Lou looked directly into Gracie's eyes and found something there which prompted her to say, 'Oh, I've missed you. So much. I was thinking of the waste. All these years gone by and not a word. What happened to us? To you? For God's sake, tell me. Where did you go after – after that night? I need to know everything.'

They sat facing each other across a small table in a dim corner of the Eagle's Head, a cosy fire burning in the old grate, and Gracie told her story. It didn't take long.

'After Erich was shot and Karl moved to another camp, I thought I would be in huge trouble too. However, since they never reached me in the clearing, and no one in authority was aware I'd planned to help them, I met with no difficulties save for losing you and all my friends among the squad.' She gave a half smile. 'I went back home for a while, needing to recuperate,

I suppose. That was a mistake which I quickly recognised. I missed you all too much.'

'We missed you.' They exchanged a telling glance, like an unspoken apology, given and accepted. 'I still hear from the others occasionally. Jeannie went back to her beloved Scotland and married a widower. Lena and Tess set up in business together, running a market garden.'

'Good for them.'

'Lena did swear she'd never go back to working inside again. But you were telling me your story. What happened next?'

'Fortunately, the Timber Corps were happy for me to stay on and sent me to Scotland. I worked there for a couple of years and then moved back down to Cornwall. Ended up pretty well where we began, would you believe? Which reminds me, remember Eddie? Rose's brother?'

'Once seen, never forgotten.' Lou pretended to tidy her bangs, though her chestnut hair had been cut years ago and now she wore it in a short, fifties-style bob. 'What a randy bugger he was! Creepy-crawly eyes.'

'They found his body in the cellar of Clovellan House. Must have got trapped in there when he was drunk one night. Nobody found him for years as Lord Clovellan was away. Didn't even know he was missing. Apparently everyone assumed he'd gone off with Rose. Makes you shudder, doesn't it?'

'No wonder she never heard from him. Oh, poor Rose. I don't think she knows. We must tell her carefully, with tact.'

'Yes, of course. She was never very fond of him, though, was she? I mean, there was far more to that story than she ever told us, don't you think? Anyway, as I was saying, there I was working back in Cornwall by the end of the war. Restrictions were lifted, at least in the respect that Karl and I were allowed to see each other, although in theory fraternisation was still not allowed. We got married in September 1946 and had a marvellous celebration with a cardboard wedding cake and everything. Even Mum and Dad came. Amazing. Not that they were speaking to each other, of course.' She laughed but the sound faded as a shadow flickered across her face.

'I had hoped my own marriage would be happier but the beginning was not particularly propitious. There were huge difficulties. Karl was still held in a camp for one thing, as were most POWs, so we spent our wedding night, every night in fact, apart.

'And, as expected, I was no longer considered to be British. When I had my first child a year later – oh, yes,' she added with a smile, 'we did manage to get together sometimes. As I said, restrictions were easing but every night he always had to go back to the camp at dusk. When I went into labour, no hospital would take me. They told me that since I had married a German, I should go to Germany to have the baby. Can you believe it? Crazy! I complained bitterly. Loud and long.'

Lou grinned. 'As only you know how.'

'But of course. I had my baby, a daughter, safe and well. They even allowed Karl to pay us a visit. Eventually, by the spring of that year, 1947, he was repatriated but wanted to stay here in England. After a flurry of letters to various MPs, courts, and goodness knows who else, he got his wish. We now have two more children, both sons, and have been as happy as Larry ever since.'

Lou grabbed her again in a fierce hug. 'I'm so pleased. And so sorry for – for how I reacted. It was just . . .'

'That's all water under the bridge now. Forget it. But what about you?' Gracie's face was suddenly serious. 'And what about Gordon?' At that instant, movement outside the pub window caught her eye. 'Oh, heavens, look. Here comes Karl now. Don't you think he's as handsome as ever? Still got those lovely thick blond lashes, and those adorable pale blue eyes. Oh, and Rose and Adam are with him, and another chap, walking with a stick. Who . . . ?'

'That's my Gordon.' Lou said proudly, her grin seeming to stretch from ear to ear. 'Bit frayed around the edges. Wounded when his ship went down in the campaign off Italy. But he still limps jauntily along, if not with quite his old sailor swagger.'

'Oh, Lou, how lucky we are! All together again, after all these years.' Then Rose was flying in through the door and they were weeping together, not even attempting to wipe away the tears that slid down their cheeks. It was some moments before Gracie could speak. 'Did you see that notice, "The Forest Code", on the board where the side entrance to the compound used to be? It says, "Leave nothing but footprints". Do you think we've left ours, in this forest?'

Lou smiled. 'I'm sure we have. Footprints in time. Some of them rather muddy ones. But I like the last line best: "take away nothing . . . except memories". For me, a memory is the most precious part of friendship, the greatest treasure of all.'